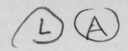

Praise for the novels of
#1 *New York Times* bestselling author
**Debbie Macomber**

"Prolific Macomber is known for her honest portrayals of ordinary women in small-town America…. [She is] an icon of the genre."
—*Publishers Weekly*

"Debbie Macomber tells women's stories in a way no one else does."
—*BookPage*

"Popular romance writer Debbie Macomber has a gift for evoking the emotions that are at the heart of the genre's popularity."
—*Publishers Weekly*

"Debbie Macomber is one of the most reliable, versatile romance writers around."
—*Milwaukee Journal Sentinel*

"No one writes better women's contemporary fiction."
—*RT Book Reviews*

"With first-class author Debbie Macomber, it's quite simple—she gives readers an exceptional, unforgettable story every time, and her books are always, always keepers!"
—*ReadertoReader.com*

# DEBBIE MACOMBER

## Looking for a Hero

mira

ISBN-13: 978-0-7783-3114-8

Recycling programs for this product may not exist in your area.

Looking for a Hero

Copyright © 2018 by Harlequin Books S.A.

The publisher acknowledges the copyright holder of the individual works as follows:

Marriage Wanted
Copyright © 1993 by Debbie Macomber

My Hero
Copyright © 1992 by Debbie Macomber

For questions and comments about the quality of this book, please contact us at CustomerService@Harlequin.com.

www.MIRABooks.com

**Printed in U.S.A.**

## Also by Debbie Macomber

### Blossom Street

The Shop on Blossom Street
A Good Yarn
Susannah's Garden
Back on Blossom Street
Twenty Wishes
Summer on Blossom Street
Hannah's List
The Knitting Diaries
   "The Twenty-First Wish"
A Turn in the Road

### Cedar Cove

16 Lighthouse Road
204 Rosewood Lane
311 Pelican Court
44 Cranberry Point
50 Harbor Street
6 Rainier Drive
74 Seaside Avenue
8 Sandpiper Way
92 Pacific Boulevard
1022 Evergreen Place
Christmas in Cedar Cove
   (5-B Poppy Lane and
   A Cedar Cove Christmas)
1105 Yakima Street
1225 Christmas Tree Lane

### The Dakota Series

Dakota Born
Dakota Home
Always Dakota
Buffalo Valley

### The Manning Family

The Manning Sisters
   (The Cowboy's Lady and
   The Sheriff Takes a Wife)

The Manning Brides
   (Marriage of Inconvenience and
   Stand-In Wife)
The Manning Grooms
   (Bride on the Loose and
   Same Time, Next Year)

### Christmas Books

A Gift to Last
On a Snowy Night
Home for the Holidays
Glad Tidings
Christmas Wishes
Small Town Christmas
When Christmas Comes
   (now retitled Trading
   Christmas)
There's Something About
   Christmas
Christmas Letters
The Perfect Christmas
Choir of Angels
   (Shirley, Goodness and Mercy,
   Those Christmas Angels and
   Where Angels Go)
Call Me Mrs. Miracle

### Heart of Texas

VOLUME 1
   (Lonesome Cowboy and
   Texas Two-Step)
VOLUME 2
   (Caroline's Child and
   Dr. Texas)
VOLUME 3
   (Nell's Cowboy and
   Lone Star Baby)
Promise, Texas
Return to Promise

# CONTENTS

# MARRIAGE WANTED

To Randall Toye,
who has supported and encouraged me
for twenty-eight wonderful years.

# One

Savannah Charles watched the young woman wandering around her bridal shop, checking prices and looking more discouraged by the moment. Her shoulders slumped and she bit her lip when she read the tag on the wedding gown she'd selected. She had excellent taste, Savannah noticed; the ivory silk-taffeta dress was one of her own favorites. A pattern of lace and pearls swirled up the puffed sleeves and bodice.

"Can I help you?" Savannah asked, moving toward her.

Startled, the woman turned. "I… It doesn't look like it. This dress is almost twice as much as my budget for the whole wedding. Are you Savannah?"

"Yes."

She smiled shyly. "Missy Gilbert told me about you. She said you're wonderful to work with and that you might be able to give Kurt and me some guidance. I'm Susan Davenport." She held out her hand and Savannah shook it, liking the girl immediately.

"When's your wedding?"

"In six weeks. Kurt and I are paying for it ourselves.

His two younger brothers are still in college and his parents haven't got much to spare." Amusement turned up the corners of her mouth as she added, "Kurt's dad claims he's becoming poor by degrees."

Savannah smiled back. "What about your family?"

"There's only my brother and me. He's fifteen years older and, well…it isn't that he doesn't like Kurt. Because once you meet Kurt, it's impossible not to love him. He's kind and generous and interesting…."

Savannah was touched by Susan's eagerness to tell her about the man she wanted to marry.

"But Nash—my brother—doesn't believe in marriage," the young woman went on to explain. "He's an attorney and he's worked on so many divorce cases over the years that he simply doesn't believe in it anymore. It doesn't help that he's divorced himself, although that was years and years ago."

"What's your budget?" Savannah asked. She'd planned weddings that went into six figures, but she was equally adept at finding reasonable alternatives. She walked back to her desk, limping on her right foot. It ached more this afternoon than usual. It always did when the humidity was this high.

Susan told her the figure she and Kurt had managed to set aside and Savannah frowned. It wasn't much, but she could work with it. She turned around and caught Susan staring at her. Savannah was accustomed to that kind of reaction to her limp, the result of a childhood accident. She generally wore pants, which disguised the scars and disfigurement, but her limp was always noticeable, and more so when she was tired. Until they knew her better, it seemed to disconcert people. Generally she ignored their hesitation and continued, hoping that her own acceptance would put them at ease.

"Even the least expensive wedding dresses would eat up the majority of the money we've worked so hard to save."

"You could always rent the dress," Savannah suggested.

"I could?" Her pretty blue eyes lit up when Savannah mentioned the rental fee.

"How many people are you inviting?"

"Sixty-seven," Susan told her, as if the number of guests had been painfully difficult to pare down. "Kurt and I can't afford more. Mostly it's his family.... I don't think Nash will even come to the wedding." Her voice fell.

Despite never having met Susan's older brother, she already disliked him. Savannah couldn't imagine a brother refusing to attend his sister's wedding, no matter what his personal views on marriage happened to be.

"Kurt's from a large family. He has aunts and uncles and, I swear, at least a thousand cousins. We'd like to invite everyone, but we can't. The invitations alone will cost a fortune."

"Have you thought about making your own invitations?"

Susan shook her head. "I'm not very artsy."

"You don't need to be." Opening a drawer, Savannah brought out a book of calligraphy. "These are fairly simple and elegant-looking and they'll add a personal touch because they're individualized." She paused. "You'll find other ideas on the internet."

"These are beautiful. You honestly think I could do this?" She looked expectantly at Savannah.

"Without a doubt," Savannah answered with a smile.

"I wish I could talk some sense into Nash," Susan muttered, then squared her shoulders as if she was ready to take him on right that minute. "He's the only family I have. We've got aunts and uncles here and there, but no one we're close to, and Nash is being so unreasonable about this. I love Kurt and nothing's going to change the way I feel. I love his family, too. It can be lonely when you don't belong to someone. That's Nash's problem. He's forgotten what it's like to belong to someone. To be in a relationship."

Loneliness. Savannah was well acquainted with the feeling. All her life she'd felt alone. The little girl who couldn't run and play with friends. The teenage girl who never got asked to the prom. The woman who arranged the happiest days of other people's lives.

Loneliness. Savannah knew more than she wanted to about long days and longer nights.

"I'm sure your brother will change his mind," Savannah said reassuringly—even though she wasn't sure at all.

Susan laughed. "That only goes to prove you don't know my brother. Once he's set on something, it takes an Act of Congress to persuade him otherwise."

Savannah spent the next hour with Susan, deciding on the details of both the wedding and the reception. With such a limited budget it was a challenge, but they did it.

"I can't believe we can do so much with so little," Susan said once they'd finished. Her face glowed with happiness. "A nice wedding doesn't mean as much to Kurt as it does to me, but he's willing to do whatever he can to make our day special."

Through the course of their conversation, Savannah

learned that Kurt had graduated from the University of Washington with an engineering degree. He'd recently been hired by a California firm and had moved to the San Francisco area, where Susan would be joining him.

After defying her brother, Susan had moved in with Kurt's family, working part-time and saving every penny she could to help with the wedding expenses.

"I can hardly wait to talk to Kurt," Susan said excitedly as she gathered her purse and the notes she'd made. "I'll get back to you as soon as he's had a chance to go over the contract." Susan paused. "Missy was right. You are wonderful." She threw both arms around Savannah in an impulsive hug. "I'll be back as soon as I can and you can take the measurements for the dress." She cast a dreamy look toward the silk-and-taffeta gown and sighed audibly. "Kurt's going to die when he sees me in that dress."

"You'll make a lovely bride."

"Thank you for everything," Susan said as she left the store.

"You're welcome." It was helping young women like Susan that Savannah enjoyed the most. The eager, happy ones who were so much in love they were willing to listen to their hearts no matter what the cost. Over the years, Savannah had worked with every kind of bride and she knew the signs. The Susans of this world were invariably a delight.

It was highly unlikely that Savannah would ever be married herself. Men were an enigma to her. Try as she might, she'd never been able to understand them. They invariably treated her differently than they did other women. Savannah assumed their attitude had to do with her damaged leg. Men either saw her as fragile, untouchable, because of it, or they viewed her as a buddy, a confidante. She supposed she should be flattered by the easy camaraderie they shared with her. They sought her advice, listened politely when she spoke, then did as they pleased.

Only a few men had seen her as a woman, a woman with dreams and desires of her own. But when it came to love, each of them had grown hesitant and afraid. Each relationship had ended awkwardly long before it had gotten close to serious.

Maybe that wasn't a fair assessment, Savannah mused sadly. Maybe it was her own attitude. She'd been terrified of ever falling in love. No matter how deeply she felt about a man, she was positive that her imperfection would come between them. It was safer to hold back, to cling to her pride than risk rejection and pain later on.

A week later, Susan came breezing through the door to Savannah's shop.

"Hello," she said, smiling broadly. "I talked to Kurt and he's as excited as I am." She withdrew a debit card from her purse. "I'd like to give you the down payment now. And I have the signed contract for you."

Savannah brought out her paperwork and Susan paid her. "My brother doesn't believe we'll be able to do it without his help, but he's wrong. We're going to have a beautiful wedding, with or without Nash, thanks to you."

This was what made Savannah's job so fulfilling. "I'll order what we need right away," she told Susan. Savannah only wished there was some way she could influence the young woman's unreasonable older brother. She knew his type—cynical, distrusting, pessimistic. A man who scoffed at love, who had no respect for marriage. How very sad. Despite her irritation with the face-less Nash, Savannah couldn't help feeling sorry for him. Whether or not he realized it, he was going to lose his sister.

There were just the two of them, so she didn't under-stand why Nash wouldn't support his sister in her de-cision. Luckily Susan had Kurt's parents. Undoubtedly this was something her brother hadn't counted on, either.

Susan left soon afterward. What remained of Savan-nah's day was busy. The summer months used to be her overburdened time, but that hadn't held true of late. Her services were booked equally throughout the year.

Around five-thirty, when Savannah was getting ready to close for the day, the bell chimed over her door, in-dicating someone had entered the shop. She looked up from her computer and found a tall, well-dressed man standing by the doorway. It had started to rain lightly; he shook off the raindrops in his hair before he stepped farther inside. She saw him glance around and scowl, as if being in such a place was repugnant to him. Even before he spoke she knew he was Susan's brother. The family resemblance was striking.

"Hello," she said.

"Hello." He slid his hands in his pockets with a con-temptuous frown. Apparently he feared that even being in this place where love and romance were honored would infect him with some dread disease. It must take a good deal of energy to maintain his cynicism, Savan-nah thought.

"Can I help you?" she asked.

"No, thanks. I was just looking." He walked slowly through the shop. His expensive leather shoes made a tapping sound against the polished hardwood floor. She noticed that he took pains not to touch anything.

Savannah nearly laughed out loud when he passed a display of satin pillows, edged in French lace, that were meant to be carried by the ring bearer. He stepped around it, giving it a wide berth, then picked up one of her business cards from a brass holder on a small antique table.

"Are you Savannah Charles?" he asked.

"Yes," she replied evenly. "I am."

"Interesting shop you have here," he said dryly. Savannah had to admit she found him handsome in a rugged sort of way. His facial features were strong and well-defined. His mouth firm, his jaw square and stubbornly set. He walked in short, clipped steps, his impatience nearly palpable. Naturally, she might be altogether wrong and this could be someone other than Susan's brother. Savannah decided it was time to find out.

"Are you about to be married?"

"No," he said disgustedly.

"This seems like an unusual shop for you to browse through, then."

He smiled in her direction, acknowledging her shrewdness. "I believe you've been talking to my sister, Susan Davenport."

So Savannah had been right. This was Susan's hard-nosed older brother. His attitude had been a dead giveaway. "Yes, Susan's been in."

"I take it she's decided to go through with this wedding nonsense, then?" He eyed her suspiciously as if to suggest his sister might have changed her mind except for Savannah's encouragement and support.

"It would be best if you discussed Susan's plans with her."

Nash clasped his hands behind his back. "I would if we were on speaking terms."

How he knew his sister was working with her, Savannah hadn't a clue. She didn't even want to know.

"So," he said conversationally, "exactly what do you do here?"

"I'm a wedding coordinator."

"Wedding coordinator," he repeated, sounding genuinely curious. He nodded for her to continue.

"Basically I organize the wedding for the bride and her family so they're free to enjoy this all-important day."

"I see," he said. "You're the one who makes sure the flowers arrive at the church on time?"

"Something like that." His version oversimplified her role, but she didn't think he'd appreciate a detailed job description. After all, he wasn't interested in her, but in what he could learn about his sister and Kurt's plans.

He wandered about the shop some more, careful not to come into contact with any of the displays she'd so carefully arranged. He strolled past a lace-covered table with an elegant heart-shaped guest book and plumed pen as if he were walking past a nest of vipers. Savannah couldn't help being amused.

"Susan hasn't got the money for a wedding," he announced. "At least, not one fancy enough to hire a co-ordinator."

"Again, this is something you need to discuss with your sister."

He didn't like her answer; that much was obvious from the way his mouth thinned and the irritation she saw in his eyes. They were the same intense blue as his sister's, but that was where the resemblance ended. Susan's eyes revealed her love and enthusiasm for life. Nash's revealed his disenchantment and skepticism. She finished up the last of her paperwork, ignoring him as much as she could.

"You're a babe in the woods, aren't you?"

"I beg your pardon?" Savannah said, looking up.

"You actually believe all this...absurdity?"

"I certainly don't think of love and commitment as absurd, if that's what you mean, Mr. Davenport."

"Call me Nash."

"All right," she agreed reluctantly. In a few minutes she was going to show him the door. He hadn't bothered to disguise the purpose of his visit. He was trying to pump her for information and hadn't figured out yet that she refused to be placed in the middle between him and his sister.

"Did you ever stop to realize that over fifty percent of the couples who marry in this day and age end up divorcing?"

"I know the statistics."

He walked purposely toward her as if approaching a judge's bench, intent on proving his point. "Love is a lame excuse for marriage."

Since he was going to make it impossible for her to concentrate, she sat back on her stool and folded her arms. "What do you suggest couples do then, Mr. Davenport? Just live together?"

"Nash," he reminded her irritably. "And, yes, living together makes a lot more sense. If a man and woman are so hot for each other, I don't see any reason to muddy the relationship with legalities when a weekend in bed would simplify everything."

Savannah resisted the urge to roll her eyes. Rejecting marriage made as much sense to her as pushing a car over a cliff because the fender was dented. Instead she asked, "Is this what you want Susan and Kurt to do? Live together indefinitely? Without commitment?"

That gave him pause. Apparently it was perfectly fine for other couples to do that, but when it came to his little sister, he hesitated. "Yes," he finally said. "Until this infatuation passes."

"What about children?"

"Susan's little more than a child herself," he argued, although she was twenty-four—and in Savannah's estimation a mature twenty-four. "If she's smart, she'll avoid adding to her mistakes," he said stiffly.

"What about someone other than your sister?" she demanded, annoyed with herself for allowing him to draw her into this pointless discussion. "Are you suggesting our society should do away with family?"

"A wedding ring doesn't make a family," he returned just as heatedly.

Savannah sighed deeply. "I think it's best for us to agree to disagree," she said, feeling a bit sad. It was unrealistic to think she'd say anything that would change his mind. Susan was determined to marry Kurt, with or without his approval, but she loved her brother, too. That was what made this situation so difficult.

"Love is a lame excuse to mess up one's life," he said, clenching his fists at his side with impotent anger. "A lame excuse."

At his third use of the word *lame,* Savannah inwardly

flinched. Because she was sitting behind her desk, he didn't realize she was "lame."

"Marriage is an expensive trap that destroys a man's soul," Nash went on to say, ignoring her. "I see the results of it each and every day. Just this afternoon, I was in court for a settlement hearing that was so nasty the judge had to pull both attorneys into chambers. Do you really believe I want my little sister involved in something like that?"

"Your sister is a grown woman, Mr. Davenport. She's old enough to make her own decisions."

"Mistakes, you mean."

Savannah sensed his frustration, but arguing with him would do no good at all. "Susan's in love. You should know by now that she's determined to marry Kurt."

"In love. Excuses don't get much worse than that."

Savannah had had enough. She stood and realized for the first time how tall Nash actually was. He loomed head and shoulders over her five-foot-three-inch frame. Standing next to him she felt small and insignificant. For all their differences, Savannah could appreciate his concerns. Nash loved his sister; otherwise he wouldn't have gone to such effort to find out her plans.

"It's been interesting," Nash said, waiting for her to walk around her desk and join him. Savannah did, limping as she went. She was halfway across the room before she saw that he wasn't following her. Half turning around, she noticed that he was looking at her leg, his features marked by regret.

"I didn't mean to be rude," he said, and she couldn't doubt his sincerity. What surprised her was his sensitivity. She might have judged this man too harshly. His attitude had irritated her, but she'd also been entertained by him—and by the vigor of their argument.

"You didn't know." She finished her trek to the door, again surprised to realize he hadn't followed her. "It's well past my closing time," she said meaningfully.

"Of course." His steps were crisp and uniform as he marched across her shop, stopping abruptly when he reached her. A frown wrinkled his brow as he stared at her again.

"What's wrong?"

He laughed shortly. "I'm trying to figure something out."

"If it has to do with Susan and Kurt—"

"It doesn't," he cut in. "It has to do with you." An odd smile lifted his mouth. "I like you. You're impertinent, sassy and stubborn."

"Oh, really!" She might have been offended if she hadn't been struggling so hard not to laugh.

"Really."

"You're tactless, irritating and overpowering," she responded.

His grin was transformed into a full-blown smile. "You're right. It's a shame, though."

"A shame? What are you talking about?"

"You being a wedding coordinator. It's a waste. With your obvious organizational skills, you might've done something useful. Instead, your head's stuck in the clouds and you've let love and romance fog up your brain. But you know what?" He rubbed the side of his jaw. "There just might be hope for you."

"Hope. Funny, I was thinking the same thing about you. There just might be a slim chance of reasoning with you. You're clearly intelligent and even a little witty. But unfortunately you're misguided. Now that you're dealing with your sister's marriage, however, there's a remote possibility someone might be able to get through to you."

"What do you mean?" he asked, folding his arms over his chest and resting his weight on one foot.

"Your judgment's been confused by your clients. By their anger and bitterness and separations. We're at opposite ends of the same subject. I work with couples when they're deeply in love and convinced the relationship will last forever. You see them when they're embittered and disillusioned. But what you don't seem to realize is that you need to see the glass as half-full and not half-empty."

He frowned. "I thought we were talking about marriage."

"We are. What you said earlier is true. Fifty percent of all married couples end up divorcing—which means fifty percent of them go on to lead fulfilling, happy lives."

Nash's snort was derisive. He dropped his arms and straightened, shaking his head. "I was wrong. There's no hope for you. The fifty percent who stay together are just as miserable. Given the opportunity, they'd gladly get out of the relationship."

Nash was beginning to irritate her again. "Why is it so difficult for you to believe that there's such a thing as a happy marriage?"

"Because I've never seen one."

"You haven't looked hard enough."

"Have you ever stopped to think that your head's so muddled with hearts and flowers and happy-ever-afters that you can't and won't accept what's right in front of your eyes?"

"Like I said, it's past my closing time." Savannah jerked open the shop door. The clanging bell marked the end of their frustrating conversation. Rarely had Savannah allowed anyone to get under her skin the way she had Nash Davenport. The man was impossible. Totally unreasonable...

The woman was impossible. Totally unreasonable.

Nash couldn't understand why he continued to mull over their conversation. Twenty-four hours had passed, and he'd thought about their verbal sparring match a dozen times.

Relaxing in his leather office chair, he rolled a pen between his palms. Obviously Savannah didn't know him well; otherwise, she wouldn't have attempted to convince him of the error of his views.

His eyes fell on the phone and he sighed inwardly. Susan was being stubborn and irrational. It was plain that he was going to have to be the one to mend fences. He'd hoped she'd come to her senses, but it wasn't going to happen. He was her older brother, her closest relative, and if she refused to make the first move, he'd have to do it.

He looked up Kurt Caldwell's parents' phone number. He resented having to contact her there. Luck was with him, however, when Susan herself answered.

"It's Nash," he said. When she was little, her voice rose with excitement whenever he called. Anytime he arrived home, she'd fly into his arms, so glad to see him she couldn't hold still. He sighed again, missing the child she once was.

"Hello, Nash," Susan said stiffly. No pleasure at hearing from him was evident now.

"How are you doing?" That was the purpose of this call, after all.

"Fine. How about you?" Her words were stilted, and her stubbornness hadn't budged an inch. He would have said as much, then thought better of it.

"I'm fine, too," he answered.

The silence stretched between them.

"I understand you have a wedding coordinator now," he said, hoping to come across as vaguely interested. She might have defied him, but he would always be her big brother.

"How do you know that?"

"Word, uh, gets around." In fact, he'd learned about it from a family friend. Still, he shouldn't have said anything. And he wouldn't have if Savannah hadn't dominated his thoughts from the moment he'd met her.

"You've had someone checking into my affairs, haven't you?" Susan lowered her voice to subzero temperatures. "You can't rule my life, Nash. I'm going to marry Kurt and that's all there is to it."

"I gathered as much from Savannah Charles...."

"You've talked to Savannah?"

Nash recognized his second mistake immediately. He'd blown it now, and Susan wasn't going to forgive him.

"Stop meddling in my life, Nash." His sister's voice quavered suspiciously and seconds later the line was disconnected. The phone droned in his ear before he dejectedly replaced the receiver.

Needless to say, that conversation hadn't gone well. He'd like to blame Savannah, but it was his fault. He'd been the one to let her name slip, a stupid error on his part.

The wedding coordinator and his sister were both too stubborn and naive for their own good. If this was how

Susan wanted it, then he had no choice but to abide by her wishes. Calling her had been another mistake in a long list he'd been making lately.

His assistant poked her head in his door, and he gave her his immediate attention. He had more important things to worry about than his sister and a feisty wedding coordinator who lived in a dreamworld.

"What did my brother say?" Susan demanded.

"He wanted to know about you," Savannah said absently as she arranged champagne flutes on the display table next to the five-tier wedding cake. She'd been working on the display between customers for the past hour.

"In other words, Nash was pumping you for information?"

"Yes, but you don't need to worry, I didn't tell him anything. What I did do was suggest he talk to you." She straightened, surprised that he'd followed her advice. "He cares deeply for you, Susan."

"I know." Susan gnawed on her lower lip. "I wish I hadn't hung up on him."

"Susan!"

"I... He told me he'd talked to you and it made me so mad I couldn't bear to speak to him another second."

Savannah was surprised by Nash's slip. She would've thought their conversation was the last thing he'd mention. But from the sound of it, he didn't get an opportunity to rehash it with Susan.

"If he makes a pest of himself," Susan said righteously, "let me know and I'll... I'll do something."

"Don't worry about it. I rather enjoyed talking to him." It was true, although Savannah hated to admit it.

She'd worked hard to push thoughts of Nash from her mind over the past couple of days. His attitude had annoyed her, true, but she'd found him intriguing and—it bothered her to confess this—a challenge. A smile came when she realized he probably saw her the same way.

"I have to get back to work," Susan said reluctantly. "I just wanted to apologize for my brother's behavior."

"He wasn't a problem."

On her way out the door, Susan muttered something Savannah couldn't hear. The situation was sad. Brother and sister loved each other but were at an impasse.

Savannah continued to consider the situation until the bell over the door chimed about five minutes later. Smiling, she looked up, deciding she wasn't going to get this display finished until after closing time. She should've known better than to try.

"Nash." His name was a mere whisper.

"Hello again," he said dryly. "I've come to prove my point."

# Two

"You want to prove your point," Savannah repeated thoughtfully. Nash Davenport was the most headstrong man she'd ever encountered. He was also one of the handsomest. That did more to confuse her than to help. For reasons as yet unclear, she'd lost her objectivity. No doubt it had something to do with that pride of his and the way they'd argued. No doubt it was also because they remained diametrically opposed on the most fundamental issues of life—love and marriage.

"I've given some thought to our conversation the other day," Nash said, pacing back and forth, "and it seems to me that I'm just the person to clear up your thinking. Besides," he went on, "if I can clear up your thinking, maybe you'll have some influence on Susan."

Although it was difficult, Savannah resisted the urge to laugh.

"To demonstrate my good faith, I brought a peace offering." He held up a white sack for her inspection. "Two lattes," he explained. He set the bag on the corner of her desk and opened it, handing her one of the paper cups. The smell of hot coffee blended with steamed milk was as welcome as popcorn in a theater. "Make yourself comfortable," he said next, gesturing toward the stool, "because it might take a while."

"I don't know if this is a good idea," Savannah felt obliged to say as she carefully edged onto the stool.

"It's a great idea. Just hear me out," he said smoothly.

"Oh, all right," she returned with an ungracious nod. Savannah might have had the energy to resist him if it hadn't been so late in the day. She was tired and the meeting with Susan had frustrated her. She'd come to her upset and unhappy, and Savannah had felt helpless, not knowing how to reassure the younger woman.

Nash pried off the lid of his latte, then glanced at his watch. He walked over to her door and turned over the sign so it read Closed.

"Hey, wait a minute!"

"It's—" he looked at his watch again "—5:29 p.m. You're officially closed in one minute."

Savannah didn't bother to disagree. "I think it's only fair for you to know that whatever you have to say isn't going to change my mind," she said.

"I figured as much."

The man continued to surprise her. "How do you intend to prove your point? Parade divorced couples through my wedding shop?"

"Nothing that drastic."

"Did it occur to you that I could do the same thing and have you meet with a group of blissful newlyweds?" she asked.

He grinned. "I'm way ahead of you. I already guessed you'd enjoy introducing me to any number of loving couples who can't keep their hands off each other."

Savannah shrugged, not denying it.

"The way I figure it," he said, "we both have a strong argument to make."

"Exactly." She nodded. "But you aren't going to change my mind and I doubt I'll change yours." She didn't know what kept some couples together against all odds or why others decided to divorce when the first little problem arose. If Nash expected her to supply the answers, she had none to offer.

"Don't be so sure we won't change each other's mind." Which only went to prove that he thought there was a chance he could influence her. "We could accomplish a great deal if we agree to be open-minded."

Savannah cocked one eyebrow and regarded him skeptically. "Can you guarantee you'll be open-minded?"

"I'm not sure," he answered, and she was impressed with his honesty. "But I'm willing to try. That's all I ask of you."

"That sounds fair."

He rubbed his palms together as though eager to get started. "If you don't object, I'd like to go first."

"Just a minute," she said, holding up her hand. "Before we do, shouldn't we set some rules?"

"Like what?"

Although it was her suggestion, Savannah didn't really have an answer. "I don't know. Just boundaries of some kind."

"I trust you not to do anything weird, and you can count on the same from me," he said. "After all—"

"Don't be so hasty," she interrupted. "If we're going to put time and effort into this, it makes sense that we have rules. And something riding on the outcome."

His blue eyes brightened. "Now there's an interesting

thought." He paused and a smile bracketed his mouth. "So you want to set a wager?"

Nash seemed to be on a one-man campaign to convince her the world would be a better place without the institution of marriage. "We might as well make it interesting, don't you think?"

"I couldn't agree more. If you can prove your point and get me to agree that you have, what would you want in exchange?"

This part was easy. "For you to attend Susan and Kurt's wedding. It would mean the world to Susan."

The easy smile disappeared behind a dark frown.

"She was in this afternoon," Savannah continued, rushing the words in her eagerness to explain. "She's anxious and confused, loving you and loving Kurt and needing your approval so badly."

Nash's mouth narrowed into a thin line of irritation.

"Would it really be so much to ask?" she ventured. "I realize I'd need to rely on your complete and total honesty, but I have faith in you." She took a sip of her latte.

"So, if you convince me my thinking is wrong on this marriage issue, you want me to attend Susan's wedding." He hesitated, then nodded slowly. "Deal," he said, and his grin reappeared.

Until that moment, Savannah was convinced Nash had no idea what he intended to use for his argument. But apparently he did. "What would you want from me?" she asked. Her question broke into his musings because he jerked his head toward her as if he'd forgotten there might be something in this for him, as well. He took a deep breath and then released it. "I don't know. Do I have to decide right now?"

"No."

"It'll be something substantial—you understand that, don't you?"

Savannah managed to hold back a smile. "I wouldn't expect anything less."

"How about home-cooked dinners for a week served on your fanciest china? That wouldn't be out of line," he murmured.

She gaped at him. Her request had been generous and completely selfless. She'd offered him an excuse to attend Susan's wedding and salvage his pride, and in return he wanted her to slave in the kitchen for days on end.

"That is out of line," she told him, unwilling to agree to anything so ridiculous. If he wanted homemade meals, he could do what the rest of the world did and cook them himself, visit relatives or get married.

Nash's expression was boyish with delight. "So you're afraid you're going to lose."

Raising her eyebrows, she said, "You haven't got a prayer, Davenport."

"Then what's the problem?" he asked, making an exaggerated gesture with both hands. "Do you agree to my terms or not?"

This discussion had wandered far from what she'd originally intended. Savannah had been hoping to smooth things over between brother and sister and at the same time prove her own point. She wasn't interested in putting her own neck on the chopping block. Any attempt to convince Nash of the error of his ways was pointless.

He finished off his latte and flung the empty container into her garbage receptacle. "Be ready tomorrow afternoon," he said, walking to the door.

Savannah scrambled awkwardly from the stool. "What for?" she called after him. She limped two steps toward him and stopped abruptly at the flash of pain that shot up her leg. She'd sat too long in the same position, something she was generally able to avoid. She wanted to rub her thigh, work the throbbing muscle, but that would reveal her pain, which she wanted to hide from Nash.

"You'll know more tomorrow afternoon," he promised, looking pleased with himself.

"How long will this take?"

"There are time restrictions? Are there any other rules we need to discuss?"

"I... We should both be reasonable about this, don't you think?"

"I was planning to be sensible, but I can't speak for you."

This conversation was deteriorating rapidly. "I'll be ready at closing time tomorrow afternoon, then," she said, holding her hand against her thigh. If he didn't leave soon, she was going to have to sit down. Disguising her pain had become a way of life, but the longer she stood, the more difficult it became.

"Something's wrong," he announced, his gaze hard and steady. "You'd argue with me if there wasn't."

Again she was impressed by his sensitivity. "Nonsense. I said I'd be ready. What more do you want?"

He left her then, in the nick of time. A low moan escaped as she sank onto her chair. Perspiration moistened her brow and she drew in several deep breaths. Rubbing her hand over the tense muscles slowly eased out the pain.

The phone was situated to the left of her desk and after giving the last of her discomfort a couple of minutes to ebb away, she reached for the receiver and dialed her parents' number. Apparently Nash had decided how to present his case. She had, too. No greater argument could be made than her parents' loving relationship. Their marriage was as solid as Fort Knox and they'd been devoted to each other for over thirty years. Nash couldn't meet her family and continue to discredit love and marriage.

Her father answered on the second ring, sounding delighted to hear from her. A rush of warm feeling washed over Savannah. Her family had been a constant source of love and encouragement to her through the years.

"Hi, Dad."

"It's always good to hear from you, sweetheart."

Savannah relaxed in her chair. "Is Mom around?"

"No, she's got a doctor's appointment to have her blood pressure checked again. Is there anything I can do for you?"

Savannah's hand tightened around the receiver. She didn't want to mislead her parents into thinking she was involved with Nash. But she needed to prove her point. "Is there any chance I could bring someone over for dinner tomorrow night?"

"Of course."

Savannah laughed lightly. "You might want to check Mom's calendar. It'd be just like you to agree to something when she's already made plans."

"I looked. The calendar's right here in the kitchen and tomorrow night's free. Now, if you were to ask about Friday, that's a different story."

Once more Savannah found herself smiling.

"Who do you want us to meet?"

"His name's Nash Davenport."

Her announcement was met with a short but noticeable silence. "You're bringing a young man home to meet your family? This is an occasion, then."

"Dad, it isn't like that." This was exactly what she'd feared would happen, that her family would misinterpret her bringing Nash home. "We've only just met...."

"It was like that with your mother and me," her father said excitedly. "We met on a Friday night and a week later I knew this was the woman I was going to love all my life, and I have."

"Dad, Nash is just a friend—not even a friend, really, just an acquaintance," Savannah said, trying to correct his mistaken impression. "I'm coordinating his sister's wedding."

"No need to explain, sweetheart. If you want to bring a young man for your mother and me to meet, we'd be thrilled, no matter what the reason."

Savannah was about to respond, but then decided that a lengthy explanation might hurt her cause rather than help it. "I'm not sure of the exact time we'll arrive."

"No problem. I'll light up the barbecue and that way you won't need to worry. Come whenever you can. We'll make an evening of it."

Oh, yes, it was going to be quite an evening, Savannah mused darkly. Two stubborn people, both convinced they were right, would each try to convert the other.

This was going to be so easy that Nash almost felt guilty. Almost... Poor Savannah. Once he'd finished with what he had to show her, she'd have no option but to accept the reality of his argument.

Nash loved this kind of debate, when he was certain

beyond a shadow of a doubt that he was right. By the time he was done, Savannah would be eating her words.

Grabbing his briefcase, he hurried out of his office, anxious to forge ahead and prove his point.

"Nash, what's your hurry?"

Groaning inwardly, Nash turned to face a fellow attorney, Paul Jefferson. "I've got an appointment this evening," Nash explained. He didn't like Paul, had never liked Paul. What bothered him most was that this brown-noser was going to be chosen over him for the partnership position that was opening up within the year. Both Paul and Nash had come into the firm at the same time, and they were both good attorneys. But Paul had a way of ingratiating himself with the powers that be and parting the waters of opportunity.

"An appointment or a date?" Paul asked with that smug look of his. One of these days Nash was going to find an excuse to wipe that grin off his face.

He looked pointedly at his watch. "If you'll excuse me, Paul, I have to leave, otherwise I'll be late."

"Can't keep her waiting, now can we?" Paul said, and finding himself amusing, he laughed at his own sorry joke.

Knotting his fist at his side, Nash was happy to escape. Anger clawed at him until he was forced to stop and analyze his outrage. He'd been working with Paul for nearly ten years. He'd tolerated his humorless jokes, his conceited, self-righteous attitude and his air of superiority without displaying his annoyance. What was different now?

He considered the idea of Paul being preferred to him for the partnership. But this was nothing new. The minute he'd learned about the opening, he'd suspected

Stackhouse and Serle would choose Paul. He'd accepted it as fact weeks ago.

Paul had suggested Nash was hurrying to meet a woman—which he was. Nash didn't bother to deny it. What upset him was the sarcastic way Paul had said it, as though Savannah—

His mind came to a grinding halt. Savannah.

So she was at the bottom of all this. Nash had taken offense at the edge in Paul's voice, as if his fellow attorney had implied that Savannah was, somehow, less than she should be. He knew he was being oversensitive. After all, Paul had never even met her. But still…

Nash recalled his own reaction to Savannah, his observations when he'd met her. She was small. Her dark, pixie-style hair and deep brown eyes gave her a fragile appearance, but that was deceptive. The woman obviously had a constitution of iron.

Her eyes… Once more his thoughts skidded to a halt. He'd never known a woman with eyes that were more revealing. In them he read a multitude of emotions. Pain, both physical and emotional. In them he saw a woman with courage. Nash barely knew Savannah and yet he sensed she was one of the most astonishing people he'd probably ever meet. He'd wanted to defend her, wanted to slam his colleague up against a wall and demand an apology for the slight, vague though it was. In fact, he admitted, if Paul was insulting anyone, it was more likely him than Savannah….

When he reached his car, Nash sat in the driver's seat with his key poised in front of the ignition for a moment, brooding about his colleague and the competitiveness between them.

His mood lightened considerably as he made his way

through the heavy traffic to the wedding shop. He'd been looking forward to this all day.

He found a parking spot and climbed out of his car, then fed the meter. As he turned away he caught sight of Savannah in the shop window, talking to a customer. Her face was aglow with enthusiasm and even from this distance her eyes sparkled. For a reason unknown to him, his pulse accelerated as joy surged through him.

He was happy to be seeing Savannah. Any man would, knowing he was about to be proven right. But this was more than that. This happiness was rooted in the knowledge that he'd be spending time with her.

Savannah must have felt his scrutiny, because she glanced upward and their eyes met briefly before she reluctantly pulled hers away. Although she continued speaking to her customer, Nash sensed that she'd experienced the same intensity of feeling he had. It was at moments such as this that he wished he could be privy to a woman's thoughts. He would gladly have forfeited their bet to know if she was as surprised and puzzled as he felt. Nash couldn't identify the feeling precisely; all he knew was that it made him uncomfortable.

The customer was leaving just as Nash entered the shop. Savannah was sitting at her desk and intuitively he realized she needed to sit periodically because of her leg. She looked fragile and confused. When she raised her eyes to meet his, he was shocked by the strength of her smile.

"You're right on time," she said.

"You would be, too, if you were about to have home-cooked meals personally served to you for the next week."

"Don't count on it, Counselor."

"Oh, I'm counting on it," he said with a laugh. "I've already got the menu picked out. We'll start the first night with broiled New York sirloin, Caesar salad and a three-layer chocolate cake."

"You certainly love to dream," she said with an effortless laugh. "I find it amusing that you never stopped to ask if I could cook. It'll probably come as a surprise to learn that not all women are proficient in the kitchen. If by some odd quirk of fate you do happen to win this wager, you'll dine on boxed macaroni and cheese or microwave meals for seven days and like it."

Nash was stunned. She was right; he'd assumed she could cook as well as she seemed to manage everything else. Her shop was a testament to her talent, appealing to the eye in every respect. True, all those wedding gowns and satin pillows were aiding and abetting romance, but it had a homey, comfortable feel, as well. This wasn't an easy thing to admit. A wedding shop was the last place on earth Nash ever thought he'd willingly visit.

"Are you ready to admit defeat?" he asked.

"Never, but before we get started I need to make a couple of phone calls. Do you mind?"

"Not in the least." He was a patient man, and never more so than now. The longer they delayed, the better. It wasn't likely that Paul would stay late, but Nash wanted to avoid introducing Savannah to him. More important, he wanted her to himself. The thought was unwelcome. This wasn't a date and he had no romantic interest in Savannah Charles, he reminded himself.

Savannah reached for the phone and he wandered around the shop noticing small displays he'd missed on his prior visits. The first time he'd felt nervous; he didn't know what to expect from a wedding coordinator, but certainly not the practical, gutsy woman he'd found.

He trained his ears not to listen in on her conversation, but the crisp, businesslike tone of her voice was surprisingly captivating.

It was happening again—that disturbing feeling was back, deep in the pit of his stomach. He'd felt it before, several years earlier, and it had nearly ruined his life. He was in trouble. Panic shot through his blood and he felt the overwhelming urge to turn and run in the opposite direction. The last time he'd had this feeling, he'd gotten married.

"I'm ready," Savannah said, and stood.

Nash stared at her for a long moment as his brain processed what was going on.

"Nash?"

He gave himself a hard mental shake. He didn't know if he was right about what had happened here, but he didn't like it. "Do you mind riding with me?" he asked, once he'd composed himself.

"That'll be fine."

The drive back to his office building in downtown Seattle was spent in relative silence. Savannah seemed to sense his reflective mood. Another woman might have attempted to fill the space with idle chatter. Nash was grateful she didn't.

After he'd parked, he led Savannah into his building and up the elevator to the law firm's offices. She seemed impressed with the plush furnishings and the lavish view of Mount Rainier and Puget Sound from his twentieth-story window.

When she'd entered his office she'd walked directly to the window and set her purse on his polished oak credenza. "How do you manage to work with a view like this?" she asked, her voice soft with awe. She seemed mesmerized by the beauty that appeared before her.

After several years Nash had become immune to its splendor, but lately he'd begun to appreciate the solace he found there. The color of the sky reflected like a mirror on the water's surface. On a gray and hazy morning, the water was a dull shade of steel. When the sun shone, Puget Sound was a deep, iridescent greenish blue. He enjoyed watching the ferries and other commercial and pleasure craft as they intersected the waterways. In the last while, he'd often stood in the same spot as Savannah and sorted through his thoughts.

"It's all so beautiful," she said, turning back to him. Hearing her give voice to his own feelings felt oddly comforting. The sooner he presented his argument, the better. The sooner he said what had to be said and put this woman out of his mind, the better.

"You ready?" he asked, flinging opening a file cabinet and withdrawing a handful of thick folders from the top drawer.

"Ready as I'll ever be," she said, taking a chair on the other side of his desk.

Nash slapped the files down on his credenza. "Let's start with Adams versus Adams," he muttered, flipping through the pages of the top folder. "Now, this was an interesting case. Married ten years, two sons. Then Martha learned that Bill was having an affair with a coworker, so she decided to have one herself, only she chose a nineteen-year-old boy. The child-custody battle lasted two months, destroyed them financially and ended so bitterly that Bill moved out of town and hasn't been heard from since. Last

I heard, Martha was clinically depressed and in and out of hospitals."

Savannah gasped. "What about their sons?" she asked. "What happened to them?"

"Eventually they went to live with a relative. From what I understand, they're both in counseling and have been for the last couple of years."

"How very sad," she whispered.

"Don't kid yourself. This is only the beginning. I'm starting with the *A*s and working my way through the file drawer. Let me know when you've had enough." He reached for a second folder. "Anderson versus Anderson... Ah, yes, I remember this one. She attempted suicide three times, blackmailed him emotionally, used the children as weapons, wiped him out financially and then sued for divorce, claiming he was an unfit father." His back was as stiff as his voice. He tossed aside that file and picked up the next.

"Allison versus Allison," he continued crisply. "By the way, I'm changing the names to protect the guilty."

"The guilty?"

"To my way of thinking, each participant in these cases is guilty of contributing to the disasters I'm telling you about. Each made a crucial mistake."

"You're about to suggest their first error was falling in love."

"No," he returned coldly, "it all started with the wedding vows. No two people should be expected to live up to that ideal. It isn't humanly possible."

"You're wrong, Nash. People live up to those vows each and every day, in small ways and in large ones."

Nash jabbed his finger against the stack of folders. "This says otherwise. Love isn't meant to last. Couples are kidding themselves if they believe commitment lasts beyond the next morning. Life's like that, and it's time the rest of the world woke up and admitted it."

"Oh, please!" Savannah cried, standing. She walked over to the window, her back to him, clenching and unclenching her fists. Nash wondered if she was aware of it, and doubted she was.

"Be honest, Savannah. Marriage doesn't work anymore. Hasn't in years. The institution is outdated. If you want to stick your head in the sand, then fine. But when others risk getting hurt, someone needs to tell the truth." His voice rose with the heat of his argument.

Slowly she turned again and stared at him. An almost pitying look came over her.

"She must have hurt you very badly." Savannah's voice was so low, he had to strain to hear.

"Hurt me? What are you talking about?"

She shook her head as though she hadn't realized she'd spoken out loud. "Your ex-wife."

The anger that burned through Nash was like acid. "Who told you about Denise?" he demanded.

"No one," she returned quickly.

He slammed the top file shut and stuffed the stack of folders back inside the drawer with little care and less concern. "How'd you know I was married?"

"I'm sorry, Nash, I shouldn't have mentioned it."

"Who told you?" The answer was obvious but he wanted her to say it.

"Susan mentioned it...."

"How much did she tell you?"

"Just that it happened years ago." Each word revealed her reluctance to drag his sister into the conversation. "She wasn't breaking any confidences, if that's what you think. I'm sure the only reason she brought it up was to explain your—"

"I know why she brought it up."

"I apologize, Nash. I shouldn't have said anything."

"Why not? My file's in another attorney's cabinet, along with those of a thousand other fools just like me who were stupid enough to think love lasts."

Savannah continued to stare at him. "You loved her, didn't you?"

"As much as any foolish twenty-four-year-old loves anyone. Would you mind if we change the subject?"

"Susan's twenty-four."

"Exactly," he said, slapping his hand against the top of his desk. "And she's about to make the same foolish choice I did."

"But, Nash..."

"Have you heard enough, or do you need to listen to a few more cases?"

"I've heard enough."

"Good. Let's get out of here." The atmosphere in the office was stifling. It was as though each and every client he'd represented over the years was there to remind him of the pain he'd lived through himself—only he'd come away smarter than most.

"Do you want me to drive you back to the office or would you prefer I take you home?" he asked.

"No," Savannah said as they walked out of the office. He purposely adjusted his steps to match her slower gait. "If you don't mind, I'd prefer to have our, uh, wager settled this evening."

"Fine with me."

"If you don't mind, I'd like to head for my parents' home. I want you to meet them."

"Sure, why not?" he asked flippantly. His anger simmered just below the surface. Maybe this wasn't such a brilliant idea after all....

Savannah gave him the address and directions. The drive on the freeway was slowed by heavy traffic, which frustrated him even more. By the time they reached the exit, his nerves were frayed. He was about to suggest they do this another evening when she instructed him to take a left at the next light. They turned the corner, drove a block and a half down and were there.

They were walking toward the house when a tall, burly man with a thinning hairline hurried out the front door. "Savannah, sweetheart," he greeted them with a huge grin. "So this is the young man you're going to marry."

# Three

"Dad!" Savannah was mortified. The heat rose from her neck to her cheeks, and she knew her face had to be bright red.

Marcus Charles raised his hands. "Did I say something I shouldn't have?" But there was still a smile on his face.

"I'm Nash Davenport," Nash said, offering Marcus his hand. Considering how her father had chosen to welcome Nash, his gesture was a generous one. She chanced a look in the attorney's direction and was relieved to see he was smiling, too.

"You'll have to forgive me for speaking out of turn," her father said, "but Savannah's never brought home a young man she wants us to meet, so I assumed you're the—"

"Daddy, that's not true!"

"Name one," he said. "And while you're inventing a beau, I'll take Nash in and introduce him to your mother."

"Dad!"

"Hush now or you'll give Nash the wrong impression."

*The wrong impression!* If only he knew. This meeting couldn't have gotten off to a worse start, especially with Nash's present mood. She'd made a drastic mistake mentioning his marriage. It was more than obvious that he'd been badly hurt and was trying to put the memory behind him.

Nash had built a strong case against marriage. The more clients he described, the harder his voice became. The grief of his own experience echoed in his voice as he listed the nightmares of the cases he'd represented.

Nash and her father were already in the house by the time Savannah walked up the steps and into the living room. Her mother had redecorated the room in a Southwestern motif, with painted clay pots and Navajo-style rugs. A recent addition was a wooden folk art coyote with his head thrown back, howling at the moon.

Every time she entered this room, Savannah felt a twinge of sadness. Her mother loved the Southwest and her parents had visited there often. Savannah knew her parents had once looked forward to moving south. She also knew she was the reason they hadn't. As an only child, and one who'd sustained a serious injury—even if it'd happened years before—they worried about her constantly. And with no other immediate family in the Seattle area, they were uncomfortable leaving their daughter alone in the big city.

A hundred times in the past few years, Savannah had tried to convince them to pursue their dreams, but they'd continually made excuses. They never came right out and said they'd stayed in Seattle because of her. They didn't need to; in her heart she knew.

"Hi, Mom," Savannah said as she walked into the kitchen. Her mother was standing at the sink, slicing tomatoes fresh from her garden. "Can I do anything to help?"

Joyce Charles set aside the knife and turned to give her a firm hug. "Savannah, let me look at you," she said, studying her. "You're working too hard, aren't you?"

"Mom, I'm fine."

"Good. Now sit down here and have something cold to drink and tell me all about Nash."

This was worse than Savannah had first believed. She should have explained her purpose in bringing him to meet her family at the very beginning, before introducing him. Giving them a misleading impression was bad enough, but she could only imagine what Nash was thinking.

When Savannah didn't immediately answer her question, Joyce supplied what information she already knew. "You're coordinating his sister's wedding and that's how you two met."

"Yes, but—"

"He really is handsome. What does he do?"

"He's an attorney," Savannah said. "But, Mom—"

"Just look at your dad." Laughing, Joyce motioned toward the kitchen window that looked out over the freshly mowed backyard. The barbecue was heating on the brick patio and her father was showing Nash his prize fishing flies. He'd been tying his own for years and took real pride in the craft; now that he'd retired, it was his favorite hobby.

After glancing out at them, Savannah sank into a kitchen chair. Her mother had poured her a glass of lemonade. Her father displayed his fishing flies only when the guest was someone important, someone he was hoping to impress. Savannah should have realized when she first mentioned Nash that her father had made completely the wrong assumption about this meeting.

"Mom," she said, clenching the ice-cold glass. "I think you should know Nash and I are friends. Nothing more."

"We know that, dear. Do you think he'll like my pasta salad? I added jumbo shrimp this time. I hope he's not a fussy eater."

Jumbo shrimp! So they were rolling out the red carpet. With her dad it was the fishing flies, with her mother it was pasta salad. She sighed. What had she let herself in for now?

"I'm sure he'll enjoy your salad." And if his anti-marriage argument—his evidence—was stronger than hers, he'd be eating seven more meals with a member of the Charles family. Her. She could only hope her parents conveyed the success of their relationship to this cynical lawyer.

"Your father's barbecuing steaks."

"T-bone," Savannah guessed.

"Probably. I forget what he told me when he took them out of the freezer."

Savannah managed a smile.

"I thought we'd eat outside," her mother went on. "You don't mind, do you, dear?"

"No, Mom, that'll be great." Maybe a little sunshine would lift her spirits.

"Let's go outside, then, shall we?" her mother said, carrying the large wooden bowl with the shrimp pasta salad.

The early-evening weather was perfect. Warm, with a subtle breeze and slanting sunlight. Her mother's prize roses bloomed against the fence line. The bright red ones were Savannah's favorite. The flowering rhododendron tree spread out its pink limbs in opulent welcome. Robins chatted back and forth like long-lost friends.

Nash looked up from the fishing rod he was holding and smiled. At least he was enjoying himself. Or seemed to be, anyway. Perhaps her embarrassment was what entertained him. Somehow, Savannah vowed, she'd find a way to clarify the situation to her parents without complicating things with Nash.

A cold bottle of beer in one hand, Nash joined her, grinning as though he'd just won the lottery.

"Wipe that smug look off your face," she muttered under her breath, not wanting her parents to hear. It was unlikely they would, busy as they were with the barbecue.

"You should've said something earlier." His smile was wider than ever. "I had no idea you were so taken with me."

"Nash, please. I'm embarrassed enough as it is."

"But why?"

"Don't play dumb." She was fast losing her patience with him. The misunderstanding delighted him and mortified her. "I'm going to have to tell them," she said, more for her own benefit than his.

"Don't. Your father might decide to barbecue hamburgers instead. It isn't every day his only daughter brings home a potential husband."

"Stop it," she whispered forcefully. "We both know how you feel about marriage."

"I wouldn't object if you wanted to live with me."

Savannah glared at him so hard, her eyes ached.

"Just joking." He took a swig of beer and held the

bottle in front of his lips, his look thoughtful. "Then again, maybe I wasn't."

Savannah was so furious she had to walk away. To her dismay, Nash followed her to the back of the yard. Glancing over her shoulder, she caught sight of her parents talking.

"You're making this impossible," she told him furiously.

"How's that?" His eyes fairly sparkled.

"Don't, please don't." She didn't often plead, but she did now, struggling to keep her voice from quavering.

He frowned. "What's wrong?"

She bit her lower lip so hard, she was afraid she'd drawn blood. "My parents would like to see me settled down and married. They…they believe I'm like every other woman and—"

"You aren't?"

Savannah wondered if his question was sincere. "I'm handicapped," she said bluntly. "In my experience, men want a woman who's whole and perfect. Their egos ride on that, and I'm flawed. Defective merchandise doesn't do much for the ego."

"Savannah—"

She placed her hand against his chest. "Please don't say it. Spare me the speech. I've accepted what's wrong with me. I've accepted the fact that I'll never run or jump or marry or—"

Nash stepped back from her, his gaze pinning hers. "You're right, Savannah," he broke in. "You are handicapped and you will be until you view yourself otherwise." Having said that, he turned and walked away.

Savannah went in the opposite direction, needing a few moments to compose herself before rejoining the others. She heard her mother's laughter and turned to see her father with his arms around Joyce's waist, nuzzling her neck. From a distance they looked twenty years younger. Their love was as alive now as it had been years earlier…and demonstrating that was the purpose of this visit.

She scanned the yard, looking for Nash, wanting him to witness the happy exchange between her parents, but he was busy studying the fishing flies her father had left out for his inspection.

Her father's shout alerted Savannah that dinner was ready. Reluctantly she joined Nash and her parents at the round picnic table. She wasn't given any choice but to share the crescent-shaped bench with him.

He was close enough that she could feel the heat radiating off his body. Close enough that she yearned to be closer yet. That was what surprised her, but more profoundly it terrified her. From the first moment she'd met him, Savannah suspected there was something different about him, about her reactions to him. In the beginning she'd attributed it to their disagreement, his heated argument against marriage, the challenge he represented, the promise of satisfaction if she could change his mind.

Dinner was delicious and Nash went out of his way to compliment Joyce until her mother blushed with pleasure.

"So," her father said, glancing purposefully toward Savannah and Nash, "what are your plans?"

"For what?" Nash asked.

Savannah already knew the question almost as well as she knew the answer. Her father was asking about her future with Nash, and she had none.

"Why don't you tell Nash how you and Mom met,"

Savannah asked, interrupting her father before he could respond to Nash's question.

"Oh, Savannah," her mother protested, "that was years and years ago." She glanced at her husband of thirty-seven years and her clear eyes lit up with a love so strong, it couldn't be disguised. "But it was terribly romantic."

"You want to hear this?" Marcus's question was directed to Nash.

"By all means."

In that moment, Savannah could have kissed Nash, she was so grateful. "I was in the service," her father explained. "An Airborne Ranger. A few days before I met Joyce, I received my orders and learned I was about to be stationed in Germany."

"He'd come up from California and was at Fort Lewis," her mother added.

"There's not much to tell. Two weeks before I was scheduled to leave, I met Joyce at a dance."

"Daddy, you left out the best part," Savannah complained. "It wasn't like the band was playing a number you enjoyed and you needed a partner."

Her father chuckled. "You're right about that. I'd gone to the dance with a couple of buddies. The evening hadn't been going well."

"I remember you'd been stood up," Savannah inserted, eager to get to the details of their romance.

"No, dear," her mother intervened, picking up the story, "that was me. So I was in no mood to be at any social function. The only reason I decided to go was to make sure Lenny Walton knew I hadn't sat home mooning over him, but in reality I was at the dance mooning over him."

"I wasn't particularly keen on being at this dance, either," Marcus added. "I thought, mistakenly, that we were going to play pool at a local hall. I've never been much of a dancer, but my buddies were. They disappeared onto the dance floor almost immediately. I was bored and wandered around the hall for a while. I kept looking at my watch, eager to be on my way."

"As you can imagine, I wasn't dancing much myself," Joyce said.

"Then it happened." Savannah pressed her palms together and leaned forward. "This is my favorite part," she told Nash.

"I saw Joyce." Her father's voice dropped slightly. "When I first caught sight of her, my heart seized. I thought I might be having a reaction to the shots we'd been given earlier in the day. I swear I'd never seen a more beautiful woman. She wore this white dress and she looked like an angel. For a moment I was convinced she was." He reached for her mother's hand.

"I saw Marcus at that precise second, as well," Joyce whispered. "My friends were chatting and their voices faded until the only sound I heard was the pounding of my own heart. I don't remember walking toward him and yet I must have, because when I looked up Marcus was standing there."

"The funny part is, I don't remember moving, either."

Savannah propped her elbows on the table, her dinner forgotten. This story never failed to move her, although she'd heard it dozens of times over the years.

"We danced," her mother continued.

"All night."

"We didn't say a word. I think we must've been afraid the other would vanish if we spoke."

"While we were on the dance floor I kept pinching myself to be sure this was real, that Joyce was real. It was like we were both in a dream. These sorts of things only happen in the movies.

"When the music stopped, I looked around and realized my buddies were gone. It didn't matter. Nothing mattered but Joyce."

"Oh, Dad, I never get tired of hearing this story."

Joyce smiled as if she, too, was eager to relive the events of that night. "As we were walking out of the hall, I kept thinking I was never going to see Marcus again. I knew he was in the army—his haircut was a dead giveaway. I was well aware that my parents didn't want me dating anyone in the military, and up until then I'd abided by their wishes."

"I was afraid I wasn't going to see her again," Savannah's father went on. "But Joyce gave me her name and phone number and then ran off to catch up with her ride home."

"I didn't sleep at all that night. I was convinced I'd imagined everything."

"I couldn't sleep, either," Marcus confessed. "Here I was with my shipping orders in my pocket—this was not the time to get involved with a woman."

"I'm glad you changed your mind," Nash said, studying Savannah.

"To tell you the truth, I don't think I had much of a choice. It was as if our relationship was preordained. By the end of the following week, I knew Joyce was the woman I'd marry. I knew I'd love her all my life, and both have held true."

"Did you leave for Germany?"

"Of course. I had no alternative. We wrote back and

forth for two years and then were married three months
after I was discharged. There was never another woman
for me after I met Joyce."

"There was never another man for me," her mother
said quietly.

Savannah tossed Nash a triumphant look and was disappointed to see that he wasn't looking her way.

"It's a romantic story." He was gracious enough to
admit that much.

"Apparently some of that romance rubbed off on Savannah." Her father's eyes were proud as he glanced at
her. "This wedding business of hers is thriving."

"So it seems." Some of the enthusiasm left Nash's
voice. He was apparently thinking of his sister, and Savannah's role in her wedding plans.

"Eat, before your dinner gets cold," Joyce said, waving her fork in their direction.

"How long did you say you've been married?" Nash
asked, cutting off a piece of his steak.

"Thirty-seven years," her father told him.

"And it's been smooth sailing all that time?"

Savannah wanted to pound her fist on the table and
insist that this cross-examination was unnecessary.

Marcus laughed. "Smooth sailing? Oh, hardly. Joyce
and I've had our ups and downs over the years like most
couples. If there's anything special about our marriage,
it's been our commitment to each other."

Savannah cleared her throat, wanting to gloat. Once
more Nash ignored her.

"You've never once entertained the idea of divorce?"
he asked.

This question was unfair! She hadn't had the opportunity to challenge his clients about their divorces, not

that she would've wanted to. Every case had saddened and depressed her.

"As soon as a couple introduces the subject of divorce, there isn't the same willingness to concentrate on communication and problem-solving. People aren't nearly as flexible," Marcus said. "Because there's always that out, that possibility."

Joyce nodded. "If there was any one key to the success of our marriage, it's been that we've refused to consider divorce an option. That's not to say I haven't fantasized about it a time or two."

"We're only human," her father agreed with a nod. "I'll admit I've entertained the notion a time or two myself—even if I didn't do anything about it."

No! It wasn't true. Savannah didn't believe it. "But you were never serious," she felt obliged to say.

Marcus looked at her and offered her a sympathetic smile, as if he knew about their wager. "Your mother and I love each other, and neither of us could say we're sorry we stuck it out through the hard times, but yes, sweetheart, there were a few occasions when I didn't know if our marriage would survive."

Savannah dared not look at Nash. Her parents' timing was incredible. If they were going to be brutally honest, why did it have to be now? In all the years Savannah was growing up she'd never once heard the word *divorce*. In her eyes their marriage was solid, always had been and always would be.

"Of course, we never stopped talking," her mother was saying. "No matter how angry we might be with each other."

Soon after, Joyce brought out dessert—a coconut cake—and coffee.

"So, what do you think of our little girl?" Marcus asked, when he'd finished his dinner. He placed his hands on his stomach and studied Nash.

"Dad, please! You're embarrassing me."

"Why?"

"My guess is Savannah would prefer we didn't give her friend the third degree, dear," Joyce said mildly.

Savannah felt like kissing her mother's cheek. She stood, eager to disentangle herself from this conversation. "I'll help with the dishes, Mom," she said as if suggesting a trip to the mall.

Nash's mood had improved considerably after meeting Savannah's parents. Obviously, things weren't going the way she'd planned. Twice now, during dinner, it was all he could do not to laugh out loud. She'd expected them to paint a rosy picture of their idyllic lives together, one that would convince him of the error of his own views.

The project had backfired in her face. Rarely had he seen anyone look more shocked than when her parents said that divorce was something they'd each contemplated at one point or another in their marriage.

The men cleared the picnic table and the two women shooed them out of the kitchen. Nash was grateful, since he had several questions he wanted to ask Marcus about Savannah.

They wandered back outside. Nash was helping Marcus gather up his fishing gear when Savannah's father spoke.

"I didn't mean to pry earlier," he said casually, carrying his fishing rod and box of flies into the garage.

A motor home was parked alongside the building. Although it was an older model, it looked as good as new.

"You don't need to worry about offending me," Nash assured him.

"I wasn't worried about you. Savannah gave me 'the look' while we were eating. I don't know how much experience you have with women, young man, but take my advice. When you see 'the look,' shut up. No matter what you're discussing, if you value your life, don't say another word."

Nash chuckled. "I'll keep that in mind."

"Savannah's got the same expression as her mother. If you continue dating her, you'll recognize it soon enough." He paused. "You are going to continue seeing my daughter, aren't you?"

"You wouldn't object?"

"Heavens, no. If you don't mind my asking, what do you think of my little girl?"

Nash didn't mince words. "She's the most stubborn woman I've ever met."

Marcus nodded and leaned his prize fishing rod against the wall. "She gets that from her mother, too." He turned around to face Nash, hands on his hips. "Does her limp bother you?" he asked point-blank.

"Yes and no." Nash wouldn't insult her father with a half-truth. "It bothers me because she's so conscious of it herself."

Marcus's chest swelled as he exhaled. "That she is."

"How'd it happen?" Curiosity got the better of him, although he'd prefer to hear the explanation from Savannah.

Her father walked to the back of the garage where a youngster's mangled bicycle was stored. "It sounds simple to say she was hit by a car. This is what was left of her bike. I've kept it all these years as a reminder of how far she's come."

"Oh, no..." Nash breathed when he viewed the mangled frame and guessed the full extent of the damage done to the child riding it. "How'd she ever survive?"

"I'm not being facetious when I say sheer nerve. Anyone with less fortitude would have willed death. She was in the hospital for months, and that was only the beginning. The doctors initially told us she'd never walk again, and for the first year we believed it.

"Even now she still has pain. Some days are worse than others. Climate seems to affect it somewhat. And her limp is more pronounced when she's tired." Marcus replaced the bicycle and turned back to Nash. "It isn't every man who recognizes Savannah's strength. You haven't asked for my advice, so forgive me for offering it."

"Please."

"My daughter's a special woman, but she's prickly when it comes to men and relationships. Somehow, she's got it in her head that no man will ever want her."

"I'm sure that's not true."

"It is true, simply because Savannah believes it is," Marcus corrected. "It'll take a rare man to overpower her defenses. I'm not saying you're that man. I'm not even saying you should try."

"You seemed to think otherwise earlier. Wasn't it you who assumed I was going to marry your daughter?"

"I said that to get a rise out of Savannah, and it worked." Marcus rubbed his jaw, eyes twinkling with delight.

"We've only just met." Nash felt he had to present some explanation, although he wasn't sure why.

"I know." He slapped Nash affectionately on the back and together they left the garage. When they returned to the house, the dinner dishes had been washed and put away.

Savannah's mother had filled several containers with leftovers and packed them in an insulated bag. She gave Savannah detailed instructions on how to warm up the leftover steak and vegetables. Attempting brain surgery sounded simpler. As it happened, Nash caught a glimpse of Marcus from the corner of his eye and nearly burst out laughing. The older man was slowly shaking his head.

"I like the coyote, Mom," Savannah said, as Nash took the food for her. She ran one hand over the stylized animal. "Are you and Dad going to Arizona this winter?"

Nash felt static electricity hit the airwaves.

"We haven't decided, but I doubt we will this year," Joyce answered.

"Why not?" Savannah asked. This was obviously an old argument. "You love it there. More and more of your friends are becoming snowbirds. It doesn't make sense for you to spend your winters here in the cold and damp when you can be with your friends, soaking up the sunshine."

"Sweetheart, we've got a long time to make that decision," Marcus reminded her. "It's barely summer."

She hugged them both goodbye, then slung her purse over her shoulder, obviously giving up on the argument with her parents.

"What was that all about?" Nash asked once they were in his car.

It was unusual to see Savannah look vulnerable, but

she did now. He wasn't any expert on women. His sister was evidence of that, and so was every other female he'd ever had contact with, for that matter. It looked as though gutsy Savannah was about to burst into tears.

"It's nothing," she said, her voice so low it was almost nonexistent. Her head was turned away from him and she was staring out the side window.

"Tell me," he insisted as he reached the freeway's on ramp. He increased the car's speed.

Savannah clasped her hands together. "They won't leave because of me. They seem to think I need a babysitter, that it's their duty to watch over me."

"Are you sure you're not being overly sensitive?"

"I'm sure. Mom and Dad love to travel, and now that Dad's retired they should be doing much more of it."

"They have the motor home."

"They seldom use it. Day trips, a drive to the ocean once or twice a year, and that's about it. Dad would love to explore the East Coast in the autumn, but I doubt he ever will."

"Why not?"

"They're afraid something will happen to me."

"It sounds like they're being overprotective."

"They are!" Savannah cried. "But I can't force them to go, and they won't listen to me."

He sensed that there was more to this story. "What's the real reason, Savannah?" He made his words as coaxing as he could, not wanting to pressure her into telling him something she'd later regret.

"They blame themselves for the accident," she whispered. "They were leaving for a weekend trip that day and I was to stay with a babysitter. I'd wanted to go with them and when they said I couldn't, I got upset. In order to appease me, Dad said I could ride my bicycle. Up until that time he'd always gone with me."

Nash chanced a look at her and saw that her eyes were closed and her body was rigid with tension.

"And so they punish themselves," she continued in halting tones, "thinking if they sacrifice their lives for me, it'll absolve them from their guilt. Instead it increases mine."

"Yours?"

"Do you mind if we don't discuss this anymore?" she asked, sounding physically tired and emotionally beaten.

The silence that followed was eventually broken by Savannah's sigh of defeat.

"When would you like me to start cooking your dinners?" she asked as they neared her shop.

"You're conceding?" He couldn't keep the shock out of his voice. "Just like that, without so much as an argument? You must be more tired than I realized."

His comments produced a sad smile.

"So you're willing to admit marriage is a thing of the past and has no part in this day and age?"

"Never!" She rallied a bit at that.

"That's what I thought."

"Are you ready to admit love can last a lifetime when it's nourished and respected?" she asked.

Nash frowned, his thoughts confused. "I'll grant there are exceptions to every rule and your parents are clearly that. Unfortunately, the love they share doesn't exist between most married couples.

"It'd be easy to tell you I like my macaroni and cheese extra cheesy," he went on to say, "but I have a feeling you'll change your mind in the morning and demand a rematch."

Savannah smiled and pressed the side of her head against the car window.

"You're exhausted, and if I accepted your defeat, you'd never forgive me."

"What do you suggest, then?"

"A draw." He pulled into the alley behind the shop, where Savannah had parked her car. "Let's call it square. I proved what I wanted to prove and you did the same. There's no need to go back to the beginning and start over, because neither of us is going to make any progress with the other. We're both too strong-minded for that."

"We should have recognized it sooner," Savannah said, eyes closed.

She was so attractive, so…delectable, Nash had to force himself to look away.

"It's very gentlemanly of you not to accept my defeat."

"Not really."

Her eyes slowly opened and she turned her head so she could meet his eyes. "Why not?"

"Because I'm about to incur your wrath."

"Really? How are you going to do that?"

He smiled. It'd been so long since he'd looked forward to anything this much. "Because, my dear wedding coordinator, I'm about to kiss you."

# *Four*

"You're...you're going to kiss me?" Savannah had been exhausted seconds earlier, but Nash's words were a shot of adrenaline that bolted her upright.

"I most certainly am," he said, parking his car behind hers in the dark alley. "Don't look so scared. The fact is, you might even enjoy this."

That was what terrified Savannah most. If ever there was a man whose touch she yearned for, it was Nash. If ever there was a man she longed to be held by, it was Nash.

He bent his head toward hers and what resistance she'd managed to amass died a sudden death as he pressed his chin to her temple and simply held her against him. If he'd been rough or demanding or anything but gentle, she might've had a chance at resisting him. She might've had the desire to resist him. But she didn't. A sigh rumbled through her and with heedless curiosity she lifted her hand to his face, her fingertips grazing his jaw. Her touch seemed to go through him like an electrical shock because he groaned and, as she tilted back her head, his mouth sought hers.

At the blast of unexpected sensation, Savannah buckled against him and whimpered, all the while clinging
to him. The kiss continued, gaining in intensity and fer-
vor until Savannah felt certain her heart would pound
straight through her chest.

Savannah closed her eyes, deep in a world of sensual pleasure.

"Savannah." Her name was a groan. His breathing,
heavy and hard, came in bursts as he struggled to regain control. Savannah was struggling, too. She finally
opened her eyes. Her fingers were in his hair; she sighed
and relaxed her hold.

Nash raised his head and took her face between his
hands, his eyes delving into hers. "I didn't mean for
that to happen."

An apology. She should've expected it, should've been
prepared for it. But she wasn't.

He seemed to be waiting for her to respond so she
gave him a weak smile, and lowered her gaze, not wanting him to guess how strong her reaction had been.

He leaned his forehead against hers and chuckled
softly. "You're a surprise a minute."

"What do you mean?"

He dropped a glancing kiss on the side of her face.
"I wouldn't have believed you'd be so passionate. The
way you kissed me..."

"In other words, you didn't expect someone like me
to experience sensual pleasure?" she demanded righteously. "It might shock you to know I'm still a woman."

"What?" Nash said. "What are you talking about?"

"You heard me," she said, frantically searching for
her purse and the bag of leftovers her mother had insisted she take home with her.

"Stop," he said. "Don't use insults to ruin something that was beautiful and spontaneous."

"I wasn't the one—"

She wasn't allowed to finish. Taking her by the arms, he hauled her toward him until his mouth was on hers. Her resistance disappeared in the powerful persuasion of his kisses.

He exhaled sharply when he finished. "Your leg has nothing to do with this. Nothing. Do you understand?"

"Why were you so surprised, then?" she asked, struggling to keep her indignation alive. It was almost impossible when she was in his arms.

His answer took a long time. "I don't know."

"That's what I thought." She broke away and held her purse against her like a shield. "We've agreed to disagree on the issue of love and marriage, isn't that correct?"

"Yes," he said without emotion.

"Then I don't see any reason for us to continue our debate. It's been a pleasure meeting you, Mr. Davenport. Goodbye." Having said that, she jerked open the car door and nearly toppled backward. She caught herself in the nick of time before she could tumble head-first into the alley.

"Savannah, for heaven's sake, will you—"

"Please, just leave me alone," she said, furious with herself for making such a dramatic exit and with him for reasons as yet unclear.

Because he made her feel, she guessed sometime later, when she was home and safe. He made her feel as if she was whole and without flaws. As if she was an attractive, desirable woman. Savannah blamed Nash for pretending she could be something she wasn't and the anger simmered in her blood long after she'd readied for bed.

Neatly folding her quilt at the foot of her bed, Savannah stood, seething, taking deep breaths to keep the tears at bay.

In the morning, after she'd downed her first cup of coffee, Savannah felt better. She was determined to put the incident and the man out of her mind. There was no reason for them to see each other again, no reason for them to continue with this farce. Not that Nash would want to see her, especially after the idiotic way she'd behaved, scrambling out of his car as if escaping a murderer.

As was so often the case of late, Savannah was wrong. Nash was waiting on the sidewalk in front of her shop, carrying a white bag, when she arrived for work.

"Another peace offering?" she asked, when she unlocked the front door and opened it for him.

"Something like that." He handed her a latte, then walked across the showroom and sat on the corner of her desk, dangling one leg, as though he had every right to make himself comfortable in her place of business.

Savannah hadn't recovered from seeing him again so soon; she wasn't prepared for another confrontation. "What can I do for you?" she asked stiffly, setting the latte aside. She sat down and leaned back in the swivel chair, hoping she looked relaxed, knowing she didn't.

"I've come to answer your question," he said, leg swinging as he pried loose the lid on his cup. He was so blasé about everything, as if the intensity of their kisses was a common thing for him. As if she was one in a long line of conquests. "You wanted to know what was different last night and I'm here to tell you."

This was the last thing Savannah expected. She

glanced pointedly at her watch. "Is this going to take long? I've got an appointment in ten minutes."

"I'll be out of here before your client arrives."

"Good." She crossed her arms, trying to hold on to her patience. Their kisses embarrassed her now. She was determined to push the whole incident out of her mind and forget him. It'd been crazy to make a wager with him. Fun, true, but sheer folly nonetheless. The best she could do was forget she'd ever met the man. Nash, however, seemed unwilling to let that happen.

"Well?" she pressed when he didn't immediately speak.

"A woman doesn't generally go to my head the way you did," he said. "When I make love to a woman I'm the one in control."

"We weren't making love," she said heatedly, heat flushing her cheeks with instant color. Her fingers bit into the soft flesh of her arms as she fought to keep the embarrassment to herself.

"What do you call it, then?"

"Kissing."

"Yes, but it would've developed into something a whole lot more complicated if we hadn't been in my car. The last time I made love in the backseat of a car, I was—"

"This may come as a surprise to you, but I have no interest in hearing about your sexual exploits," she interjected.

"Fine," he snapped.

"Besides, we were nowhere near making love."

Nash's responding snort sent ripples of outrage through Savannah. "You overestimate your appeal, Mr. Davenport."

He laughed outright this time. "Somehow or other, I thought you'd say as much. I was hoping you'd be a bit more honest, but then, I've found truth an unusual trait in most women."

The bell above her door chimed just then, and her appointment strolled into the shop. Savannah was so grateful to have this uncomfortable conversation interrupted, she almost hugged her client.

"I'd love to continue this debate," she lied, "but as you can see, I have a customer."

"Perhaps another time," Nash suggested.

She hesitated. "Perhaps."

He snickered disdainfully as he stood and sipped from the take-out cup. "As I said, women seem to have a hard time dealing with the truth."

Savannah pretended not to hear him as she walked toward her customer, a welcoming smile on her face. "Good morning, Melinda. I'm so glad to see you."

Nash said nothing as he sauntered past her and out the door. Not until he was out of sight did Savannah relax her guard. He claimed she went to his head. What he didn't know was that his effect on her was startlingly similar. Then again, perhaps he did know....

The woman irritated him. No, Nash decided as he hit the sidewalk, his stride clipped and fast, she more than irritated him. Savannah Charles incensed him. He didn't understand this oppressive need he felt to talk to her, to explain, to hear her thoughts. He'd awakened wishing things hadn't ended so abruptly between them, wishing he'd known what to say to convince her of his sincerity. Morning had felt like a second chance.

In retrospect, he suspected he was looking for help himself in working through the powerful emotions that had evolved during their embrace. Instead, Savannah claimed he'd miscalculated her reaction. The heck he had.

He should've realized she was as confused as he was about their explosive response to each other.

Nash arrived at his office half an hour later than usual. As he walked past his assistant's desk, she handed him several telephone messages. He was due in court in twenty minutes, and wouldn't have time to return any calls until early afternoon. Shuffling through the slips, he stopped at the third one.

Susan.

His sister had called him, apparently on her cell. Without further thought he set his briefcase aside and reached for the phone, punching out the number listed.

"Susan, it's Nash," he said when she answered. If he hadn't been so eager to talk to her, he might have mulled over the reason for her call. Something must have happened; otherwise she wouldn't have swallowed her pride to contact him.

"Hello, Nash."

He waited a moment in vain for her to continue. "You called me?"

"Yes," she said abruptly. "I wanted to apologize for hanging up on you the other day. It was rude and unnecessary. Kurt and I had a…discussion about it and he said I owed you an apology."

"Kurt's got a good head on his shoulders," he said, thinking his sister would laugh and the tension between them would ease. It didn't.

"I thought about what he had to say and Kurt's right. I'm sorry for the way I reacted."

"I'm sorry, too," Nash admitted. "I shouldn't have checked up on you behind your back." If she could be so generous with her forgiveness, then so could he. After all, Susan was his little sister. He had her best interests at heart, although she wouldn't fully appreciate his concern until later in life, when she was responsible for children of her own. He wasn't Susan's father, but he was her closest relative. Although she was twenty-four, he felt she still needed his guidance and direction.

"I was thinking we might have lunch together some afternoon," she ventured, and the quaver in her voice revealed how uneasy she was making the suggestion.

Nash had missed their lunches together. "Sounds like a great idea to me. How about Thursday?"

"Same place as always?"

There was a Mexican restaurant that was their favorite, on a steep side street not far from the King County courthouse. They'd made a point of meeting there for lunch at least once a month for the past several years. The waitresses knew them well enough to greet them by name.

"All right. See you Thursday at noon."

"Great."

Grinning, Nash replaced the receiver.

He looked forward to this luncheon date with his sister the way a kid anticipates the arrival of the Easter bunny. They'd both said and done things they regretted. Nash hadn't changed his mind about his sister marrying Kurt Caldwell. Kurt was decent, intelligent, hardworking and sincere, but they were both too young for marriage. Too uninformed about it. Judging by Susan's reaction, she wasn't likely to heed his advice. He hated to think of her making the same mistakes he had, but there didn't seem to be any help for it. He might as well mend the bridges of communication before they became irreparable.

\* \* \*

"Is something wrong?" Susan asked Savannah as they went over the details for the wedding. It bothered her how careful Susan and Kurt had to be with their money, but she admired the couple's discipline. Each decision had been painstaking.

"I'm sorry." Savannah's mind clearly wasn't on the subject at hand. It had taken a sharp turn in another direction the moment Susan had shown up for their appointment. She reminded Savannah so much of her brother. Susan and Nash had the same eye and hair color, but they were alike in other ways, as well. The way Susan smiled and her easy laugh were Nash's trademarks.

Savannah had worked hard to force all thoughts of Nash from her mind. Naively, she felt she'd succeeded, until Susan had come into the shop.

Savannah didn't know what it was about this hard-headed cynic that attracted her so strongly. She resented the fact that he was the one to ignite the spark of her sensual nature. There was no future for them. Not when their views on love and marriage were so diametrically opposed.

"Savannah," Susan asked, "are you feeling okay?"

"Of course. I'm sorry, my thoughts seem to be a thousand miles away."

"I noticed," Susan said with a laugh.

Her mood certainly seemed to have improved since their previous meeting, Savannah noticed, wishing she could say the same. Nash hadn't contacted her since their last disastrous confrontation a few days earlier. Not that she'd expected he would.

Susan had entered the small dressing room and stepped into the wedding gown. She came out, lifting her hair at the back so Savannah could fasten the long row of pearl buttons.

"I'm having lunch with Nash on Thursday," Susan announced unexpectedly.

"I'm glad you two have patched up your differences."

Susan's shoulders moved in a reflective sigh. "We haven't exactly—at least, not yet. I called him to apologize for hanging up on him. He must have been eager to talk to me because his assistant told me he was due in court and I shouldn't expect to hear from him until that afternoon. He phoned back no more than five minutes later."

"He loves you very much." Savannah's fingers expertly fastened the pearl buttons. Nash had proved he was capable of caring deeply for another human being, yet he staunchly denied the healing power of love, wouldn't allow it into his own life.

*Perhaps you're doing the same thing.*

The thought came at her like the burning flash from a laser gun, too fast to avoid, and too painful to ignore. Savannah shook her head to chase away the doubts. It was ridiculous. She'd purposely chosen a career that was steeped in romance. To suggest she was blocking love from her own life was ludicrous. Yet the accusation repeated itself over and over....

"Savannah?"

"I'm finished," she said quickly. Startled, she stepped back.

Susan dropped her arms and shook her hair free before slowly turning around to face Savannah. "Well?" she asked breathlessly. "What do you think?"

Although she was still preoccupied with a series of haunting doubts, Savannah couldn't help admiring how beautiful Nash's sister looked in the bridal gown. "Oh, Susan, you're lovely."

The young woman viewed herself in the mirror, staring at her reflection for several minutes as if she wasn't sure she could believe what she was seeing.

"I'm going to ask Nash to attend the wedding when we have lunch," she said. Then, biting her lip, she added, "I'm praying he'll agree to that much."

"He should." Savannah didn't want to build up Susan's expectations. She honestly couldn't predict what Nash would say; she only knew what she thought he should do.

"He seemed pleased to hear from me," Susan went on to say.

"I'm sure he was." They stood beside each other in front of the mirror. Neither seemed inclined to move. Savannah couldn't speak for Susan, but for her part, the mirror made the reality of her situation all too clear. Her tailored pants might not reveal her scarred and twisted leg, but she remained constantly aware of it, a not-so-gentle reminder of her deficiency.

"Let me know what Nash says," Savannah said impulsively just before Susan left the shop.

"I will." Susan's eyes shone with a childlike enthusiasm as she turned and walked away.

Savannah sat at her desk and wrote down the pertinent facts about the wedding gown she was ordering for Susan, but as she moved the pen across the paper, her thoughts weren't on dress measurements. Instead they flew straight to Nash. If nothing else, he'd given her cause to think over her life and face up to a few uncomfortable truths. That wasn't a bad day's work for a skeptical divorce attorney. It was unfortunate he'd never realize the impact he'd had on her.

Nash was waiting in the booth at quarter after twelve on Thursday, anxiously glancing at his watch every fifteen seconds, convinced Susan wasn't going to show, when she strolled into the restaurant. A smile lit her face when she saw him. It was almost as if they'd never disagreed, and she was a kid again coming to her big brother for advice.

"I'm sorry I'm late," she said, slipping into the vinyl seat across from him. "I'm starved." She reached for a salted chip, weighing it down with spicy salsa.

"It's good to see you," Nash ventured, taking the first step toward reconciliation. He'd missed Susan and he said so.

"I've missed you, too. It doesn't feel right for us to fight, does it?"

"Not at all."

"You're the only real family I have."

"I feel the same way. We've both made mistakes and we should learn from them." He didn't cast blame. There was no point.

The waitress brought their menus. Nash didn't recognize the young woman, which made him consider just how long it was since he'd had lunch with Susan. Frowning, he realized she'd been the one to approach him about a reconciliation, when as the older, more mature adult, he should've been working toward that end himself.

"I brought you something," Susan said, setting her handbag on the table. She rooted through it until she found what she was looking for. Taking the envelope from her purse, she handed it to him.

Nash accepted the envelope, peeled it open and pulled out a handcrafted wedding invitation, written on antique-white parchment paper in gold letters. He didn't realize his sister knew calligraphy. Although it was obviously handmade, the effort was competent and appealing to the eye.

"I wrote it myself," Susan said eagerly. "Savannah suggested Kurt and I would save money by making our own wedding invitations. It's much more personal this way, don't you think?"

"Very nice."

"The gold ink on the parchment paper was Kurt's idea. Savannah gave me a book on calligraphy and I've been practicing every afternoon."

He wondered how many more times his sister would find an excuse to drag the wedding coordinator's name into their conversation. Each time Susan mentioned Savannah it brought up unwelcome memories of their few short times together. Memories Nash would rather forget.

"Do you like it?" Susan asked eagerly. She seemed to be waiting for something more.

"You did a beautiful job," he said.

"I'm really glad you think so."

Susan was grinning under the warmth of his praise.

The waitress returned and they placed their order, although neither of them had looked at the menu. "We're certainly creatures of habit, aren't we?" his sister teased.

"So," he said, relaxing in the booth, "how are the wedding plans going?"

"Very well, thanks to Savannah." She folded her hands on top of the table, flexing her long fingers against each other, studying him, waiting.

Nash read over the invitation a second time and saw

that it had been personally written to him. So this was the purpose of her phone call, the purpose of this lunch. She was asking him if he'd attend her wedding, despite his feelings about it.

"I don't expect you to change your mind about me marrying Kurt," Susan said anxiously, rushing the words together in her eagerness to have them said. "But it would mean the world to me if you'd attend the ceremony. There won't be a lot of people there. Just a few friends and Kurt's immediate family. That's all we can afford. Savannah's been wonderful, showing us how to get the most out of our limited budget. Will you come to my wedding, Nash?"

Nash knew when he was involved in a losing battle. Susan would marry Kurt with or without his approval. His kid sister was determined to do this her way. He'd done his best to talk some sense into her, but to no avail. He'd made the mistake of threatening her, and she'd called his bluff. The past weeks had been miserable for them both.

"I'll come."

"Oh, Nash, thank you." Tears brimmed and spilled over her lashes. She grabbed her paper napkin, holding it beneath each eye in turn. "I can't begin to tell you how much this means to me."

"I know." He felt like crying himself, but for none of the same reasons. He didn't want to see his sister hurt and that was inevitable once she was married. "I still don't approve of your marrying so young, but I can't stop you."

"Nash, you keep forgetting, I'm an adult, over twenty-one. You make me sound like a little kid."

He sighed expressively. That was the way he saw her, as his kid sister. It was difficult to think of her married, with a family of her own, when it only seemed a few years back that she was in diapers.

"You'll love Kurt once you get to know him better," she said excitedly, wiping the moisture from her cheek. "Look at what you've done to me," she muttered. Her mascara streaked her face in inky rows.

His hand reached for hers and he squeezed her fingers. "We'll get through this yet, kid," he joked.

Nash suspected, in the days that followed, that it was natural to feel good about making his sister so happy. All he'd agreed to do was attend the ceremony. He hadn't figured out what was going to keep him in his seat when the minister asked anyone who opposed the union to speak now or forever hold their peace. Attending the ceremony itself, regardless of his personal feelings toward marriage, was the least he could do for causing the rift between them.

The card from Savannah that arrived at his office took him by surprise. He stared at the return address on the envelope for a moment before turning it over and opening it with eager fingers. Her message was straightforward: "Thank you." Her elegant signature appeared below.

Nash gazed at the card for several minutes before slapping it down on his desk. The woman was driving him crazy.

He left the office almost immediately, shocking his assistant, who rushed after him, needing to know what she was supposed to do about his next appointment. Nash suggested she entertain him with some law journals and coffee. He promised to be back in half an hour.

Luckily he found a parking spot on the street. Climbing out of his car, he walked purposely toward the bridal shop. Savannah was sitting at her desk intent on her task. When she glanced up and saw him, she froze.

"I got your card," he said stiffly.

"I... It made Susan so happy to know you'd attend her wedding. I wanted to thank you," she said, her eyes following his every move.

He marched to her desk, not understanding even now what force had driven him to her. "How many guests is she inviting?"

"I...believe the number's around sixty."

"Change that," he instructed harshly. "We're going to be inviting three hundred or more. I'll have the list to you in the morning."

"Susan and Kurt can't afford—"

"They won't be paying for it. I will. I want the best for my sister, understand? We'll have a sit-down dinner, a dance with a ten-piece orchestra, real flowers and a designer wedding dress. We'll order invitations because there'll be too many for Susan to make herself. Have you got that?" He motioned toward her pen, thinking she should write it all down.

Savannah looked as if she hadn't heard him. "Does Susan know about all this?"

"Not yet."

"Don't you think you should clear it with her first?"

"It might be too soon, because a good deal of this hinges on one thing."

Savannah frowned. "What's that?"

"If you'll agree to attend the wedding as my date."

# Five

"Your date?" Savannah repeated as she leapt to her feet. No easy task when one leg was as unsteady as hers. She didn't often forget that, but she did now in her incredulity. "That's emotional blackmail," she cried, before slumping back in her chair.

"You're right, it is," Nash agreed, leaning forward and pressing his hands against the edge of her oak desk. His face was scant inches from her own, and his eyes cut straight through her defenses. "It's what you expect of me, isn't it?" he demanded. "Since I'm so despicable."

"I never said that!"

"Maybe not, but you thought it."

"No, I didn't!" she snapped, then decided she probably had. She'd been shaken by his kiss, and then he'd apologized as if he'd never meant it to happen. And, perhaps worse, maybe he wished it hadn't.

A slow, leisurely smile replaced Nash's dark scowl. "That's what I thought," he said as he raised his hand and brushed a strand of hair from her forehead. His fingertips lingered at her face. "I wish I knew what's happening to us."

"Nothing's happening," Savannah insisted, but her voice lacked conviction even to her own ears. She was fighting the powerful attraction she felt for him for all she was worth, which at the moment wasn't much. "You aren't really going to blackmail me, are you?"

He gently traced the outline of her face, pausing at her chin and tilting it upward. "Do you agree to attend the wedding with me?"

"Yes, only—"

"Then you should know I had no intention of following through with my threat. Susan can have the wedding of her dreams."

Savannah stood, awkwardly placing her weight on her injured leg. "I'm sure there are far more suitable dates for you," she said crisply.

"I want you."

He made this so difficult. "Why me?" she asked. By his own admission, there were any number of other women who'd jump at the chance to date him. Why had he insisted on singling her out? It made no sense.

Nash frowned as if he wasn't sure himself, which lent credence to Savannah's doubts. "I don't know. As for this wedding, it seemed to me I could be wrong. It doesn't happen often, but I have been known to make an error in judgment now and again." He gave her a quick, self-deprecating grin. "Susan's my only sister—the only family I've got. I don't want there to be any regrets between us. Your card helped, too, and the way I see it, if I'm going to sit through a wedding, I'm not going to suffer alone. I want you there with me."

"Then I suggest you ask someone who'd appreciate the invitation," she said defiantly, straightening her shoulders.

"I want to be with you," he insisted softly, his eyes revealing his confusion. "Darned if I know why. You're stubborn, defensive and argumentative."

"One would think you'd rather…oh, wrestle a rattle-snake than go out with me."

"One would think," he agreed, smiling boyishly, "but if that's the case, why do I find myself listening for the sound of your voice? Why do I look forward to spending time with you?"

"I…wouldn't know." Except that she found herself in the same situation. Nash was never far from her thoughts; she hadn't been free of him from the moment they'd met.

His eyes, dark and serious, wandered over her face. Before she could protest, he lowered his head and nuzzled her ear. "Why can't I get you out of my mind?"

"I can't answer that, either." He was going to kiss her again, in broad daylight, where they could be interrupted by anyone walking into the shop. Yet Savannah couldn't bring herself to break away, couldn't offer so much as a token resistance.

A heartbeat later, his mouth met hers. Despite her own hesitation, she kissed him back. Nash groaned, drawing her more securely into his embrace.

"Savannah," he whispered as he broke off the kiss. "I can hardly believe this, but it's even better than before."

Savannah said nothing, although she agreed. She was trembling, and prayed Nash hadn't noticed, but that was too much to ask. He slid his fingers into her hair and brought her face close to his. "You're terrified, aren't you?" he asked, his cheek touching hers.

"Don't be ridiculous," she muttered. She felt his smile against her flushed skin and realized she hadn't fooled him any more than she had herself. "I don't know what I am."

"I don't know, either. Somehow I wonder if I ever will. I don't suppose you'd make this process a lot easier and consider just having an affair with me?"

Savannah stiffened, not knowing if he meant what he was saying. "Absolutely not."

"That's what I thought," he said with a lengthy sigh. "It's going to be the whole nine yards with you, isn't it?"

"I have no idea what you mean," she insisted.

"Perhaps not." Pulling away, he checked his watch and seemed surprised at the time. "I've got to get back to the office. I'll give Susan a call this afternoon and the three of us can get together and make the necessary arrangements."

Savannah nodded. "We're going to have to move quickly. Planning a wedding takes time."

"I know."

She smiled shyly, wanting him to know how pleased she was by his change of heart. "This is very sweet of you, Nash."

He gestured weakly with his hands, as if he wasn't sure he was doing the right thing. "I still think she's too young to be married. I can't help thinking she'll regret this someday."

"Marriage doesn't come with guarantees at any age," Savannah felt obliged to tell him. "But then, neither does life. Susan and Kurt have an advantage you seem to be overlooking."

"What's that?"

"They're in love."

"Love." Nash snickered loudly. "Generally it doesn't last more than two or three weeks."

"Sometimes that's true, but not this time," Savannah said. "However, I've worked with hundreds of couples over the years and I get a real sense about the people who come to me. I can usually tell if their marriages will last or not."

"What about Kurt and Susan?"

"I believe they'll have a long, happy life together."

Nash rubbed the side of his face, his eyes intense. He obviously didn't believe that.

"Their love is strong," she said, trying to bolster her argument.

Nash raised his eyebrows. "Spoken like a true romantic."

"I'm hoping the skeptic in you will listen."

"I'm trying."

Savannah could see the truth in that. He was trying, for Susan's sake and perhaps hers. He'd come a long way from where he was when they'd first met. But he had a lot farther to go.

Nash had no idea weddings could be so demanding, so expensive or so time-consuming. The one advantage of all this commotion and bother was all the hours he was able to spend with Savannah. As the weeks progressed, Nash came to know Savannah Charles, the businesswoman, as well as he did the lovely, talented woman who'd attracted him from the beginning. He had to admit she knew her stuff. He doubted anyone else could have arranged so large and lavish a wedding on such short notice. It was only because she had long-standing relationships with those involved—the florists, photographers, printers, hotel managers and so on—that Nash was able to give Susan an elaborate wedding.

As the days passed, Nash lost count of how often he asked Savannah out to dinner, a movie, a baseball game. She found a plausible excuse each and every time. A less determined man would have grown discouraged and given up.

But no more, he mused, looking out his office window. As far as she was concerned, he held the trump card in the palm of his hand. Savannah had consented to attend Susan's wedding with him, and there was no way he was letting her out of the agreement.

He sat at his desk thinking about this final meeting scheduled for later that afternoon. He'd been looking forward to it all week. Susan's wedding was taking place Saturday evening, and Savannah had flat run out of excuses.

Nash arrived at the shop before his sister. He was grateful for these few moments alone with Savannah.

"Hello, Nash." Her face lit up with a ready smile when he walked into the shop. She was more relaxed with him now. She stood behind a silver punch bowl, decorating the perimeter with a strand of silk gardenias.

Her knack for making something ordinary strikingly beautiful was a rare gift. In some ways she'd done that with his life these past few weeks, giving him something to anticipate when he got out of bed every morning. She'd challenged him, goaded him, irritated and bemused him. It took quite a woman to have such a powerful effect.

"Susan's going to be a few minutes late," Nash told her. "I was hoping she'd changed her mind and decided to call off the whole thing." He'd hoped nothing of the sort, but enjoyed getting a reaction out of Savannah.

"Give it up. Susan's going to be a beautiful bride."

"Who's going to be working the wedding?" he asked, advancing toward her.

"I am, of course. Together with Nancy. You met her last week."

He nodded, remembering the pleasant, competent young woman who'd come to one of their meetings. Savannah often contracted her to help out at larger events.

"Since Nancy's going to be there, you can attend as my date and leave the work to her."

"Nash, will you please listen to reason? I can't be your date.... I know it's short notice but there are plenty of women who'd enjoy—"

"We have an agreement," he reminded her.

"I realize that, but—"

"I won't take no for an answer, Savannah, not this time."

She stiffened. Nash had witnessed this particular reaction on numerous occasions. Whenever he asked her out, her pride exploded into full bloom. Nash was well acquainted with how deeply entrenched that pride was.

"Nash, please."

He reached for her hand and raised it to his lips. His mouth grazed her fingertips. "Not this time," he repeated. "I'll pick you up just before we meet to have the pictures taken."

"Nash..."

"Be ready, Savannah, because I swear I'll drag you there in your nightgown if I have to."

Savannah was in no mood for company, nor was she keen on talking to her mother when Joyce phoned that same evening. She'd done everything she could to persuade Nash to change his plans. But he insisted she be his date for Susan's wedding. Indeed, he'd blackmailed her into agreeing to it.

"I haven't heard from you in ages," her mother said.

"I've been busy with the last-minute details of Susan Davenport's wedding."

"She's Nash's sister, isn't she?"

Her mother knew the answer to that. She was looking for an excuse to bring Nash into the conversation, which she'd done countless times since meeting him. If Savannah had to do that wager over again, she'd handle it differently. Her entire day had been spent contemplating various regrets. She wanted to start over, be more patient, finish what she'd begun, control her tongue, get out of this ridiculous "date" with Nash.

But she couldn't.

"Your father's talking about taking a trip to the ocean for a week or two."

"That sounds like an excellent idea." Savannah had been waiting all summer for them to get away.

"I'm not sure we should go…."

"For heaven's sake, why not?"

"Oh, well, I hate to leave my garden, especially now. And there've been a few break-ins in the neighborhood the last few weeks. I'd be too worried about the house to enjoy myself." The excuses were so familiar, and Savannah wanted to scream with frustration. But her mother had left out the real reason for her uncertainty. She didn't want to leave Savannah. Naturally, her parents had never come right out and said that, but it was their underlying reason for staying close to the Seattle area.

Savannah had frequently tried to discuss this with them. However, both her parents just looked at her blankly as if they didn't understand her concerns. Or they changed the subject. They didn't realize what poor liars they were.

"Have you seen much of Nash lately?" Her mother's voice rose expectantly.

"We've been working together on the wedding, so we've actually been seeing a lot of each other."

"I meant socially, dear. Has he taken you out? He's such a nice young man. Both your father and I think so."

"Mother," Savannah said, hating this, "I haven't been dating Nash."

Her mother's sigh of disappointment cut through Savannah. "I see."

"We're friends, nothing more. I've told you that."

"Of course. Be sure and let me know how the wedding goes, will you?"

Seeing that Nash had spared little expense, it would be gorgeous. "I'll give you a call early next week and tell you all about it."

"You promise?"

"Yes, Mom, I promise."

Savannah replaced the receiver with a heavy heart. The load of guilt she carried was enough to buckle her knees. How could one accident have such a negative impact on so many people for so long? It wasn't fair that her parents should continue to suffer for what had happened to her. Yet they blamed themselves, and that guilt was slowly destroying the best years of their lives.

Nash arrived at Savannah's house to pick her up late Saturday afternoon. He looked tall and distinguished in his black tuxedo and so handsome that for an awkward moment, Savannah had trouble taking her eyes off him.

"What's wrong?" he said, running his finger along

the inside of his starched collar. "I feel like a concert pianist."

Savannah couldn't keep from smiling. "I was just thinking how distinguished you look."

His hand went to his temple. "I'm going gray?"

She laughed. "No."

"*Distinguished* is the word a woman uses when a man's entering middle age and losing his hair."

"If you don't get us to this wedding, we're going to miss it, and then you really will lose your hair." She placed her arm in his and carefully set one foot in front of the other. She rarely wore dress shoes. It was chancy, but she didn't want to ruin the effect of her full-length dress with flats. Nash couldn't possibly know the time and effort she'd gone to for this one date, which would likely be their first and last. She'd ordered the dress from New York, a soft, pale pink gown with a pearl-studded yoke. The long, sheer sleeves had layered pearl cuffs. She wore complementary pearl earrings and a single-strand necklace.

It wasn't often in her life that Savannah felt beautiful, but she did now. She'd worked hard, wanting to make this evening special for Susan—and knowing it would be her only date with Nash. She suspected there was a bit of Cinderella in every woman, the need to believe in fairy tales and happy endings, in true love conquering against impossible odds. For this one night, Savannah longed to forget she was crippled. For this one night, she wanted to pretend she was beautiful. A princess.

Nash helped her across the yard and held open the door for her. She was inside the car, seat belt buckled, when he joined her. His hands gripped the steering wheel, but when he didn't start the car, she turned to him.

"Is something wrong?"

He smiled at her, but she saw the strain in his eyes and didn't understand it. "It's just that you're so beautiful, I can hardly keep my hands off you."

"Oh, Nash," she whispered, fighting tears. "Thank you."

"For what?"

She shook her head, knowing she'd never be able to explain.

The church was lovely. Savannah had rarely seen a sanctuary decorated more beautifully. The altar was surrounded with huge bouquets of pink and white roses, and their scent drifted through the room. The end of each pew was decorated with a small bouquet of white rosebuds and gardenias with pink and silver bows. The effect was charming.

Seated in the front row, Savannah closed her eyes as the organ music swelled. She stood, and from the rustle of movement behind her, she knew the church was filled to capacity.

Savannah turned to see Nash escort his sister slowly down the center aisle, their steps in tune to the music. They were followed by the bridesmaids and groomsmen, most of them recruited late, every one of them delighted to share in Susan and Kurt's happiness.

Savannah had attended a thousand or more weddings in her years as a coordinator. Yet it was always the same. The moment the music crescendoed, her eyes brimmed with tears at the beauty and emotion of it all.

This wedding was special because the bride was Nash's sister. Savannah had felt a part of it from the beginning, when Susan had approached her, desperate for assistance. Now it was all coming together and Susan was about to marry Kurt, the man she truly loved.

Nash was uncomfortable with love, and a little jealous, too, although she doubted he recognized that. Susan, the little sister he adored, would soon be married and would move to California with her husband.

When they reached the steps leading to the altar, Susan kissed Nash's cheek before placing her hand on Kurt's arm. Nash hesitated as if he wasn't ready to surrender his sister. Just when Savannah was beginning to get worried, he turned and entered the pew, standing next to her. Either by accident or design, his hand reached for hers. His grip was tight, his face strained with emotion.

Savannah was astonished to see that his eyes were bright with tears. She could easily be mistaken, though, since her own were blurred. A moment later, she was convinced she was wrong.

The pastor made a few introductory comments about the sanctity of marriage. Holding his Bible open, he stepped forward. "I'd like each couple who's come to celebrate the union of Susan and Kurt to join hands," he instructed.

Nash took both of Savannah's hands so that she was forced to turn sideways. His eyes delved into hers, and her heart seemed to stagger to a slow, uneven beat at what she read in them. Nash was an expert at disguising his feelings, yes, but also at holding on to his anger and the pain of his long-dead marriage, at keeping that bitterness alive. As he stared down at her, his eyes became bright and clear and filled with an emotion so strong, it transcended anything she'd ever seen.

Savannah was barely aware of what was going on around them. Sounds faded; even the soloist who was singing seemed to be floating away. Savannah's peripheral vision became clouded, as if she'd stepped into a dreamworld. Her sole focus was Nash.

With her hands joined to Nash's, their eyes linked, she heard the pastor say, "Those of you wishing to renew your vows, repeat after me."

Nash's fingers squeezed hers as the pastor intoned the words. "I promise before God and all gathered here this day to take you as my wife. I promise to love and cherish you, to leave my heart and my life open to you."

To Savannah's amazement, Nash repeated the vow in a husky whisper. She could hear others around them doing the same. Once again tears filled her eyes. How easy it would be to pretend he was devoting his life to hers.

"I'll treasure you as a gift from God, to encourage you to be all He meant you to be," Savannah found herself repeating a few minutes later. "I promise to share your dreams, to appreciate your talents, to respect you. I pledge myself to you, to learn from and value our differences." As she spoke, Savannah's heart beat strong and steady and sure. Excitement rose up in her as she realized that what she'd said was true. These were the very things she yearned to do for Nash. She longed for him to trust her enough to allow her into his life, to help him bury the hurts of the past. They were different, as different as any couple could be. That didn't make their relationship impossible. It added flavor, texture and challenge to their attraction. Life together would never be dull for them.

"I promise to give you the very best of myself, to

be faithful to you, to be your friend and your partner," Nash whispered next, his voice gaining strength. Sincerity rang through his words.

"I offer you my heart and my love," Savannah repeated, her own heart ready to burst with unrestrained joy.

"You are my friend," Nash returned, "my lover, my wife."

It was as if they, too, were part of the ceremony, as if they, too, were pledging their love and their lives to each other.

Through the minister's words, Savannah offered Nash all that she had to give. It wasn't until they'd finished and Kurt was told to kiss his bride that Savannah remembered this wasn't real. She'd stepped into a dreamworld, the fantasy she'd created out of her own futile need for love. Nash had only been following the minister's lead. Mortified, she lowered her eyes and tugged her trembling fingers free from Nash's.

He, too, apparently harbored regrets. His hands clasped the pew in front of them until his knuckles paled. He formed a fist with his right hand. Savannah dared not look up at him, certain he'd recognize her thoughts and fearing she'd know his. She couldn't have borne the disappointment. For the next several hours they'd be forced to share each other's company, through the dinner and the dance that followed the ceremony. Savannah wasn't sure how she was going to manage it now, after she'd humiliated herself.

Thankfully she was spared having to face Nash immediately after the ceremony was over. He became a part of the reception line that welcomed friends and relatives. Savannah was busy herself, working with the woman she'd hired to help coordinate the wedding and reception. Together they took down the pew bows, which would serve as floral centerpieces for the dinner.

"I don't think I've ever seen a more beautiful ceremony," Nancy Mastell told Savannah, working furiously. "You'd think I'd be immune to this after all the weddings we attend."

"It…was beautiful," Savannah agreed. Her stomach was in knots, and her heart told her how foolish she'd been; nevertheless, she couldn't make herself regret what had happened. She'd learned something about herself, something she'd denied far too long. She needed love in her life. For years she'd cut herself off from opportunity, content to live off the happiness of others. She'd moved from one day to the next, carrying her pain and disappointment, never truly happy, never fulfilled. Pretending.

This was why Nash threatened her. She couldn't pretend with him. Instinctively he knew. For reasons she'd probably never understand, he saw straight through her.

"Let me get those," Nancy said. "You're a wedding guest."

"I can help." But Nancy insisted otherwise.

When Savannah returned to the vestibule, she found Nash waiting for her. They drove in silence to the high-end hotel, where Nash had rented an elegant banquet room for the evening.

Savannah prayed he'd say something to cut the terrible tension. She could think of nothing herself. A long list of possible topics presented itself, but she couldn't come up with a single one that didn't sound silly or trite.

Heaven help her, she didn't know how they'd be able to spend the rest of the evening in each other's company.

Dinner proved to be less of a problem than Savannah expected. They were seated at a table with two delightful older gentlemen whom Nash introduced as John Stack-house and Arnold Serle, the senior partners of the law firm that employed him. John was a widower, she gathered, and Arnold's wife was in England with her sister.

"Mighty nice wedding," Mr. Stackhouse told Nash.

"Thank you. I wish I could take credit, but it's the fruit of Savannah's efforts you're seeing."

"Beautiful wedding," Mr. Serle added. "I can't remember when I've enjoyed one more."

Savannah was waiting for a sarcastic remark from Nash, but one never came. She didn't dare hope that he'd changed his opinion, and guessed it had to do with the men who were seated with them.

Savannah spread the linen napkin across her lap. When she looked up, she discovered Arnold Serle watching her. She wondered if her mascara had run or if there was something wrong with her makeup. Her doubts must have shown in her eyes, because he grinned and winked at her.

Savannah blushed. A sixty-five-year-old corporate attorney was actually flirting with her. It took her a surprisingly short time to recover enough to wink back at him.

Arnold burst into loud chuckles, attracting the attention of Nash and John Stackhouse, who glanced disapprovingly at his partner. "Something troubling you, Arnold?"

"Just that I wish I were thirty years younger. Savannah here's prettier than a picture."

"You been at the bottle again?" his friend asked. "He

becomes quite a flirt when he has," the other man explained. "Especially when his wife's out of town."

Arnold's cheeks puffed with outrage. "I most certainly do not."

Their salads were delivered and Savannah noted, from the corner of her eye, that Nash was studying her closely. Taking her chances, she turned and met his gaze. To her astonishment, he smiled and reached for her hand under the table.

"Arnold's right," he whispered. "Every other woman here fades compared to you." He paused. "With the exception of Susan, of course."

Savannah smiled.

The orchestra was tuning their instruments in the distance and she focused her attention on the group of musicians, feeling a surge of regret and frustration. "I need to tell you something," she said.

"What?"

"I'm sorry, I can't dance. But please don't let that stop you."

"I'm not much of a dancer myself. Don't worry about it."

"Anything wrong?" Arnold asked.

"No, no," Nash was quick to answer. "Savannah just had a question."

"I see."

"That reminds me," John began. "There's something we've been meaning to discuss with you, Nash. It's about the position for senior partner opening up at the firm," he said.

"Can't we leave business out of this evening?" Arnold asked, before Nash could respond. Arnold frowned.

"It's difficult enough choosing another partner without worrying about it day and night."

Nash didn't need to say a word for Savannah to know how much he wanted the position. She felt it in him, the way his body tensed, the eager way his head inclined. But after Arnold's protest, John hadn't continued the discussion.

The dinner dishes were cleared from the table by the expert staff. The music started, a wistful number that reminded Savannah of sweet wine and red roses. Susan, in her flowing silk gown, danced with Kurt as their guests looked on, smiling.

The following number Kurt danced with his mother and Nash with Susan. His assurances that he wasn't much of a dancer proved to be false. He was skilled and graceful.

Savannah must have looked more wistful than she realized because when the next number was announced, Arnold Serle reached for her hand. "This dance is mine."

Savannah was almost too flabbergasted to speak. "I... can't. I'm sorry, but I can't."

"Nonsense." With that, the smiling older man all but pulled her from her chair.

# Six

Savannah was close to tears. She couldn't dance and now she was being forced onto the ballroom-style floor by a sweet older man who didn't realize she had a limp. He hadn't even noticed it. Humiliation burned her cheeks. The wonderful romantic fantasy she was living was about to blow up in her face. Then, when she least expected to be rescued, Nash was at her side, his hand at her elbow.

"I believe this dance is mine, Mr. Serle," he said, whisking Savannah away from the table.

Relief rushed through her, until she saw that he was escorting her onto the dance floor himself. "Nash, I can't," she said in a heated whisper. "Please don't ruin this day for me."

"Do you trust me?"

"Yes, but you don't seem to understand...."

Understand or not, he led her confidently onto the crowded floor, turned and gathered her in his arms. "All I want you to do is relax. I'll do the work."

"Nash!"

"Relax, will you?"

"No... Please take me back to the table."

Instead he grasped her hands and raised them, tucking them around his neck. Savannah turned her face away from him. Their bodies fit snugly against each other and Nash felt warm and substantial. His thigh moved against hers, his chest grazed her breasts and a slow excitement began to build within her. After holding her breath, she released it in a long, trembling sigh.

"It feels good, doesn't it?"

"Yes." Lying would be pointless.

"We're going to make this as simple and easy as possible. All you have to do is hold on to me." He held her close, his hands clasped at the base of her spine. "This isn't so bad now, is it?"

"I'll never forgive you for this, Nash Davenport." Savannah was afraid to breathe again for fear she'd stumble, for fear she'd embarrass them both. She'd never been on a dance floor in her life and try as she might, she couldn't make herself relax the way he wanted. This was foreign territory to her, the girl who'd never been asked to a school dance. The girl who'd watched and envied her friends from afar. The girl who'd only waltzed in her dreams with imaginary partners. And not one of them had been anything like Nash.

"Maybe this will help," Nash whispered. He bent his head and kissed the side of her neck with his warm, moist mouth.

"Nash!" She squirmed against him.

"I've wanted to do that all night," he whispered. Goose bumps shivered up her arms as his tongue made lazy circles along one ear. Her legs felt as if they'd collapse, and she involuntarily pressed her weight against him.

"Please stop that!" she said from between clenched teeth.

"Not on your life. You're doing great." He made all the moves and, holding her the way he was, took the weight off her injured leg so she could slide with him.

"I'll embarrass us both any minute," she muttered.

"Just close your eyes and enjoy the music."

Since they were in the middle of the floor, Savannah had no choice but to follow his instructions. Her chance to escape gracefully had long since passed.

The music was slow and easy, and when she lowered her lashes, she could pretend. This was the night, she'd decided earlier, to play the role of princess. Only she'd never expected her Cinderella fantasy to make it all the way to the ballroom floor.

"You're a natural," he whispered. "Why have you waited so long?"

She was barely moving, which was all she could manage. This was her first experience, and although she was loath to admit it, Nash was right; she was doing well. This must be a dream, a wonderful romantic dream. If so, she prayed it'd be a very long time before she woke.

As she relaxed, Nash's arms moved to a more comfortable position. She lowered her own arm just a little, and her fingers toyed with the short hair at his neck. It was a small but intimate gesture, to run her fingers through his hair, and she wondered at her courage. It might be just another facet of her fantasy, but it seemed the action of a lover or a wife.

Wife.

In the church, when they'd repeated the vows, Nash had called her his friend, his lover, his wife. But it wasn't real. But for now, she was in his arms and they were dancing cheek to cheek, as naturally as if they'd been partners for years. For now, she would make it real, because she so badly wanted to believe it.

"Who said you couldn't dance?" he asked her after a while.

"Shh." She didn't want to talk. These moments were much too precious to waste on conversation. This time was meant to be savored and enjoyed.

The song ended, and when the next one started almost without pause, the beat was fast. Her small bubble of happiness burst. Her disappointment must have been obvious because Nash chuckled. "Come on," he said. "If we can waltz, we can do this."

"Nash... I could do the slow dance because you were holding me, but this is impossible."

Nash, however, wasn't listening. He was dancing. Without her. His arms jerked back and forth, and his feet seemed to be following the same haphazard course. He laughed and threw back his head. "Go for it, Savannah!" He shouted to be heard above the music. "Don't just stand there. Dance!"

She was going to need to move—off the dance floor. She was about to turn away when Nash clasped her around the waist, holding her with both hands. "You can't quit now."

"Oh, yes, I can. Just watch me."

"All you need to do is move a little to the rhythm. You don't need to leap across the dance floor."

There was no talking to him, so she threw her arms in the air in abject frustration.

"That's it," he shouted enthusiastically.

"Excuse me, excuse me," Arnold Serle's voice said

from behind her. "Nash, would you mind if I danced with Savannah now?" he shouted.

Nash looked at Savannah and grinned, as cheerful as a six-year-old pulling a prank on his first-grade teacher. "Savannah would love to. Isn't that right?" With that, he danced his way off the floor.

"Ready to rock 'n' roll?" Arnold asked.

Savannah didn't mean to laugh, but she couldn't stop herself. "I'm not very good at this."

"Shall we?" he said, holding out his palm to her.

Reluctantly she placed her hand in his. She didn't want to offend Nash's boss, but she didn't want to embarrass herself, either. Taking Nash's advice, she moved her arms, just a little at first, swaying back and forth, convinced she looked like a chicken attempting flight. Others around her were wiggling and twisting in every which direction. Savannah's movements, or lack of them, weren't likely to be noticed.

To her utter amazement, Mr. Serle began to twist vigorously. His dancing was reminiscent of 1960s teen movies she'd seen on TV. With each jerking motion he sank closer to the floor, until he was practically kneeling. After a moment he stopped moving. He hunkered there, one arm stretched forward, one elbow back.

"Mr. Serle, are you all right?"

"Would you mind helping me up? My back seems to have gone out on me."

Savannah looked frantically around for Nash, but he was nowhere to be seen. She was silently calling him several colorful names for getting her into this predicament. With no other alternative, she bent forward, grabbed the older man's elbow and pulled him into an upright position.

"Thanks," he said, with a bright smile. "I got carried away there and forgot I'm practically an old man. Sure felt good. My heart hasn't beaten this fast in years."

"Maybe we should sit down," she suggested, praying he'd agree.

"Not on your life, young lady. I'm only getting started."

Nash made his way back to the table, smiling to himself. He hadn't meant to embarrass Savannah. His original intent had been to rescue her. Taking her onto the dance floor was pure impulse. All night he'd been looking for an excuse to hold her, and he wasn't about to throw away what might be his only chance.

*Beautiful* didn't begin to describe Savannah. When he'd first met her, he'd thought of her as cute. He'd dated women far more attractive than she was. On looks alone, she wasn't the type that stood out in a crowd. Nor did she have a voluptuous body. She was small, short and proportioned accordingly. If he was looking for long shapely legs and an ample bust, he wouldn't find either in Savannah. She wasn't a beauty, and yet she was the most beautiful woman he'd ever known.

That didn't make a lot of sense. He decided it was because he'd never met anyone quite like Savannah Charles. He didn't fully understand why she appealed to him so strongly. True, she had a compassionate heart, determination and courage—all qualities he admired.

"Is Arnold out there making a world-class fool of himself?" John Stackhouse asked, when Nash joined the elder of the two senior partners at their table.

"He's dancing with Savannah."

John Stackhouse was by far the most dignified and reserved of the two. Both were members of the executive committee, which had the final say on the appointment of the next senior partner. Stackhouse was often the most disapproving of the pair. Over the years, Nash had been at odds with him on more than one occasion. Their views on certain issues invariably clashed. Although he wasn't particularly fond of the older man, Nash respected him, and considered him fair-minded.

John Stackhouse sipped from his wineglass. "Actually, I'm pleased we have this opportunity to talk," he said to Nash, arching an eyebrow. "A wedding's not the place to bring up business, as Arnold correctly pointed out, but I believe now might be a good time for us to talk about the senior partnership."

Nash's breath froze in his lungs, and he nodded. "I'd appreciate that."

"You've been with the firm a number of years now, and worked hard. We've won some valuable cases because of you, and that's in your favor."

"Glad to hear that." So Paul Jefferson didn't have it sewn up the way he'd assumed.

"I don't generally offer advice..."

This was true enough. Stackhouse kept his opinions to himself until asked, and it boded well that he was willing to make a few suggestions to Nash. Although he badly wanted the position, Nash still didn't think he had a chance against Paul. "I'd appreciate any advice you care to give me."

"Arnold and a couple of the other members of the executive committee were discussing names. Yours was raised almost immediately."

Nash moved forward, perching on the end of his chair. "What's the consensus?"

"Off the record."

"Off the record," Nash assured him.

"You're liked and respected, but there's a problem, a big one as far as the firm's concerned. The fact is, I'm the one who brought it up, but the others claimed to have noticed it, as well."

"Yes?" Nash's mind zoomed over the list of potential areas of trouble.

"You've been divorced for years now."

"Yes."

"This evening's the first time I've seen you put that failure behind you. I've watched you chew on your bitterness like an old bone, digging it up and showing it off like a prized possession when it suited you. You've developed a cutting, sarcastic edge. That's fine in the courtroom, but a detriment in your professional life as well as your private life. Especially if you're interested in this senior partnership."

"I'm interested," Nash was quick to tell him, too quick perhaps because Stackhouse smiled. That happened so rarely it was worth noting.

"I'm glad to hear you say that."

"Is there anything I could do to help my chances?" This conversation was unprecedented, something Nash had never believed possible.

The attorney hesitated and glanced toward the dance floor, frowning. "How serious are you about this young woman?"

Of all the things Nash had thought he might hear, this was the one he least expected. "Ah…" Nash was rarely at a loss for words, but right now he had no idea how to answer. "I don't know. Why do you ask?"

"I realize it's presumptuous of me, and I do hope

you'll forgive me, but it might sway matters if you were to marry again."

"Marry?" he repeated, as if the word was unfamiliar to him.

"It would show the committee that you've put the past behind you," John continued, "and that you're trying to build a more positive future."

"I...see."

"Naturally, there are no guarantees and I certainly wouldn't suggest you consider marriage if you weren't already thinking along those lines. I wouldn't have said anything, but I noticed the way you were dancing with the young lady and it seemed to me you care deeply for her."

"She's special."

The other man nodded. "Indeed she is. Would you mind terribly if I danced with her myself? I see no reason for Arnold to have all the fun." Not waiting for Nash to respond, he stood and made his way across the dance floor to Savannah and his friend.

Nash watched as John Stackhouse tapped his fellow attorney on the shoulder and cut in. Savannah smiled as the second man claimed her.

Marry!

Nash rubbed his face. A few months earlier, the suggestion would have infuriated him. But a few months earlier, he hadn't met Savannah.

Nor had he stood in a church, held hands with an incredible woman and repeated vows. Vows meant for his sister and the man she loved. Not him. Not Savannah. Yet these vows had come straight from his heart to hers. He hadn't intended it to be that way. Not in the beginning. All he'd wanted to do was show Savannah how far he'd come. Repeating a few words seemed a small thing at the time.

But it wasn't as simple as all that. Because everything had changed from that moment forward. He'd spoken in a haze, not fully comprehending the effect it was having on him. All he understood was that he was tired. Tired of being alone. Tired of pretending he didn't need anyone else. Tired of playing a game in which he would always be the loser. Those vows he'd recited with Savannah had described the kind of marriage she believed in so strongly. It was an ideal, an uncommon thing, but for the first time in years he was willing to admit it was possible. A man and a woman could share this loving, mutually respectful partnership. Savannah had made it real to him the moment she'd repeated the vows herself.

Marry Savannah.

He waited for the revulsion to hit him the way it usually did when someone mentioned the word *marriage*. Nothing happened. Of course, that was perfectly logical. He'd spent time in a wedding shop, making a multitude of decisions that revolved around Susan's wedding. He'd become immune to the negative jolt the word always struck in him.

But he expected some adverse reaction. A twinge, a shiver of doubt. Something.

It didn't come.

Marriage. He repeated it slowly in his mind. No, he'd never consider anything so drastic. Not for the sole reason of making senior partner. He'd worked hard. It was a natural progression; if he didn't get the appointment now, he would later.

Marriage to Savannah. If there was ever a time the wine was talking, it was now.

* * *

Savannah had never experienced a night she'd enjoyed more. She'd danced and drunk champagne, then danced again. Every time she'd turned around, there was someone waiting to dance with her or fill her glass.

"Oh, Nash, I had the most incredible night of my life," she said, leaning against the headrest in his car and closing her eyes. It was a mistake, because the world went on a crazy spin.

"That good, was it?"

"Yes, oh, yes. I hate to see it end."

"Then why should it? Where would you like to go?"

"You'll take me anywhere?"

"Name it."

"The beach. I want to go to the beach." She was making a fool of herself, but she didn't care. She wanted to throw out her arms and sing. Where was a mountaintop when she needed one?

"Your wish is my command," Nash said to her.

She slipped her hand around his upper arm and hugged him, resting her head on his shoulder. "That's how I feel about tonight. It's magical. I could ask for anything and somehow it would be given to me."

"I believe it would."

Excited now that her fantasy had become so real, she lowered the car window and let out a wild whoop of joy.

Nash laughed. "What was that for?"

"I'm so happy! I never dreamed I could dance like that. Did you see me? Did you see all the men who asked me?" She brought her hand to her chest. "Me. I always thought I couldn't dance, and I did, and I owe it all to you."

"I knew you could do it."

"But how…"

"You can walk, can't you?"

"Yes, but I assumed it was impossible to dance." The champagne had affected her, but she welcomed the light-headedness it produced. "Oh, did you see Mr. Stackhouse? I thought I'd burst out laughing. I'm convinced he's never done the twist in his life." The memory made her giggle.

"I couldn't believe my eyes," Nash said and she heard the amusement in his voice. "Neither could Arnold Serle. Arnold said they've been friends for thirty-five years and he's never seen John do anything like it, claimed he was just trying to outdo him. That's when he leapt onto the dance floor, too, and the three of you started a conga line."

"There's magic to this night, isn't there?"

"There must be," he agreed.

Her leg should be aching, and would be soon, but she hadn't felt even a twinge. Perhaps later, when adrenaline wasn't pumping through her body and she was back on planet Earth, she'd experience the familiar discomfort. But it hadn't happened yet.

"Your beach," Nash announced, edging into the parking space at Alki Beach in West Seattle. A wide expanse of sandy shore stretched before them. Seattle's lights glittered in the distance like decorations on a gaily lit Christmas tree. Gentle waves lapped the driftwood-strewn sand, and the scents of salt and seaweed hung in the air. "Make all your wishes this easy to fulfill, will you?"

"I'll do my best," she promised. Her list was short, especially for a woman who, on this one night, was a princess in disguise.

"Any other easy requests?" Nash asked. He moved closer and draped his arm across her shoulders.

"A full moon would be nice."

"Will a crescent-shaped one do, instead?"

"It'll have to."

"Perhaps I could find a way to take your mind off the moon," Nash suggested, his voice low and oddly breathless.

"Oh?" *Oh, please let him kiss me,* Savannah pleaded. The night would be perfect if only Nash were to take her in his arms and kiss her....

"Do you know what I'm thinking?" he asked.

She closed her eyes and nodded. "Kiss me, Nash. Please kiss me."

His mouth came down on hers and she thought she was ready for his sensual invasion, since she'd yearned for it so badly. But nothing could have prepared her for the greed they felt for each other. She linked her arms around his neck and gave herself to his touch.

"Why is it," Nash groaned, long minutes later as he breathed kisses across her cheeks, "that we seem to be forever kissing in a car?"

"I...don't know."

His lips toyed with hers. "You're making this difficult."

"I am." Her effect on him made Savannah giddy. It made her feel strong, and for a woman who'd felt weak most of her life, this was a potent aphrodisiac.

"You're so beautiful," Nash whispered, just before he kissed her again.

"Tonight I'm invincible," she murmured. Privately she wondered if Cinderella had spent time like this with her prince before rushing off and leaving him with a single glass slipper. She wondered if her counterpart had the opportunity to experience such unexpected pleasure.

Nash kissed her again and again, until a host of dizzying sensations accosted her from all sides. She broke away and buried her face in his chest in a desperate effort to clear her head.

"Savannah." Taking her by the shoulders, he eased back. "Look at me."

Blindly she obeyed him, running her tongue over lips that were swollen from the urgency of their kisses. "Touch me," she pleaded, gazing at the desire in his eyes, the desire that was a reflection of her own.

Nash went still, his breathing labored. "I can't.... We're on a public beach." He closed his eyes. "That does it," he said forcefully, pulling away from her. "We're going to do this right. We're not teenagers anymore. I want to make love to you, Savannah, and I'm not willing to risk being interrupted by a policeman who'll arrest me for taking indecent liberties." He reached for the ignition and started the car. She saw how badly his hand shook.

"Where are we going?"

"My house."

"Nash..."

"Don't argue with me."

"Kiss me first," she said, not understanding his angry impatience. They had all night. She wouldn't stop being a princess for hours yet.

"I have every intention of kissing you. A lot."

"That sounds nice," she whispered, and with a soft sigh pressed her head against his shoulder.

After several minutes of silence, she said, "I'm not always beautiful." She felt she should remind him of that.

"I hate to argue with you, especially now," he said,

planting one last kiss on the corner of her mouth, "but I disagree."

"I'm really not," she insisted, although she thought it was very kind of him to disagree.

"I want you more than I've ever wanted any other woman in my life."

"You do?" It was so nice of him to say such things, but it wasn't necessary. Unexpected tears filled her eyes. "No one's ever said things like that to me before."

"Stupid fools." They stopped at a red light and Nash reached for her and kissed her as if he longed to make up for a lifetime of rejection. Savannah brought her arms around his neck and sighed when he finally broke off the kiss.

"You're not drunk, are you?" Nash demanded, turning a corner sharply. He shot a wary glance at her, as if this was a recent suspicion.

"No." She was, just a little, but not enough to affect her judgment. "I know exactly what I'm doing."

"Right, but do you know what I intend on doing?"

"Yes, you're taking me home so we can make love in your bed. You'd prefer that to being arrested for doing it publicly."

"Smart girl."

"I'm not a girl!"

"Sorry, slip of the tongue. Trust me, I know exactly how much of a woman you are."

"No, you don't. You haven't got a clue, Nash Davenport, but that's all right because no one else does, either." Herself included, but she didn't say that.

Nash pulled into his driveway and was apparently going faster than he realized, because when he hit his brakes the car jerked to an abrupt stop. "The way I've been driving, it's a miracle I didn't get a ticket," he mumbled as he leapt out of the car. He opened her door, and Savannah smiled lazily and lifted her arms to him.

"I don't know if I can walk," she said with a tired sigh. "I can dance, though, if anyone cares to ask."

He scooped her effortlessly into his arms and carried her to his front porch. Savannah was curious to see his home, curious to learn everything she could about him. She wanted to remember every second of this incredible night.

It was a bit awkward getting the key in the lock and holding her at the same time, but Nash managed. He threw open the door and walked into the dark room. He hesitated, kicked the door closed and traipsed across the living room, not bothering to turn on the lights.

"Stop," she insisted.

"For what? Savannah, you're driving me crazy."

Languishing in his arms, she arched back her head and kissed his cheek. "What a romantic thing to say."

"Did you want something?" he asked impatiently.

"Oh, yes, I want to see your home. A person can find out a great deal about someone just by seeing the kind of furniture he buys. Little things, too, like his dishes. And books and music and art." She gave a tiny shrug. "I've been curious about you from the start."

"You want to know the pattern of my china?"

"Well, yes…"

"Can it wait until tomorrow? There are other things I'd rather be doing…."

Nash moved expertly down the darkened hallway to his room. Gently he placed her on the mattress and knelt over her. She smiled up at him. "Oh, Nash, you have a four-poster bed. But…tomorrow's too late."

"For what?"

"Us. This—being together—will only work for one night. Then the princess disappears and I go back to being a pumpkin." She frowned. "Or do I mean scullery maid?" She giggled, deciding her fracturing of the fairy tale didn't matter.

Nash froze and his eyes met hers, before he groaned and fell backward onto the bed. "You are drunk, aren't you?"

"No," she insisted. "Just happy. Now kiss me and quit asking so many questions." She was reaching for him when it happened. The pain shot like fire through her leg and, groaning, she fell onto her side.

# *Seven*

Nash recognized the effort Savannah made to hide her agony. It must have been excruciating; it was certainly too intense to disguise. Lying on her back, she squeezed her eyes tightly shut, gritted her teeth and then attempted to manage the pain with deep-breathing exercises.

"Savannah," he whispered, not wanting to break her concentration and at the same time desperately needing to do something, anything, to ease her discomfort. "Let me help," he pleaded.

She shook her head. "It'll pass in a few minutes."

Even in the moonlight, Nash could see how pale she'd become. He jumped off the bed and was pacing like a wild beast, feeling the searing grip of her pain himself. It twisted at his stomach, creating a mental torment unlike anything he'd ever experienced.

"Let me massage your leg," he insisted, and when she didn't protest he lifted the skirt of her full-length gown and ran his hands up and down her thigh. Her skin was hot to the touch and when he placed his chilled hands on her, she groaned anew.

"It'll pass." He repeated her own words, praying he

was right. His heart was pounding double-time in his anxiety. He couldn't bear to see Savannah endure this unbearable pain, and stand by and do nothing.

Her whole leg was terribly scarred and his heart ached at the agony she'd endured over the years. Her muscles were tense and knotted but gradually began to relax as he gently worked her flesh with both hands, easing them up and down her thigh and calf. He saw the marks of several surgeries; the scars were testament to her suffering and her bravery.

"There are pills in my purse," she whispered, her voice barely discernible.

Nash quickly surveyed the room, jerking his head from left to right, wondering where she'd put it. He found the small clutch purse on the carpet. Grasping it, he emptied the contents on top of the bed. The brown plastic bottle filled with a prescription for pain medication rolled into view.

Hurrying into his bathroom, he ran her a glass of water, then dumped a handful of the thick chalky tablets into the palm of his hand. "Here," he said.

Levering herself up on one elbow, Savannah took three of the pills. Her hands were trembling, he noted, and he could hardly resist taking her in his arms. Once she'd swallowed the pills, she closed her eyes and laid her head on the pillow.

"Take me home, please."

"In a few minutes. Let's give those pills a chance to work first."

She was sobbing openly now. Nash lay down next to her and gathered her in his arms.

"I'm sorry," she sobbed.

"For what?"

"For ruining everything."

"You didn't ruin anything." He brushed his lips over the crown of her head.

"I...didn't want you to see my leg." Her tears came in earnest now and she buried her face in his shoulder.

"Why?"

"It's ugly."

"You're beautiful."

"For one night..."

"You're wrong, Savannah. You're beautiful every minute of every day." He cradled her head against him, whispering softly in her ear. Gradually he felt her tension diminish, and he knew by the even sound of her breathing that she was drifting off to sleep.

Nash held her for several minutes, wondering what he should do. She'd asked that he take her home, but waking her seemed cruel, especially now that the terrible agony had passed. She needed her sleep, and movement might bring back the pain.

What it came down to, he admitted reluctantly, was one simple fact. He wanted Savannah with him and was unwilling to relinquish her.

Kissing her temple, he eased himself from her arms and crawled off the bed. He got a blanket from the top shelf in his closet and covered her with it, careful to tuck it about her shoulders.

Looking down on her, Nash shoved his hands in his pockets and stared for several minutes.

He wandered into the living room, slumped into his recliner and sat in the dark while the night shadows moved against the walls.

He'd been selfish and inconsiderate, but above all he'd

been irresponsible. Bringing Savannah to his home had been the most recent in a long list of errors in judgment.

He was drunk, but not on champagne. His intoxication was strictly due to Savannah. The idealist. The romantic. Attending his sister's wedding hadn't helped matters any. Susan had been a beautiful bride and if there was ever a time he could believe in the power of love and the strength of vows, it was at her wedding.

It'd started early in the evening when he'd exchanged vows with Savannah as if *they* were the ones being married. It was a moment out of time—dangerous and unreal.

He'd attempted to understand what had happened, offered a litany of excuses, but he wasn't sure he'd ever find one that would satisfy him. He wished there was someone or something he could blame, but that wasn't likely. The best he could hope for was to forget the whole episode and pray Savannah did the same.

Savannah. She was so beautiful. He'd never enjoyed dancing with a woman like he did with her. Smiling to himself, he recalled the way he'd been caught up in the magic of her joy. Being with her, sharing this night with her, was like being drawn into a fairy tale, impossible to resist even if he'd tried. And he hadn't.

Before he knew it, they were parked at Alki Beach, kissing like there was no tomorrow. He'd never desired a woman more.

Wrong. There'd been a time, years earlier, when he'd been equally enthralled with a woman. In retrospect it was easy to excuse his naïveté. He'd been young and impressionable. And because of that, he'd fallen hopelessly in love.

Love. He didn't even like the sound of the word. He'd found love to be both painful and dangerous.

Nash didn't love Savannah. He refused to allow himself to wallow in that destructive emotion a second time. He was attracted to her, but love was out of the question. Denise had taught him everything he needed to know about that.

He hadn't thought of her, except in passing, in years. Briefly he wondered if she was happy, and doubted his ex-wife would ever find what she was searching for. Her unfaithfulness continued to haunt him even now, years after their divorce. For too long he'd turned a blind eye to her faults, all in the glorious name of love.

He'd made other mistakes, too. First and foremost he'd married the wrong woman. His father had tried to tell him, but Nash had refused to listen, discrediting his advice, confident his father's qualms about Nash's choice in women were part and parcel of being too old to understand true love. Time had proved otherwise.

Looking back, Nash realized he'd shared only one thing with Denise. Incredible sex. He'd mistaken her physical demands for love. Within a few weeks of meeting, they were living together and their sexual relationship had become addictive.

It was ironic that she'd been the one to bring up the subject of marriage. Until then she'd insisted she was a "free spirit." Not until much later did he understand this sudden need she had for commitment. With his father seriously ill, there was the possibility of a large inheritance.

They'd been happy in the beginning. Or at least Nash had attempted to convince himself of that, and perhaps they were, but their happiness was short-lived.

He'd first suspected something was wrong when he arrived home late one evening after a grueling day in court and caught the scent of a man's cologne. He'd asked Denise and she'd told him he was imagining things. Because he wanted to believe her, because the thought of her being unfaithful was so completely foreign, he'd accepted her word. He had no reason to doubt her.

His second clue came less than a month later when a woman he didn't know met him outside his apartment. She was petite and fragile in her full-length coat, her hands deep in the pockets, her eyes downcast. She hated to trouble him, she said, but could Nash please keep his wife away from her husband. She'd recently learned she was pregnant with their second child and wanted to keep the marriage together if she could.

Nash had been stunned. He'd tried to ask questions, but she'd turned and fled. He didn't say anything to Denise, not that night and not for a long time afterward. But that was when he started to notice the little things that should've been obvious.

Nash hated himself for being so weak. He should have demanded the truth then and there, should have kicked her out of his home. Instead he did nothing. Denial was comfortable for a week and then two, while he wrestled with his doubts.

Savannah's scarred leg was a testament to her bravery, her endless struggle to face life each and every day. His scarred emotions were a testament to his cowardice, to knowing that his wife was cheating on him and accepting it rather than confronting her with the truth.

His wife had been *cheating* on him. What an ineffectual word that was for what he felt. It sounded so... trivial. So insignificant. But the sense of betrayal was sharper than any blade, more painful than any incision. It had slashed his ego, punctured his heart and forever changed the way he viewed love and life.

Nash had loved Denise; he must have, otherwise she wouldn't have had the power to hurt him so deeply. That love had burned within him, slowly twisting itself into a bitter desire to get even.

The divorce had been ugly. Nash attempted to use legal means to retaliate for what Denise had done to him emotionally. Unfortunately there was no compensation for what he'd endured. He'd learned this countless times since from other clients. He'd wanted to embarrass and humiliate her the way she had him, but in the end they'd both lost.

Following their divorce, Denise had married again almost immediately. Her new husband was a man she'd met three weeks earlier. Nash kept tabs on her for some time afterward and was downright gleeful when he learned she was divorcing again less than a year later.

For a long while Nash was convinced he hated Denise. In some ways he did; his need for revenge had been immature. But as the years passed, he was able to put their short marriage in perspective, and he was grateful for the lessons she'd taught him. Paramount was the complete unreliability of love and marriage.

Denise had initiated him into this kind of thinking, and the hundreds of divorce cases he'd handled since then had reinforced it.

Then he'd met Savannah. In the beginning, she'd irritated him no end. With her head in the clouds, subsisting on the thin air of romance, she'd met each of his arguments as if she alone was responsible for defending the institution of marriage. As if she alone was responsible for changing his views.

Savannah irritated him—that was true enough—but she'd worn down his defenses until he was doing more than listening to her; he was beginning to believe again. It took some deep soul-searching to admit that.

He must believe, otherwise she wouldn't be sleeping in his bed. Otherwise they wouldn't have come within a heartbeat of making love.

What a drastic mistake that would have been, Nash realized a second time. He didn't know when common sense had abandoned him, but it had. Perhaps he'd started breathing that impossibly thin air Savannah had existed on all these years. Apparently it had tricked him as it had her.

Nash should have known better than to bring Savannah into his home. He couldn't sleep with her and expect their relationship to remain the same. Everything would change. Savannah wasn't the type of woman to engage in casual affairs and that was all Nash had to offer. A few hours in bed would have been immensely pleasurable, but eventually disastrous to them both.

Savannah woke when dawn light crept through a nearby window. Opening her eyes, she needed a moment to orient herself. She was in a strange bed. Alone. It didn't take long to remember the events of the night before. She was in Nash's home.

Sitting up required an effort. The contents of her purse were strewn across the bed and, gathering them together as quickly as possible, she went in search of her shoes.

Nash was nowhere to be seen. If her luck held, she

could call a cab and be out of his home before he realized she'd gone.

Her folly weighed heavily on her. She'd never felt more embarrassed in her life.

She moved stealthily from the bedroom into the living room. Pausing, she saw Nash asleep in his recliner. Her breath caught in her throat as she whispered a silent prayer of thanksgiving that he was asleep.

Fearing the slightest sound would wake him, she decided to sneak out the back door, find a phone elsewhere and call for a cab. Her cell phone was at home; there hadn't been room for it in the tiny beaded purse she'd brought with her yesterday.

Her hand was on the lock to the back door, a clean escape within her reach, when Nash spoke from behind her.

"I thought you wanted to check out my china pattern."

Savannah closed her eyes in frustration. "You were sleeping," she said without turning around.

"I'm awake now."

Her face was so hot, it was painful. Dropping her hands, she did her best to smile before slowly pivoting around.

"How were you planning on getting home?" he asked.

"A taxi."

"Did you bring your cell?"

He knew perfectly well she hadn't. "No, I was going to locate a phone somewhere and call a cab."

"I see." He began to make a pot of coffee as if this morning was no different from any other. "Why did you find it so important to leave now?" he asked in what she was sure were deceptively calm tones.

"You were sleeping...."

"And you didn't want to disturb me."

"Something like that."

"We didn't make love, so there's no need to behave like an outraged virgin."

"I'm well aware of what we did and didn't do," Savannah said stiffly. He was offended that she was sneaking out of his home. That much was apparent.

Nash was an experienced lover, but she doubted he'd ever dealt with a situation similar to what had happened to them. Most women probably found pleasure in his touch, not excruciating pain. Most women sighed with enjoyment; they didn't *sob* in agony. Most women lived the life of a princess on a day-to-day basis, while her opportunity came once in a lifetime.

"How's your leg feel?"

"It's fine."

"You shouldn't have danced—"

"Nothing on this earth would have stopped me," she told him, her voice surprisingly strong. "The pain's something I live with every day. It's the price I paid for enjoying myself. I had a wonderful time last night, Nash. Don't take that away from me."

He hesitated, then said, "Sit down and have a cup of coffee. We'll talk and then I'll drive you home." He poured two cups and set them on the round kitchen table. "Cream and sugar?"

She shook her head.

He sat casually in one of the chairs.

"I... I'm not much of a conversationalist in the morning," she said.

"No problem. We can wait until afternoon if you'd rather."

She didn't and he knew that. All she wanted was to escape.

Reluctantly she pulled out the chair opposite his and sat down. The coffee was too hot to drink, but just the right temperature to warm her hands. She cradled the cup between her palms and focused her attention on it. "I want you to know how sorry I am for—"

He interrupted her. "If you're apologizing for last night, don't bother."

"All right, I won't."

"Good."

Savannah took her first tentative sip of coffee. "Well," she said, looking up but avoiding his eyes, "what would you suggest we talk about?"

"What happened."

"Nothing happened," she said.

"It almost did."

"I know that better than you think, Nash. So why are we acting like strangers this morning? Susan's wedding was beautiful. Dancing with you and the two gentlemen from your office was wonderful. For one incredible night I played the glamorous role of a princess. Unfortunately, it ended just a little too soon."

"It ended exactly where it should have. Our making love would have been a mistake."

Savannah was trying to put everything in perspective, but his statement felt like a slap in the face. It shouldn't have hurt so much, but it did. Unwanted tears sprang to her eyes.

"You don't agree?"

"Does it matter?" she asked, refusing to let him know how deeply he'd hurt her.

"I suppose not."

"It doesn't," she said more forcefully. She was having a difficult time holding back the tears. They threatened to spill down her face any second. "I'd like to go home now," she said.

"It wouldn't have worked, you know."

"Of course I know that," she flared.

She felt more than saw Nash's hesitation. "Are you all right?" he asked.

"I've never been better," she snapped. "But I want to go home. Sitting around here in this dress is ridiculous. Now either you drive me or I'm calling a cab."

"I'll drive you."

The ride back to her place was a nightmare for Savannah. Nash made a couple of attempts at conversation, but she was in no mood to talk and certainly in no mood to analyze the events of the night before. She'd been humiliated enough and didn't want to make things worse.

The minute Nash pulled into her driveway, Savannah opened the car door, eager to make her escape. His hand at her elbow stopped her.

Savannah groaned inwardly and froze. But Nash didn't seem to have anything to say.

"Susan's wedding was very nice. Thank you," he finally told her.

She nodded, keeping her back to him and her head lowered.

"I enjoyed our time together."

"I...did, too." Even though that time was over now. It was daylight, and the magic of last night was gone.

"I'll give you a call later in the week."

She nodded, although she didn't believe it. This was probably a line he used often. Just another way of saying goodbye, she figured.

"What about Thursday?" he asked unexpectedly, after he'd helped her out of the car.

"What about it?"

"I'd like to take you out.... A picnic or something."

He couldn't have surprised her more. Slowly she raised her head, studying him, confident she'd misunderstood.

He met her gaze steadily. "What's wrong?"

"Are you asking me out on a date?"

"Yes," he said, taking her house keys from her lifeless hand and unlocking her front door. "Is that a problem?"

"I... I don't know."

"Would you prefer it if we went dancing instead?" he asked, his mouth lifting in a half smile.

Despite their terrible beginning that morning, Savannah smiled. "It'd be nice, but I don't think so."

"I'll see what I can arrange. I'll pick you up around six at the shop. Okay?"

Savannah was too shocked to do anything but nod.

"Good." With that he leaned forward and brushed his lips over hers. It wasn't much as kisses went, but the warmth of his touch went through her like a bolt of lightning.

Savannah stood on her porch, watching him walk away. He was at his car before he turned back. "You were a beautiful princess," he said.

Nash wasn't sure what had prompted the invitation for a picnic for Thursday. It wasn't something he'd given any thought to suggesting. In fact, he felt as surprised as Savannah looked when he'd asked her.

A date. That was simple enough. It wasn't as if he hadn't gone out on dates before, but it had been a long while since he'd formally asked a woman out. He was making more of this than necessary, he decided.

By Wednesday he would have welcomed an excuse to get out of it. Especially after John Stackhouse called him into his office. The minute he received the summons, Nash guessed this was somehow linked to Savannah.

"You wanted to see me?" Nash asked, stepping inside the senior partner's office later that afternoon.

"I hope I'm not calling you away from something important?"

"Not at all," Nash assured him. It might have been his imagination, but Stackhouse's attitude seemed unusually friendly. Although they were always polite to each other, he wasn't John's favorite, not the way Paul Jefferson was. But then, Paul wasn't prone to disagree with anyone who could advance his career.

"I have a divorce I want you to handle," his boss said casually.

These cases were often assigned to him. He'd built his reputation on them. Lately, though, they hadn't held his interest and he was hoping to diversify.

"This man is a friend of mine by the name of Don Griffin. It's a sad case, very sad." John paused, shaking his head.

"Don Griffin," Nash repeated. The name was familiar, but he couldn't place it.

"You might have heard of him. Don owns a chain of seafood restaurants throughout the Pacific Northwest."

"I think I read something about him not long ago."

"You might have," John agreed. "He's mentioned in the paper every now and then. But getting back to the divorce… Don and Janice have been married a lot of years. They have two college-age children and then Janice learned a few years back that she was pregnant. You can imagine their shock."

Nash nodded sympathetically.

"Unfortunately the child has Down syndrome. This came as a second blow, and Don took it hard. So did Janice."

Nash couldn't blame the couple for that. "They're divorcing?"

"Yes." John's expression was filled with regret. "I don't know all the details, but apparently Janice was devoting all her time and attention to little Amy and, well, in a moment of weakness, Don got involved with another woman. Janice found out and filed for divorce."

"I see. And is this what Don wants?"

The senior partner's face tightened with disappointment. "Apparently so. I'm asking you, as a personal favor, to handle this case, representing Don. My late wife and I were good friends with both Don and Janice."

"I'll help in any way I can," Nash said, but without real enthusiasm. Another divorce case, more lives ripped apart. He'd anesthetize his feelings as best he could and struggle to work out the necessary details, but only because John had asked him.

"I'll make an appointment to have Don come in for the initial consultation Friday morning, if that's agreeable?" Once more he made it a question, as if he expected Nash to decline.

This was the first personal favor Stackhouse had ever asked of him.

"I'll be happy to take the case," Nash said again. So he'd been wrong; this had nothing to do with Savannah.

"Good." John reached for his phone. "I'll let Don know I got him the best divorce attorney in town."

"Thank you." Compliments were few and far between from the eldest of the senior partners. Nash suspected he should feel encouraged that the older man trusted him with a family friend.

On his way out of the office, Nash ran into Arnold Serle. "Nash," the other man said, his face lighting up. "I haven't seen you all week."

"I've been in court."

"So I heard. I just wanted you to know how much I enjoyed your sister's wedding."

"We enjoyed having you." So he wasn't going to escape hearing about Savannah after all.

"How's Savannah?" Arnold asked eagerly.

"Very well. I'll tell her you asked about her."

"Please do. My niece is thinking about getting married. I'd like to steer her to Savannah's shop. If your sister's wedding is evidence of the kind of work Savannah does, I'd like to hire her myself." He chuckled then. "I sincerely hope you appreciate what a special woman she is."

"I do."

"Pleased to hear it," Arnold said, grinning broadly.

By Thursday evening, Nash had run through the full range of emotions. Knowing he'd be seeing Savannah later was both a curse and a blessing. He looked forward to being with her and at the same time dreaded it.

He got there right at six. Savannah was sitting at her desk, apparently working on her computer; she didn't hear him enter the shop because she didn't look up. She was probably entertaining second thoughts of her own.

"Savannah." He said her name lightly, not wanting to frighten her.

She jerked her head up, surprise written on her face.

But it wasn't the shock in her eyes that unnerved him, it was the tears.

"It's Thursday," he reminded her. "We have a date."

Nash wondered if she'd forgotten.

"Are you going to tell me what's upset you so much?" he asked.

"No," she said with a warm smile, the welcome in her eyes belying her distress. "I'm glad to see you, Nash. I could do with a friend just now."

# *Eight*

Savannah hadn't forgotten about her date with Nash. She'd thought of little else in the preceding days, wondering if she should put any credence in his asking. One thing she knew about Nash Davenport—he wasn't the type to suggest something he didn't want.

"I had the deli pack us dinner," he told her. "I hope you're hungry."

"I am," she said, wiping the last tears from her face. Nash was studying her with undisguised curiosity and she was grateful he didn't press her for details. She wouldn't have known how to explain, wouldn't have found the words to tell him about the sadness and guilt she felt.

"Where are we going?" she asked, locking the shop. If ever there was a time she needed to get away, to abandon her woes and have fun, it was now.

"Lake Sammamish."

The large lake east of Lake Washington was a well-known and well-loved picnic area. Savannah had been there several times over the years, mostly in the autumn, when she went to admire the spectacular display of fall color. She enjoyed walking along the shore and feeding the ducks.

"I brought a change of clothes," she said. "It'll only take me a minute to get out of this suit."

"Don't rush. We aren't in any hurry."

Savannah moved into the dressing room and replaced her business outfit with jeans and a large sweatshirt with Einstein's image. She'd purchased it earlier in the week with this outing in mind. When she returned, she discovered Nash examining a silk wedding dress adorned with a pearl yoke. She smiled to herself, remembering the first time he'd entered her shop and the way he'd avoided getting close to anything that hinted of romance. He'd come a long way in the past few months, further than he realized, much further than she'd expected.

"This gown arrived from New York this afternoon. It's lovely, isn't it?"

She thought he'd shrug and back away, embarrassed that she'd commented on his noticing something as symbolic of love as a wedding dress.

"It's beautiful. Did one of your clients order it?"

"No. It's from a designer I've worked with in the past and I fell in love with it myself. I do that every once in a while—order a dress that appeals to me personally. Generally they sell, and if they don't, there's always the possibility of renting it out."

"Not this one," he said in a voice so low, she had to strain to hear him. He seemed mesmerized by the dress.

"Why not?" she asked.

"This is the type of wedding gown…" He hesitated.

"Yes?" she prompted.

"When a man sees the woman he loves wearing this dress, he'll cherish the memory forever."

Savannah couldn't believe what she was hearing. This was Nash? The man who'd ranted and raved that love was a wasted emotion? The man who claimed marriage was for the deluded?

"That's so romantic," Savannah murmured. "If you don't object, I'd like to advertise it that way."

Nash's eyes widened and he shook his head. "You want to use that in an ad?"

"If you don't mind. I won't mention your name, unless you want me to."

"No! I mean... Can we just drop this?"

"Of course. I'm sorry, I didn't mean to embarrass you."

"You didn't," he said, when it was clear that she had. "I seem to have done this to myself." He made a point of looking at his watch. "Are you ready?"

Savannah nodded. This could prove to be an interesting picnic....

They drove to Lake Sammamish in Nash's car and he seemed extra talkative. "Arnold Serle asked about you the other day," he told her as he wove in and out of traffic.

"He's a darling," Savannah said, savoring the memories of the two older men who'd worked so hard to bolster her self-confidence, vying for her the way they had. "Mr. Stackhouse, too," she added.

"You certainly made an impression on them."

Although the night had ended in disaster, she would always treasure it. Dancing with John and Arnold. Dancing with Nash...

"What's the smile about?" Nash asked, momentarily taking his eyes off the road.

"It's nothing."

"The tears were nothing, too?"

The tears. She'd almost forgotten she'd been crying when he arrived. "I was talking to my parents this afternoon," she said as the misery returned. "It's always the same. They talk about traveling, but they never seem to leave Seattle. Instead of really enjoying life, they smother me with their sympathy and their sacrifices, as if that could bring back the full use of my leg." She was speaking fast and furiously, and not until she'd finished did she realize how close she was to weeping again.

Nash's hand touched hers for a moment. "You're a mature adult, living independently of them," he said. "You have for years."

"Which I've explained so many times, I get angry just thinking about it. Apparently they feel that if something were to happen, no one would be here to take care of me."

"What about other relatives?"

"There aren't any in the Seattle area. I try to reassure them that I'm fine, that no disasters are about to strike and even if one did, I have plenty of friends to call on, but they just won't leave."

"Was that what upset you this afternoon?" he asked.

Savannah dropped her gaze to her hands, now clenched tightly in her lap. "They've decided to stay in Seattle this winter. Good friends of theirs asked if they'd travel with them, leaving the second week of September and touring the South before spending the winter in Arizona. My dad's always wanted to visit New Orleans and Atlanta. They said they'll go another year," Savannah muttered, "but I know they won't. They know it, too."

"Your parents love you. I understand their concern."

"How can you say that?" she demanded angrily. "They're doing this because they feel guilty about my accident. Now I'm the one who's carrying that load. When will it ever end?"

"I don't know," he said quietly.

"I just wish they loved me enough to trust me to take care of myself. I've been doing exactly that for a long time now."

Nodding, he exited the freeway and took the road leading into Lake Sammamish State Park. He drove around until he found a picnic table close to the parking lot. The gesture was a thoughtful one; he didn't want her to have a long way to walk.

It might not be very subtle, but Savannah didn't care. She was determined to enjoy their outing. She needed this. She knew it was dangerous to allow herself this luxury. She was well aware that Nash could be out of her life with little notice. That was something she'd always taken into account in other relationships, but her guard had slipped with Nash.

He helped her out of the car and carried the wicker basket to the bright blue picnic table. The early evening was filled with a symphony of pleasant sounds. Birds chirped in a nearby tree, their song mingling with the laughter of children.

"I'm starved," Nash said, peering inside the basket. He raised his head and waggled his eyebrows. "My, oh, my, what goodies."

Savannah spread a tablecloth across one end of the table and Nash handed her a large loaf of French bread, followed by a bottle of red wine.

"That's for show," he said, grinning broadly. "This is for dinner." He took out a bucket of fried chicken and a six-pack of soda.

"I thought you said the deli packed this."

"They did. I made a list of what I wanted and they packed it in the basket for me."

"You're beginning to sound like a tricky defense attorney," she said, enjoying this easy banter between them. It helped take her mind off her parents and their uncomfortable conversation that afternoon.

They sat across from each other and with a chicken leg in front of her mouth, Savannah looked out over the blue-green water. The day was perfect. Not too warm and not too cool. The sun was shining and a gentle breeze rippled off the lake. A lifeguard stood sentinel over a group of preschool children splashing in the water between bursts of laughter. Farther out, a group of teens dived off a large platform. Another group circled the lake in two-seater pedal boats, their wake disrupting the serenity of the water.

"You're looking thoughtful," Nash commented.

Savannah blushed, a little embarrassed to be caught so enraptured with the scene before her. "When I was a teenager I used to dream a boy would ask me to pedal one of the boats with him."

"Did anyone?"

"No...." A sadness attached itself to her heart, dredging up the memories of a difficult youth. "I can't pedal."

"Why not? You danced, didn't you?"

"Yes, but that's different."

"How?"

"Don't you remember what happened after the dance?"

"We could rent a pedal boat and I'll do the work," he said. "You just sit back and enjoy the ride."

She lowered her gaze, not wanting him to see how badly she longed to do what he'd suggested.

"Come on," he wheedled. "It'll be fun."

"We'd go around in circles," she countered. She

wasn't willing to try. "It won't work if we don't each do our share of the pedaling. I appreciate what you're doing, but I simply can't hold up my part."

"You won't know that until you try," he said. "Remember, you didn't want to dance, either." His reminder was a gentle one and it hit its mark.

"We might end up looking like idiots."

"So? It's happened before. To me, anyway." He stood and offered her his hand. "You game or not?"

She stared up at him, and indecision kept her rooted to the table. "I don't know if it's a good idea."

"Come on, Savannah, prove to me that you can do this. But more importantly, prove it to yourself. I'm not going to let you overdo it, I promise."

His confidence was contagious. "If you're implying that you could've kept me off the dance floor, think again. I danced every dance."

"Don't remind me. The only way I could dance with you was to cut in on someone else. At least this way I'll have you to myself."

Savannah placed her hand firmly in his, caught up in his smile.

"If anyone else comes seeking the pleasure of your company this time," he said, "they'll have to swim."

Savannah's mood had been painfully introspective when Nash arrived. Now, for the first time in what seemed like days, she experienced the overwhelming urge to laugh. Hugging Nash was a spontaneous reaction to the lightheartedness she felt with him.

He stiffened when her arms went around him, but recovered quickly, gripping her about her waist, picking her up and twirling her around until she had to beg him to stop. Breathless, she gazed at him, and said, "You make me want to sing."

"You make me want to—"

"What?" she asked.

"Sing," he muttered, relaxing his hold enough for her feet to touch the ground.

Savannah could have sworn his ears turned red. "I make you want to do what?" she pressed.

"Never mind, Savannah," he answered. "It's better that you don't know. And please, just this once, is it too much to ask that you don't argue with me?"

"Fine," she said, pretending to be gravely disappointed. She mocked him with a deep sigh.

They walked down to the water's edge, where Nash paid for the rental of a small pedal boat. He helped her board and then joined her, the boat rocking precariously as he shifted his weight.

Savannah held tightly to her seat. She remained skeptical of this idea, convinced they were going to look like a pair of idiots once they left the shore. She didn't mind being laughed at, but she didn't want him laughed at because of her.

"I...don't think we should do this," she whispered, struck by an attack of cowardice.

"I'm not letting you out of this now. We haven't even tried."

"I'll embarrass you."

"Let me worry about that."

"Nash, please."

He refused to listen to her and began working the pedals, making sure the pace he set wasn't too much for her. Water rustled behind them and Savannah jerked around to see the paddle wheel churning up the water. Before she realized it, they were speeding along.

"We're moving," she shouted. "We're actually moving."

It seemed that everyone on the shore had turned to watch them. In sheer delight, Savannah waved her arms. "We're actually moving."

"I think they've got the general idea," Nash teased.

"I could just kiss you," Savannah said, resisting the urge to throw her arms around his neck and do exactly that.

"You'll need to wait a few minutes." His hand reached for hers and he entwined their fingers.

"Let's go fast," she urged, cautiously pumping her feet. "I want to see how fast we can go."

"Savannah...no."

"Yes, please, just for a little bit."

He groaned and then complied. The blades of the paddle behind them churned the water into a frothy texture as they shot ahead. Nash was doing most of the work. Her efforts were puny compared to his, but it didn't seem to matter. This was more fun than she'd dared to dream. As much fun as dancing.

Savannah laughed boisterously. "I never knew," she said, squeezing his upper arm with both hands and pressing her head against his shoulder. "I never thought I could do this."

"There's a whole world out there just waiting to be explored."

"I want to skydive next," Savannah said gleefully.

"Skydive?"

"All right, roller-skate. I wanted to so badly when I was growing up. I used to skate before the accident, you know. I was pretty good, too."

"I'm sure you were."

"All my life I've felt hindered because of my leg and suddenly all these possibilities are opening up to me." She went from one emotional extreme to the other. First joy and laughter and now tears and sadness. "Meeting you was the best thing that's ever happened to me," she said, and sniffled. "I could cry, I'm so happy."

Nash stiffened and Savannah wondered if she'd offended him. His reaction would have been imperceptible if they hadn't been sitting side by side.

Nash was pedaling harder now; her own feet were set in motion by his efforts. "Where are we going?" she asked, noting that he seemed to be steering the craft toward shore. She didn't want to stop, not when they were just getting started. This was her one fear, that she'd embarrass him, and apparently she had.

"See that weeping willow over on the far side of the bank?" he asked, motioning down the shoreline. She did, noting the branches draped over the water like a sanctuary. It appeared to be on private property.

"Yes."

"We're headed there."

"Why?" she asked, thinking of any number of plausible reasons. Perhaps he knew the people who lived there and wanted to stop and say hello.

"Because that weeping willow offers a little more privacy than out here on the lake. And I intend to take you up on your offer, because frankly, I'm not going to be able to wait much longer."

Offer, she mused. What offer?

Nash seemed to enjoy her dilemma and raised her hand to his mouth, kissing the inside of her palm. "I seem to remember you saying you wanted to kiss me. So I'm giving you the opportunity."

"Now?"

"In a moment." He steered the boat under the drooping limbs of the tree. The dense growth cut off the sunlight and cooled the late-afternoon air.

Nash stopped and the boat settled, motionless, in the water. He turned to her and his gaze slid across her face.

"Has anyone ever told you how beautiful you are?"

Besides him and her parents? And they had to praise her, didn't they? No one. Not ever. "No."

"Is the rest of the world blind?"

His words were followed by silence. A silence that spanned years for Savannah. No man had looked past her flaw and seen the desirable woman she longed to be. No man but Nash.

His mouth came down on hers, shattering the silence with his hungry need, shattering the discipline she'd held herself under all these years. She wrapped herself in his embrace and returned the kiss with the potency of her own need.

Nash moaned and kissed her hard, and she responded with every ounce of her being. She kissed him as if she'd been waiting all her life for this moment, this man. In ways too numerous to count, she had been.

She moaned softly, thinking nothing seemed enough. Nash made her greedy. She wanted more. More of life. More of laughter. More of him.

Dragging his mouth from hers, he trailed a row of moist kisses down her neck. "If we were anyplace but here, do you know what we'd be doing now?"

"I… I think so." How odd her voice sounded.

"We'd be in bed making love."

"I..."

"What?" he prompted. "Were you about to tell me you can't? Because I'll be more than happy to prove otherwise." He directed her mouth back to his.... Then, slowly, reluctantly, as though remembering this was a public place and they could be interrupted at any time, he ended the kiss.

Savannah had more difficulty than Nash in returning to sanity. She needed the solid reality of him close to her. When he eased himself from her arms, his eyes searched out hers.

"If you say that shouldn't have happened, I swear I'll do something crazy," she whispered.

"I don't think I could make myself say it."

"Good," she breathed.

Nash pressed his forehead to hers. "I wish I knew what it is you do to me." She sensed that it troubled him that she could break through that facade of his. She was beginning to understand this man. She was physically handicapped, but Nash was crippled, too. He didn't want love, but he couldn't keep himself from needing it, from caring about her, and that worried him. It worried her, too.

"You don't like what I do to you." That much was obvious, but she wanted to hear him admit it.

Nash gave a short laugh. "That's the problem, I like it too much. There's never been anyone who affects me this way. Not since Denise."

"Your ex-wife?"

"Yes." He regretted mentioning her name, Savannah guessed, because he made a point of changing the subject immediately afterward.

"We should go back to the pier."

"Not yet," Savannah pleaded. "Not so soon. We just got started."

"I don't want you to strain your leg. You aren't accustomed to this much exercise."

"I won't, I promise. Just a little while longer." This was so much fun, she didn't want it to ever end. It wasn't every day that she could turn a dream into reality. It wasn't every day a man kissed her as if she were his cherished love.

Love. Love. Love. The word repeated itself in her mind. She was falling in love with Nash. It had begun weeks earlier, the first time he'd kissed her, and had been growing little by little. Love was a dangerous emotion when it came to Nash. He wouldn't be an easy man to care about.

He steered them away from the tree and into the sunlight. Savannah squinted against the glare, but it didn't seem to affect Nash. He pedaled now as if he was escaping something. The fun was gone.

"I'm ready to go back," Savannah said after several minutes of silence.

"Good." He didn't bother to disguise his relief.

The mood had changed so abruptly that Savannah had trouble taking it all in. Nash couldn't seem to get back to shore fast enough. He helped her out of the boat and placed his arm, grudgingly it seemed, around her waist to steady her. Once he was confident she had her balance, he released her.

"I think we should leave," he said when they returned to the picnic table.

"Sure," she agreed, disappointed and sad. She folded up the tablecloth and handed it to him. He carried the basket to the car and loaded it in the trunk.

Savannah knew what was coming; she'd been through it before. Whenever a man feared he was becoming—or might become—emotionally attached to her, she could count on the same speech. Generally it began with what an exceptional woman she was, talented, gifted, fun, that sort of thing. The conclusion, however, was always the same. Someday a special man would come into her life. She'd never expected her relationship with Nash to get even that far. She'd never expected to see him after Susan's wedding. This outing was an unforeseen bonus.

They were on the freeway, driving toward Seattle, before Savannah found the courage to speak. It would help if she broached the subject first.

"Thank you, Nash, for a lovely picnic."

He said nothing, which was just as well.

"I know what you're thinking," she said, clasping her hands tightly together.

"I doubt that."

She smiled to herself. "I've seen this happen with other men, so you don't need to worry about it."

"Worry about what?"

"You're attracted to me and that frightens you— probably more than the other men I've dated because a woman you once loved has deeply hurt you."

"I said I don't want to talk about Denise."

"I'm not going to ask about her, if that's what concerns you," she said quickly, wanting to relieve him about that. "I'm going to talk about us. You may not realize it now, but I'm saving you the trouble of searching for the right words."

He jerked his head away from traffic and scowled at her. "I beg your pardon?"

"You heard me right. You see, it's all familiar to me, so you needn't worry about it. This isn't the first time."

"It isn't?" The question was heavy with sarcasm.

"I've already explained it's happened before."

"Go on. I'd be interested in hearing this." The hard muscles of his face relaxed and the beginnings of a smile came into play.

"You like me."

"That should be fairly obvious," he commented.

"I like you, too."

"That's a comfort." The sarcastic edge was back, but it wasn't as biting.

"In fact, you're starting to like me a little too much."

"I'm not sure what that means, but go on."

"We nearly made love once."

"Twice," he corrected. "We were closer than you think a few minutes ago."

"Under a tree in a pedal boat?" she asked with a laugh.

"Trust me, honey, where there's a will, there's a way."

Savannah blushed and looked pointedly away. "Let's not get sidetracked."

"Good idea."

He was flustering her, distracting her train of thought. "It becomes a bit uncomfortable whenever a man finds me attractive."

"Why's that?"

"Because…well, because they have to deal with my problem, and most people are more comfortable ignoring it. If you deny that there's anything different, it might go away."

"Have I done that?" This question was more serious than the others.

"No," she admitted. "You've been accepting of my… defect. I'm just not sure—"

"I've never viewed you as defective," he interrupted.

It seemed important to him that she acknowledge that,

so she did. "I'm grateful to have met you, Nash, grateful for the fun we've had."

"This is beginning to sound like a brush-off."

"It is," she murmured. "Like I said, I'm saving you the trouble of coming up with an excuse for not seeing me again. This is the better-to-be-honest-now-instead-of-cruel-later scenario."

"Saving me the trouble," he exploded, and then burst into gales of laughter. "So that's what this is all about."

"Yes. You can't tell me that isn't what you were thinking. I know the signs, Nash. Things got a bit intense between us and now you're getting cold feet. It happened the night of Susan's wedding, too. We didn't make love and you were grateful, remember?"

He didn't agree or disagree.

"Just now...at the lake, we kissed, and you could feel it happening a second time, and that's dangerous. You couldn't get away from me fast enough."

"That's not entirely true."

"Your mood certainly changed."

"Okay, I'll concede that, but not for the reasons you're assuming. My mood changed because I started thinking about something and frankly it threw me for a loop."

"Thinking about what?" she pressed.

"A solution."

"To what?"

"Hold on, Savannah, because I don't know how you're going to react. Probably about the same way I did."

"Go on," she urged.

"It seems to me..."

"Yes?" she said when he didn't immediately finish.

"It seems to me that we might want to think about getting married."

# Nine

"Married," Savannah repeated in a husky whisper.

Nash knew he'd shocked her, but no more than he had himself. The notion of marriage went against the grain. Something was either very wrong—or very right. He hadn't decided yet.

"I don't understand." Savannah shook her head, making a vague gesture with her hands.

"Unfortunately, I don't know if I'll do a decent job of explaining it," Nash said.

"Try." Her hands were at her throat now, fingering the collar of her sweatshirt.

"This could work, Savannah, with a little effort on both our parts."

"Marriage? You hate the very word…. I've never met anyone with a more jaded attitude toward love and romance. Is this some kind of joke?"

"Trust me. I was just as shocked at the idea as you are, but the more I thought about it, the more sense it made. I wish it was a joke." Nash's choice of words must have been poor because Savannah recoiled from him. "It would be a marriage of convenience," he added, hoping that might reassure her—or at least not scare her off.

"What?" she cried. "In other words, you intend to take what I consider sacred and make a mockery of it."

It was difficult not to be defensive when Savannah was acting so unreasonable. "If you'll listen, you might see there are advantages for both of us."

"Take me back to my shop," she said in a icy voice.

"I'm going there now, but I was hoping we could talk first."

She said nothing, which didn't bode well. Nash wanted to explain, ease her mind, ease his own, but he wasn't sure he could. He'd spoken prematurely without giving the matter sufficient consideration. It was after they'd kissed under the weeping willow that the idea had occurred to him. It had shocked him so completely that for a time he could barely function. He'd needed to escape and now that they were on their way back into Seattle, he realized he needed to talk this over with her.

"I know this comes as a surprise," he said, looking for a way to broach the subject once again. He exited from the freeway and was within a mile of Savannah's shop.

Savannah looked steadfastly out the window, as if the houses they were passing mesmerized her.

"Say something," Nash demanded. He drove into the alley where her car was parked and turned off the engine. He kept his hands tightly on the steering wheel.

"You wouldn't want to hear what I'm thinking," Savannah told him through clenched teeth.

"Maybe not," he agreed. "But would you listen to what I have to say?"

She crossed her arms and glared at him. "I don't know if I can and keep a straight face."

"Try," he said, just as she had earlier.

"All right, go on, explain." She closed her eyes.

"When I came to pick you up this afternoon, you were upset."

She shrugged, unwilling to acknowledge even that much. It wasn't an encouraging sign. He'd been premature in mentioning marriage. He wasn't sure why he'd considered it so urgent that he couldn't take the night to sleep on it first. Perhaps he was afraid he'd change his mind. Perhaps this was what he'd always wanted, and he needed to salvage his pride with the marriage-of-convenience proposal. Either way, it didn't matter; he'd already shown his hand.

"You love your parents and want them to go after their dream, isn't that right?"

"Would you simply make your point?"

"Fine, I will," he said, his argument gaining momentum. "I'm offering you the perfect solution. You marry me."

"In other words, you're suggesting we mislead my parents into believing this is a love match?"

"I hadn't thought of it in those terms, but, yes, I guess we would be misleading them. If that makes you uncomfortable, tell them the truth. Keep your maiden name if you want. That wouldn't bother me at all. The point is, if you were married, your father and mother would feel free to move south for the winters the way they've always wanted."

"What's in this for you?" she demanded. "Don't try to tell me you're doing it out of the goodness of your heart, either. I know better."

"You're right, there're advantages to me, too."

She snickered softly. "Somehow I thought there would be."

"That's the beauty of my idea," he said, trying to keep his irritation in check. Savannah was treating this like a joke while he was dead serious. A man didn't mention the word *marriage* lightly. Nash had been through this before, but this time marriage would be on his terms.

"Go on," Savannah snapped.

"As I said, there are certain advantages in this marriage for me, as well. The night of Susan's wedding, John Stackhouse pulled me aside and told me that I was being considered for the position of senior partner."

"But it would help if you were married."

Savannah wasn't slow-witted, that was for sure. "Something like that," he admitted. "It seems the other senior partners are afraid that my bitterness about my own divorce has spilled over into other areas of my life."

"Imagine that."

Nash tried to hide his annoyance. Savannah was making this extremely difficult.

"There're no guarantees for either of us, of course. If you agree to the terms of this marriage, that doesn't mean your parents will pack up and head south. If we did go ahead with it, there's nothing to say I'll be made senior partner. There's an element of risk for us both. You might get what you want and I might not. Or vice versa."

"Ah, now I understand," Savannah said in a slow, singsong voice. "That's where the convenience part comes into play. You want an out."

"That has nothing to do with it," Nash flared.

"Do you think I'm stupid, Nash? Of course it does. No one wants a cripple for a wife," she said furiously, "and if you can put an escape clause in the marriage contract, all the better."

"That's ridiculous! It has nothing to do with this."

"Would you have proposed marriage to any other woman this way, suggesting a short-term relationship for the sake of convenience? Heaven forbid that you might feel some genuine affection for me!"

It took Nash a moment to compose himself. He'd acted on impulse, which was not only uncharacteristic but a huge mistake, one that had only led to greater confusion. "Maybe this wasn't such a bright idea after all," he began. "I should've ironed out the details before talking to you about it. If you want to find fault with me for that, then I'll accept it with a heartfelt apology, but this business about me using you because I consider you less of a woman—you couldn't be more wrong. Your suggestion insults us both."

"Why do I have a hard time believing that?" Savannah asked. She sounded suspiciously close to tears, which grieved him more than her anger had.

"All I'm looking for here is a way of being fair to us both," Nash argued. "Despite what you think, I didn't mean to insult you."

"I'm sure you didn't. You're probably thinking people will admire you. Imagine Nash Davenport taking pity on that—"

"Savannah, stop." He pressed his lips tightly together. She was making a mockery of his proposal, a mockery of herself.

"Are you saying I'm wrong?"

His self-control was stretched to the limit. "Don't even suggest that," he said.

"I have to go," Savannah whispered. She turned from him, her fingers closing around the door handle. "It'd be best if we didn't see each other again."

Nash knew that the minute she left his car it would

be over between them. He couldn't allow that to happen, couldn't let her leave, not without righting the wrong. He needed to do something, anything, to convince her he was sincere.

"Not yet," Nash said, taking her by the shoulder.

"Let go of me."

"Not without this." He locked his arms around her waist and pulled her against him.

She didn't resist, not for a second. Her own arms crept around his neck, and then they were kissing again, with the same passion as before.

He didn't know how long they were in each other's arms—or what brought him back to sanity. Possibly a noise from the street, or Savannah herself. He jerked his head up and buried his face in her shoulder, which was heaving with the strength of her reaction. Her fingers were buried in his hair.

"I find it amazing," she whispered brokenly, "that you're looking for a marriage in name only."

He wasn't sure if she was being humorous or not, but he wasn't taking any chances. "We might need to revise that part of the agreement."

"There won't be any agreement, Nash."

He was afraid of that. "Would you kindly listen to reason, Savannah? I wasn't trying to insult you… I thought you'd like the idea."

"Think again." She was breathing deeply, clearly fighting to regain her composure.

"Are you willing to listen to reason?" he asked again, hoping he'd reached her, if on no other level than the physical.

"I've had to deal with a certain amount of cruelty in my life," she said in a low voice. "Children are often brutal with their taunts and their name-calling. It was something I became accustomed to as a child. It hurt. Sticks and stones may break your bones, but words cut far deeper."

"Savannah, stop." That she'd compare his proposal to the ridicule she'd endured as a child was too painful to hear.

She stiffened, her back straight. "I don't want to see you again."

The words hit him hard. "Why not?"

She opened the car door and stepped awkwardly into the alley. Her leg seemed to be bothering her and with some effort she shifted her weight. "I don't trust myself with you...and I don't trust you with me. I've got to take care of myself."

"I want to help you, not hurt you," he insisted.

She hung her head and Nash suspected she did so to hide the fact that she was crying. "Goodbye, Nash. Please don't try to see me again.... Don't make this any more difficult than it already is."

Two weeks later, Nash's sister, Susan, strolled into Savannah's shop. Savannah felt a sense of awe at the happiness that shone from the young woman's eyes.

"What are you doing here?" she asked. "You're supposed to be on your honeymoon."

"We've been back for several days."

Following the wedding, Savannah rarely saw her clients. Whenever someone made the effort to stop in, it was a special treat. More so with Susan because Savannah had been so actively involved in the wedding. Actively involved with Nash, if she was willing to be honest, which at the moment she wasn't.

"You look—" Savannah searched for the right word "—serene." The two women hugged and Savannah held her friend tightly as unexpected tears moistened her eyes. She didn't allow them to fall, not wanting Susan to see how emotional she'd become. "I've missed you," she said. She had, but more than that, she'd missed Nash.

"Nash said the same thing. You both knew before I was married that I'd be moving to California with Kurt. Now you're acting like it's a big shock. By the way, Kurt sends his love."

Savannah eased from Susan's embrace. "What are you doing back in Seattle so soon? Kurt's with you, isn't he?"

"Why I'm here is a long story. As to your second question, Kurt couldn't come. With the wedding and the honeymoon, he couldn't get away. It's the first time we've been apart since the wedding and I miss him dreadfully." A wistful look came over her.

"What brings you to Seattle?"

Susan hesitated just a fraction of a second. "Nash."

So her big brother had sent her. This was exactly what she should have expected from Nash. The man wasn't fair—he'd use any means at his disposal to achieve his purpose.

"He doesn't know I'm here," Susan said as if reading Savannah's thoughts. "He'd be furious if he ever found out. I phoned him when Kurt and I got home from our honeymoon and he said he was having several pieces of furniture shipped to us. Things that belonged to our parents. I was a little surprised, since we're living in a small apartment and don't have much space. Nash knows that. Kurt talked to him, too, and afterward we agreed something was wrong. The best way to handle the situation was for me to visit."

"I see." Savannah made busywork around her desk, turning off her computer, straightening papers, rearranging pens in their holder. "How is Nash?"

"Miserable. I don't know why and he's doing an admirable job of pretending otherwise. He's spending a lot of time at the office. Apparently he's tied up with an important case."

"Divorce?" Savannah asked unnecessarily. That was his specialty—driving a wedge deeper and deeper between two people who'd once loved each other, increasing misery and heartache. Each divorce he handled lent credence to his pessimistic views. That wasn't going to change, and she was a fool if she believed otherwise.

"You might have read about this case. It's the one with Don Griffin, the man who owns all those great seafood restaurants. It's really sad."

Savannah did remember reading something about it. Apparently Mr. Griffin had an affair with a much younger woman. It was a story as old as time. She hadn't realized Nash was involved, but should have. He was Seattle's top divorce attorney, and naturally a man as wealthy and influential as Don Griffin would hire the very best.

"I know the case," Savannah admitted.

"Nash's been working late every night." Susan paused and waited for Savannah to comment.

"He enjoys his work."

"He used to, but I'm not so sure anymore. Something's really bothering him."

Their conversation was making Savannah uncomfortable. "I'm sorry to hear that."

"It's more than what's going on at the law firm, though. Kurt and I both think it has something to do with you, but when I asked him, Nash nearly bit my head off. He wouldn't even talk about you."

Savannah smiled to herself. "Neither will I. Sometimes it's better to leave well enough alone. We both appreciate your love and support, but what's going on between Nash and me is our own business. Leave it at that, please."

"All right." Susan wasn't happy about it, Savannah could tell, but the last thing she and Nash wanted or needed was Susan and Kurt meddling in their lives. Susan looked regretfully at the time. "I have to get back. The movers are coming this afternoon. I'm not taking much—we simply don't have room for it. And with the stuff Nash is shipping... I don't know why he insisted on sending us the rocking horse. Dad built it for him when he was a little kid and it was understood that Nash would hand it down to his own children. It's been in the basement for years. I don't know why he sent it to me. Kurt and I aren't planning to start a family for a couple of years. Men just don't make sense sometimes."

"You're only discovering that now?" Savannah teased.

Susan laughed. "I should know better after living with my brother all those years."

They hugged and Susan left shortly afterward.

The day was exceptionally slow, and with time on her hands, Savannah sat at her desk and drew a design for a flower arrangement. Intent on her task, she worked for several minutes before she saw that it wasn't a flower arrangement that was taking shape, but a child's rocking horse.

\* \* \*

"What do you mean Janice turned down our settlement proposal?" Don Griffin shouted. He propelled his large frame from the chair across from Nash's desk and started pacing. His movements were abrupt and disjointed. "It was a fair offer, more than fair. You said so yourself."

"That's how these things work, Mr. Griffin. As I explained earlier, if you'll recall, it was unlikely that your wife and her attorney would accept our first offer. It's just the way the game's played. Your wife's attorney wouldn't be earning his fee if he didn't raise some objections."

"How much longer is this going to drag on?" his client demanded. "I want this over with quickly. Give Janice what she wants. If she insists on taking control of the restaurants, fine, she can have them. She can have the house, the cars, our investments, too, for all I care."

"I can't allow you to do that."

"Why not?" He slammed his hand down on the desk.

"You've hired me to represent you in a court of law, to look after your interests. If you make a decision now based on emotion, you'll regret it later. These matters take time."

"I haven't got time," the tall, stocky man said. Don Griffin was in his fifties, and beginning to show his age.

"Is there a reason we need to rush?" Nash hated surprises. If Don's ex-girlfriend was pregnant, he didn't want to find out about it in the courtroom.

"Yes!" the other man shouted. "There's a very good reason. I hate this constant fighting, hate having my reputation raked over the coals in the press. Twenty-seven years of marriage—and after one indiscretion,

Janice makes me look like a serial murderer. The restaurant's receipts actually dropped ten percent after that story was leaked."

Nash didn't know who was responsible for that, but he could make an educated guess. Janice Griffin's attorney, Tony Pound, stirred up controversy whenever possible, especially if it helped his case.

Nash made a note of the lost revenue and decided that when he phoned Tony later this afternoon, he'd tell him Janice's compensation might not be as big as she'd hoped—not if the business failed due to negative publicity.

"If it goes on like this," Don continued, "we may be filing for bankruptcy next."

"I'll make sure Mr. Pound learns this."

"Good, and while you're at it," Don said, waving his finger at Nash, "do what you can about me seeing my daughter. Janice can't keep me away from Amy, and this bull about me being a negative influence on our daughter is exactly that—bull."

"I'll arrange visitation rights for you as soon as I can."

"See if I can have her this weekend. I'm going to the beach and Amy's always loved the beach."

"I'll see what I can do. Is there anything else?"

His client paced, rubbing his hands together. "Have you seen my wife and daughter recently?" he asked.

"No. That would be highly unusual. Is there a reason you're asking?"

"I… I was just wondering how they looked, that's all. If they're well."

It was there in his eyes, Nash saw, the way it always was. The pain, the loneliness, the sense of loss so strong it brought powerful men and women to their knees. Nash thought of these moments when clients realized they were about to lose what they'd once considered their anchor. The chains were broken. With the anchors gone, it became a struggle to keep from drifting. Storms rose up, and that was when Nash learned the truth about his clients. Some weathered these tempests and came out stronger and more confident. Others struggled to stay afloat and eventually drowned.

Sadly, he didn't know which kind of person Don Griffin would prove to be.

The urgency in her father's voice frightened Savannah. His phone call came during her busiest time of day. It took her a moment to decipher what he was saying.

"Mom's in the hospital?" Savannah repeated. Her blood ran cold at the thought.

"Yes." Her father, who was always so calm and collected, was near panic. "She collapsed at home.... I didn't know what to do so I called an aid car and they've brought her to the hospital. The doctors are with her now."

"I'll be there in five minutes," Savannah promised. Fortunately, Nancy had come in to help her, so she didn't have to close the shop.

She'd always hated the smell of hospitals, she thought as she rushed into the emergency entrance of Northend Memorial. It was a smell that resurrected memories she'd pushed to the back of her mind.

Savannah found her father in the emergency waiting room, his shoulders hunched, his eyes empty. "Daddy," she whispered, "what happened?"

"I...don't know. We were working in the yard when your mother called out to me. By the time I turned around she'd passed out. I was afraid for a moment that she was dead. I nearly panicked."

Savannah sat in the seat beside him and reached for his hand.

"I forgot about you not liking hospitals," her father said apologetically.

"It's all right. I wouldn't want to be anyplace else but here with you."

"I'm scared, sweetheart, really scared."

"I know." Savannah was, too. "Have you talked to the doctors yet?"

He shook his head. "How long will it take? She's been in there for over an hour."

"Anytime now, I'm sure." At the moment, Savannah wasn't sure of anything, least of all how her father would cope without her mother if it turned out that something was seriously wrong....

"Mr. Charles." The doctor approached them, his face revealing concern.

Automatically Savannah and her father got to their feet, bracing themselves for whatever he might say.

"Your wife's suffered a stroke."

In the past few weeks, Nash had made a habit of staying late at the office. He no longer liked spending time at the house. It'd been nearly a month since Savannah had been inside his home and he swore that whenever he walked inside, he caught a whiff of her perfume. He knew it was ridiculous, but he'd taken to placing air fresheners at strategic points.

His bed was also a problem. Savannah had left her imprint there, as well. When he woke in the morning, he could sense her presence. He could almost hear her breathing, feel her breath, her mouth scant inches from his own. It bothered him that a woman could have this powerful an effect on him.

She'd meant what she said about ending the relationship. Not that he'd expected to hear from her again. He hoped he would, but that was entirely different from expecting her to call.

More times than he cared to count, he'd resisted the urge to contact her. He'd considered sending flowers with a humorous note, something to break the ice, to salvage his pride and hers, then decided against it.

She'd made herself clear and he had no option but to abide by her wishes. She didn't want to see him again. So she wouldn't. The next move, if there was one, would have to be hers.

As for that absurd proposal of marriage… Seldom had he regretted anything more. It embarrassed him to think about it, so he avoided doing so whenever possible.

Someone knocked softly on his office door. He checked his watch, surprised to discover he wasn't alone at 10:00 p.m.

"Come in."

The door opened and Savannah stood there. She was pale, her features ashen, her eyes red-rimmed as if she'd recently been crying.

"Savannah," he said, hurrying around his desk. "What's wrong?" He didn't reach for her, much as he wanted to, not knowing if she'd welcome his touch.

"I've come," she said in a voice that was devoid of emotion, "to tell you I've reconsidered. I'll accept your offer of a marriage of convenience…. That is, if it's still open."

# Ten

"You're sure about this?" Generally Nash wasn't one to look a gift horse in the mouth, but this time was the exception. Something had happened to cause Savannah to change her mind, something drastic. Nash was convinced of that.

"I wouldn't be here if I wasn't sure." Nervously she reached inside her purse and took out a well-creased slip of paper. "I've made up a list of issues we need to discuss first...if you're willing."

"All right." He gestured toward the guest chair and sat down himself. "But first tell me what happened."

"My mother," she began, and paused as her lower lip began to tremble. She needed a moment to compose herself enough to continue speaking. "Mom's in the hospital.... She had a stroke."

"I'm sorry to hear that."

Savannah nodded. "Her prognosis for a complete recovery is excellent, but it frightened me terribly—Dad, too."

"I understand."

"Mom's stroke helped me realize I might not have my

parents much longer. I refuse to allow them to sacrifice their dreams because of me."

"I see."

She unfolded the piece of paper in her hands. "Are you ready to discuss the details?"

"By all means." He reached for his gold pen and a fresh legal pad.

"There will be no…lovemaking. You mentioned earlier that you preferred this to be a marriage of convenience, and I'm in full agreement."

That had been a hasty suggestion, certainly not one he'd carefully thought out. In light of their strong physical attraction, Nash didn't believe this stipulation would hold up for more than a few days, a week at the most. The minute he kissed her, or took her in his arms, the chemistry they shared would return.

"You're sure about this?" he asked.

"Positive."

Suggesting they wouldn't be able to keep their hands off each other would inevitably trigger a heated argument. Savannah would accuse him of being arrogant. Nash decided to agree with her for the present and let time prove him right.

"Do you agree?" Her eyes challenged him to defy her.

Nash rolled the pen between his palms and relaxed in his leather chair, not wanting to give her any reason to suspect that he had reservations or what they were. "If a marriage in name only is what you want, then naturally I'll agree to those terms."

"Good." She nodded, much too enthusiastically to suit him.

"Unless we mutually agree otherwise at some point," he added.

Savannah's eyes darted back to his. "I wouldn't count on that if I were you. I'm agreeing to this marriage for one reason and one reason only. I want to be sure you understand that."

"In other words, you don't plan to trick me into falling in love with you." He heard the edge in his own voice and regretted it. Savannah had sacrificed her pride the minute she'd walked through his door; goading wasn't necessary.

"This isn't a game to me, Nash," she said, her voice sharp. "I'm serious. If you aren't, maybe we should call it quits right now."

"I was the one who suggested this," he reminded her, not bothering to mention that it had been a spur-of-the-moment idea he'd deplored ever since. He stared at Savannah, noting the changes in her. He'd always viewed her as delicate, feminine. But there was a hardness to her now, a self-protective shell. She didn't trust him not to hurt her. Didn't trust him not to destroy her once-unshakable faith in love and marriage.

"I'll draw up the papers to read that this will be a marriage of convenience unless we mutually agree otherwise. Does that wording satisfy you?"

"All right, as long we understand each other." Her gaze fell to her list. "The second item I have here has to do with our living arrangements. I'll move in with you for a brief period of time."

"How brief?" This didn't sound any more encouraging than her first stipulation.

"Until my mother's well enough to travel south. That's the reason I'm willing to go through with this, after all. But to be as fair as possible, I'll stay with you until a senior partner's named."

"I'd appreciate that." The announcement would come within the month, Nash was certain, although it was taking much longer than he'd assumed. He'd like nothing better than to pull a fast one on Paul. The pompous ass would likely leave the firm. Nash smiled just thinking about it.

"After that there won't be any need for us to continue this farce. I'll move back to my home and we can have the marriage, such as it is, dissolved. Of course, I'll make no claims on you financially and expect the same."

"Of course," Nash agreed. Yet this talk of divorce so soon after marriage grated on him. It wouldn't look good to John Stackhouse and Arnold Serle if he was only married for a few weeks. And a quick divorce—any divorce—was the last thing he wanted. "For propriety's sake, I'd like to suggest we stay married a year," he said.

"A year," she repeated, making it sound as long as a lifetime. She sighed. "Fine. I'll accept that, provided we both adhere to all the other conditions."

"Anything else?" he asked, after making a second notation on the legal pad.

"Yes, as a matter of fact, I have a few more points."

Nash groaned inwardly, but presented a calm exterior.

"While I'm living with you, I insist we sleep in separate bedrooms. The less we have to do with each other, the better. You live your life the same as always and I'll live mine."

Nash wrote this down, as well, but made a point of hesitating, making sure she was aware of his uneasiness about this latest dictate. This would be the ideal setup if he was looking for a roommate, but Nash was seeking a deeper commitment.

"Since you mention propriety…" Savannah began.

"Yes?" he prompted when she didn't immediately continue.

"Although our marriage will be one of convenience, I feel strongly that we should practice a certain code of ethics." The words were rushed, as if she thought he'd disagree. "I expect you to stop dating other women," she said, speaking more slowly now. "If I were to discover that you'd been seeing someone else, I would consider that immediate grounds for divorce."

"The same would hold true for you," he returned calmly. It made him wonder what kind of man she thought he was. "If I found out you were interested in another man, then I'd see no reason to continue our agreement."

"That isn't likely to happen," she blurted out defensively.

"Any more than it is with me."

She clamped her mouth shut and Nash guessed she didn't believe him. Where had she gotten the impression that he was a playboy? It was true that after his divorce he'd occasionally dated, but there'd never been anyone he was serious about—until Savannah. "We'll need to be convincing," she said next, her voice quavering slightly, "otherwise my parents, especially my father, will see through this whole thing in an instant. They aren't going to be easily fooled, and it's important we persuade them we're getting married because we're in love."

"I can be convincing." He'd gained his reputation swaying twelve-member juries; an elderly couple who wanted to believe he was in love with their daughter would be a piece of cake.

"I'll do my best to be the same," Savannah assured him, relaxing slightly. She neatly folded the sheet of paper, running her fingers along the crease. "Was there anything you wanted to add?"

Without time to think over their agreement, Nash was at a disadvantage. "I might later."

"I...was hoping we could come to terms quickly so I can tell my parents right away."

"We'll tell them together," Nash said. "Otherwise they'll find it odd. What do you want to do about the actual wedding ceremony?"

She looked away, then lowered her gaze. "I wasn't sure you'd agree so I hadn't given it much thought. I guess I should have, since I arrange weddings for a living."

"Don't look so chagrined. This isn't a normal, run-of-the-mill marriage."

"Exactly," she was quick to concur. "I'd like a small gathering. My parents and a few good friends—no more than ten or so. What about you?"

"About that number." He'd make sure Serle and Stackhouse received invitations.

"I'll arrange for the ceremony, then, followed by dinner. Is that agreeable?"

He shrugged, not really caring. Small and private appealed to him far more than the lavish gathering Susan had had. At least Savannah wasn't going to subject him to that, although he felt mildly guilty about cheating her out of a fancy wedding.

"How long do you think you'll need to come up with any further stipulations?" she asked.

"Not long," he promised, but he had one thought that he mentioned before he could censure it. "I'd like us to make a habit of eating dinner together."

"Dinner?" Savannah sounded incredulous.

His sole condition did seem surprising. But he felt that if they were going to the trouble of getting married, they shouldn't remain strangers. "We need to spend some time together, don't you think?"

"I don't see why that's necessary."

"It will be if we're going to create the facade of being married. We'll need to know what's going on in each other's lives."

Her nod was reluctant. "I see your point."

"We can share the housework, so you don't need to worry about me sticking you with the cooking and the cleanup afterward. I want to be fair about this."

"That seems equitable."

"I don't intend to take advantage of you, Savannah." It was important she believe that, although it was obvious she didn't. Even married to Savannah, he didn't hold out much hope of becoming a senior partner. Not when Paul Jefferson was ingratiating himself with anyone and everyone who could advance his career. But if there was the slightest possibility that he might beat out Paul, Nash was willing to risk it. His dislike for the man increased daily, especially since Paul resented that Nash had been given the Don Griffin case and had made his feelings obvious.

"What day should I arrange the wedding for?" Savannah asked, flipping through the pages of a small pocket calendar.

"In a week, if at all possible." He could tell by the way her eyes widened that she expected more time. "Is that too soon?"

"Not really.... A week shouldn't be a problem, although people are going to ask questions."

"So? Does that bother you?"

"Not exactly."

"Good." Nash had little success in hiding a smile.

"In that case, I think you should write up the agreement right away," she said. "You can add whatever provisions you want and if I disagree, I'll cross them out."

"Okay. When would you like to tell your parents?"

"As soon as possible. Tomorrow evening?"

Nash stood and replaced his pen in the marble holder. "Is your mother still in the hospital?"

Savannah nodded. "Dad spends almost every minute with her. The nurses told me they tried to send him home the first night, but he refused and ended up sleeping on a cot beside her."

"He's taken this hard, hasn't he?"

Savannah nodded. "He's worried sick.... That's the main reason I decided to accept your proposal. Mom loves the sunshine and I can't think of any place she'd enjoy recuperating more than in Arizona with her friends."

"In that case, we'll do everything we can to be sure that happens."

"Oh, Savannah." Her mother's eyes glistened with the sheen of tears as she sat up in her hospital bed early the next evening. "You're going to be married."

Nash slid his arm around Savannah's waist with familiar ease and smiled down on her. "I know my timing couldn't be worse," he murmured, "but I hope you'll forgive me."

"There's nothing to forgive. We're thrilled, aren't we, Marcus?" Her mother smiled blissfully. Nash was eating up the attention, nuzzling Savannah's neck, planting kisses on her cheek when he was sure her parents would notice. These open displays of affection were unlike him and were fast beginning to irritate Savannah.

"This does seem rather sudden, though, doesn't it?" her father asked. He might have embarrassed her by acting as if Nash was practically her fiancé that first evening, but he was astute about people, and Savannah knew that convincing him would be much more difficult than persuading her mother. Nash must have realized it, too, because he was playing the role as if he expected to earn an award for his performance as the besotted lover.

"Savannah and I've been dating off and on all summer." He brought her close to his side and dropped a quick kiss on the side of her neck. The moment they were alone, she'd tell him to keep his kisses to himself. Every time he touched his lips to her skin, a shiver of awareness raced up her spine. Nash knew it; otherwise he wouldn't take every opportunity to make her so uncomfortable.

"Are you in love?" her father asked her directly.

"Marcus, what a thing to ask," her mother said with a flustered laugh. "Savannah and Nash have come to us wanting to share their wonderful news. This isn't any time to ask a lot of silly questions."

"Would I marry Nash if I didn't love him?" Savannah asked, hoping that would be enough to reassure her father.

"We'd like to have the wedding as soon as possible," Nash added, looking down at her adoringly.

"There's a rush?" her father asked.

His attitude surprised Savannah. She was prepared for a bit of skepticism, but not this interrogation. Once he was convinced Savannah loved Nash—and vice versa—she didn't figure there would be any problems.

"I want Savannah with me," Nash answered. "It took me a long time to decide to marry again and now that I have, each day without her feels like an eternity." He reached for her hand and raised it to his lips, then placed a series of soft kisses on her knuckles. He was overdoing it, making fools of them both, and Savannah fumed.

"You feel the same way about Nash?"

"Yes, Daddy," she returned smoothly.

"I've waited all my life for a woman like Savannah."

Savannah couldn't help it; she stepped on Nash's foot and he yelped, then glared at her accusingly.

"I'm sorry, darling, did I hurt you?" she asked sweetly.

"No, I'm fine." His eyes questioned her, but she ignored the silent entreaty.

Her father stood at the head of the bed, which was angled up so that her mother was in a sitting position. They were holding hands.

"Do you object to Savannah marrying Nash?" her father questioned.

Her mother's sigh was filled with relief and joy. "Savannah's far too old to require our approval, and you know it. She can do as she pleases. I don't understand why you're behaving as if this is some...some tragedy when our little girl is so happy. Isn't this what we've prayed for all these years?"

"I know it's come at you out of the blue, Daddy," Savannah whispered, the words sticking in her throat, "but you know me well enough to know I'd never marry a man I didn't love with all my heart."

"The sooner Savannah's in my life, the sooner I can be complete," Nash added with a dramatic sigh.

Although he was clearly making an effort to sound sincere, it was all Savannah could do not to elbow him in the ribs. Anyone who knew Nash would recognize that he was lying, and doing a poor job of it. Presumably he was more effective in front of a jury.

"I should be out of the hospital by Friday," her mother said excitedly. "That'll give me a couple of days to rest at home before the wedding."

"If you need a few extra days to rest, we don't mind waiting. It's important that you be there, isn't that right, darling?"

Savannah felt him nudging her and quickly nodded. "Of course. Having you both there is more important than anything."

Her father shook his head. "I don't understand why you insist on having the wedding so soon. You've only known each other for a few months."

"We know each other better than you think," Nash said. The insinuation that they were lovers was clear. Savannah bit her tongue to keep from claiming otherwise. If Nash was trying to embarrass her, he'd surpassed his wildest expectations. Her face burned, and she couldn't meet her parents' eyes.

"I don't think we need to question Savannah and Nash any longer," her mother said. "They know their own minds. You have my blessing."

"Daddy?" Savannah whispered, holding her breath.

He didn't say anything, then nodded.

"There are a thousand things to do before Wednesday," Savannah said abruptly, bending over to kiss her mother's pale cheek. "If you don't mind, Nash and I'll leave now."

"Of course," her father said.

"Thank you so much for the wonderful news, sweetheart." Her mother was tiring; their departure came at the opportune moment.

Savannah couldn't wait until they were well outside the hospital room before turning on Nash. "How dare you," she flared, hands clenched at her sides. The man had no sense of decency. She'd told him how important it was to be convincing, but Nash cheerfully went about making fools of them both. His behavior angered her so much she could hardly speak.

"What did I do?" he demanded, wearing a confused, injured look that was meant to evoke sympathy. It wouldn't work—not this time.

"You implied...you—you let my parents believe we were lovers," she sputtered. And that was just for starters.

"So?" Nash asked. "Good grief, Savannah, you're thirty years old. They know you're not a virgin."

She punched the elevator button viciously. The rush of tears was a mingling of outrage and indignation, and she blinked furiously in an effort to keep them from spilling.

Nash exhaled softly and rubbed the back of his neck. "You are a virgin, aren't you?"

"Do you mind if we don't discuss such private matters in a public place?" she ground out. The elevator arrived just then, and Savannah eagerly stepped on.

There were a couple of other people who stared at her. Her limp sometimes made her the center of attention, but right now she suspected it was her tears that prompted their curiosity.

She managed to keep quiet until they reached the parking lot. "As for that stupid declaration of being so crazy about me you couldn't wait another minute to make me yours—I wanted to throw up."

"Why? You should be praising me instead of getting all bent out of shape."

"Praising you? For what?"

"Convincing your father we're in love."

"Oh, please," Savannah whispered, gazing upward.

The sun had begun to set, spreading shades of gold and pink across the sky. It was all so beautiful, when she felt so ugly. Nash was saying the things every woman longs to hear—beautiful words. Only, his were empty. Perhaps that was what troubled her so much, the fact that he didn't mean what he was saying when she wanted it to be true.

"You're not making any sense." His patience was clearly gone as he unlocked the passenger door, then slammed it shut. "Let's have this out right here and now."

"Fine!" she shouted.

"I was doing everything I could think of to convince your parents we're madly in love. Correct me if I'm wrong, but wasn't that the objective?"

"You didn't need to lay it on so thick, did you?"

"What do you mean?"

"Did you have to hold on to me like you couldn't bear to be separated from me for a single second? The kissing has got to stop. I won't have you fawning all over me like…like a lovesick calf."

"Fine. I won't lay another hand on you as long as we're together. Not unless you ask."

"You make that sound like a distinct possibility and trust me, it's not."

He laughed shrewdly, but didn't reply. The look he gave her just then spoke volumes. Savannah found herself getting even angrier.

"You could practice being a bit more subtle, couldn't you?" she went on. "If anyone should know the power of subtlety, it's you. I thought you were this top-notch attorney. Don't you know anything about human nature?"

"I know a little." He went strangely quiet for a moment. "You don't think we fooled your father?"

"No, Nash, I don't," she said, calmer now. "The only

people we seem capable of fooling are ourselves. I'm afraid this simply isn't going to work."

"You want out already?" he demanded, sounding shocked and surprised. "Our engagement isn't even three hours old and already you're breaking it."

"We don't have any choice," she insisted. "Anyone with sense is going to see through this charade in a heartbeat. If we can't handle announcing the news to my parents, how do you expect to get through the wedding ceremony?"

"We'll manage."

"How can you be so sure of that?"

"We did before, didn't we?" he asked softly. "At Susan's wedding."

He would bring that up. The man didn't fight fair. Her behavior at the wedding ceremony had been a slip of judgment and now he was waving it in front of her like a red flag, challenging her to a repeat performance. "But that wasn't real…we weren't the center of attention."

"Like I said, we'll manage very well—just wait and see."

Nash walked around to the front of his car and leaned against the hood, crossing his arms. "Your parents are okay with it, so I suggest we continue as planned. Are you game?"

Savannah nodded, feeling she had no other choice. She suspected she could convince her father that she was in love with Nash; she wasn't sure he'd believe Nash was in love with her.

Nash was busy at his desk, reviewing the latest settlement offer from Don Griffin, when his secretary buzzed him and announced that a Mr. Marcus Charles was there to see him without an appointment.

"Send him in," Nash instructed. He closed the file, set it aside and stood.

Savannah's dad was a gentle, reflective man who reminded him a little of his own father. "Come in, please," Nash said pleasantly. "This is a surprise."

"I should have phoned."

"We all behave impulsively at one time or another," Nash said, hoping Savannah's father would catch his meaning. He'd tried hard to make it sound as if their wedding plans were impulsive, which was more or less the truth. He'd tried to convince her family that he was crazy in love with her and, according to Savannah, he'd overplayed his hand. Perhaps she was right.

"Do you mind if I sit down?"

"Of course not," Nash said immediately, dismayed by his own lack of manners. Apparently he was more shaken by this unforeseen visit than he'd realized. "Is there anything I can get you? Coffee, tea, a cold drink?"

"No, thanks." He claimed the chair across from Nash's and crossed his legs. "It looks like Joyce will be released from the hospital a day early."

Nash was relieved. "That's wonderful news."

"The news from you and Savannah rivaled that. The doctor seems to think it's what helped Joyce recover so quickly."

"I'm pleased to hear that."

"It's going to take several months before she's fully recovered, but that's to be expected."

Nash nodded, not thinking any comment was necessary. He was rarely nervous, but he felt that way now.

Marcus was silent for a moment. "So you want to marry Savannah."

"Yes, sir." This much was true and his sincerity must

have rung clear in his response because it seemed to him that Savannah's father relaxed.

"My daughter's accident damaged her confidence, her self-image, at least in emotional situations." He paused. "Do you know what I mean?"

"Yes," he said honestly.

Marcus stood and walked over to the window. "I'm not going to ask if you love Savannah," he said abruptly. "For a number of reasons that doesn't matter to me as much as it did earlier. If you don't love her, you will soon enough.

"You came to me the other night seeking my blessing and I'm giving it to you." He turned and held out his hand.

The two men exchanged handshakes. When they'd finished, Marcus Charles reached inside his suit jacket, withdrew a business-size envelope and set it on Nash's desk.

"What's that?"

Marcus smiled. "Savannah's mother and I thought long and hard about what we should give you as a wedding present, then decided the best gift would be time alone. Inside is a map to a remote cabin in the San Juan Islands that we've rented for you. We're giving you one week of uninterrupted peace."

# *Eleven*

"What did you expect me to do?" Nash demanded as they drove off the Washington State ferry. "Refuse your parents' wedding gift?" This marriage was definitely getting off to a rocky start. They'd been husband and wife less than twelve hours and already they were squabbling.

"A remote cabin...alone together," she groaned. "I've never heard of anything more ridiculous."

"Most newlyweds would be thrilled with the idea," he said.

"We're not most newlyweds."

"I don't need you to remind me of that," Nash snapped. "You try to do someone a favor..."

"Are you insinuating that marrying me was a favor?" Savannah was huddled close to the door. "That you were doing it out of kindness?"

Nash prayed for patience. So this was what their marriage was going to be like—this constant barrage of insults, nit-picking, faultfinding.

"No, Savannah, I don't consider marrying you a favor and I didn't do it out of kindness. You're my wife and—"

"In name only," she said in icy tones.

"Does that mean we're enemies now?"

"Of course not."

"Then why have we been at each other's throats from the moment we left the wedding dinner? I'm sorry your family insisted on giving us a honeymoon. I'm well aware that you'd rather spend time with anyone but me. I was hoping we'd make the best of this."

She didn't respond, for which he was grateful. The silence was a welcome contrast to the constant bickering.

"It was a beautiful wedding," she said softly, unexpectedly.

"Yes, it was." Savannah was beautiful in her ivory silk suit with a short chiffon veil decorated with pearls. Nash had barely been able to take his eyes off her. It was a struggle to remember this wasn't a real, till-death-do-us-part marriage.

"I've been acting defensive," she added apologetically. "I'm sorry, Nash, for everything. It isn't your fault we're stuck together like this."

"Well, it was my idea, after all. And our marriage could be a good thing in lots of ways."

"You're right," she said, but she didn't sound convinced. "We might find we enjoy each other's company."

Nash was offended by the comment. He'd enjoyed being with Savannah from the beginning, enjoyed goading her, challenging her views on marriage. He'd found himself seeking her out, looking for excuses to be with her, until she'd insisted she didn't want to see him again. He'd abided by her wishes, but he'd missed her, far more than he cared to admit.

"I saw Mr. Serle and Mr. Stackhouse talking to you after the ceremony."

Nash grinned, feeling a sense of satisfaction. Both of the senior partners had been delighted to see Nash marry Savannah. She'd managed to completely captivate those two. Arnold Serle had been acutely disappointed that they'd decided against a wedding dance. He'd been counting on another spin around the floor with Savannah.

"Did they say anything about the senior partnership?" Savannah asked.

He was annoyed that she already seemed eager to get out of their arrangement. "No, but then, a wedding isn't exactly the place to be discussing business." He didn't mention that it was at his sister's reception that John Stackhouse had originally introduced the subject.

"I see." She sounded disappointed, and Nash's hands tightened on the steering wheel. Luckily the drive was a beautiful one through lush green Lopez Island. Although Nash had lived in Washington all his life, he'd never ventured into the San Juan Islands. When they drove off the ferry he was surprised by the quiet coves and breathtaking coastline. In an effort to fill their time, he'd arranged for him and Savannah to take a cruise and explore the northernmost boundary islands of Susia and Patos, which were the closest to the Canadian border. He'd wanted their honeymoon to be a memorable experience; he'd planned a shopping excursion to Friday Harbor for another day. He'd read about the quaint shops, excellent restaurants and a whale museum. Women liked those sorts of things. It seemed now that his efforts were for naught. Savannah had no intention of enjoying these days together.

"Have your parents said anything about traveling south?"

"Not yet," she said, her voice disheartened.

"They might not, you know." In other words, she could find herself living with him for the next few years, like it or not. The thought didn't appeal to him any more than it did her, especially if she continued with this attitude.

"How much farther is it to the cabin?" she asked stiffly. Nash wasn't sure. He didn't have GPS but he had a detailed map and instructions. However, since he'd never been on Lopez Island, he wasn't any expert. "Soon, I suspect."

"Good."

"You're tired?"

"A little."

It'd been a full day. First the wedding, then the dinner followed by the drive to the ferry and the ride across Puget Sound. Darkness would fall within the hour and Nash had hoped they'd be at the cabin before then.

He reached the turnoff in the road and took a winding, narrow highway for several miles. Savannah was suspiciously silent, clutching her wedding bouquet. He was surprised she'd chosen to bring it with her.

He found the dirt road that led to the cabin and slowly drove down it, grateful he'd rented a four-wheel-drive vehicle. The route was filled with ruts, which didn't lend him much confidence about this remote cabin. If this was any indication of what the house would be like, they'd be lucky to have electricity and running water.

He was wrong and knew it the minute he drove into the clearing. This was no cabin, but a luxurious house, built with a Victorian flair, even to the turret and wrap-around porch.

"Oh, my…it's lovely," Savannah whispered.

The house was a sight to behold all on its own, but the view of the water was majestic.

"I'll get the luggage," Nash said, hopping out of the Jeep. He thought better of it, hurried around to Savannah's side and helped her down.

With his hands around her waist, he lifted her onto the ground. He longed to hold her against him, to swing her into his arms and carry her over the threshold like any new husband, but he didn't dare. Savannah would assume he was making a mockery of this traditional wedding custom. That was how she seemed to be dealing with everything lately, distrusting him and his motives. She made marriage feel like an insult. If this attitude lasted much longer, they'd have the shortest marriage on record.

"I'll get the luggage," he said again, unnecessarily. At least if his hands were full, he wouldn't be tempted to reach for Savannah.

"I'll open the door," she said, and for the first time she sounded enthusiastic. She hurried ahead of him and he noticed that she favored her injured leg more than usual. Sitting for any length of time must make movement more difficult. She rarely spoke about her leg—about the accident, her long rehabilitation or the pain she still suffered. He wished he knew how to broach the subject, but every attempt had been met with bristly pride, as if she believed that sharing this imperfect part of herself would make her too vulnerable.

She had the door open when he joined her. Stepping inside the house was like stepping into the nineteenth century. The warmth and beauty of this house seemed to greet them with welcoming arms.

The living room was decorated with a mix of antiques, and huge windows created a room that glowed in the setting sun.

"Oh, Nash," Savannah said, "I don't think I've ever seen anything more beautiful."

"Me, neither."

"Dad must have seen an ad for this house, maybe on a vacation website. He knows how much I love anything Victorian, especially houses."

Nash stashed that away in his storehouse of information about Savannah. When it was time to celebrate her birthday or Christmas, he'd know what to buy her.

"I'll put these in the bedrooms," he said. He didn't like the idea of them sleeping separately, but he didn't have any choice. He'd agreed to do so until she changed her mind, and from the look of things that could be a decade from now—if ever.

The master bedroom was equally attractive, with a huge four-poster mahogany bed. French lace curtains hung from the windows and the walls were papered in pale yellow. He set down Savannah's suitcase and headed for the second bedroom, which would be his. It was originally intended as a children's room, he realized. Instead of spending his wedding night with the woman he'd just married, he was destined to stare at row after row of tin soldiers. So much for romance!

Savannah woke early the next morning. The sunlight spilling in from the window was filtered through the lace curtains until a spidery pattern reflected against the floor. She yawned and sat up in bed. Surprisingly, she'd fallen asleep right away without the sadness or tears she'd expected.

"You're a married woman," she said aloud, thinking

she might believe it if she heard herself say it. Her wedding and all that led up to it was still unreal to her. Afterward she'd been awful to Nash.

It took her a long time to understand why she'd behaved in such an uncharacteristic manner. Just before she went to bed, she'd realized what was going on. She was lashing out at him, blaming him for making a farce of what she considered holy. Only, he wasn't to blame; they were in this together. Marriage was advantageous to them both.

She heard him rummaging around in the kitchen. The aroma of coffee urged her out of bed. She threw on her robe and shoved her feet into slippers.

"'Morning," she said when she joined him. He'd obviously been up for hours. His jacket hung on a peg by the back door with a pair of rubber boots on the mat. His hair was wet, and he held a mug of steaming coffee and leaned against the kitchen counter.

"'Morning," he said, grinning broadly.

"You've been exploring." It hurt a little that he'd gone outside without her, but she couldn't really fault him. She hadn't been decent company in the past week or so. And walking along the beach with her wouldn't be much fun, since her gait was slow and awkward.

"I took a walk along the beach. I found you something." He reached behind him and presented her with a perfectly formed sand dollar.

Savannah's hand closed around her prize.

"I'm not sure, but I think I saw a pod of whales. It's a little difficult to tell from this distance."

Savannah made busywork about the kitchen, pouring herself a cup of coffee and checking the refrigerator for milk, all the while struggling to hold back her disappointment. She would've loved to see a pod of whales, even from a distance.

"What would you like for breakfast?" she asked, hoping to get their day off to a better start.

"Bacon, eggs, toast and a kiss."

Savannah froze.

"You heard me right. Come on, Savannah, loosen up. We're supposed to be madly in love, remember? This isn't going to work if you act the part of the outraged virgin."

What he said was true, but that didn't make it any easier. She turned away from him and fought down a confused mixture of anger and pain. She wanted to blame him, and knew she couldn't. She longed to stamp her foot, as she had when she was a little girl, and cry out, "Stop! No more." No more discord. No more silliness. But it wouldn't do any good. She was married but resigned to a life of loneliness. These were supposed to be the happiest days of her life and here she was struggling not to weep.

Nash had moved behind her and placed his hands on her shoulders. "Do you find me so repugnant?" he whispered close to her ear.

His warm breath was moist. She shut her eyes and shook her head.

"Then why won't you let me kiss you?"

She shrugged, but was profoundly aware of the answer. If Nash kissed her, she'd remember how much she enjoyed his touch. It'd been like that from the beginning. He knew it. She knew it. Now he intended to use that against her.

He brought his mouth down to her neck and shivers of awareness moved up and down her spine. Needing something to hold on to, Savannah reached for the kitchen counter.

"One kiss," he coaxed. "Just one."

"Y-you promise?"

"Of course. Anything you say."

She made a small, involuntary movement to turn around. His hands on her shoulders aided the process. She quivered when his mouth met hers and a familiar heat began to warm her. As always, their need for each other was so hot and intense, it frightened her.

Slowly, he lifted his mouth from hers. "Do you want me to stop?" he asked in a husky whisper.

Savannah made an unintelligible sound.

"That's what I thought," he said, claiming her mouth again.

She locked her arms around his neck. Soon the kissing wasn't enough....

Savannah felt as though her body was on fire. She'd been empty and lonely for so long. No man had ever kissed her like this. No man had ever wanted her so badly.

"You don't want me to stop, do you?" he begged. "Don't tell me you want me to stop."

Incapable of a decision, she made a second unintelligible sound.

"If we continue like this, we're going to end up making love on the kitchen floor," Nash whispered.

"I don't know what I want," she whimpered.

"Yes, you do. Savannah. If it gets much hotter, we're both going to explode. Let me make love to you."

She started to protest, but he stopped her, dragging his mouth back to hers. Only she could satisfy him, his kisses seemed to be saying. Savannah didn't know if he was telling her this or if she was hearing it in her mind. It didn't matter; she got the message.

"No," she said with a whimper. She couldn't give him her body. If they made love, he'd own her completely, and she couldn't allow that to happen. Someday he was going to walk away from her. Someday he was going to announce that it was over and she was supposed to go on her merry way without him. She was supposed to pretend it didn't matter.

"You don't mean that," Nash pleaded. "You can't tell me you don't want me." The words were issued in a heated whisper. "Don't do this, Savannah."

She buried her face in his shoulder. "Please...don't. You promised. You said you'd stop...whenever I asked."

He released her then, slowly, her body dragging against his as her feet slid back to the floor. She stepped away from him, anxious to break the contact, desperately needing room to breathe. She pressed her hand to the neckline of her gown and drew in several deep breaths.

Nash's eyes were squeezed shut as he struggled to bring himself under control. When he opened them, Savannah swore they were filled with fire.

Without a word to her, he reached for his jacket, opened the door and walked out.

She was trembling so hard, she had to pull out a chair and sit down. She didn't know how long she was there before she felt strong enough to stand, walk back into the bedroom and dress.

It was a mistake to let him kiss her; she'd known it even as she agreed, known it would be like this between them. Gnawing on her lower lip, she argued with herself. She and Nash had created an impossible situation, drawn up a list of rules and regulations and then insisted on testing each one to the limits of their endurance.

She'd just placed their coffee cups in the dishwasher when the back door opened and Nash appeared. She studied him. He looked calm and outwardly serene, but she wasn't fooled. She could see the angry glint in his eyes.

"If you're looking for an apology, you can forget it," he said.

"I'm...not."

"Good."

Now didn't seem the time to mention that he hadn't helped matters any by suggesting the kiss. Both of them knew what would happen when they started flirting with the physical aspect of their relationship.

Nash poured himself a cup of coffee. "Let's sit down and talk this over."

"I...don't know what there is to say," she said, preferring to avoid the issue completely. "It was a very human thing to happen. You're an attractive, healthy man with...needs."

"And you're a red-blooded woman. You have *needs,* too. But admitting that takes real honesty, doesn't it?"

Savannah found the remark insulting, but then, Nash didn't seem inclined to be generous with her. Since she didn't have an argument to give him, she let it pass.

"I did some thinking while I walked off my frustration."

"Oh?" She was curious about what he'd decided, but didn't want to press him.

"The way I see it, I'm setting myself up for constant frustration if we have any more bouts like this last one. If you want to come out of this marriage as pristine as

the freshly fallen snow, then far be it from me to hit my
head against a brick wall."

"I'm not sure I understand."

"You don't need to. You have your wish, Savannah.
I won't touch you again, not until you ask me, and the
way I feel right now, you're going to have to do a whole
lot more than ask. You're going to have to beg."

Nash hadn't known it was possible for two human
beings to live the way he and Savannah had spent the
past two weeks. The so-called honeymoon had been bad
enough, but back in civilization, living in his house, the
situation had gone from unbearable to even worse. The
electricity between them could light up a small city. Yet
they continued to ignore their mutual attraction.

They lived as brother and sister. They slept in separate rooms, inquired about each other's day, sat at the
dinner table every night and made polite conversation.

In two weeks Nash hadn't so much as held her hand.
He dared not for fear he'd get burned. Not by her rejection, but by their need for each other.

Part of the problem was the fact that Savannah was a
virgin. She didn't know what she was missing, but she
had a fairly good idea, and that added a certain amount
of intrigue. He sincerely hoped she was miserable, at
least as miserable as he was.

"Mr. Griffin is here to see you," his assistant announced.

Nash stood to greet his client. Don Griffin had lost
weight in the past month. Nash had, too, come to think
of it. He didn't have much of an appetite and was working out at the gym most nights after dinner.

"Did you hear from Janice's attorney?" Don demanded.

"Not yet."

"Does he normally take this long to return phone calls?" Agitated, Don started to pace.

"He does when he wants us to sweat," he said.

"Raise Janice's monthly allotment by five hundred dollars."

Nash sighed inwardly. This was a difficult case and not for the usual reasons. "Sit down, Mr. Griffin," he said. "Please."

Don complied and sat down. He bounced his fingers against each other and studied Nash as he leaned back in his chair.

"Janice hasn't requested any extra money," Nash said.

"She might need it. Amy, too. There are a hundred unexpected expenses that crop up. I don't want her having to scrimp. It's important to me that my wife and daughter live comfortably."

"You've been more than generous."

"Just do as I say. I'm not paying you to argue with me."

"No, you're paying me for advice and I'm about to give you some, so kindly listen. It doesn't come cheap."

Don snorted loudly. "No kidding. I just got your last bill."

Nash smiled. His clients were often shocked when they learned how expensive divorce could be. Not only financially, but emotionally. Nash had seen it happen more times than he cared to think about. Once his clients realized how costly a divorce could be, they were already embroiled in bitterness and it was impossible to undo the damage.

"Do you know what you're doing, giving Janice extra money?" he asked.

"Sure I do. I'm attempting to take care of my wife and daughter."

"You're already doing that. Offering them more money is more about easing your conscience. You want to absolve your guilt because you had an affair."

"It wasn't an affair," Don shouted. "It was a one-night thing, a momentary lapse that I've regretted every moment since. Janice would never have found out about it if it hadn't been for—never mind, that doesn't matter now. She found out about it and immediately called an attorney."

"My point is, she learned about your indiscretion and now you want to buy peace of mind. Unfortunately, it doesn't work like that."

"All I'm trying to do is get this divorce over with."

Tony Pound, Janice's attorney, wasn't a fool. He knew exactly what he was doing, dragging the proceedings out as long as possible to prolong the guilt and the agony. To Nash's way of thinking, his client had been punished enough.

"This is one mistake you aren't going to be paying monetarily for the rest of your life," Nash assured him. "And I plan to make sure of it. That's why John Stackhouse asked me to take your case. You've lost your wife, your home, your daughter. You've paid enough. Now go back to your apartment and relax. I'll contact you when I hear from Mr. Pound."

Don Griffin nodded reluctantly. "I don't know how much more of this I can take."

"It shouldn't be much longer," Nash assured him.

He rose slowly from the chair. "You'll be in touch soon?"

Nash said he would. Don left the office and Nash sat down to review his file for the hundredth time. He was missing something, he realized. That cold-blooded instinct for the kill.

He wasn't enjoying this, wasn't even close to experiencing the satisfaction he usually gained from bringing his opponents to their knees. Somewhere along the line he'd changed. He'd sensed things were different shortly after he'd met Savannah. Now there was no hiding his feelings. He'd lost it. Only, he wasn't sure what he'd found in exchange.

"Have you got a moment?" John Stackhouse stuck his head in Nash's office.

"Sure. What can I do for you?"

The senior partner was smiling from ear to ear. "Would you mind coming down to the meeting room?"

Nash's pulse accelerated wildly. The executive committee had been meeting with the other senior partners that afternoon to make their recommendation for new senior partner.

"I got the position?" Nash asked hesitantly.

"I think that would be a fair assessment," the older man said, slapping Nash on the shoulder. "It wasn't a hard decision, Nash. You're a fine attorney and an asset to this firm."

A half hour later, Nash rushed out of the office and drove directly to Savannah's shop. As luck would have it, she was busy with a customer. He tried to be patient, tried to pretend he was some stranger who'd casually strolled in.

Savannah looked at him with wide, questioning eyes and he delighted in unnerving her by blowing her a kiss.

"When did you say the wedding was?" she asked the smartly dressed businesswoman who was leafing through a book of invitations.

"In December."

"You have plenty of time, but it's a good idea to set your budget now. I'll be happy to assist you in any way I can."

"I appreciate that," Nash heard the woman say.

He wandered over to her desk and sorted through her mail. Without being obvious, Savannah walked over to where he was sitting, took the envelopes from him and gently slapped his hands. "Behave yourself," she said under her breath.

"I have a few extra expenses coming up," he said in a low whisper. "I hope you're doing well. I might need a loan."

"What expenses?" she asked in the same low voice.

"New business cards, stationery and the like."

"New stationery?" she repeated more loudly.

The customer turned around. "I'm sorry," Savannah said apologetically. "I was commenting on something my husband said."

The woman smiled graciously. "I thought you two must be married. I saw the way you looked at each other when he walked in the door."

Neither Nash nor Savannah responded.

Savannah started to walk away when Nash caught her hand. It was the first time he'd purposely touched her since the morning after their wedding. Apparently it caught her by surprise, because she turned abruptly, her gaze seeking out his.

"I'm the new senior partner."

Savannah's eyes lit up with undisguised delight.

"Nash, oh, Nash." She covered her mouth with both hands and blinked back tears. "Congratulations."

"If you don't mind, I'll come back another time with my fiancé," Savannah's customer said.

"I'm sorry," Savannah said, limping toward the woman.

"Don't apologize. Celebrate with your husband. You both deserve it." When she reached the front door, she turned the sign to "Closed," winked at Nash and walked out of the store.

"When did you find out?" Savannah asked, rubbing her index finger beneath her eye.

"About half an hour ago. I thought we'd go out to dinner and celebrate."

"I...don't know what to say. I'm so happy for you."

"I'm happy, too." It was difficult not to take her in his arms. He stood and walked away from her rather than break his self-imposed restriction.

"Where are you going?" Savannah asked, sounding perplexed.

"I need to keep my distance from you."

"Why?"

"Because I want to hold you so much, my arms ache."

Savannah broke into a smile. "I was just thinking the same thing," she said, opening her arms to him.

# *Twelve*

Nash checked his watch for the time, set aside the paper and hurried into the kitchen. It was his night to cook and he'd experimented with a new recipe. If anyone had told him he'd be hanging around a kitchen, fretting over elaborate recipes, he would've stoutly denied such a thing could even happen.

Marriage had done this to him, and to his surprise Nash wasn't complaining. He enjoyed their arrangement, especially now that they were on much friendlier terms. The tension had lessened considerably following the evening they'd celebrated his appointment as senior partner. It felt as if the barriers were gradually being lowered.

He was bent over the oven door when he heard Savannah come into the house. She'd called him at the office to let him know she'd be late, which had become almost a nightly occurrence.

"I'm home," she said, entering the kitchen. She looked pale and worn-out. He'd never have guessed September would be such a busy month for weddings. Savannah had overbooked herself and spread her time and energy much too thin. He'd resisted the urge to lecture her, although it'd been difficult.

"Your timing couldn't be better," he said, taking the sausage, cabbage and cheese casserole out of the oven and setting it on the counter. The scent of spicy meat filled the kitchen.

"That smells delicious," Savannah said, and Nash beamed proudly. He'd discovered, somewhat to his surprise, that he enjoyed cooking. Over the years he'd learned a culinary trick or two, creating a small repertoire of dinners. Nothing, however, that required an actual recipe. Now he found himself reading cookbooks on a regular basis.

"I've got the table set if you're ready to eat," he told her.

"You must've known I was starving."

"Did you skip lunch again today?" he asked, using oven mitts to carry the glass casserole dish to the table. Once again he had to stop himself from chastising her. Their peace was too fragile to test. "Sit down and I'll bring you a plate."

It looked as if Savannah was in danger of falling asleep as he joined her at the table.

"Nash," she said after the first taste, "this is wonderful!"

"I'm glad you approve."

"Keep this up and you can do all the cooking," she teased, smiling over at him.

Nash set his fork aside and folded his hands. He couldn't keep silent any longer. "You're working too hard."

She lowered her gaze and nodded. "I know. I scheduled the majority of these weddings soon after our own. I... I thought it would be a good idea if I spent as much time at the shop as possible."

In other words, less time with him. "I hope you've changed your mind."

"I have." Her hand closed around her water glass. "I assumed our...arrangement would be awkward, but it hasn't been, not since the beginning."

"I've enjoyed spending time with you." It frustrated him, living as they did, like polite strangers, but that, too, had changed in the past couple of weeks. Their relationship had become that of good friends. Their progress was slow but steady, which gave Nash hope that eventually Savannah would be comfortable enough with him to make love. He realized his attitude was shortsighted. Breaching that barrier had been a challenge from the first, but he hadn't thought beyond it. He didn't want to think about it now.

When they finished eating, Savannah carried their plates to the sink. They had an agreement about cleanup, one of many. When one of them did the cooking, the other washed the dishes.

"Sit down," Nash ordered, "before you collapse."

"This will only take a couple of minutes," she insisted, opening the dishwasher.

Nash took her by the hands and led her into the living room. Pushing her down on the sofa, he said, "I want you to relax."

"If I do that, I'll fall asleep, and I need to go back to the shop later to finish up a few things."

"Don't even think about it, Savannah." Those were fighting words, but he counted on her being too tired to argue with him. "You're exhausted. I'm your husband, and I may not be a very good one, but I refuse to allow you to work yourself this hard."

She closed her eyes and leaned her head against the

Dear Debbie Macomber Fan,

**IT'S A FACT:** if you answer 4 quick questions, we'll send you 4 FREE REWARDS!

I'm not kidding you. As a leading publisher of women's fiction, we value your opinions... and your time. That's why we are prepared to **reward** you handsomely for completing our mini-survey. In fact, we have 4 Free Rewards for you, including 2 free books and 2 free gifts.

As you may have guessed, that's why our mini-survey is called **"4 for 4".** Answer 4 questions and get 4 Free Rewards. It's that simple!

Thank you for participating in our survey,

*Pam Powers*

# To get your 4 FREE REWARDS:
## Complete the survey below and return the insert today to receive 2 FREE BOOKS and 2 FREE GIFTS guaranteed!

## "4 for 4" MINI-SURVEY

**1** Is reading one of your favorite hobbies?
☐ YES ☐ NO

**2** Do you prefer to read instead of watch TV?
☐ YES ☐ NO

**3** Do you read newspapers and magazines?
☐ YES ☐ NO

**4** Do you enjoy trying new book series with FREE BOOKS?
☐ YES ☐ NO

**YES!** I have completed the above Mini-Survey. Please send me my 4 FREE REWARDS (worth over $20 retail). I understand that I am under no obligation to buy anything, as explained on the back of this card.

### 194/394 MDL GMYQ

| | |
|---|---|
| FIRST NAME | LAST NAME |

ADDRESS

| | |
|---|---|
| APT.# | CITY |

| | |
|---|---|
| STATE/PROV. | ZIP/POSTAL CODE |

## READER SERVICE—Here's how it works:

◄ If offer card is missing write to: Reader Service, P.O. Box 1341, Buffalo, NY 14240-8531 or visit www.ReaderService.com ◄

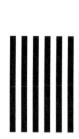

**BUSINESS REPLY MAIL**
FIRST-CLASS MAIL    PERMIT NO. 717    BUFFALO, NY

POSTAGE WILL BE PAID BY ADDRESSEE

**READER SERVICE**
PO BOX 1341
BUFFALO NY 14240-8571

NO POSTAGE
NECESSARY
IF MAILED
IN THE
UNITED STATES

sofa cushion. She gave him a small smile. "You are a good husband, Nash. Thoughtful and considerate."

"Right." He hoped she wasn't expecting an argument. As it was, he should be awarded some kind of medal.

He reached for her legs and placed them on his lap. "Just relax," he urged again when she opened her eyes, silently questioning him. He removed her shoes and massaged her tired feet. She sighed with pleasure and wiggled her toes.

"I haven't been to my place in a week," she said, and Nash found that an odd comment until he thought about it. She was admitting how comfortable she'd gotten living with him. It was a sign, a small one, that she was willing to advance their relationship. Nash didn't intend to waste it.

"I've moved nearly all my clothes here," she continued in sleepy tones.

"That's very good, don't you think?" he asked, not expecting her to reply.

"Hmm."

He continued to rub her feet and ankles, marveling at the delicate bone structure. He let his hands venture upward over her calves. She sighed and nestled farther down in the sofa. Gaining confidence, Nash risked going higher, where her skin was silky warm and smooth. He wasn't sure how this was affecting Savannah, but it was having a strong effect on him. His breathing went shallow and his heart started to thunder in his ears. He'd promised himself that he wouldn't ask her to make love again. She'd have to come to him. He wanted her to beg—but if anyone was going to do any begging, it was him.

"It's very relaxing," Savannah murmured with a sigh.

Funny, it wasn't relaxing for him....

"Nash." His name was released on a harshly indrawn breath.

His hands froze. His heart went still and his breath caught. "Yes?" He struggled to sound expressionless, although that was nearly impossible. The less she recognized how critical his need was for her, the better.

"I think I should stop, don't you?" Where he dredged up the strength to suggest that was beyond him.

"It feels good."

"That's the problem. It feels so good."

"For you, too?"

Sometimes he forgot what an innocent she was. "For me, too."

Her head was propped against the back of the sofa, her eyes closed. Her mouth was slightly parted and she moistened her lips with the tip of her tongue. Nash groaned inwardly and forced himself to look away.

"Maybe we should kiss," she whispered.

Nash wasn't interested in a repeat performance of what had taken place earlier, but at the same time he wasn't about to turn down her offer. She wasn't begging, but this was close enough.

He shifted his weight and brought her into his arms.

Perspiration broke out on his forehead and he held his breath while he reined in his desire. "If we start kissing, we might not be able to stop."

"I know."

"You know that?" Something was wrong with him. He should be carrying her into the bedroom and not asking questions until afterward. A long time afterward.

"We can follow through with our agreement, can't we?" she asked. Her eyes fluttered open.

"What agreement?" His mind could only hold one

thing at the moment, and that was his painful physical need for her.

"We'll separate once my parents decide to travel," she said, and it sounded more like a reassurance. "In the meantime, I'm not going to be trapped in a loveless marriage. As per the contract, we can initiate divorce proceedings when the year's up."

"Fine," he said, willing to agree to any terms. "Whatever you want."

"Do you think it would be a mistake to make love?" she asked.

"No." He sounded as if he'd choked on something. "That seems like a good idea to me," he said a couple of seconds later. He got off the sofa, reached down and scooped her into his arms.

She gave a small cry of surprise when he lifted her up and marched down the darkened hallway. He walked into his bedroom and placed her on his bed.

He was afraid of going too fast—and of not going fast enough. Afraid of not lasting long enough, of cheating her out of what lovemaking should be for her first time. His fears managed to make him feel indecisive.

"Is something wrong?" she asked, staring up at him, her eyes wide and questioning.

Unable to answer, he shook his head.

She smiled then, softly, femininely, and stretched her arms up, bringing him down next to her. He noticed that her breathing was as quick and shallow as his own. Carefully he peeled open the front of her shirt and eased it from her shoulders. Her bra and everything else soon followed....

They fell asleep afterward, their arms and legs intertwined, their bodies joined in the most elemental of ways. Nash had never known such peace, never experienced such serenity, and it lulled him into a deep sleep.

It was after midnight when he woke. The lights were still on in the living room and the kitchen. Carefully, so as not to wake Savannah, he crawled out of the bed and reached for his robe. Shuffling barefoot out of the bedroom, he yawned.

He felt good. Like he could run a marathon or swim a mile in world-record time. He finished the dinner dishes and was turning off the kitchen light when he looked up and saw Savannah standing inside the living room. Her hair was tousled, yet he'd never seen her look more beautiful. She'd donned her blouse, which covered precious little of her body.

"I woke up and you were gone," she said in a small voice.

"I was coming back to bed."

"Good." She led him back, not that he required any coaxing. The room was dark, but streaks of moonlight floated against the wall as they made their way to the bed.

Nash held back the covers and Savannah climbed in. He followed, gathering her in his arms, cradling her head against his shoulder.

He waited for her to speak, wondering what she was thinking, afraid to ask. With utter contentment he kissed her hair. She squirmed against him, nestling in as close as possible, and breathed out a long, womanly sigh.

Although he was an experienced lover, Nash had never heard a woman sigh the way Savannah did just then. It seemed to come from deep inside her, speaking of pleasure and the surprise of mutual satisfaction.

"Thank you," he whispered.

"No," she said. "Thank you." And then she snuggled

up to him again, as if she needed this closeness as much as he did. As if she craved these peaceful moments, too.

He waited a few more minutes, wanting to be sure she hadn't drifted off to sleep. "We should talk."

"I know," she whispered. "I thought about that, too."

"And?"

"I planned on discussing things with you, reassessing the issues, that sort of thing."

"Why didn't you?" He couldn't help being curious.

He felt her lips move in a smile. "When the time came, all I wanted was you."

His chest rose with an abundance of fierce male pride. "I wanted you, too."

Serenity surrounded him and he sank into its warmth.

"Should we talk now?" Savannah asked after a while.

The last thing Nash wanted right this minute was a lengthy conversation about their marriage. Words would destroy the tranquillity, and these moments were too precious to waste.

"This doesn't have to change anything, if you don't want it to," he murmured, rubbing his chin over her head, loving the silky feel of her hair.

Savannah went still, and he wondered if he'd said something wrong. "You're content with our arrangement the way it is?" she asked.

"For now I am. We don't have to make any decisions tonight, do we?"

"No," she agreed readily.

"Then relax and go back to sleep." His eyes drifted shut as he savored this closeness.

"Nash."

"Hmm?"

"It was nothing like I expected," she told him.

"Better, I hope."

"Oh, yes." And then she kissed him.

Don and Janice Griffin's meeting before Judge Wilcox was scheduled for two in the afternoon. Nash was well prepared for this final stage of the divorce proceedings.

Don Griffin arrived at his office an hour early and—in what was fast becoming a habit—started pacing the room.

"I'm ready anytime you are," his client said.

"If we leave now, we'll end up sitting outside in the hallway," Nash told him.

"I don't care. I want this over with as quickly and cleanly as possible, understand?"

"That message came through loud and clear," Nash assured him. "Settle down and relax, will you?"

Don thrust both hands into his hair. "Relax? Are you crazy, man? You might've gone through this a thousand times, but it's almost thirty years of my life we're throwing out the window. The stress is getting to me."

"What's this I hear about putting a divorce special on your restaurants' menu?" Nash asked in an effort to take the older man's mind off the coming proceedings. "Anyone who comes into any of your restaurants the day his divorce is final eats for free."

"That's right, and I'd rather you didn't say anything derogatory about it. I've met a number of men just like me. Some of 'em married twenty, thirty years and all of a sudden it's gone. Poof. Suddenly they're lost and alone and don't know what to do with the rest of their lives."

"I'm not going to say anything negative. I think it's a generous thing you're doing."

Don Griffin eyed him as if he wasn't sure he should believe that.

When they arrived at the courtroom, Mr. Griffin and Nash took their seats behind one table. Janice Griffin and Tony Pound sat behind the other. Nash noticed the way Don stole a look at his almost ex-wife. Next, he caught a glimpse of Janice looking at Don. It wasn't anything he hadn't seen countless times before. One last look, so to speak, before the ties were severed. A farewell. An acceptance that it was soon to be over— the end was within sight. This marriage was about to breathe its last breath.

Judge Wilcox entered the room and everyone stood. In a crisp, businesslike manner, he asked a series of questions of each party. Janice responded, her voice shaking. Don answered, sounding like a condemned man. They sat back down and the final decree was about to be pronounced when Nash vaulted out of his seat.

For a moment he didn't know what had forced him into action. "If you'll pardon me, Your Honor," he said, with his back to his client, "I'd like to say a few words."

He could hear Tony begin to object. Nash didn't give him the opportunity.

"My client doesn't want this divorce, and neither does his wife."

A string of hot words erupted behind him as Tony Pound flew out of his chair. The judge's gavel pounded several times, the noise deafening.

"Your Honor, if you'll indulge me for just a moment."

No one was more surprised than Nash when he was given permission. "Proceed."

"My client has been married for almost thirty years. He made a mistake, Your Honor. Now, he'll be the first to admit it was a foolish, stupid mistake. But he's human and so is his wife. They've both paid dearly for this blunder and it seems to me they've paid enough."

He turned to face Janice Griffin, who was shredding a tissue in her hand. "You've made mistakes in your life, too, haven't you, Mrs. Griffin?"

Janice lowered her gaze and nodded.

"You can't cross-examine my client," Pound yelled.

Nash ignored him, and thankfully so did Judge Wilcox.

"My client has loved his wife and family for nearly thirty years. He still loves her. I saw the way he looked at Mrs. Griffin when she walked into the courtroom. I also saw the way she looked at him. These two people care deeply for each other. They've been driven apart by their pain and their pride. Thirty years is a very long time out of a person's life, and I don't believe anyone should be in a rush to sign it away."

"Your Honor, I find this outburst extremely unprofessional," Tony Pound protested.

Nash didn't dare turn around.

"Don Griffin has suffered enough for his indiscretion. Mrs. Griffin has been through enough agony, too. It's time to think about rebuilding lives instead of destroying them."

There wasn't a sound in the courtroom. Having had his say, Nash returned to his seat.

Judge Wilcox held his gavel with both hands. "Is what Mr. Davenport said true, Mr. Griffin? Do you love your wife?"

Don Griffin rose slowly to his feet. "A thousand times more than I thought possible."

"Mrs. Griffin?"

She, too, stood, her eyes watering, her lips trembling. "Yes, Your Honor."

The judge glared at them both and set down the gavel. "Then I suggest you try to reconcile your differences and stop wasting the court's time."

Nash gathered together the papers he'd removed from his briefcase and slipped them back inside. Don Griffin walked behind him and was met halfway by his wife. From his peripheral vision, Nash watched as Janice Griffin, sobbing, walked into her husband's arms. They held on to each other, weeping and laughing and kissing all at once.

Not bad for an afternoon's work, Nash decided.

He picked up his briefcase and walked out of the courtroom. He hadn't taken two steps when Tony Pound joined him.

"That was quite a little drama you put on just now."

"I couldn't see two people who were obviously in love end their marriage," Nash said. They marched side by side through the halls of justice.

"It's true, then," Tony commented.

"What is?"

"That you've lost your edge, that killer instinct you're famous for. I have to admit I'm glad to see it. People said it'd happen when they learned you were married, but no one expected it to be this soon. Whoever took you on as a husband must be one heck of a woman."

Nash smiled to himself. "She is."

"It doesn't look like I'll be seeing you in court all that often."

"Probably not. I'm not taking on any new divorce cases."

"Dad, what an unexpected surprise," Savannah said, delighted that her father had decided to drop in at her store. He didn't visit often and his timing was perfect. She was about to take a break, sit down and rest her leg. "How's Mom?"

"Much better," he said, pulling out a chair as Savannah poured him a cup of coffee.

"Good."

"That's what I've come to talk to you about."

Savannah poured herself a cup and joined him. Her mother had made impressive progress in the past six weeks. Savannah called and visited often, and several times Nash had accompanied her. Joyce was growing stronger each day. She was often forgetful and that frustrated her, but otherwise she was recuperating nicely.

"I thought it'd be a good idea if I talked to you first," her father said.

"About what?"

"Your mother and I traveling."

It was the welcome news she'd been waiting to hear. At the same time it was the dreaded announcement that would end the happiest days of her life.

"I think you should travel. I always have."

"I was hoping to take your mother south. We might even look for a place to buy."

"Arizona," she suggested, raising the cup to her lips. "Mom's always loved the Southwest."

"The sunshine will do her good," her father agreed.

Savannah didn't know how she'd be able to pull this off, when she felt like she was dying on the inside. Over the years she'd become proficient at disguising her pain. Pain made others uncomfortable, so she'd learned to live with it.

"You wouldn't object to our going?" Her father didn't often sound hesitant but he did now.

"Of course I don't! I want you to travel and enjoy your

retirement years. I've got Nash now, so there's no need to worry about me. None whatsoever."

"You're sure?"

"Dad! Go and enjoy yourselves," Savannah said and managed to laugh.

Three hours later, she sat in the middle of Nash's living room, staring aimlessly into space. All that was left now was the waiting—that, and telling him....

Nash got home shortly after six. His eyes were triumphant as he marched into the house. "Savannah," he said, apparently delighted to see her. "You didn't work late tonight."

"No," she responded simply.

He lifted her off the sofa as if she weighed nothing and twirled her around. "I had the most incredible day."

"Me, too."

"Good. We'll celebrate." Tucking his arm beneath her knees, he started for the bedroom. He stopped abruptly when he saw her suitcase sitting at the end of the hallway. His eyes were filled with questions as they met hers.

"Are you going somewhere?"

She nodded. "My parents have decided to take an extended trip south."

"So?"

"So, according to the terms of our marriage agreement, I'm moving back into my own home."

# *Thirteen*

"You're moving out just like that?" Nash asked, lowering her feet to the ground. He stepped away from her as if he needed to put some distance between them. His eyes narrowed and he studied her, his expression shocked.

Savannah hadn't expected him to look at her like that. This was what they'd decided in the beginning, it was what he said he wanted after the first time they'd made love. She'd asked, wanting to be clear on exactly what her role in his life was to be, and Nash had said that making love changed nothing.

"This shouldn't come as a surprise," she said, struggling to keep her voice as even as possible.

"Is it what you want?" He thrust his hands deep inside his pockets and glared at her icily.

"Well?" he demanded when she didn't immediately answer.

"It doesn't matter what I think. I'm keeping my end of the bargain. What do you want me to do?"

Nash gave a nonchalant shrug of his shoulders. "I'm

not going to hold you prisoner here against your wishes, if that's what you're asking."

That wasn't what she was asking. She wanted some indication that he loved her and wanted her living with him. Some indication that he intended to throw out their stupid prenuptial agreement and make this marriage real. Apparently Nash wasn't interested.

"When are your parents leaving?"

"Friday morning, at dawn."

"So soon?"

She nodded. "Dad wanted to wait until Mom was strong enough to travel comfortably...and evidently she is now."

"I see." Nash wandered into the kitchen. "So you're planning to move out right away?"

"I...thought I'd take some clothes over to my house this evening."

"You certainly seem to be in a rush."

"Not really. I've managed to bring quite a few of my personal things here. I...imagine you'll want me out as quickly as possible." The smallest sign that he loved her would be enough to convince her to stay. A simple statement of need. A word. A look. Anything.

Nash offered nothing.

He opened the refrigerator and took out a cold soda, popping it open.

"I started dinner while I was waiting for you," she said. "The casserole's in the oven."

Nash took a long swallow of his soda. "I appreciate the effort, but I don't seem to have much of an appetite."

Savannah didn't, either. Calmly she walked over and turned off the oven. She stood with her back to Nash and bit her lip.

What a romantic fool she was, hoping the impossible would happen. She'd known when she agreed to marry him that it would be like this. He was going to break her heart. She'd tried to protect herself from exactly this, but it hadn't worked.

These past few weeks had been the happiest of her life and nothing he said now would take them away from her. He loved her, she knew he did, as much as it was possible for Nash to love anyone. He'd never said the words, but he didn't need to. She felt them when she slept in his arms. She experienced them each time they made love.

Her heart constricted with fresh pain. She didn't want to leave Nash, but she couldn't stay, not unless he specifically asked, and it was clear he had no intention of doing so.

She heard him leave the room, which was just as well since she was having a hard time not breaking into tears.

She was angry then. Unfortunately there wasn't a door to slam or anything handy to throw. Having a temper tantrum was exactly what she felt like doing.

Dinner was a waste. She might as well throw the whole thing in the garbage. Opening the oven door, she reached inside and grabbed the casserole dish.

Intense, unexpected pain shot through her fingers as she touched the dish.

She cried out and jerked her hand away. Stumbling toward the sink, she held her fingers under cold running water.

"Savannah?" Nash rushed into the kitchen. "What happened?"

"I'm all right," she said, fighting back tears by taking deep breaths. If she was lucky, her fingers wouldn't blister, but she seemed to be out of luck lately.

"What happened?" Nash demanded again.

"Nothing." She shook her head, not wanting to answer him because that required concentration and effort, and all she could think of at the moment was pain. Physical pain. Emotional agony. The two were intermingled until she didn't know where one stopped and the other started.

"Let me look at what you've done," he said, moving close to her.

"No," Savannah said, jerking her arm away from him. "It's nothing."

"Let me be the judge of that."

"Leave me alone," she cried, sobbing openly now, her shoulders heaving. "Just leave me alone. I can take care of myself."

"I'm your husband."

She whirled on him, unintentionally splashing him with cold water. "How can you say that when you can hardly wait to be rid of me?"

"What are you talking about?" he shouted. "I wasn't the one who packed my bags and casually announced I was leaving. If you want to throw out questions, then you might start by asking yourself what kind of wife you are!"

Savannah rubbed her uninjured hand beneath her nose. "You claimed you didn't want a wife."

"I didn't until I married you." Nash opened the freezer portion of the refrigerator and brought out a tub of ice cubes. "Sit down," he said in tones that brooked no argument. She complied. He set the tub on the table and gently placed her burned fingers inside it. "The first couple of minutes will be uncomfortable, but after that you won't feel much," he explained calmly.

Savannah continued to sob.

"What did you do?" he asked.

"I was taking out the baking dish."

Nash frowned. "Did the oven mitt slip?"

"I forgot to use one," she admitted.

He took a moment to digest this information before kneeling down at her feet. His eyes probed hers and she lowered her gaze. Tucking his finger beneath her chin, he leveled her eyes to his.

"Why?"

"Isn't it obvious? I...was upset."

"About what?"

She shrugged, not wanting to tell him the truth. "These things happen and..."

"Why?" he repeated softly.

"Because you're an idiot," she flared.

"I know you're upset about me not wanting dinner, but—"

"Dinner?" she cried, incredulous. "You think this is because you didn't want dinner? How can any man be so dense?" She vaulted to her feet, her burned fingers forgotten. "You were just going to let me walk out of here."

"Wrong."

"Wrong? And how did you plan to stop me?"

"I figured I'd move in with you."

She blinked. "I beg your pardon?"

"You heard me. The agreement, as originally written, states that you'll move out of my premises after your parents decide to travel and you—"

"I know what that stupid piece of paper says," Savannah said, frowning.

"If you don't want to live with me, then it makes perfect sense for me to—"

"I do want to live with you, you idiot," she broke in.

"I was hoping you'd do something—anything—to convince me to stay."

Nash was quiet for a few seconds. "Let me see if I have this straight. You were going to move out, although you didn't want to. Is that right?"

She nodded.

"Why?"

"Because I wanted you to ask me to stay."

"Ah, I understand now. You do one thing, hoping I'll respond by asking you to do the opposite."

She shrugged, realizing how silly it sounded in the cold light of reason. "I...guess so."

"Let this be a lesson to you, Savannah Davenport," Nash said, taking her in his arms. "If you want something, all you need to do is ask for it. If you'd simply sought my opinion, you'd have learned an important fact."

"Oh?"

"I'm willing to move heaven and earth to make sure we're together for the rest of our natural lives."

"You are?"

"In case you haven't figured it out yet, I'm in love with you." A surprised look must have come over her because he added, "You honestly didn't know?"

"I...prayed you were, but I didn't dare hope you'd admit it. I've been in love with you for so long I can't remember when I didn't love you."

He kissed her gently, his mouth coaxing and warm. "Promise you won't ever stop loving me. I need you so badly. It wasn't until you were in my life that I saw how jaded I'd become. Taking on so many divorce cases didn't help my attitude any. I've made a decision that's due to your influence on me. When I graduated from law school, I specialized in tax and tax laws. I'm going back to that."

"Oh, Nash, I'm so pleased."

He kissed her with a hunger that left her weak and clinging.

"I can ask for anything?" she murmured between kisses.

"Anything."

"Throw away that stupid agreement."

He smiled boyishly and pressed his forehead against hers. "I already have.... The first night, after we made love."

"You might have told me!"

"I intended to when the time was right."

"And when did you calculate that to be?" she asked, having difficulty maintaining her feigned outrage.

"Soon. Very soon."

She smiled and closed her eyes. "But not soon enough."

"I had high hopes for us from the first. I opened my mouth and stuck my foot in it at the beginning by suggesting that ludicrous marriage-of-convenience idea. Marriage, the second time around, is a lot more frightening because you've already made one mistake."

"Our marriage isn't a mistake," she assured him. "I won't let it be."

"I felt that if I had control of the situation, I might be able to control my feelings for you, but after Susan's wedding I knew that was going to be impossible."

"Why didn't you follow your own advice and ask how I felt?" she said, thinking of all the weeks they'd wasted.

"We haven't been on the best of terms, have we?" he murmured.

Savannah was embarrassed now by what a shrew

she'd been. She slid her arms around his neck and kissed him soundly in an effort to make up for those first weeks.

"You said I can ask for anything I want?" she said against his lips.

"Hmm...anything," he agreed.

"I'd like a baby."

Nash's eyes flew open with undisguised eagerness. "How soon?"

"Well... I was thinking we could start on the project tonight."

A slow, lazy smile came into place. "That's a very good idea. Very good indeed."

*Three years later...*

"I can't believe the changes in Nash," Susan commented to Savannah. She and Kurt had flown up from California to spend the Christmas holiday with them this year. The two women were working in the kitchen.

"He's such a good father to Jacob," Savannah said, blinking back tears. She cried so easily when she was pregnant, and she was entering her second trimester with this baby. If the ultrasound was accurate, they were going to have a little girl.

"Nash is doing so well and so are you. But don't you miss working at the shop?"

"No, I've got a wonderful manager and you can imagine how busy a fourteen-month-old keeps me. I've thought about going back part-time and then decided not to, not yet at any rate. What about you? Will you continue teaching?" Savannah softly patted Susan's slightly distended stomach.

"No, but I'll probably work on a substitute basis to

keep up my credentials so when our family's complete, I can return without a lot of hassle."

"That's smart."

"She's my sister, isn't she?" Nash said, walking into the kitchen, cradling his son in his arms. Jacob babbled happily, waving his rattle in every direction. He'd been a contented baby from the first. Their joy.

Kurt's arms surrounded his wife and he flattened his hands over her stomach. "We've decided to have our two close together, the same way you and Savannah planned your family."

Savannah and Nash exchanged smiles. "Planned?" she teased her husband.

"The operative word there is *two,*" Nash said, eyeing her suspiciously.

"Sweetheart, we've been over this a hundred times. I really would like four."

"Four!" Nash cried. "The last time we talked you said three."

"I've changed my mind. Four is a nice even number."

"Four children is out of the question," Nash said with a disgruntled look, then seemed to notice Kurt and Susan staring at him. "We'll talk about this later, all right? But we will talk."

"Of course we will," Savannah promised, unable to hold back a smile.

"She's going to do it," Nash grumbled to his sister and brother-in-law. "Somehow, before I've figured out how she's managed it, we'll be a family of six."

"You'll love it, Nash, I promise." The oven timer rang and Savannah glanced at the clock. "Oh, dear, I've got to get busy. Mr. Serle and Mr. Stackhouse will be here any minute."

"This is something else she didn't tell me before we were married," Nash said, his eyes shining with love. "She charms the most unexpected people...."

"They love Jacob," Savannah reminded him.

"True," Nash said wryly. "I've never seen two old men more taken with a toddler."

"And I've never seen a man more taken with his wife," Susan added. "I could almost be jealous, but there's no need." She turned to her husband and put her arms around his neck. "Still, it doesn't do any harm to keep him on his toes."

"No, it doesn't," Savannah agreed. And they all laughed.

\* \* \* \* \*

# MY HERO

For Virginia Myers, my mentor—
thanks for your friendship and encouragement!

# *One*

The man was the source of all her problems, Bailey York decided. He just didn't cut it. The first time around he was too cold, too distant. Only a woman "who loved too much" could possibly fall for him.

The second time, the guy was a regular Milquetoast. A wimp. He didn't seem to have a single thought of his own. This man definitely needed to be whipped into shape, but Bailey wasn't sure she knew how to do it.

So she did the logical thing. She consulted a fellow romance writer. Jo Ann Davis and Bailey rode the subway together every day, and Jo Ann had far more experience in this. Three years of dealing with men like Michael.

"Well?" Bailey asked anxiously when they met on a gray, drizzly January morning before boarding San Francisco's Bay Area Rapid Transit system, or BART for short.

Jo Ann shook her head, her look as sympathetic as her words. "You're right—Michael's a wimp."

"But I've worked so hard." Bailey couldn't help feeling discouraged. She'd spent months on this, squeezing in every available moment. She'd sacrificed lunches, given up nighttime television and whole weekends. Even Christmas had seemed a mere distraction. Needless to say, her social life had come to a complete standstill.

"No one told me writing a romance novel would be so difficult," Bailey muttered, as the subway train finally shot into the station. It screeched to a halt and the doors slid open, disgorging a crowd of harried-looking passengers.

"What should I do next?" Bailey asked as she and Jo Ann made their way into one of the cars. She'd never been a quitter, and already she could feel her resolve stiffening.

"Go back to the beginning and start over again," Jo Ann advised.

"Again," Bailey groaned, casting her eyes about for a vacant seat and darting forward, Jo Ann close behind, when she located one. When they were settled, Jo Ann handed Bailey her battle-weary manuscript.

She thumbed through the top pages, glancing over the notes Jo Ann had made in the margins. Her first thought had been to throw the whole project in the garbage and put herself out of her misery, but she hated to admit defeat. She'd always been a determined person; once she set her mind to something, it took more than a little thing like characterization to put her off.

It was ironic, Bailey mused, that a woman who was such a failure at love was so interested in writing about it. Perhaps that was the reason she felt so strongly about selling her romance novel. True love had scurried past her twice, stepping on her toes both times. She'd learned her lesson the hard way. Men were wonderful to read about and to look at from afar, but when it came to involving herself in a serious relationship, Bailey simply wasn't interested. Not anymore.

"The plot is basically sound," Jo Ann assured her. "All you really need to do is rework Michael."

The poor man had been reworked so many times it was a wonder Janice, her heroine, even recognized him. And if *Bailey* wasn't in love with Michael, she couldn't very well expect Janice to be swept off her feet.

"The best advice I can give you is to re-read your favorite romances and look really carefully at how the author portrays her hero," Jo Ann went on.

Bailey heaved an expressive sigh. She shouldn't be complaining—not yet, anyway. After all, she'd only been at this a few months, unlike Jo Ann who'd been writing and submitting manuscripts for more than three years. Personally, Bailey didn't think it would take *her* that long to sell a book. For one thing, she had more time to write than her friend. Jo Ann was married, the mother of two school-age children, plus she worked full-time. Another reason Bailey felt assured of success was that she had a romantic heart. Nearly everyone in their writers' group had said so. Not that it had done her any good when it came to finding a man of her own, but in the romance-writing business, a sensitive nature was clearly an asset.

Bailey prayed that all her creative whimsy, all her romantic perceptions, would be brilliantly conveyed on the pages of *Forever Yours*. They were, too—except for Michael, who seemed bent on giving her problems.

Men had always been an enigma to her, Bailey mused, so it was unreasonable to expect that to be any different now.

"Something else that might help you…" Jo Ann began thoughtfully.

"Yes?"

"Writers' Input recently published a book on characterization. I read a review of it, and as I recall, the author claims the best way to learn is to observe. It sounded rather abstract at the time, but I've had a chance to think about it, and you know? It makes sense."

"In other words," Bailey mused aloud, "what I really need is a model." She frowned. "I sometimes think I wouldn't recognize a hero if one hit me over the head."

No sooner had the words left her mouth than a dull object smacked the side of her head.

Bailey let out a sharp cry and rubbed the tender spot, twisting around to glare at the villain who was strolling casually past. She wasn't hurt so much as surprised.

"Hey, watch it!" she cried.

"I beg your pardon," a man said crisply, continuing down the crowded aisle. He carried a briefcase in one hand, with his umbrella tucked under his arm. As far as Bailey could determine, the umbrella handle had been the culprit. She scowled after him. The least he could've done was inquire if she'd been hurt.

"You're coming to the meeting tonight, aren't you?" Jo Ann asked. The subway came to a stop, which lowered the noise level enough for them to continue their conversation without raising their voices. "Libby McDonald's going to be there." Libby had published several popular romances and was in the San Francisco area visiting relatives. Their romance writers' group was honored that she'd agreed to speak.

Bailey nodded eagerly. Meeting Jo Ann couldn't have come at a better time. They'd found each other on the subway when Bailey noticed they were both reading the same romance, and began a conversation. She soon learned that they shared several interests; they began to meet regularly and struck up a friendship.

A week or so after their first meeting, Bailey sheepishly admitted how much she wanted to write a romance novel herself, not telling Jo Ann she'd already finished and submitted a manuscript. It was then that Jo Ann revealed that she'd written two complete manuscripts and was working on her third historical romance.

In the months since they'd met, Jo Ann's friendship had been invaluable to Bailey. Her mentor had introduced her to the local writers' group, and Bailey had discovered others all striving toward the same ultimate goal—publishing their stories. Since joining the group, Bailey had come to realize she'd made several mistakes, all typical of a novice writer, and had started the rewriting project. But unfortunately that hadn't gone well, at least not according to Jo Ann.

Bailey leafed through her manuscript, studying the notes her friend had made. What Jo Ann said made a lot of sense. "A romance hero is larger than life," Jo Ann had written in bold red ink along one margin. "Unfortunately, Michael isn't."

In the past few months, Bailey had been learning about classic romance heroes. They were supposed to be proud, passionate and impetuous. Strong, forceful men who were capable of tenderness. Men of excellent taste and impeccable style. That these qualities were too good to be true was something Bailey knew for a fact. A hero was supposed to have a burning need to find the one woman who would make his life complete. That sounded just fine on paper, but Bailey knew darn well what men were *really* like.

She heaved an exasperated sigh and shook her head. "You'd think I'd know all this by now."

"Don't be so hard on yourself. You haven't been at this as long as I have. Don't make the mistake of thinking I have all the answers, either," Jo Ann warned. "You'll notice I haven't sold yet."

"But you will." Bailey was convinced of that. Jo Ann's historical romance was beautifully written. Twice her friend had been a finalist in a national writing competition, and everyone, including Bailey, strongly believed it was only a matter of time before a publishing company bought *Fire Dream*.

"I agree with everything you're saying," Bailey added. "I just don't know if I can do it. I put my heart and soul into this book. I can't do any better."

"Of course you can," Jo Ann insisted.

Bailey knew she'd feel differently in a few hours, when she'd had a chance to muster her resolve; by tonight she'd be revising her manuscript with renewed enthusiasm. But for now, she needed to sit back and recover her confidence. She was lucky, though, because she had Jo Ann, who'd taken the time to read *Forever Yours* and give much-needed suggestions.

Yet Bailey couldn't help thinking that if she had a model for Michael, her job would be much easier. Jo Ann used her husband, Dan. Half their writers' group was in love with him, and no one had even met the man.

Reading Jo Ann's words at the end of the first chapter, Bailey found herself agreeing once more. "Michael should be determined, cool and detached. A man of substance."

Her friend made it sound so easy. Again Bailey reflected on how disadvantaged she was. In all her life, she hadn't dated a single hero, only those who thought they were but then quickly proved otherwise.

Bailey was mulling over her dilemma when she noticed him. He was tall and impeccably dressed in a gray pin-striped suit. She wasn't an expert on men's clothing, but she knew quality when she saw it.

The stranger carried himself with an air of cool detachment. That was good. Excellent, in fact. Exactly what Jo Ann had written in the margin of *Forever Yours*.

Now that she was studying him, she realized he looked vaguely familiar, but she didn't know why. Then she got it. This was "a man of substance." The very person she was looking for…

Here she was, bemoaning her sorry fate, when lo and behold a handsome stranger strolled into her life. Not just any stranger. This man was Michael incarnate. The embodiment of everything she'd come to expect of a romantic hero. Only this version was living and breathing, and standing a few feet away.

For several minutes, Bailey couldn't keep her eyes off him. The subway cars were crowded to capacity in the early-morning rush, and while other people looked bored and uncomfortable, her hero couldn't have been more relaxed. He stood several spaces ahead of her, holding the overhead rail and reading the morning edition of the paper. His raincoat was folded over his arm and, unlike some of the passengers, he seemed undisturbed by the train's movement as it sped along.

The fact that he was engaged in reading gave Bailey the opportunity to analyze him without being detected. His age was difficult to judge, but she guessed him to be in his mid-thirties. Perfect! Michael was thirty-four.

The man in the pin-striped suit was handsome, too.

But it wasn't his classic features—the sculpted cheek-bones, straight nose or high forehead—that seized her attention.

It was his jaw.

Bailey had never seen a more determined jaw in her life. Exactly the type that illustrated a touch of arrogance and a hint of audacity, both attributes Jo Ann had mentioned in her critique.

His rich chestnut-colored hair was short and neatly trimmed, his skin lightly tanned. His eyes were dark. As dark as her own were blue.

His very presence seemed to fill the subway car. Bailey was convinced everyone else sensed it, too. She couldn't understand why the other women weren't all staring at him just as raptly. The more she studied him, the better he looked. He was, without a doubt, the most masculine male Bailey had ever seen—exactly the way she'd always pictured her hero. Unfortunately she hadn't succeeded in transferring him from her imagination to the page.

Bailey was so excited she could barely contain herself. After months of writing and rewriting *Forever Yours,* shaping and reshaping the characters, she'd finally stumbled upon a real-life Michael. She could hardly believe her luck. Hadn't Jo Ann just mentioned this great new book that suggested learning through observing?

"Do you see the man in the gray pin-striped suit?" Bailey whispered, elbowing Jo Ann. "You know who he is, don't you?"

Jo Ann's eyes narrowed as she identified Bailey's hero and studied him for several seconds. She shook her head. "Isn't he the guy who clobbered you on the head with his umbrella a few minutes ago?"

"He is?"

"Who did you think he was?"

"You mean you don't know?" Bailey had been confident Jo Ann would recognize him as quickly as she had.

"*Should* I know him?"

"Of course you should." Jo Ann had read *Forever Yours*. Surely she'd recognize Michael in the flesh.

"Who do *you* think he is?" Jo Ann asked, growing impatient.

"That's Michael—my Michael," she added when Jo Ann frowned.

"Michael?" Jo Ann echoed without conviction.

"The way he was meant to be. The way Janice, my heroine, and I want him to be." Bailey had been trying to create him in her mind for weeks, and now here he was! "Can't you feel the sexual magnetism radiating from him?" she asked out of the corner of her mouth.

"Frankly, no."

Bailey decided to ignore that. "He's absolutely perfect. Can't you sense his proud determination? That commanding presence that makes him larger than life?"

Jo Ann's eyes narrowed again, the way they usually did when she was doing some serious contemplating.

"Do you see it now?" Bailey pressed.

Jo Ann's shoulders lifted in a regretful shrug. "I'm honestly trying, but I just don't. Give me a couple of minutes to work on it."

Bailey ignored her fellow writer's lack of insight. It didn't matter if Jo Ann agreed with her or not. The man in the gray suit was Michael. Her Michael. Naturally she'd be willing to step aside and give him to Janice, who'd been waiting all these weeks for Michael to straighten himself out.

"It hit me all of a sudden—what you were saying about observing in order to learn. I need a model for Michael, someone who can help me gain perspective," Bailey explained, her gaze momentarily leaving her hero.

"Ah…" Jo Ann sounded uncertain.

"If I'm ever going to sell *Forever Yours* I've got to employ those kinds of techniques." Bailey's eyes automatically returned to the man. Hmm, a little over six feet tall, she estimated. He really was a perfect specimen. All this time she'd been feeling melancholy, wondering how she could ever create an authentic hero, then, almost by magic, this one appeared in living color.…

"Go on," Jo Ann prodded, urging Bailey to finish her thought.

"The way I figure it, I may never get this characterization down right if I don't have someone to pattern Michael after."

Bailey half expected Jo Ann to argue with her. She was pleasantly surprised when her friend agreed with a quick nod. "I think you're right. It's an excellent idea."

Grinning sheepishly, Bailey gave herself a mental pat on the back. "I thought so myself."

"What are you planning to do? Study this guy—research his life history, learn what you can about his family and upbringing? That sort of thing? I hope you understand that this may not be as easy as it seems."

"Nothing worthwhile ever is," Bailey intoned solemnly. Actually, how she was going to do any of this research was a mystery to her, as well. Eventually she'd come up with some way of learning what she needed to know without being obvious about it. The sooner the better, of course. "I should probably start by finding out his name."

"That sounds like a good idea," Jo Ann said as though she wasn't entirely sure this plan was such a brilliant one, after all.

The train came to a vibrating halt, and a group of people moved toward the doors. Even while they disembarked, more were crowding onto the train. Bailey kept her gaze on the man in the pin-striped suit for fear he'd step off the subway without her realizing it. When she was certain he wasn't leaving, she relaxed.

"You know," Jo Ann said thoughtfully once the train had started again. "My Logan's modeled after Dan, but in this case, I'm beginning to have—"

"Did you see that?" Bailey interrupted, grabbing her friend's arm in her enthusiasm. The longer she studied the stranger, the more impressed she became.

"What?" Jo Ann demanded, glancing around her.

"The elegant way he turned the page." Bailey was thinking of her own miserable attempts to read while standing in a moving train. Any endeavor to turn the unwieldy newspaper page resulted in frustration to her and anyone unfortunate enough to be standing nearby. Yet he did it as gracefully and easily as if he were sitting at his own desk, in his own office.

"You're really hung up on this guy, aren't you?"

"You still don't see it, do you?" Bailey couldn't help being disappointed. She would've expected Jo Ann, of all her friends, to understand that this stranger was everything she'd ever wanted in Michael, from the top of his perfect hair to the tip of his (probably) size-eleven shoe.

"I'm still trying," Jo Ann said squinting as she stared at Bailey's hero, "but I don't quite see it."

"That's what I thought." But Bailey felt convinced

she was right. This tall, handsome man was Michael, and it didn't matter if Jo Ann saw it or not. She did, and that was all that mattered.

The subway train slowed as it neared the next stop. Once again, passengers immediately crowded the doorway. Her hero slipped the newspaper into his briefcase, removed the umbrella hooked around his forearm and stood back, politely waiting his turn.

"Oh, my," Bailey said, panic in her voice. This could get complicated. Her heart was already thundering like a Midwest storm gone berserk. She reached for her purse and vaulted to her feet.

Jo Ann looked at her as though she suspected Bailey had lost her wits. She tugged the sleeve of Bailey's coat. "This isn't our stop."

"Yes, I know," Bailey said, pulling an unwilling Jo Ann to her feet.

"Then what are you doing getting off here?"

Bailey frowned. "We're following him, what else?"

"We? But what about our jobs?"

"You don't expect me to do this alone, do you?"

# Two

"You don't mean we're actually going to *follow* him?"

"Of course we are." They couldn't stand there arguing. "Are you coming or not?"

For the first time in recent history, Jo Ann seemed at a complete loss for words. Just when Bailey figured she'd have to do this on her own, Jo Ann nodded. The two dashed off the car just in time.

"I've never done anything so crazy in all my life," Jo Ann muttered.

Bailey ignored her. "He went that way," she said, pointing toward the escalator. Grabbing Jo Ann by the arm, she hurried after the man in the pin-striped suit, maintaining a safe distance.

"Listen, Bailey," Jo Ann said, jogging in order to keep up, but still two steps behind her. "I'm beginning to have second thoughts about this."

"Why? Not five minutes ago you agreed that modeling Michael on a real man was an excellent approach to characterization."

"I didn't know you planned to stalk the guy! Don't you think we should stay back a little farther?"

"No." Bailey was adamant. As it was, her hero's long, powerful strides were much faster than Bailey's normal walking pace. Jo Ann's short-legged stride was even slower.

By the time they reached the corner, Jo Ann was panting. She leaned against the street lamp and placed her hand over her heart, inhaling deeply. "Give me a minute, would you?"

"We might lose him." The look Jo Ann gave her suggested that might not be so bad. "Think of this as research," Bailey added, looping her arm through Jo Ann's again and dragging her forward.

Staying in the shadow of the buildings, the two trailed Bailey's hero for three more blocks. Fortunately he was walking in the direction of the area where Bailey and Jo Ann both worked.

When he paused for a red light, Bailey stayed several feet behind him, wandering aimlessly toward a widow display while glancing over her shoulder every few seconds. She didn't want to give him an opportunity to notice her.

"Do you think he's married?" Bailey demanded of her friend.

"How would I know?" Jo Ann snapped.

"Intuition."

The light changed and Bailey rushed forward. A reluctant Jo Ann followed on her heels. "I can't believe I'm doing this."

"You already said that."

"What am I going to tell my boss when I'm late?" Jo Ann groaned.

Bailey had to wait when Jo Ann came to a sudden

halt, leaned against a display window and removed her high heel. She shook it out, then hurriedly put it back on.

"Jo Ann," Bailey said in a heated whisper, urging her friend to hurry.

"There was something in my shoe," she said from between clenched teeth. "I can't race down the streets of San Francisco with a stone in my shoe."

"I don't want to lose him," Bailey stopped abruptly, causing Jo Ann to collide with her. "Look, he went into the Cascade Building."

"Oh, good," Jo Ann muttered on the tail end of a sigh that proclaimed relief. "Does that mean we can go to work now?"

"Of course not." It was clear to Bailey that Jo Ann knew next to nothing about detective work. She probably didn't read mysteries. "I have to find out what his name is."

"What?" Jo Ann sounded as though Bailey had suggested they climb to the top of Coit Tower and leap off. "How do you plan to do that?"

"I don't know. I'll figure it out later." Clutching her friend's arm, Bailey urged her forward. "Come on, we can't give up now."

"Sure we can," Jo Ann muttered as they entered the Cascade Building.

"Hurry," Bailey whispered, releasing Jo Ann's elbow. "He's getting into the elevator." Bailey slipped past several people, mumbling. "Excuse me, excuse me" as she struggled to catch the same elevator, Jo Ann stumbling behind her.

They managed to make it a split second before the doors closed. There were four or five others on board, and Jo Ann cast Bailey a frown that doubted her intelligence.

Bailey had other concerns. She tried to remain as unobtrusive as possible, not wanting to call attention to herself or Jo Ann. Her hero seemed oblivious to them, which served her purposes nicely. All she intended to do was find out his name and what he did for a living, a task that shouldn't require the FBI.

Jo Ann jerked Bailey's sleeve and nodded toward the stranger's left hand. It took Bailey a moment to realize her friend was pointing out the fact that he wasn't wearing a wedding ring. The realization cheered Bailey and she made a circle with thumb and finger, grinning broadly.

As the elevator sped upward, Bailey saw Jo Ann anxiously check her watch. Then the elevator came to a smooth halt. A few seconds passed before the doors slid open and two passengers stepped out.

Her hero glanced over his shoulder, then moved to one side. For half a second, his gaze rested on Bailey and Jo Ann.

Half a second! Bailey straightened, offended at the casual way in which he'd dismissed her. She didn't want him to notice her, but at the same time, she felt cheated that he hadn't recognized the heroine in her—the same way she'd seen the hero in him. She was, after all, heroine material. She was attractive and... Well, *attractive* might be too strong a word. Cute and charming had a more comfortable feel. Her best feature was her thick dark hair that fell straight as a stick across her shoulders. The ends curved under just a little, giving it shape and bounce. She was taller than average, and slender, with clear blue eyes and a turned-up nose. As for her personality, she had spunk enough not to turn away from a good argument and spirit enough to follow a stranger around San Francisco.

Bailey noted that once again his presence seemed to fill the cramped quarters. His briefcase was tucked under his arm, while his hand gripped the curved handle of his umbrella. For all the notice he gave those around him, he might have been alone.

When Bailey turned to her friend, she saw that Jo Ann's eyes were focused straight ahead, her teeth gritted as though she couldn't wait to tell Bailey exactly what she thought of this crazy scheme. It *was* crazy, Bailey would be the first to admit, but these were desperate times in the life of a budding romance writer. She would stop at nothing to achieve her goal.

Bailey grinned. She had to agree that traipsing after her hero was a bit unconventional, but *he* didn't need to know about it. He didn't need to ever know how she intended to use him.

Her gaze moved from Jo Ann, then to the man with the umbrella. The amusement drained out of her as she found herself staring into the darkest pair of eyes she'd ever seen. Bailey was the first to look away, her pulse thundering in her ears.

The elevator stopped several times until, finally, only the three of them were left. Jo Ann had squeezed into the corner. Behind the stranger's back she mouthed several words that Bailey couldn't hope to decipher, then tapped one finger against the face of her watch.

Bailey nodded and raised her hand, fingers spread, to plead for five more minutes.

When the elevator stopped again, her hero stepped out, and Bailey followed, with Jo Ann trailing behind her. He walked briskly down the wide hallway, then entered a set of double doors marked with the name of a well-known architectural firm.

"Are you satisfied now?" Jo Ann burst out. "Honestly, Bailey, have you gone completely nuts?"

"You told me I need a hero who's proud and determined and I'm going to find one."

"That doesn't answer my question. Has it occurred to you yet that you've gone off the deep end?"

"Because I want to find out his name?"

"And how do you plan to do that?"

"I don't know yet," Bailey admitted. "Why don't I just ask?" Having said that, she straightened her shoulders and walked toward the same doors through which the man had disappeared.

The pleasant-looking middle-aged woman who sat at the reception desk greeted her with a warm smile. "Good morning."

"Good morning," Bailey returned, hoping her smile was as serene and trusting as the older woman's. "This may seem a bit unusual, but I… I was on the subway this morning and I thought I recognized an old family friend. Naturally I didn't want to make a fool of myself in case I was wrong. He arrived in your office a few minutes ago and I was wondering… I know it's unusual, but would you mind telling me his name?"

"That would be Mr. Davidson. He's been taking BART the last few months because of the freeway renovation project."

"Mr. Davidson," Bailey repeated slowly. "His first name wouldn't be Michael, would it?"

"No." The receptionist frowned slightly. "It's Parker."

"Parker," Bailey repeated softly. "Parker Davidson."

She liked the way it sounded, and although it wasn't a name she would've chosen for a hero, she could see that it fit him perfectly.

"Is Mr. Davidson the man you thought?"

It took Bailey a second or two to realize the woman was speaking to her. "Yes," she answered with a bright smile. "I do believe he is."

"Why, that's wonderful." The woman was obviously delighted. "Would you like me to buzz him? I'm sure he'd want to talk to you himself. Mr. Davidson is such a nice man."

"Oh, no, please don't do that." Bailey hoped she was able to hide the panic she felt at the woman's suggestion. "I wouldn't want to disturb him and I really have to be getting to work. Thank you for your trouble."

"It was no trouble whatsoever." The receptionist glanced down at her appointment schedule and shook her head. "I was going to suggest you stop in at noon, but unfortunately Mr. Davidson's got a lunch engagement."

Bailey sighed as though with regret and turned away from the desk. "I'll guess I'll have to talk to him another time."

"That's really too bad. At least give me your name." The woman's soft brown eyes went from warm to sympathetic.

"Janice Hampton," Bailey said, mentioning the name of her heroine. "Thank you again for your help. You've been most kind."

Jo Ann was in the hallway pacing and muttering when Bailey stepped out of Parker's office. She stopped abruptly as Bailey appeared, her eyes filled with questions. "What happened?"

"Nothing. I asked the receptionist for his name and

she told me. She even let it slip that he's got a lunch engagement…"

"Are you satisfied *now?*" Jo Ann sounded as though she'd passed from impatience to resignation. "In case you've forgotten, we're both working women."

Bailey glanced at her watch and groaned. "We won't be too late if we hurry." Jo Ann worked as an insurance specialist in a doctor's office and Bailey was a paralegal.

Luckily their office buildings were only a few blocks from the Cascade Building. They parted company on the next corner and Bailey half jogged the rest of the way.

No one commented when she slipped into the office ten minutes late. She hoped the same held true for Jo Ann, who'd probably never been late for work in her life.

Bailey settled down at her desk with her coffee and her files, then hesitated. Jo Ann was right. Discovering Parker's name was useless unless she could fill in the essential details about his life. She needed facts. Lots of facts. The kinds of people he associated with, his background, his likes and dislikes, everyday habits.

It wasn't until later in the morning that Bailey started wondering where someone like Parker Davidson would go for lunch. It might be important to learn that. The type of restaurant a man chose—casual? elegant? exotic?— said something about his personality. Details like that could make the difference between a sale and a rejection, and frankly, Bailey didn't know if Michael could tolerate another spurning.

At ten to twelve Bailey mumbled an excuse about having an appointment before she headed out the door. Her boss gave her a funny look, but Bailey made sure she escaped before anyone could ask any questions. It wasn't like Bailey to take her duties lightly.

Luck was with her. She'd only been standing at the street corner for five minutes when Parker Davidson came out of the building. He was deeply involved in conversation with another man, yet when he raised his hand to summon a taxi, one appeared instantly, as if by magic. If she hadn't seen it with her own eyes, Bailey wouldn't have believed it. Surely this was the confidence, the command, others said a hero should possess. Not wanting to miss a single detail, Bailey took a pen and pad out of her purse and started jotting them down.

As Parker's cab slowly pulled away, she ventured into the street and flagged down a second cab. In order to manage that, however, she'd had to wave her arms above her head and leap up and down.

She yanked open the door and leapt inside. "Follow that cab," she cried, pointing toward Parker's taxi.

The stocky driver twisted around. "Are you serious? You want me to follow that cab?"

"That's right," she said anxiously, afraid Parker's taxi would soon be out of sight.

Her driver laughed outright. "I've been waiting fifteen years for someone to tell me that. You got yourself a deal, lady." He stepped on the accelerator and barreled down the street, going well above the speed limit.

"Any particular reason, lady?"

"I beg your pardon?" The man was doing fifty in a thirty-mile-an-hour zone.

"I want to know why you're following that cab." The car turned a corner at record speed, the wheels screeching, and Bailey slid from one end of the seat to the other. If she'd hoped to avoid attention, it was a lost cause. Parker Davidson might not notice her, but nearly everyone else in San Francisco did.

"I'm doing some research for a romance novel," Bailey explained.

"You're doing *what?*"

"Research."

Apparently her answer didn't satisfy him, because he slowed to a sedate twenty miles an hour. "Research for a romance novel," he repeated, his voice flat. "I thought you were a private detective or something."

"I'm sorry to disappoint you. I write romance novels and— Oh, stop here, would you?" Parker's cab had pulled to the curb and the two men were climbing out.

"Sure, lady, don't get excited."

Bailey scrambled out of the cab and searched through her purse for her money. When she couldn't find it, she slapped the large bag onto the hood of the cab and sorted through its contents until she retrieved her wallet. "Here."

"Have a great day, lady," the cabbie said sardonically, setting his cap farther back on his head. Bailey offered him a vague smile.

She toyed with the idea of following the men into the restaurant and having lunch. She would have, too, if it weren't for the fact that she'd used all her cash to pay for the taxi.

But there was plenty to entertain her while she waited—although Bailey wasn't sure exactly what she was waiting for. The streets of Chinatown were crowded. She gazed about her at the colorful shops with their produce stands and souvenirs and rows of smoked ducks hanging in the windows. Street vendors displayed their wares and tried to coax her to come examine their goods.

Bailey bought a fresh orange with some change she scrounged from the bottom of her purse. Walking across the street, she wondered how long her hero would dawdle over his lunch. Most likely he'd walk back to the office. Michael would.

His lunch engagement didn't last nearly as long as Bailey had expected. When he emerged from the restaurant, he took her by surprise. Bailey was in the process of using her debit card to buy a sweatshirt she'd found at an incredibly low price and had to rush in an effort to keep up with him.

He hadn't gone more than a couple of blocks when she lost him. Stunned, she stood in the middle of the sidewalk, wondering how he could possibly have disappeared.

One minute he was there, and the next he was gone. Tailing a hero wasn't nearly as easy as she'd supposed.

Discouraged, Bailey clutched her bag with the sweatshirt and slung her purse over her shoulder, then started back toward her office. Heaven only knew what she was going to say to her boss once she arrived—half an hour late.

She hadn't gone more than a few steps when someone grabbed her arm and jerked her into the alley. She opened her mouth to scream, but the cry died a sudden death when she found herself staring up at Parker Davidson.

"I want to know why the hell you're following me."

# Three

"Ah... Ah..." For the life of her, Bailey couldn't string two words together.

"Janice Hampton, I presume?"

Bailey nodded, simply because it was easier than explaining herself.

Parker's eyes slowly raked her from head to foot. He obviously didn't see anything that pleased him. "You're not an old family friend, are you?"

Still silent, she answered him with a shake of her head.

"That's what I thought. What do you want?"

Bailey couldn't think of a single coherent remark.

"Well?" he demanded since she was clearly having a problem answering even the most basic questions. Bailey had no idea where to start or how much to say. The truth would never do, but she didn't know if she was capable of lying convincingly.

"Then you leave me no choice but to call the police," he said tightly.

"No...please." The thought of explaining everything to an officer of the law was too mortifying to consider.

"Then start talking." His eyes were narrow and as cold as the January wind off San Francisco Bay.

Bailey clasped her hands together, wishing she'd never given in to the whim to follow him on his lunch appointment. "It's a bit…complicated," she mumbled.

"Isn't it always?"

"Your attitude isn't helping any," she returned, straightening her shoulders. He might be a high-and-mighty architect—and her behavior might have been a little unusual—but that didn't give him the right to treat her as if she were some kind of criminal.

"*My* attitude?" he said incredulously.

"Listen, would you mind if we shorted this inquisition?" she asked, checking her watch. "I've got to be back at work in fifteen minutes."

"Not until you tell why you've been my constant shadow for the past hour. Not to mention this morning."

"You're exaggerating." Bailey half turned to leave when his hand flew out to grip her shoulder.

"You're not going anywhere until you've answered a few questions."

"If you must know," she said at the end of a protracted sigh, "I'm a novelist…"

"Published?"

"Not yet," she admitted reluctantly, "but I will be."

His mouth lifted at the corners and Bailey couldn't decide if the movement had a sardonic twist or he didn't believe a word she was saying. Neither alternative did anything to soothe her ego.

"It's true!" she said heatedly. "I am a novelist, only I've been having trouble capturing the true nature of a classic hero and, well, as I said earlier, it gets a bit involved."

"Start at the beginning."

"All right." Bailey was prepared now to do exactly that. He wanted details? She'd give him details. "It all began several months back when I was riding BART and I met Jo Ann—she's the woman I was with this morning. Over the course of the next few weeks I learned that she's a writer, too, and she's been kind enough to tutor me. I'd already mailed off my first manuscript when I met Jo Ann, but I quickly learned I'd made some basic mistakes. All beginning writers do. So I rewrote the story and—"

"Do you mind if we get to the part about this morning?" he asked, clearly impatient.

"All right, fine, I'll skip ahead, but it probably won't make much sense." She didn't understand why he was wearing that beleaguered look, since he was the one who'd insisted she start at the beginning. "Jo Ann and I were on the subway this morning and I was telling her I doubted I'd recognize a hero. You see, Michael's the hero in my book and I'm having terrible problems with him. The first time around he was too harsh, then I turned him into a wimp. I just can't seem to get him to walk the middle of the road. He's got to be tough, but tender. Strong and authoritative, but not so stubborn or arrogant the reader wants to throttle him. I need to find a way to make Michael larger than life, but at the same time the kind of man any woman would fall in love with and—"

"Excuse me for interrupting you again," Parker said, folding his arms across his chest and irritably tapping his foot, "but could we finish this sometime before the end of the year?"

"Oh, yes. Sorry." His sarcasm didn't escape her, but she decided to be generous and overlook it. "I was telling Jo Ann I wouldn't recognize a hero if one hit me over the head, and no sooner had I said that than your umbrella whacked me." The instant the words were out, Bailey realized she should have passed over that part.

"I like the other version better," he said with undisguised contempt. He shook his head and stalked past her onto the busy sidewalk.

"What other version?" Bailey demanded, marching after him. She was only relaying the facts, the way *he'd* insisted!

"The one where you're an old family friend. This nonsense about being a novelist is—"

"The absolute truth," she finished with all the dignity she could muster. "You're the hero—well, not exactly the hero, don't get me wrong, but a lot like my hero, Michael. In fact, you could be his twin."

Parker stopped abruptly and just as abruptly turned around to face her. The contempt in his eyes was gone, replaced by some other emotion Bailey couldn't identify.

"Have you seen a doctor?" he asked gently.

"A doctor?"

"Have you discussed this problem with a professional?"

It took Bailey a moment to understand what he was saying. Once she did, she was so furious she couldn't formulate words fast enough to keep pace with her speeding mind.

"You think...mental patient...on the loose?"

He nodded solemnly.

"That's the most ridiculous thing I've ever heard in my life!" Bailey had never been more insulted. Parker Davidson thought she was a crazy person! She waved her arms haphazardly as she struggled to compose her thoughts. "I'm willing to admit that following you is a bit eccentric, but...but I did it in the name of research!"

"Then kindly research someone else."

"Gladly." She stormed ahead several paces, then whirled suddenly around, her fists clenched. "You'll have to excuse me, I'm new to the writing game. There's a lot I don't know yet, but obviously I have more to learn than I realized. I was right the first time—you're no hero."

Not giving him the opportunity to respond, she rushed back to her office, thoroughly disgusted with the man she'd assumed to be a living, breathing hero.

Max, Bailey's cat, was waiting anxiously for her when she arrived home that evening, almost an hour later than usual since she'd stayed to make up for her lengthy lunch. Not that Max would actually deign to let her think he was pleased to see her. Max had one thing on his mind and one thing only.

Dinner.

The sooner she fed him, the sooner he could go back to ignoring her.

"I'm crazy about you, too," Bailey teased, bending over to playfully scratch his ears. She talked to her cat the way she did her characters, although Michael had been suspiciously quiet of late—which was fine with Bailey, since a little time apart was sure to do them both good. She wasn't particularly happy with her hero after the Parker Davidson fiasco that afternoon. Once again Michael had led her astray. The best thing to do was lock him in the desk drawer for a while.

Max wove his fat fluffy body between Bailey's legs while she sorted through her mail. She paused, staring into space as she reviewed her confrontation with Parker Davidson. Every time she thought about the things he'd said, she felt a flush of embarrassment. It was all she could do not to cringe at the pitying look he'd given her as he asked if she was seeking professional help. Never in her life had Bailey felt so mortified.

"Meow." Max seemed determined to remind her that he was still waiting for his meal.

"All right, all right," she muttered, heading for the refrigerator. "I don't have time to argue with you tonight. I'm going out to hear Libby McDonald speak." She removed the can of cat food from the bottom shelf and dumped the contents on the dry kibble. Max had to have his meal moistened before he'd eat it.

With a single husky purr, Max sauntered over to his dish and left Bailey to change clothes for the writers' meeting.

Once she was in her most comfortable sweater and an old pair of faded jeans, she grabbed a quick bite to eat and was out the door.

Jo Ann had already arrived at Parklane College, the site of their meeting, and was rearranging the classroom desks to form a large circle. Bailey automatically helped, grateful her friend didn't question her about Parker Davidson. Within minutes, the room started to fill with members of the romance writers' group.

Bailey didn't know if she should tell Jo Ann about the meeting with Parker. No, she decided, the whole sorry episode was best forgotten. Buried under the heading of Mistakes Not to Be Repeated.

If Jo Ann did happen to ask, Bailey mused, it would be best to say nothing. She didn't make a habit of lying, but her encounter with that man had been too humiliating to describe, even to her friend.

The meeting went well, and although Bailey took copious notes, her thoughts persisted in drifting away from Libby's speech, straying to Parker. The man had his nerve suggesting she was a lunatic. Who did he think he was, anyway? Sigmund Freud? But then, to be fair, Parker had no way of knowing that Bailey didn't normally go around following strange men and claiming they were heroes straight out of her novel.

Again and again throughout the talk, Bailey had to stubbornly refocus her attention on Libby's speech. When Libby finished, the twenty or so writers who were gathered applauded enthusiastically. The sound startled Bailey, who'd been embroiled in yet another mental debate about the afternoon's encounter.

There was a series of questions, and then Libby had to leave in order to catch a plane. Bailey was disappointed that she couldn't stay for coffee. It had become tradition for a handful of the group's members to go across the street to the all-night diner after their monthly get-together.

As it turned out, everyone else had to rush home, too, except Jo Ann. Bailey was on the verge of making an excuse herself, but one glance told her Jo Ann was unlikely to believe it.

They walked across the street to the brightly lit and almost empty restaurant. As they sat down in their usual booth, the waitress approached them with menus. Jo Ann ordered just coffee, but Bailey, who'd eaten an orange for lunch and had a meager dinner of five pretzels, a banana and two hard green jelly beans left over from Christmas, was hungry, so she asked for a turkey sandwich.

"All right, tell me what happened," Jo Ann said the moment the waitress left their booth.

"About what?" Bailey tried to appear innocent as she toyed with the edges of the paper napkin. She carefully avoided meeting Jo Ann's eyes.

"I phoned your office at lunchtime," her friend said in a stern voice. "Do I need to go into the details?" She studied Bailey, who raised her eyes to give Jo Ann a brief look of wide-eyed incomprehension. "Beth told me you'd left before noon for a doctor's appointment and weren't back yet." She paused for effect. "We both know you didn't have a doctor's appointment, don't we?"

"Uh…" Bailey felt like a cornered rat.

"You don't need to tell me where you were," Jo Ann went on, raising her eyebrows. "I can guess. You couldn't leave it alone, could you? My guess is that you followed Parker Davidson to his lunch engagement."

Bailey nodded miserably. So much for keeping one of her most humiliating moments a secret. She hadn't even told Max! Her cat generally heard everything, but today's encounter was best forgotten.

If only she could stop thinking about it. For most of the afternoon she'd succeeded in pushing all thoughts of that man, that unreasonable insulting architect, out of her mind. Not so this evening.

"And?" Jo Ann prompted.

Bailey could see it was pointless to continue this charade with her friend. "And he confronted me, wanting to know why the hell I was following him."

Jo Ann closed her eyes, then slowly shook her head. After a moment, she reached for her coffee. "I can just imagine what you told him."

"At first I had no idea what to say."

"That part I can believe, but knowing you, I'd guess you insisted on telling him the truth and nothing but the truth."

"You're right again." Not that it had done Bailey any good.

"And?" Jo Ann prompted again.

Bailey's sandwich arrived and for a minute or so she was distracted by that. Unfortunately she wasn't able to put off Jo Ann's questions for long.

"Don't you dare take another bite of that sandwich until you tell me what he said!"

"He didn't believe me." Which was putting it mildly.

"He didn't believe you?"

"All right, if you have to know, he thought I was an escaped mental patient."

Anger flashed in Jo Ann's eyes, and Bailey was so grateful she could have hugged her.

"Good grief, why'd you do anything so stupid as to tell him you're a writer?" Jo Ann demanded vehemently.

So much for having her friend champion her integrity, Bailey mused darkly.

"I can't understand why you'd do that," Jo Ann continued, raking her hand furiously through her hair. "You were making up stories all over the place when it came to discovering his name. You left me speechless with the way you walked into his office and spouted that nonsense about being an old family friend. Why in heaven's name didn't you make up something plausible when he confronted you?"

"I couldn't think." That, regrettably, was the truth.

Not that it would've made much difference even if she'd been able to invent a spur-of-the-moment excuse. She was convinced of that. The man would have known she was lying, and Bailey couldn't see the point of digging herself in any deeper than she already was. Of course she hadn't had time to reason that out until later. He'd hauled her into the alley and she'd simply followed her instincts, right or wrong.

"It wasn't like you didn't warn me," Bailey said, half her turkey sandwich poised in front of her mouth. "You tried to tell me from the moment we followed him off the subway how dumb the whole idea was. I should've listened to you then."

But she'd been so desperate to get a real hero down on paper. She'd been willing to do just about anything to straighten out this problem of Michael's. What she hadn't predicted was how foolish she'd end up feeling as a result. Well, no more—she'd learned her lesson. If any more handsome men hit her on the head, she'd hit them back!

"What are you going to do now?" Jo Ann asked.

"Absolutely nothing," Bailey answered without a second's hesitation.

"You mean you're going to let him go on thinking you're an escaped mental patient?"

"If that's what he wants to believe." Bailey tried to create the impression that it didn't matter to her one way or the other. She must have done a fairly good job because Jo Ann remained speechless, raising her coffee mug to her mouth three times without taking a single sip.

"What happens if you run into him on the subway again?" she finally asked.

"I don't think that'll be a problem," Bailey said blithely, trying hard to sound unconcerned. "What are the chances we'll be on the same car again at exactly the same time?"

"You're right," Jo Ann concurred. "Besides, after what happened today, he'll probably go back to driving, freeway renovation or not."

It would certainly be a blessing if he did, Bailey thought.

He didn't.

Jo Ann and Bailey were standing at the end of the crowded subway car, clutching the metal handrail when Jo Ann tugged hard at the sleeve of Bailey's bulky-knit cardigan.

"Don't turn around," Jo Ann murmured.

They were packed as tight as peas in a pod, and Bailey had no intention of moving in any direction.

"He's staring at you."

"Who?" Bailey whispered back.

She wasn't a complete fool. When she'd stepped onto the train earlier, she'd done a quick check and was thankful to note that Parker Davidson wasn't anywhere to be seen. She hadn't run into him in several days and there was no reason to think she would. He might have continued to take BART, but if that was the case their paths had yet to cross, which was fine with her. Their second encounter would likely prove as embarrassing as the first.

"He's here," Jo Ann hissed. "The architect you followed last week."

Bailey was convinced everyone in the subway car had turned to stare at her. "I'm sure you're mistaken," she muttered, furious with her friend for her lack of discretion.

"I'm not. Look." She motioned with her head.

Bailey did her best to be nonchalant about it. When she did slowly twist around, her heart sank all the way to her knees. Jo Ann was right. Parker stood no more than ten feet from her. Fortunately, they were separated by a number of people—which didn't disguise the fact that he was staring at Bailey as if he expected men in white coats to start descending on her.

She glared back at him.

"Do you see him?" Jo Ann asked.

"Of course. Thank you so much for pointing him out to me."

"He's staring at you. What else was I supposed to do?"

"Ignore him," Bailey suggested sarcastically. "I certainly intend to." Still, no matter how hard she tried to concentrate on the advertising posted above the seats, she found Parker Davidson dominating her thoughts.

A nervous shaky feeling slithered down her spine. Bailey could *feel* his look as profoundly as a caress. This was exactly the sort of look she struggled to describe in *Forever Yours*.

Casually, as if by accident, she slowly turned her head and peeked in his direction once more, wondering if she'd imagined the whole thing. For an instant the entire train seemed to go still. Her blue eyes met his brown ones, and an electric jolt rocked Bailey, like nothing she'd ever felt before. A breathless panic filled her and she longed to drag her eyes away, pretend she didn't recognize him, anything to escape this fluttery sensation in the pit of her stomach.

This was exactly how Janice had felt the first time she met Michael. Bailey had spent days writing that scene, studying each word, each phrase, until she'd achieved the right effect. That was the moment Janice had fallen in love with Michael. Oh, she'd fought it, done everything but stand on her head in an effort to control her feelings, but Janice had truly fallen for him.

Bailey, however, was much too wise to be taken in by a mere look. She'd already been in love. Twice. Both times were disasters and she wasn't willing to try it again soon. Her heart was still bleeding from the last go-round.

Of course she was leaping to conclusions. She was the one with the fluttery stomach. Not Parker. He obviously hadn't been affected by their exchange. In fact, he seemed to be amused, as if running into Bailey again was an unexpected opportunity for entertainment.

She braced herself, and with a resolve that would've impressed Janice, she dropped her gaze. She inhaled sharply, then twisted her mouth into a sneer. Unfortunately, Jo Ann was staring at her in complete—and knowing—fascination.

"What's with you—and him?"

"Nothing," Bailey denied quickly.

"That's not what I saw."

"You're mistaken," Bailey replied in a voice that said the subject was closed.

"Whatever you did worked," Jo Ann whispered a couple of minutes later.

"I don't know what you're talking about."

"Fine, but in case you're interested, he's coming this way."

"I beg your pardon?" Bailey's forehead broke out in a cold sweat at the mere prospect of being confronted by Parker Davidson again. Once in a lifetime was more than enough, but twice in the same week was well beyond her capabilities.

Sure enough, Parker Davidson boldly stepped forward and squeezed himself next to Bailey.

"Hello again," he said casually.

"Hello," she returned stiffly, refusing to look at him.

"You must be Jo Ann," he said, turning his attention to Bailey's friend.

Jo Anne's eyes narrowed. "You told him my name?" she asked Bailey in a loud distinct voice.

"I... Apparently so."

"Thank you very much," she muttered in a sarcastic voice. Then she turned toward Parker and her expression altered dramatically as she broke into a wide smile. "Yes, I'm Jo Ann."

"Have you been friends with Janice long?"

"Janice? Oh, you mean..." Bailey quickly nudged her friend in the ribs with her elbow. "Janice," Jo Ann repeated in a strained voice. "You mean *this* Janice?"

Parker frowned. "So that was a lie, as well?"

"As well," Bailey admitted coolly, deciding she had no alternative. "That was my problem in the first place. I told you the truth. Now, for the last time, I'm a writer and so is Jo Ann." She gestured toward her friend. "Tell him."

"We're both writers," Jo Ann confirmed with a sad lack of conviction. It wasn't something Jo Ann willingly broadcast, though Bailey had never really understood why. She supposed it was a kind of superstition, a fear of offending the fates by appearing too presumptuous— and thereby ruining her chances of selling a book.

Parker sighed, frowning more darkly. "That's what I thought."

The subway stopped at the next station, and he moved toward the door.

"Goodbye," Jo Ann said, raising her hand. "It was a pleasure to meet you."

"Me, too." He glanced from her to Bailey; she could have sworn his eyes hardened briefly before he stepped off the car.

"You told him your name was Janice?" Jo Ann cried the minute he was out of sight. "Why'd you do that?"

"I... I don't know. I panicked."

Jo Ann wiped her hand down her face. "Now he *really* thinks you're nuts."

"It might have helped if you hadn't acted like you'd never heard the word 'writer' before." Before Jo Ann could heap any more blame on her shoulders, Bailey had some guilt of her own to spread around.

"That isn't information I tell everyone, you know. I'd appreciate if you didn't pass it out to just anyone."

"Oh, dear," Bailey mumbled, feeling wretched. Not only was Jo Ann annoyed with her, Parker thought she was a fool. And there was little she could do to redeem herself in his eyes. The fact that it troubled her so much was something for the men with chaise longues in their offices to analyze. But trouble her it did.

If only Parker hadn't looked at her with those dark eyes of his—as if he was willing to reconsider his first assessment of her.

If only she hadn't looked back and felt that puzzling sensation come over her—the way a heroine does when she's met the man of her dreams.

The weekend passed, and although Bailey spent most of her time working on the rewrite of *Forever Yours,* she couldn't stop picturing the disgruntled look on Parker's face as he walked off the subway car. It hurt her pride that he assumed she was a liar. Granted, introducing herself as Janice Hampton had been a lie, but after that, she'd told only the truth. She was sure he didn't believe a single word she'd said. Still, he intrigued her so much she spent a couple of precious hours on Saturday afternoon on the Internet, learning everything she could about him, which unfortunately wasn't much.

When Monday's lunch hour arrived, she headed directly for Parker's building. Showing up at his door should merit her an award for courage—or one for sheer stupidity.

"May I help you?" the receptionist asked when Bailey walked into the architectural firm's outer office. It was the same woman who'd helped her the week before. The nameplate on her desk read Roseanne Snyder. Bailey hadn't noticed it during her first visit.

"Would it be possible to see Mr. Davidson for just a few minutes?" she asked in her most businesslike voice, hoping the woman didn't recognize her.

Roseanne glanced down at the appointment calendar. "You're the gal who was in to see Mr. Davidson the first part of last week, aren't you?"

So much for keeping her identity a secret. "Yes." It was embarrassing to admit that. Bailey prayed Parker hadn't divulged the details of their encounter to the firm's receptionist.

"When I mentioned your name to Mr. Davidson, he didn't seem to remember your family."

"Uh… I wasn't sure he would," Bailey answered vaguely.

"If you'll give me your name again, I'll tell him you're here."

"Bailey. Bailey York," she said with a silent sigh of relief. Parker didn't know her real name; surely he wouldn't refuse to see her.

"Bailey York," the friendly woman repeated. "But aren't you—?" She paused, staring at her for a moment before she pressed the intercom button. After a quick exchange, she nodded, smiling tentatively. "Mr. Davidson said to go right in. His office is the last one on the left," she said, pointing the way.

The door was open and Parker sat at his desk, apparently engrossed in studying a set of blueprints. His office was impressive, with a wide sweeping view of the Golden Gate Bridge and Alcatraz Island. As she stood in the doorway, Parker glanced up. His smile faded when he recognized her.

"What are you doing here?"

"Proving I'm not a liar." With that, she strode into his office and slapped a package on his desk.

"What's that?" he asked.

"Proof."

# *Four*

Parker stared at the manuscript box as though he feared it was a time bomb set to explode at any moment.

"Go ahead and open it," Bailey said. When he didn't, she lifted the lid for him. Awkwardly she flipped through the first fifteen pages until she'd gathered up the first chapter, which she shoved into his hands. "Read it."

"Now?"

"Start with the header," she instructed, and then pointed to the printed line on the top right-hand side of each page.

"York... Forever Yours... Page one," he read aloud, slowly and hesitantly.

Bailey nodded. "Now move down to the text." She used her index finger to indicate where she wanted him to read.

"Chapter one. Janice Hampton had dreaded the business meeting for weeks. She was—"

"That's enough," Bailey muttered, ripping the pages out of his hands. "If you want to look through the rest of the manuscript, you're welcome to."

"Why would I want to do that?"

"So you no longer have the slightest doubt that I wrote it," she answered in a severe tone. "So you'll believe that I *am* a writer—and not a liar or a maniac. The purpose of this visit, though, why I find it necessary to prove I'm telling you the truth, isn't clear to me yet. It just seemed...important."

As she spoke, she scooped up the loose pages and stuffed them back into the manuscript box, closing it with enough force to crush the lid.

"I believed you before," Parker said casually, leaning back in his chair as if he'd never questioned her integrity. Or her sanity. "No one could've made up that story about being a romance writer and kept a straight face."

"But you—"

"What I didn't appreciate was the fact that you called yourself by a false name."

"You caught me off guard! I gave you the name of my heroine because...well, because I saw you as the hero."

"I see." He raised one eyebrow—definitely a hero-like mannerism, Bailey had to admit.

"I guess you didn't appreciate being followed around town, either," she said in a small voice.

"True enough," he agreed. "Take my advice, would you? The next time you want to research details about a man's life, hire a detective. You and your friend couldn't have been more obvious if you'd tried."

Bailey's ego had already taken one beating from this man, and she wasn't game for round two. "Don't worry, I've given up the chase. I've discovered there aren't any real heroes left in this world. I thought you might be one, but—" she shrugged elaborately "—alas, I was wrong."

"Ouch." Parker placed his hand over his heart as though her words had wounded him gravely. "I was just beginning to feel flattered. Then you had to go and ruin it."

"I know what I'm talking about when it comes to this hero business. They're extinct, except between the pages of women's fiction."

"Correct me if I'm wrong, but do I detect a note of bitterness?"

"I'm not bitter," Bailey denied vehemently. But she didn't mention the one slightly yellowed wedding dress hanging in her closet. She'd used her savings to pay for the elegant gown and been too mortified to return it unused. She tried to convince herself it was an investment, something that would gain value over the years, like gold. Or stocks. That was what she told herself, but deep down she knew better.

"I'm sorry to have intruded upon your busy day," she said, reaching for her manuscript. "I won't trouble you again."

"Do you object to my asking you a few questions before you go?" Parker asked, standing. He walked around to the front of his desk and leaned against it, crossing his ankles. "Writers have always fascinated me."

Bailey made a show of glancing at her watch. She had forty-five minutes left of her lunch hour; she supposed she could spare a few moments. "All right."

"How long did it take you to write *Forever and a Day?*"

*"Forever Yours,"* Bailey corrected. She suspected he was making fun of her. "Nearly six months, but I worked on it every night after work and on weekends. I felt like I'd completed a marathon when I finished." Bailey knew Janice and Michael were grateful, too. "Only I made a beginner's mistake."

"What's that?"

"I sent it off to a publisher."

"That's a mistake?"

Bailey nodded. "I should've had someone read it first, but I was too new to know that. It wasn't until later that I met Jo Ann and joined a writers' group."

Parker folded his arms across his broad chest. "I'm not sure I understand. Isn't having your work read by an editor the whole point? Why have someone else read it first?"

"Every manuscript needs a final polishing. It's important to put your best foot forward."

"I take it *Forever Yours* was rejected."

Bailey shook her head. "Not yet, but I'm fairly certain it will be. It's been about four months now, but meanwhile I've been working on revisions. And like Jo Ann says—no news is no news."

Parker arched his brows. "That's true."

"Well," she said, glancing at her watch again, but not because she was eager to leave. She felt foolish standing in the middle of Parker's plush office talking about her novel. Her guard was slipping and the desire to secure it firmly in place was growing stronger.

"I assume Jo Ann read the manuscript after you mailed it off?"

"Yes." Bailey punctuated her comment with a shrug. "She took it home and returned it the next morning with margin notes and a list of comments three pages long. When I read them over, I could see how right she was and, well, mainly the problem was with the hero."

"Michael?"

Bailey was surprised he remembered that. "Yes, with Michael. He's a terrific guy, but he needs a little help figuring out what women—in this case Janice Hampton—want."

"That's where I came in?"

"Right."

"How?"

Bailey made an effort to explain. "A hero, at least in romantic fiction, is determined, forceful and cool. When I saw you the first time, you gave the impression of being all three."

"Was that before or after I hit you in the head?"

"After."

Parker grinned. "Did you ever consider that my umbrella might have caused a temporary lack of, shall we say, good judgment? My guess is that you don't normally follow men around town, taking notes about their behavior, do you?"

"No, you were my first," she informed him coldly. This conversation was becoming downright irritating.

"I'm pleased to hear that," he said with a cocky grin.

"Perhaps you're right. Perhaps I *was* hit harder than I realized." Just when she was beginning to feel reasonably comfortable around Parker, he'd do or say something to remind her that he was indeed a mere mortal. Any effort to base Michael's personality on his would only be a waste of time.

Bailey clutched her manuscript to her chest. "I really have to go now. I apologize for the intrusion."

"It's fine. I found our discussion…interesting."

No doubt he had. But it didn't help Bailey's dignity to know she was a source of amusement to one of the city's most distinguished architects.

"What else did he say?" Jo Ann asked early the following morning as they sat side by side on the crowded subway car.

Even before Bailey could answer, Jo Ann asked another question. "Did you get a chance to tell him that little joke about your story having a beginning, a *muddle* and an end?"

Jo Ann's reaction had surprised her. When Bailey admitted confronting Parker with her completed manuscript, Jo Ann had been enthusiastic, even excited. Bailey had supposed that her friend wouldn't understand her need to see Parker and correct his opinion of her. Instead, Jo Ann had been approving—and full of questions.

"I didn't have time to tell Parker any jokes," Bailey answered. "Good grief, I was only in his office, I don't know, maybe ten minutes."

"Ten minutes! A lot can happen in ten minutes."

Bailey crossed her long legs and prayed silently for patience. "Believe me, nothing happened. I accomplished what I set out to prove. That's it."

"If you were in there a full ten minutes, surely the two of you talked."

"He had a few questions about the business of writing."

"I see." Jo Ann nodded slowly. "So what did you tell him?"

Bailey didn't want to think about her visit with Parker. Not again. She'd returned from work that afternoon and, as was her habit, went directly to her computer. Usually she couldn't wait to get home to write. But that afternoon, she'd sat there, her hands poised on the keys, and instead of composing witty sparkling dialogue for Michael and Janice, she'd reviewed every word of her conversation with Parker.

He'd been friendly, cordial. And he'd actually sounded interested—when he wasn't busy being amused. Bailey hadn't expected that. What she'd expected was outright rejection. She'd come prepared to talk to a stone wall.

Michael, the first time around, had been like that. Gruff and unyielding. Poor Janice had been in the dark about his feelings from page one. It was as though her hero feared that revealing emotion was a sign of weakness.

In the second version Michael was so…amiable, so pleasant, that any conflict in the story had been watered down almost to nonexistence.

"As you might have guessed," Jo Ann said, breaking into her thoughts, "I like Parker Davidson. You were right when you claimed he's hero material. You'll have to forgive me for doubting you. It's just that I've never followed a man around before."

"You like Parker?" Bailey's musing about Michael and his shifting personality came to a sudden halt. 'You're married," Bailey felt obliged to remind her.

"I'm not interested in him for *me,* silly," Jo Ann said, playfully nudging Bailey with her elbow. "He's all yours."

"Mine!" Bailey couldn't believe what she was hearing. "You're nuts."

"No, I'm not. He's tall, dark and handsome, and we both know how perfect that makes him for a classic romance. And the way you zeroed in on Parker the instant you saw him proves he's got the compelling presence a hero needs."

"The only *presence* I noticed was his umbrella's! He nearly decapitated me with the thing."

"You know what I think?" Jo Ann murmured, nibbling on her bottom lip. "I think that something inside you, some innate sonar device, was in action. You're hungering to find Michael. Deep within your subconscious you're seeking love and romance."

"Wrong!" Bailey declared adamantly. "You couldn't be more off course. Writing and selling a romance are my top priorities right now. I'm not interested in love, not for myself."

"What about Janice?"

The question was unfair and Bailey knew it. So much of her own personality was invested in her heroine.

The train finally reached their station, and Bailey and Jo Ann stood up and made their way toward the exit.

"Well?" Jo Ann pressed, clearly unwilling to drop the subject.

"I'm not answering that and you know why," Bailey said, stepping onto the platform. "Now kindly get off this subject. I doubt I'll ever see Parker Davidson again, and if I do I'll ignore him just the way he'll ignore me."

"You're sure of that?"

"Absolutely positive."

"Then why do you suppose he's waiting for you? That *is* Parker Davidson, isn't it?"

Bailey closed her eyes and struggled to gather her wits. Part of her was hoping against hope that Parker would saunter past without giving either of them a second's notice. But another part of her, a deep womanly part, hoped he was doing exactly what Jo Ann suggested.

"Good morning, ladies," Parker said to them as he approached.

"Hello," Bailey returned, suspecting she sounded in need of a voice-box transplant.

"Good morning!" Jo Ann said with enough enthusiasm to make up for Bailey's sorry lack.

Parker bestowed a dazzling smile on them. Bailey

felt the impact of it as profoundly as if he'd bent down and brushed his mouth over hers. She quickly shook her head to dispel the image.

"I considered our conversation," he said, directing his remark to Bailey. "Since you're having so many problems with your hero, I decided I might be able to help you, after all."

"Is that right?" Bailey knew she was coming across as defensive, but she couldn't seem to help it.

Parker nodded. "I assume you decided to follow me that day to learn pertinent details about my habits, personality and so on. How about if the two of us sit down over lunch and you just ask me what you want to know?"

Bailey recognized a gift horse when she saw one. Excitement welled up inside her; nevertheless she hesitated. This man was beginning to consume her thoughts already, and she'd be asking for trouble if she allowed it to continue.

"Would you have time this afternoon?"

"She's got time," Jo Ann said without missing a beat. "Bailey works as a paralegal and she can see you during her lunch hour. This afternoon would be perfect."

Bailey glared at her friend, resisting the urge to suggest *she* have lunch with Parker since she was so keen on the idea.

"Bailey?" Parker asked, turning his attention to her.

"I...suppose." She didn't sound very gracious, and the look Jo Ann flashed her told her as much. "This is, um, very generous of you, Mr. Davidson."

"Mr. Davidson?" Parker said. "I thought we were long past being formal with each other." He dazzled her with another smile. It had the same effect on Bailey as before, weakening her knees—and her resolve.

"Shall we say noon, then?" Parker asked. "I'll meet you on Fisherman's Wharf at the Sandpiper."

The Sandpiper was known for its wonderful seafood, along with its exorbitant prices. Parker might be able to afford to eat there, but it was far beyond Bailey's meager budget.

"The Sandpiper?" she repeated. "I... I was thinking we could pick up something quick and eat on the wharf. There are several park benches along Pier 39..."

Parker frowned. "I'd prefer the Sandpiper. I'm doing some work for them, and it's good business practice to return the favor."

"Don't worry, she'll meet you there," Jo Ann assured Parker.

Bailey couldn't allow her friend to continue speaking for her. "Jo Ann, if you don't mind, I'll answer for myself."

"Oh, sure. Sorry."

Parker returned his attention to Bailey, who inhaled sharply and nodded. "I can meet you there." Of course it would mean packing lunches for the next two weeks and cutting back on Max's expensive tastes in gourmet cat food, but she supposed that was a small sacrifice.

Parker was waiting for Bailey when she arrived at the Sandpiper at a few minutes after noon. He stood when the maitre d' ushered her to his table. The room's lighting, its thick dark red carpet and rich wood created a sense of intimacy and warmth that appealed to Bailey despite her nervousness.

She'd been inside the Sandpiper only once before, with her parents when they were visiting from Oregon. Her father had wanted to treat her to the best restaurant in town, and Bailey had chosen the Sandpiper, renowned for its elegance and its fresh seafood.

"We meet again," Parker said, raising one eyebrow—that hero quirk again—as he held out her chair.

"Yes. It's very nice of you to do this."

"No problem." The waiter appeared with menus. Bailey didn't need to look; she already knew what she wanted. The seafood Caesar salad, piled high with shrimp, crab and scallops. She'd had it on her last visit and thoroughly enjoyed every bite. Parker ordered sautéed scallops and a salad. He suggested a bottle of wine, but Bailey declined. She needed to remain completely alert for this interview, so she requested coffee instead. Parker asked for the same.

After they'd placed their order, Bailey took a pen and pad from her purse, along with her reading glasses. She had a list of questions prepared. "Do you mind if we get started?"

"Sure," Parker said, leaning forward. He propped his elbows on the table and stared at her intently. "How old are you, Bailey? Twenty-one, twenty-two?"

"Twenty-seven."

He nodded, but was obviously surprised. "According to Jo Ann you work as a paralegal."

"Yes." She paused. "You'll have to excuse Jo Ann. She's a romantic."

"That's what she said about *you*—that you're a romantic."

"Yes, well, I certainly hope it works to her advantage *and* to mine."

"Oh?" His eyebrows lifted.

"We're both striving to becoming published novelists. It takes a lot more than talent, you know."

Hot crisp sourdough rolls were delivered to the table and Bailey immediately reached for one.

"The writer has to have a feel for the genre," she continued. "For Jo Ann and me, that means writing from the heart. I've only been at this for a few months, but there are several women in our writers' group who've been submitting their work for five or six years without getting published. Most of them are pragmatic about it. There are plenty of small successes we learn to count along the way."

"Such as?"

Bailey swallowed before answering. "Finishing a manuscript. There's a real feeling of accomplishment in completing a story."

"I see."

"Some people come into the group thinking they're going to make a fast buck. They think anyone should be able to throw together a romance. Generally they attend a couple of meetings, then decide writing is too hard, too much effort."

"What about you?"

"I'm in this for the long haul. Eventually I will sell because I won't stop submitting stories until I do. My dad claims I'm like a pit bull when I want something. I clamp on and refuse to let go. That's how I feel about writing. I'm going to succeed at this if it's the last thing I ever do."

"Have you always wanted to be a writer?" Parker helped himself to a roll.

"No. I wasn't even on my high-school newspaper, although now I wish I had been. I might not have so much trouble with sentence structure and punctuation if I'd paid more attention back then."

"Then what made you decide to write romances?"

"Because I read them. In fact, I've been reading romances from the time I was in college, but it's only been in the past year or so that I started creating my own. Meeting Jo Ann was a big boost for me. I might have gone on making the same mistakes for years if it wasn't for her. She encouraged me, introduced me to other writers and took me under her wing."

The waiter arrived with their meals and Bailey sheepishly realized that she'd been doing all the talking. She had yet to ask Parker a single question.

The seafood Caesar salad was as good as Bailey remembered. After one bite she decided to treat herself like this more often. An expensive lunch every month or so wouldn't sabotage her budget.

"You were telling me it only took you six months to write *Forever Yours*," Parker commented between forkfuls of his salad. "Doesn't it usually take much longer for a first book?"

"I'm sure it does, but I devoted every spare minute to the project."

"I see. What about your social life?"

It was all Bailey could do not to snicker. What social life? She'd lived in San Francisco for more than a year, and this lunch with Parker was as close as she'd gotten to a real date. Which was exactly how she wanted it, she reminded herself.

"Bailey?"

"Oh, I get out occasionally," but she didn't mention that it was always with women friends. Since her second broken engagement, Bailey had given up on the opposite sex. Twice she'd been painfully forced to accept that men were not to be trusted. After fifteen months, Tom's deception still hurt.

Getting over Tom might not have been so difficult if it hadn't been for Paul. She'd been in love with him, too, in her junior year at college. But like Tom, he'd found someone else he loved more than he did her. The pattern just kept repeating itself, so Bailey, in her own sensible way, had put an end to it. She no longer dated.

There were times she regretted her decision. This afternoon was an excellent example. She could easily find herself becoming romantically interested in Parker. She wouldn't, of course, but the temptation was there.

Parker with his coffee-dark eyes and his devastating smile. Fortunately Bailey was wise to the fickle hearts of men. Of one thing she was sure: Parker Davidson hadn't reached his mid-thirties, still single, without breaking a few hearts along the way.

There were other times she regretted her decision to give up on dating. No men equaled no marriage. And no children. It was the children part that troubled her most, especially when she was around babies. Her decision hit her hard then. Without a husband she wasn't likely to have a child of her own, since she wasn't interested in being a single mother. But so far, all she had to do was avoid places where she'd run into mothers and infants. Out of sight, out of mind....

"Bailey?"

"I'm sorry," she mumbled, suddenly aware that she'd allowed her thoughts to run unchecked for several minutes. "Did I miss something?"

"No. You had a...pained look and I was wondering if your salad was all right?"

"Yes. It's wonderful. As fantastic as I remember."

She briefly relayed the story of her parents treating her to dinner at the Sandpiper. What she didn't explain was that their trip south had been made for the express purpose of checking up on Bailey. Her parents were worried about her. They insisted she worked too hard, didn't get out enough, didn't socialize.

Bailey had listened politely to their concerns and then hugged them both, thanked them for their love and sent them back to Oregon.

Spotting her pad and pen lying beside her plate, Bailey sighed. She hadn't questioned Parker once, which was the whole point of their meeting. Glancing at her watch, she groaned inwardly. She only had another fifteen minutes. It wasn't worth the effort of getting started. Not when she'd just have to stop.

"I need to get back to the office," she announced regretfully. She looked around for the waiter so she could ask for her check.

"It's been taken care of."

It took Bailey a moment to realize that Parker was talking about her meal. "I can't let you do that," she insisted, reaching for her purse.

"Please."

If he'd argued with her, shoveled out some chauvinistic challenge, Bailey would never have allowed him to pay. But that one word, that one softly spoken word, was her undoing.

"All right," she agreed, her own voice just as soft.

"You didn't get a chance to ask your questions."

"I know." She found that frustrating, but had no one to blame but herself. "I got caught up talking about romance fiction and writing and—"

"Shall we try again? Another time?"

"It looks like we'll have to." She needed to be careful that lunch with Parker didn't develop into a habit.

"I'm free tomorrow evening."

"Evening?" Somehow that seemed far more threatening than meeting for lunch. "Uh… I generally reserve the hours after work for writing."

"I see."

Her heart reacted to the hint of disappointment in his voice. "I might be able to make an exception." Bailey was horrified as soon as the words were out. She couldn't believe she'd said that. For the entire hour, she'd been lecturing herself about the dangers of getting close to Parker. "No," she said firmly. "It's crucial that I maintain my writing schedule."

"You're sure?"

"Positive."

Parker took a business card from his coat pocket. He scribbled on the back and handed it to her. "This is my home number in case you change your mind."

Bailey accepted the card and thrust it into her purse, together with her notepad and pen. "I really have to write… I mean, my writing schedule is important to me. I can't be running out to dinner just because someone asks me." She stood, scraping back her chair in her eagerness to escape.

"Consider it research."

Bailey responded by shaking her head. "Thank you for lunch."

"You're most welcome. But I hope you'll reconsider having dinner with me."

She backed away from the table, her purse held tightly in both hands. "Dinner?" she echoed, still undecided.

"For the purposes of research," he added.

"It wouldn't be a *date*." It was important to make that point clear. The only man she had time for was Michael. But Parker was supposed to help her with Michael, so maybe… "Not a date, just research," she repeated in a more determined voice. "Agreed?"

He grinned, his eyes lighting mischievously. "What do you think?"

# Five

Max was waiting at the door when Bailey got home from work that evening. His striped yellow tail pointed straight toward the ceiling as he twisted and turned between her legs. His not-so-subtle message was designed to remind her it was mealtime.

"Just a minute, Maxie," she muttered. She leafed through the mail as she walked into the kitchen, pausing when she found a yellow slip.

"Meow."

"Max, look," she said, waving the note at him. "Mrs. Morgan's holding a package for us." The apartment manager was always kind enough to accept deliveries, saving Bailey more than one trip to the post office.

Leaving a disgruntled Max behind, Bailey hurried down the stairs to Mrs. Morgan's first-floor apartment, where she was greeted with a warm smile. Mrs. Morgan was an older woman, a matronly widow who seemed especially protective of her younger tenants.

"Here you go, dear," she said, handing Bailey a large manila envelope.

Bailey knew the instant she saw the package that this

wasn't an unexpected surprise from her parents. It was her manuscript—rejected.

"Thank you," she said, struggling to disguise her disappointment. From the moment Bailey had read Jo Ann's critique she'd realized *Forever Yours* would probably be rejected. What she hadn't foreseen was this stomach-churning sensation, this feeling of total discouragement. Koppen Publishing had kept the manuscript for nearly four months. Jo Ann had insisted no news was no news, and so Bailey had begun to believe that the editor had held on to her book for so long because she'd seriously considered buying it.

Bailey had fully expected that she'd have to revise her manuscript; nonetheless, she'd *hoped* to be doing it with a contract in her pocket, riding high on success.

Once again Max was waiting by the door, more impatient this time. Without thinking, Bailey walked into the kitchen, opened the refrigerator and dumped food into his bowl. It wasn't until she straightened that she realized she'd given her greedy cat the dinner she was planning to cook for herself.

No fool, Max dug into the ground turkey, edging his way between her legs in his eagerness. Bailey shrugged. The way she was feeling, she didn't have much of an appetite, anyway.

It took her another five minutes to find the courage to open the package. She carefully pried apart the seam. Why she was being so careful, she couldn't even guess. She had no intention of reusing the envelope. Once the padding was separated, she removed the manuscript box. Inside was a short letter that she quickly read, swallowing down the emotion that clogged her throat. The fact that the letter was personal, and not simply a standard

*Debbie Macomber*

rejection letter, did little to relieve the crushing disappointment.

Reaching for the phone, Bailey punched out Jo Ann's number. Her friend had experienced this more than once and was sure to have some words of wisdom to help Bailey through this moment. Jo Ann would understand how badly her confidence had been shaken.

After four rings, Bailey was connected to her friend's answering machine. She listened to the message, but didn't want to leave Jo Ann such a disheartening message, so she mumbled, "It's Bailey," and hung up.

Pacing the apartment in an effort to sort out her emotions didn't seem to help. She eyed her computer, which was set up in a corner of her compact living room, but the desire to sit down and start writing was nil. Vanished. Destroyed.

Jo Ann had warned her. So had others in their writers' group. Rejections hurt. She just hadn't expected it to hurt so much.

Searching in her purse for a mint, she felt her fingers close around a business card. *Parker's* business card. She slowly drew it out. He'd written down his phone number....

Should she call him? No, she decided, thrusting the card into her pocket. Why even entertain the notion? Talking to Parker now would be foolish. And risky. She was a big girl. She could take rejection. Anyone who became a writer had to learn how to handle rejection.

Rejections were rungs on the ladder of success. Someone had said that at a meeting once, and Bailey had written it down and kept it posted on the bottom edge of her computer screen. Now was the time to act on that belief. Since this was only the first rung, she had a long way to climb, but the darn ladder was much steeper than she'd anticipated.

With a fumbling resolve, she returned to the kitchen and reread the letter from Paula Albright, the editor, who wrote that she was returning the manuscript "with regret."

"Not as much regret as I feel," Bailey informed Max, who was busy enjoying *her* dinner.

"She says I show promise." But Bailey noted that she didn't say promise of what.

The major difficulty, according to the editor, was Michael. This wasn't exactly a surprise to Bailey. Ms. Albright had kindly mentioned several scenes that needed to be reworked with this problem in mind. She ended her letter by telling Bailey that if she revised the manuscript, the editorial department would be pleased to reevaluate it.

Funny, Bailey hadn't even noticed that the first time she'd read the letter. If she reworked Michael, there was still a chance.

With sudden enthusiasm, Bailey grabbed the phone. She'd changed her mind—calling Parker now seemed like a good idea. A great idea. He might well be her one and only chance to straighten out poor misguided Michael.

Parker answered on the second ring, sounding distracted and mildly irritated at being interrupted.

"Parker," Bailey said, desperately hoping she wasn't making a first-class fool of herself, "this is Bailey York."

"Hello." His tone was a little less disgruntled.

Her mouth had gone completely dry, but she rushed ahead with the reason for her call. "I want you to know I've… I've been thinking about your dinner invitation. Could you possibly meet me tonight instead of tomorrow?" She wanted to start rehabilitating Michael as soon as possible.

"This is Bailey York?" He sounded as though he didn't remember who she was.

"The writer from the subway," she said pointedly, feeling like more of an idiot with every passing second. She should never have phoned him, but the impulse had been so powerful. She longed to put this rejection behind her and write a stronger romance, but she was going to need his help. Perhaps she should call him later. "Listen, if now is inconvenient, I could call another time." She was about to hang up when Parker spoke.

"Now is fine. I'm sorry if I seem rattled, but I was working and I tend to get absorbed in a project."

"I do that myself," she said, reassured by his explanation. Drawing a deep breath, she explained the reason for her unexpected call. "*Forever Yours* was rejected today."

"I'm sorry to hear that." His regret seemed genuine, and the soft fluttering sensation returned to her stomach at the sympathy he extended.

"I was sorry, too, but it didn't come as a big shock. I guess I let my hopes build when the manuscript wasn't immediately returned, which is something Jo Ann warned me about." She shifted the receiver to her other ear, surprised by how much better she felt having someone to talk to.

"What happens when a publisher turns down a manuscript? Do they critique the book?"

"Heavens, no. Generally manuscripts are returned with a standard rejection letter. The fact that the editor took the time to personally write me about revising is sort of a compliment. Actually, it's an excellent sign. Especially since she's willing to look at *Forever Yours* again." Bailey paused and inhaled shakily. "I was wondering if I could take you up on that offer for dinner. I realize this is rather sudden and I probably shouldn't have phoned, but tonight would be best for me since…since I inadvertently gave Max my ground turkey and there's really nothing else in the fridge, but if you can't I understand…." The words had tumbled out in a nervous rush; once she'd started, she couldn't seem to make herself stop.

"Do you want me to pick you up, or would you rather meet somewhere?"

"Ah…" Despite herself, Bailey was astounded. She hadn't really expected Parker to agree. "The restaurant where you had lunch a couple of weeks ago looked good. Only, please, I insist on paying for my own meal this time."

"In Chinatown?"

"Yes. Would you meet me there?"

"Sure. Does an hour give you enough time?"

"Oh, yes. An hour's plenty." Once again Bailey found herself nearly tongue-tied with surprise—and pleasure.

Their conversation was over so fast that she was left staring at the phone, half wondering if it had really happened at all. She took a couple of deep breaths, then dashed into her bedroom to change, renew her makeup and brush her hair.

Bailey loved Chinese food, especially the spicy Szechuan dishes, but she wasn't thinking about dinner as the taxi pulled up in front of the restaurant. She'd decided to indulge herself by taking a cab to Chinatown. It did mean she'd have to take the subway home, though.

Parker, who was standing outside the restaurant waiting for her, hurried forward to open the cab door. Bailey was terribly aware of his hand supporting her elbow as he helped her out.

"It's good of you to meet me like this on such short notice," she said, smiling up at Parker.

"No problem. Who's Max?"

"My cat."

Parker grinned and, clasping her elbow more firmly, led her into the restaurant. The first thing that caught Bailey's attention was a gigantic, intricately carved chandelier made of dark polished wood. She'd barely had a chance to examine it, however, when they were escorted down a long hallway to a narrow room filled with wooden booths, high-backed and private, each almost a little room of its own.

"Oh, my, this is nice," she breathed, sliding into their booth. She slipped the bag from her shoulder and withdrew the same pen and notepad she'd brought with her when they'd met for lunch.

The waiter appeared with a lovely ceramic teapot and a pair of tiny matching cups. The menus were tucked under his arm.

Bailey didn't have nearly as easy a time making her choice as she had at the Sandpiper. Parker suggested they each order whatever they wished and then share. There were so many dishes offered, most of them sounding delectable and exciting, that it took Bailey a good ten minutes to make her selection—spicy shrimp noodles. Parker chose the less adventurous almond chicken stir-fry.

"All right," Bailey said, pouring them each some tea. "Now let's get down to business."

"Sure." Parker relaxed against the back of the booth, crossing his arms and stretching out his legs. "Ask away," he said, motioning with his hand when she hesitated.

"Maybe I'd better start by giving you a brief outline of the story."

"However you'd like to do this."

"I want you to understand Michael," she explained. "He's a businessman, born on the wrong side of the tracks. He's a little bitter, but he's learned to forgive those who've hurt him through the years. Michael's in his mid-thirties, and he's never been married."

"Why not?"

"Well, for one thing he's been too busy building his career."

"As what?"

"He's in the exporting business."

"I see."

"You're frowning." Bailey hadn't asked a single one of her prepared questions yet, and already Parker was looking annoyed.

"It's just that a man doesn't generally reach the ripe old age of thirty-five without a relationship or two. If he's never had any, then there's a problem."

"You're thirty-something and you're not married," she felt obliged to point out. "What's your excuse?"

Parker shrugged. "My college schedule was very heavy, which didn't leave a lot of time for dating. Later I traveled extensively, which again didn't offer much opportunity. Oh, there were relationships along the way, but nothing ever worked out. I guess you could say I haven't found the right woman. But that doesn't mean I'm not interested in marrying and settling down some day."

"Exactly. That's how Michael feels, except he thinks getting married would only complicate his life. He's ready to fall in love with Janice, but he doesn't realize it."

"I see," Parker said with a nod, "go on. I shouldn't have interrupted you."

"Well, basically, Michael's life is going smoothly until he meets Janice Hampton. Her father has retired and she's taking over the operation of his manufacturing firm. A job she's well qualified for, I might add."

"What does she manufacture?"

"I was rather vague about that, but I let the reader assume it has something to do with computer parts. I tossed in a word here and there to give that suggestion."

Parker nodded. "Continue. I'll try not to butt in again."

"That's okay," she said briskly. "Anyway, Janice's father is a longtime admirer of Michael's, and the old coot would like to get his daughter and Michael together. Neither one of them's aware of it, of course. At least not right away."

Parker reached for the teapot and refilled their cups. "That sounds good."

Bailey smiled shyly. "Thanks. One of the first things that happens is Janice's father maneuvers Michael and Janice under the mistletoe at a Christmas party. Everyone's expecting them to kiss, but Michael is furious and he—"

"Just a minute." Parker held up one hand, stopping her. "Let me see if I've got this straight. This guy is standing under the mistletoe with a beautiful woman and he's furious. What's wrong with him?"

"What do you mean?"

"No man in his right mind is going to object to kissing a beautiful woman."

Bailey picked up her teacup and leaned against the hard back of the wooden booth, considering. Parker was right. And Janice hadn't been too happy about the situation herself. Was that any more believable? Imagine standing under the mistletoe with a man like Parker Davidson. Guiltily she shook off the thought and returned her attention to his words.

"Unless…" he was saying pensively.

"Yes?"

"Unless he recognizes that he was manipulated into kissing her and resents it. He may even think she's in cahoots with her father."

Brightening, Bailey nodded, making a note on her pad. "Yeah, that would work." Parker was as good at tossing ideas around as Jo Ann, which was a pleasant surprise.

"Still…" He hesitated, sighing. "A pretty woman is a pretty woman and he isn't going to object too strongly, regardless of the circumstances. What happens when he does kiss her?"

"Not too much. He does it grudgingly, but I've decided I'm going to change that part. You're right. He shouldn't make too much of a fuss. However, this happens early on in the book and neither of them's aware of her father's scheme. I don't want to tip the reader off so soon as to what's happening."

Bailey's mind was spinning as she reworked the scene. She could picture Michael and Janice standing under the mistletoe, both somewhat uneasy with the situation, but as Parker suggested, not objecting too strongly. Janice figures they'll kiss, and that'll be the end of it… until they actually do the kissing.

That was the part Bailey intended to build on. When Michael's and Janice's lips met it would be like…like throwing a match on dry tinder, so intense would be the reaction.

The idea began to gather momentum in her mind. Then, not only would Janice and Michael be fighting her father's outrageous plot, they'd be battling their feelings for each other.

"This is great," Bailey whispered, "really great." She

started to tell Parker her plan when they were interrupted by the waiter who brought their dinner, setting the steaming dishes before them.

By then, Bailey's appetite had fully recovered and she reached eagerly for the chopsticks. Parker picked up his own. They both reached for the shrimp noodles. Bailey withdrew her chopsticks.

"You first."

"No, you." He waved his hand, encouraging her.

She smiled and scooped up a portion of the noodles. The situation felt somehow intimate, comfortable, and yet they were still basically strangers.

They ate in silence for several minutes and Bailey watched Parker deftly manipulate the chopsticks. It was the first time she'd dated a man who was as skilled at handling them as she was herself.

*Dated a man.*

The words leapt out at her. Bright red warning signs seemed to be flashing in her mind. Her head shot up and she stared wide-eyed at the man across the table from her.

"Bailey? Are you all right?"

She nodded and hurriedly looked away.

"Did you bite into a hot pepper?"

"No," she assured him, quickly shaking her head. "I'm fine. Really, I'm all right." Only she wasn't, and she suspected he knew it.

The remainder of their meal passed with few comments.

Naturally Parker had no way of knowing about her experiences with Paul and Tom. Nor would he be aware that there was an unused wedding dress hanging in her closet, taunting her every morning when she got ready for work. The wedding gown was an ever-present reminder of why she couldn't put any faith in the male of the species.

The danger came when she allowed her guard to slip. Before she knew it, she'd be trusting a man once again, and that was a definite mistake. Parker made her feel somehow secure; she felt instinctively that he was a man of integrity, of candor—and therein lay the real risk. Maybe he *was* a real live breathing hero, but Bailey had been fooled twice before. She wasn't going to put her heart on the line again.

They split the tab. Parker clearly wasn't pleased about that, but Bailey insisted. They were about to leave the restaurant when Parker said, "You started to say something about rewriting that scene under the mistletoe."

"Yes," she answered, regaining some of her former enthusiasm. "I'm going to have that kiss make a dynamite impact on them both. Your suggestions were very helpful. I can't tell you how much I appreciate your willingness to meet with me like this."

It was as though Parker hadn't heard her. His forehead creased as he held open the door for her and they stepped onto the busy sidewalk.

"You're frowning again," Bailey noted aloud.

"Have you ever experienced that kind of intense sensation when a man kissed you?"

Bailey didn't have to think about it. "Not really."

"That's what I thought."

"But I like the idea of that happening between Janice and Michael," she argued. "It adds a whole new dimension to the plot. I can use that. Besides, there's a certain element of fantasy in a traditional romance novel, a larger-than-life perspective."

"Oh, I'm not saying a strong reaction between them shouldn't happen. I'm just wondering how you plan to write such a powerfully emotional scene without any real experience of it yourself."

"That's the mark of a good writer," Bailey explained, ignoring his less-than-flattering remark. She'd been kissed before! Plenty of times. "Being able to create an atmosphere of romance just takes imagination. You don't expect me to go around kissing strange men, do you?"

"Why not? You had no qualms about *following* a strange man. Kissing me wouldn't be any different. It's all research."

"Kissing you?"

"It'll add credibility to your writing. A confidence you might not otherwise have."

"If I were writing a murder mystery would you suggest I go out and kill someone?" Bailey had to argue with him before she found herself *agreeing* to this craziness!

"Don't be ridiculous! Murder would be out of the question, but a kiss…a kiss is very much within your grasp. It would lend authenticity to your story. I suggest we go ahead with it, Bailey."

They were strolling side by side. Bailey was deep in thought when Parker casually turned into a narrow alley. She guessed it was the same one he'd hauled her into the day she'd followed him.

"Well," he said, resting his hands on her shoulders and staring down at her. "Are you game?"

Was she? Bailey didn't know anymore. He was right; the scene would have far more impact if she were to experience the same sensations as Janice. Kissing Parker would be like Janice kissing Michael. The sale of her book could hinge on how well she developed the attraction between hero and heroine in that all-important first chapter.

"Okay," she said, barely recognizing her own voice.

No sooner had she spoken than Parker gently cupped her chin and directed her mouth toward his. "This is going to be good," she heard him whisper just before his lips settled over hers.

Bailey's eyes drifted shut. This *was* good. In fact, it was wonderful. So wonderful, she felt weak and dizzy—and yearned to feel even weaker and dizzier. Despite herself, she clung to Parker, literally hanging in his arms. Without his support, she feared she would have slumped to the street.

He tasted so warm and familiar, as if she'd spent a lifetime in his arms, as if she were *meant* to spend a lifetime there.

The fluttering sensation in her stomach changed to a warm heaviness. She felt strange and hot. Bailey was afraid that if this didn't end soon, she'd completely lose control.

"No more," she pleaded, breaking off the kiss. She buried her face in his shoulder and dragged in several deep breaths in an effort to stop her trembling.

It wasn't fair that Parker could make her feel this way. For Janice and Michael's sake, it was the best thing that could have happened, but for her own sake, it was the worst. She didn't *want* to feel any of this. The protective numbness around her heart was crumbling just when it was so important to keep it securely in place.

The hot touch of his lips against her temple caused her to jump away from him. "Well," she said, rubbing her palms briskly together once she found her voice. "That was certainly a step in the right direction."

"I beg your pardon?" Parker was staring at her as though he wasn't sure he'd heard her accurately.

"The kiss. It had pizzazz and a certain amount of charm, but I was looking for a little more…something. The kiss between Michael and Janice has got to have spark."

"Our kiss had spark." Parker's voice was deep, brooding.

"Charm," she corrected, then added brightly, "I will say one thing, though. You're good at this. Lots of practice, right?" Playfully she poked his ribs with her elbow. "Well, I've got to be going. Thanks again for meeting me on such short notice. I'll be seeing you around." Amazingly the smile on her lips didn't crack. Even more amazing was the fact that she managed to walk away from him on legs that felt like overcooked pasta.

She was about five blocks from the BART station, walking as fast as she could, mumbling to herself all the way. She behaved like an idiot every time she even came near Parker Davidson!

She continued mumbling, chastising herself, when he pulled up at the curb beside her in a white sports car. She didn't know much about cars, but she knew expensive when she saw it. The same way she knew his suit hadn't come from a department store.

"Get in," he said gruffly, slowing to a stop and leaning over to open the passenger door.

"Get in?" she repeated. "I was going to take BART."

"Not at this time of night you're not."

"Why shouldn't I?" she demanded.

"Don't press your luck, Bailey. Just get in."

She debated whether she should or not, but from the stubborn set of his jaw, she could see it would do no good to argue. She'd never seen a more obstinate-looking jaw in her life. As she recalled, it was one of the first things she'd noticed about Parker.

"What's your address?" he asked after she'd slipped inside.

Bailey gave it to him as she fiddled with the seat belt, then sat silently while he sped down the street, weaving his way in and out of traffic. He braked sharply at a red light and she glanced in his direction.

"Why are you so angry?" she demanded. "You look as if you're ready to bite my head off."

"I don't like it when a woman lies to me."

"When did I lie?" she asked indignantly.

"You lied a few minutes ago when you said our kiss was…lacking." He laughed humorlessly and shook his head. "We generated more electricity with that one kiss than the Hoover Dam does in a month. You want to kid yourself, then fine, but I'm not playing your game."

"I'm not playing any game," she informed him primly. "Nor do I appreciate having you come at me like King Kong because my assessment of a personal exchange between us doesn't meet yours."

"A personal exchange?" he scoffed. "It was a kiss, sweetheart."

"I only agreed to it for research purposes."

"If that's what you want to believe, fine, but we both know better."

"Whatever," she muttered. Parker could think what he wanted. She'd let him drive her home because he seemed to be insisting on it. But as far as having anything further to do with him—out of the question. He was obviously placing far more significance on their kiss than she'd ever intended.

Okay, so she *had* felt something. But to hear him tell it, that kiss rivaled the great screen kisses of all time.

Parker drove up in front of her apartment building and turned off the engine. "All right," he said coolly. "Let's go over this one last time. Do you still claim our kiss was merely a 'personal exchange'? Just research?"

"Yes," she stated emphatically, unwilling to budge an inch.

"Then prove it."

Bailey sighed. "How exactly am I supposed to do that?"

"Kiss me again."

Bailey could feel the color drain out of her face. "I'm not about to sit outside my apartment kissing you with half the building looking on."

"Fine, then invite me in."

"Uh…it's late."

"Since when is nine o'clock late?" he taunted.

Bailey was running out of excuses. "There's nothing that says a woman is obligated to invite a man into her home, is there?" she asked in formal tones. Her spine was Sunday-school straight and her eyes were focused on the street ahead of her.

Parker's laugh took her by surprise. She twisted around to stare at him and found him smiling roguishly. "You little coward," he murmured, pulling her toward him for a quick peck on the cheek. "Go on. Run home before I change my mind."

# Six

"I like it," Jo Ann said. "The way you changed that first kissing scene under the mistletoe is a stroke of genius." She smiled happily. "This is exactly the kind of rewriting you'll need to turn that rejection into a sale. You've taken Michael and made him proud and passionate, but very real and spontaneous. He's caught off guard by his attraction to Janice and is reacting purely by instinct." Jo Ann tapped her fingers on the top page of the revised first chapter. "This is your most powerful writing yet."

Bailey was so pleased she could barely restrain herself from leaping up and dancing a jig down the center of the congested subway-car aisle. Through sheer determination, she managed to confine her response to a smile.

"It's interesting how coming at this scene from a slightly different angle puts everything in a new light, isn't it?"

"It sure is," Jo Ann concurred. "If the rest of the book reads as well as this chapter, I honestly think you might have a chance."

It was too much to hope for. Bailey had spent the entire weekend in front of her computer. She must have rewritten the mistletoe scene no less than ten times, strengthening emotions, exploring the heady response Michael and Janice had toward each other. She'd worked hard to capture the incredulity they'd experienced, the shock of their unexpected fascination. Naturally, neither one could allow the other to know what they were feeling yet—otherwise Bailey wouldn't have any plot.

Michael had been dark and brooding afterward. Janice had done emotional cartwheels in an effort to diminish the incident. But neither of them could forget it.

If the unable-to-forget part seemed particularly realistic, there was a reason. Bailey's reaction to Parker had been scandalously similar to Janice's feelings about Michael's kiss. The incredulity was there. The wonder. The shock. And it never should have happened.

Unfortunately Bailey had suspected that even before she'd agreed to the "research." Who did she think she was fooling? Certainly not herself. She'd wanted Parker to kiss her long before he'd offered her the excuse.

Halfway through their dinner, Bailey had experienced all the symptoms. She knew them well. The palpitating heart, the sweating palms, the sudden loss of appetite. She'd tried to ignore them, but as the meal had progressed she'd thought of little else.

Parker had gone suspiciously quiet, too. Then, later, he'd kissed her and everything became much, much worse. She'd felt warm and dizzy. A tingling sensation had slowly spread through her body. It seemed as though every cell in her body was aware of him. The sensations had been so overwhelming, she'd had to pretend nothing had happened. The truth was simply too risky.

"What made you decide to rework the scene that way?" Jo Ann asked, breaking into her thoughts.

Bailey stared at her friend and blinked rapidly.

"Bailey?" Jo Ann asked. "You look as if your mind's soaring through outer space."

"Uh… I was just thinking."

"A dangerous habit for a writer. We can't seem to get our characters out of our minds, can we? They insist on following us everywhere."

Characters, nothing! It was Parker Davidson she couldn't stop thinking about. As for the *following* part… Had her thoughts conjured him up? There he was, large as life, casually strolling toward them as though he'd sought her out. He hadn't, she told herself sternly. Nonetheless she searched for him every morning. She couldn't seem to help it. She'd never been so frighteningly aware of a man before, so eager—yet so reluctant to see him. Often she found herself scanning the faces around her, hoping to catch a glimpse of him.

Now here he was. Bailey quickly looked out the window into the tunnel's darkness, staring at the reflections in the glass.

"Good morning, ladies," Parker said jovially, standing directly in front of them, his feet braced slightly apart. The morning paper was tucked under his arm, and he looked very much as he had the first time she'd noticed him. Forceful. Appealing. Handsome.

"Morning," Bailey mumbled. She immediately turned back to the window.

"Hello again," Jo Ann replied warmly, smiling up at him.

For one wild second Bailey experienced a flash of resentment. Parker was *her* hero, not Jo Ann's! Her friend was greeting him like a long-lost brother or something. But what bothered Bailey even more was how delighted *she* felt. These were the very reactions she'd been combating all weekend.

"So," Parker said smoothly, directing his words to Bailey, "have you followed any strange men around town lately?"

She glared at him, annoyed at the way his words drew the attention of those sitting nearby. "Of course not," she snapped.

"I'm glad to hear it."

She'd just bet! She happened to glance at the man standing next to Parker. He was a distinguished-looking older gentleman who was peeking at her curiously over the morning paper.

"Did you rewrite the kissing scene?" Parker asked next.

The businessman gave up any pretense of reading, folded his paper and studied Bailey openly.

"She did a fabulous job of it," Jo Ann said with a mentor's pride.

"I was sure she would," Parker remarked. A hint of a smile raised the corners of his mouth and made his eyes sparkle. Bailey wanted to demand that he cease and desist that very instant. "I suspect it had a ring of sincerity to it," Parker added, his eyes meeting Bailey's. "A depth, perhaps, that was missing in the first account."

"It did," Jo Ann confirmed, looking mildly surprised. "The whole scene is beautifully written. Every emotion, every sensation, is right there, so vividly described it's difficult to believe the same writer is responsible for both versions."

Parker's expression reminded Bailey of Max when he'd discovered ground turkey in his dish instead of soggy cat food. His full sensuous mouth curved with satisfaction.

"I only hope Bailey can do as well with the dancing scene," Jo Ann said.

"The dancing scene?" Parker asked intently.

"That's several chapters later," Bailey explained, jerking the manuscript out of Jo Ann's lap. She shoved it inside a folder and slipped it into her spacious shoulder bag.

"It's romantic the way it's written, but there's something lacking," said Jo Ann. "Unfortunately I haven't been able to put my finger on what's wrong."

"The problem is and always has been Michael," Bailey inserted, not wanting the conversation to continue in this vein. She hoped her hero would forgive her for blaming her shortcomings as a writer on him.

"You can't fault Michael for the dancing scene," Jo Ann disagreed. "Correct me if I'm wrong, but as I recall, Michael and Janice were manipulated—by Janice's father—into attending a Pops concert. The only reason they went was that they couldn't think of a plausible excuse."

"Yes," she admitted grudgingly. "A sixties rock group was performing."

"Right. Then, as the evening went on, several couples from the audience started to dance. The young man sitting next to Janice asked her—"

"The problem is with Michael," Bailey insisted again. She glanced hopefully at the older gentleman, but he just shrugged, eyes twinkling.

"What did Michael do that was so wrong?" Jo Ann asked with a puzzled frown.

"He...he should never have let Janice dance with another man," Bailey said in a desperate voice.

"Michael couldn't have done anything else," Jo Ann argued, "otherwise he would've looked like a jealous fool." She turned to Parker for confirmation.

"I may be new to this hero business, but I can't help agreeing."

Bailey was irritated with both of them. This was *her* story and she'd write it as she saw fit. However, she refrained from saying so—just in case they were right. She needed time to mull over their opinions.

The train screeched to a halt and people surged toward the door. Bailey noted, gratefully, that this was Parker's stop.

"I'll give you a call later," he said, looking directly into Bailey's eyes. He didn't wait for a response.

He knew she didn't want to hear from him. She was frightened. Defensive. Guarded. With good reason. Only he didn't fully understand what that reason was. But a man like Parker wouldn't let her attitude go unchallenged.

"He's going to call you." Jo Ann sighed enviously. "Isn't that thrilling? Doesn't that excite you?"

Bailey shook her head, contradicting everything she was feeling inside. "Excite me? Not really."

Jo Ann frowned at her suspiciously. "What's the matter?"

"Nothing," Bailey answered with calm determination. She'd strolled down the path of romantic delusion twice before, but this time her eyes were wide open. Romance was wonderful, exciting, inspiring—and it was best limited to the pages of a well-crafted novel. Men, at least the men in her experience, inevitably proved to be terrible disappointments. Painful disappointments.

"Don't you like Parker?" Jo Ann demanded. "I mean, who wouldn't? He's hero material. You recognized it immediately, even before I did. Remember?"

Bailey wasn't likely to forget. "Yes, but that was in the name of research."

"Research?" Jo Ann cocked her eyebrows in flagrant disbelief. "Be honest, Bailey. You saw a whole lot more than Michael in Parker Davidson. You're not the type of woman who dashes off subways to follow a man. Some deep inner part of your being was reaching out to him."

Bailey forced a short laugh. "I hate to say it, Jo Ann, but I think you've been reading too many romances lately."

Jo Ann shrugged in a lie-to-yourself-if-you-insist manner. "Maybe, but I doubt it."

Nevertheless, her friend had given Bailey something to ponder.

The writing didn't go well that evening. Bailey, dressed in warm gray sweats, sans makeup and shoes, sat in front of her computer, staring blankly at the screen. "Inspiration is on vacation," she muttered, and that bit of doggerel seemed the best she could manage at the moment. Her usual warmth and humor escaped her. Every word she wrote sounded flat. She was tempted to erase the entire chapter.

Max, who had appointed himself the guardian of her printer, was curled up fast asleep on top of it. Bailey had long ago given up trying to keep him off. She'd quickly surrendered and taken to folding a towel over the printer to protect its internal workings from cat hair. Whenever she needed to print out a chapter, she nudged him awake; Max was always put out by the inconvenience and let her know it.

"Something's wrong," she announced to her feline companion. "The words just aren't flowing."

Max didn't reveal the slightest concern. He stretched out one yellow striped leg and examined it carefully, then settled down for another lengthy nap. He was fed and content and that was all that mattered.

Crossing her ankles, Bailey leaned back and clasped her hands behind her head. Chapter two of *Forever Yours* was just as vibrant and fast-paced as chapter one. But chapter three... She groaned and reread Paula Albright's letter for the umpteenth time, wanting desperately to capture the feelings and emotions the editor had suggested.

The phone rang in the kitchen, startling her. Bailey sighed irritably, then got up and rushed into the other room.

"Hello," she said curtly, realizing two important things at the same time. The first was how unfriendly and unwelcoming she sounded, and the second...the second was that she'd been unconsciously anticipating this call the entire evening.

"Hello," Parker returned in an affable tone. He didn't seem at all perturbed by her disagreeable mood. "I take it you're working, but from the sound of your voice I'd guess the rewrite isn't going well."

"It's coming along nicely." Bailey didn't know why she felt the need to lie. She was immediately consumed by guilt, then tried to disguise that by being even less friendly. "In fact, you interrupted a critical scene. I have so little time to write as it is, and my evenings are important to me."

There was an awkward silence. "Then I won't keep you," Parker said with cool politeness.

"It's just that it would be better if you didn't phone me." Her explaining didn't seem to improve the situation.

"I see," he said slowly.

And Bailey could tell that he *did* understand. She'd half expected him to argue, or at least attempt to cajole her into a more responsive mood. He didn't.

"Why don't you call me when you have a free moment," was all he said.

"I will," she answered, terribly disappointed and not sure why. It *was* better this way, with no further contact between them, she reminded herself firmly. "Goodbye, Parker."

"Goodbye," he said after another uncertain silence.

Bailey was still gripping the receiver when she heard a soft click followed by the drone of the disconnected line. She'd been needlessly abrupt and standoffish—as if she was trying to prove something. Trying to convince herself that she wanted nothing more to do with Parker.

*Play it safe, Bailey. Don't involve your heart. You've learned your lesson.* Her mind was constructing excuses for her tactless behavior, but her heart would accept none of it.

Bailey felt wretched. She went back to her chair and stared at the computer screen for a full five minutes, unable to concentrate.

*He's only trying to help,* her heart told her.

*Men aren't to be trusted,* her mind said. *Haven't you learned that yet? How many times does it take to teach you something?*

*Parker isn't like the others,* her heart insisted.

Her mind, however, refused to listen. *All men are alike.*

But if she'd done the right thing, why did she feel so rotten? Yet she knew that if she gave in to him now, she'd regret it. She was treading on thin ice with this relationship; she remembered how she'd felt when he kissed her. Was she willing to risk the pain, the heartache, all over again?

Bailey closed her eyes and shook her head. Her thoughts were hopelessly tangled. She'd done what she knew was necessary, but she didn't feel good about it. In fact, she was miserable. Parker had gone out of his way to help her with this project, offering her his time and his advice. He'd given her valuable insights into the male point of view. And when he kissed her, he'd reminded her how it felt to be a desirable woman....

Bailey barely slept that night. On Tuesday morning she decided to look for Parker, even if it meant moving from one subway car to the next, something she rarely did. When she did run into him, she intended to apologize, crediting her ill mood to creative temperament.

"Morning," Jo Ann said, meeting her on the station platform the way she did every morning.

"Hello," Bailey murmured absently, scanning the windows of the train as it slowed to a stop, hoping to spot Parker. If Jo Ann noticed anything odd, she didn't comment.

"I heard back from the agent I wrote to a couple of months back," Jo Ann said, grinning broadly. Her eyes fairly sparkled.

"Irene Ingram?" Bailey momentarily forgot about

Parker as she stared at her friend. Her sagging spirits lifted with the news. For weeks Jo Ann had been poring over the agent list, trying to decide whom to approach first. After much deliberation and thought, Jo Ann had decided to aim high. Many of the major publishers were no longer accepting non-agented material, and finding one willing to represent a beginner had been a serious concern. Irene was listed as one of the top romance-fiction agents in the industry. She represented a number of prominent names.

"And?" Bailey prompted, although she was fairly sure the news was positive.

"She's read my book and—" Jo Ann tossed her hands in the air "—she's crazy about it!"

"Does that mean she's going to represent you?" They were both aware how unusual it was for an established New York agent to represent an unpublished author. It wasn't unheard of, but it didn't happen all that often.

"You know, we never got around to discussing that— I assume she is. I mean, she talked to me about doing some minor revisions, which shouldn't take more than a week. Then we discussed possible markets. There's an editor she knows who's interested in historicals set in this time period. Irene wants to send it to her first, just as soon as I've finished with the revisions."

"Jo Ann," Bailey said, clasping her friend's hands tightly, "this is fabulous news!"

"I'm still having trouble believing it. Apparently Irene phoned while I was still at work and my eight-year-old answered. When I got home there was this scribbled message that didn't make any sense. All it said was that a lady with a weird name had phoned."

"Leave it to Bobby."

"He wasn't even home for me to question."

"He didn't write down the phone number?" Bailey asked.

"No, but he told Irene I was at work and she phoned me at five-thirty, our time."

"Weren't you the one who told me that being a writer means always knowing what time it is in New York?"

"The very one," Jo Ann teased. "Anyway, we spoke for almost an hour. It was crazy. Thank goodness Dan was home. I was standing in the kitchen with this stunned look on my face, frantically taking down notes. I didn't have to explain anything. Dan started dinner and then raced over to the park to pick up Bobby from Little League practice. Sarah set the table, and by the time I was off the phone, dinner was ready."

"I'm impressed." Several of the women in their writers' group had complained about their husbands' attitudes toward their creative efforts. But Jo Ann was fortunate in that department. Dan believed in her talent as strongly as Jo Ann did herself.

Jo Ann's dream was so close to being realized that Bailey could feel her own excitement rise. After three years of continuous effort, Jo Ann deserved a sale more than anyone she knew. She squeezed her writing in between dental appointments and Little League practices, between a full-time job and the demands of being a wife and mother. In addition, she was the driving force behind their writers' group. Jo Ann Webster had paid her dues, and Bailey sincerely hoped that landing Irene Ingram as her agent would be the catalyst to her first sale.

"I refuse to get excited," Jo Ann said matter-of-factly.

Bailey stared at her incredulously. "You're kidding, aren't you?"

"I suppose I am. It's impossible not to be thrilled, but there's a saying in the industry we both need to remember. Agents don't sell books, good writing does. Plotting and characterization are what interest an editor. Agents negotiate contracts, but they don't sell books."

"You should've phoned and told me she called," Bailey chastised.

"I meant to. Honest, I did, but when I'd finished the dinner dishes, put the kids to bed and reviewed my revision notes, it was too late. By the way, before I forget, did Parker call you?"

He was the last person Bailey wanted to discuss. If she admitted he had indeed phoned her, Jo Ann was bound to ask all kinds of questions Bailey preferred not to answer. Nor did she want to lie about it.

So she compromised. "He did, but I was writing at the time and he suggested I call him back later."

"Did you?" Jo Ann asked expectantly.

"No," Bailey said in a small miserable voice. "I should have, but... I didn't."

"He's marvelous, you know."

"Would it be okay if we didn't discuss Parker?" Bailey asked. She'd intended to seek him out, but she decided against it, at least for now. "I've got so much on my mind and I... I need to clear away a few cobwebs."

"Of course." Jo Ann's look was sympathetic. "Take your time, but don't take too long. Men like Parker Davidson don't come along often. Maybe once in a lifetime, if you're lucky."

This wasn't what Bailey wanted to hear.

Max was curled up on Bailey's printer later that same evening. She'd worked for an hour on the rewrite and

wasn't entirely pleased with the results. Her lack of satisfaction could be linked, however, to the number of
times she'd inadvertently typed Parker's name instead
of Michael's.

That mistake was simple enough to understand. She
was tired. Parker had been in her thoughts most of the
day. Good grief, when *wasn't* he in her thoughts?

Then, when she decided to take a break and scan the
evening paper, Parker's name seemed to leap right off
the page. For a couple of seconds, Bailey was convinced
the typesetter had made a mistake, just as she herself had
a few minutes earlier. Peering at the local-affairs page,
she realized that yes, indeed, Parker was in the news.

She sat down on the kitchen stool and carefully
read the brief article. Construction crews were breaking ground for a high-rise bank in the financial district.
Parker Davidson was the project's architect.

Bailey read the item twice and experienced a swell-
ing sense of pride and accomplishment.

She had to phone Parker. She owed him an explanation, an apology; she owed him her gratitude. She'd
known it the moment she'd abruptly ended their conversation the night before. She'd known it that morning when she spoke with Jo Ann. She'd known it the
first time she'd substituted Parker's name for Michael's.
Even the afternoon paper was telling her what she already knew.

Something so necessary shouldn't be so difficult, Bailey told herself, standing in front of her telephone. Her
hand still on the receiver, she hesitated. What could she
possibly say to him? Other than to apologize for her behavior and congratulate him on the project she'd read

about, which amounted to about thirty seconds of conversation.

Max sauntered into the kitchen, no doubt expecting to be fed again.

"You know better," she muttered, glaring down at him.

Pacing the kitchen didn't lend her courage. Nor did examining the contents of her refrigerator. The only thing that did was excite Max, who seemed to think she'd changed her mind, after all.

"Oh, for heaven's sake," she muttered, furious with herself. She picked up the phone, punched out Parker's home number—and waited. The phone rang once, twice, three times.

Parker was apparently out for the evening. Probably with some tall blond bombshell, celebrating his success. Every woman's basic nightmare. Four rings. Well, what did she expect? He was handsome, appealing, generous, kind—

"Hello?"

He caught her completely off guard. "Parker?"

"Bailey?"

"Yes, it's me," she said brightly. "Hello." The things she'd intended to say had unexpectedly disintegrated.

"Hello." His voice softened a little.

"Am I calling at a bad time?" she asked, wrapping the telephone cord around her index finger, then her wrist and finally her elbow. "I could call back later if that's more convenient."

"Now is fine."

"I saw your name in the paper and wanted to congratulate you. This project sounds impressive."

He shrugged it off, as she knew he would. Silence

fell between them, the kind of silence that needed to be filled or explained or quickly extinguished.

"I also wanted to apologize for the way I acted last night, when you phoned," Bailey said, the cord so tightly drawn around her hand that her fingers had gone numb. She loosened it now, her movements almost frantic. "I was rude and tactless and you didn't deserve it."

"So you ran into a snag with your writing?"

"I beg your pardon?"

"You're having a problem with your novel."

Bailey wondered how he knew that. "Uh…"

"I suggest it's time to check out the male point of view again. Get my insights. Am I right or wrong?"

"Right or wrong? Neither. I called to apologize."

"How's the rewrite coming?"

"Not too well." She sighed.

"Which tells me everything I need to know."

Bailey was mystified. "If you're implying that the only reason I'm calling is to ask for help with *Forever Yours* you couldn't be more mistaken."

"Then why *did* you call?"

"If you must know, it was to explain."

"Go on, I'm listening."

Now that she had his full attention, Bailey was beginning to feel foolish. "My mother always told me there's no excuse for rudeness, so I wanted to tell you something— something that might help you understand." Suddenly she couldn't utter another word.

"I'm listening," Parker repeated softly.

Bailey took a deep breath and closed her eyes. "Uh, maybe you *won't* understand, but you should know there's…there's a slightly used wedding dress hanging in my closet."

# Seven

Of all the explanations Bailey could have given, all the excuses she could have made to Parker, she had no idea why she'd mentioned the wedding dress. Sheer embarrassment dictated her next action.

She hung up the phone.

Immediately afterward it started ringing and she stared at it in stupefied horror. Placing her hands over her ears, she walked into the living room, sank into the overstuffed chair and tucked her knees under her chin.

Seventeen rings.

Parker let the phone ring so many times Bailey was convinced he was never going to give up. The silence that followed the last peal seemed to reverberate loudly through the small apartment.

She was just beginning to gather her thoughts when there was an impatient pounding on her door.

Max imperiously raised his head from his position on her printer as though to demand she do something. Obviously all the disruptions this evening were annoying him.

"Bailey, open this door," Parker ordered in a tone even she couldn't ignore.

Reluctantly she got up and pulled open the door, knowing intuitively that he would've gotten in one way or another. If she'd resisted, Parker would probably have had Mrs. Morgan outside her door with a key.

He stormed into her living room as though there was a raging fire inside that had to be extinguished. He stood in the center of the room and glanced around, running his hand through his hair. "What was that you said about a wedding dress?"

Bailey, who still clutched the doorknob, looked up at him and casually shrugged. "You forgot the slightly used part."

"Slightly used?"

"That's what I tried to explain earlier," she returned, fighting the tendency to be flippant.

"Are you married?" he asked harshly.

The question surprised her, although she supposed it shouldn't have. After all, they were talking about wedding dresses. "Heavens, no!"

"Then what the hell did you mean when you said it was slightly used?"

"I tried it on several times, paid for it, walked around in it. I even had my picture taken in it, but that dress has never, to the best of my knowledge, been inside a church." She closed the door and briefly leaned against it.

"Do you want to tell me what happened?"

"Not particularly," she said, joining him in the middle of the room. "I really don't understand why I even brought it up. But now that you're here, do you want a cup of coffee?" She didn't wait for his response, but went into her kitchen and automatically took down a blue ceramic mug.

"What was his name?"

"Which time? The first time around it was Paul. Tom followed a few years later," Bailey said with matter-of-fact sarcasm as she filled the mug and handed it to him. She poured a cup for herself.

"I take it you've had to cancel two weddings, then?"

"Yes," she said leading the way back into her living area. She curled up on the couch, her feet tucked beneath her, leaving the large overstuffed chair for Parker. "This isn't something I choose to broadcast, but I seem to have problems holding on to a man. To be accurate, I should explain I bought the dress for Tom's and my wedding. He was the second fiancé. Paul and I hadn't gotten around to the particulars before he...left." The last word was barely audible.

"Why'd you keep the dress?" Parker asked, his dark eyes puzzled.

Bailey looked away. She didn't want his pity any more than she needed his tenderness, she told herself. But if that was the case, why did she feel so cold and alone?

"Bailey?"

"It's such a beautiful dress." Chantilly lace over luxurious white silk. Pearls along the full length of the sleeves. A gently tapered bodice; a gracefully draped skirt. It was the kind of dress every woman dreamed she'd wear once in a lifetime. The kind of dress that signified love and romance...

Instead of leaving the wedding gown with her parents, Bailey had packed it up and transported it to San Francisco. Now Parker was asking her why. Bailey supposed there was some psychological reason behind her actions. Some hidden motive buried in her subconscious. A reminder, perhaps, that men were not to be trusted?

"You loved them?" Parker asked carefully.

"I thought I did," she whispered, staring into her coffee. "To be honest, I... I don't know anymore."

"Tell me about Paul."

"Paul," she repeated in a daze. "We met our junior year of college." That seemed like a lifetime ago now.

"And you fell in love," he finished for her.

"Fairly quickly. He intended to go into law. He was bright and fun and opinionated. I could listen to him for hours. Paul seemed to know exactly what he wanted and how to get it."

"He wanted you," Parker inserted.

"At first." Bailey hesitated, struggling against the pain before it could tighten around her heart the way it once had. "Then he met Valerie. I don't think he intended to fall in love with her." Bailey had to believe that. She knew Paul had tried to hold on to his love for her, but in the end it was Valerie he chose. "I dropped out of college afterward," she added, her voice low and trembling. "I couldn't bear to be there, on campus, seeing the two of them together." It sounded cowardly now. Her parents had been disappointed, but she'd continued her studies at a business college, graduating as a paralegal a year later.

"I should've known Paul wasn't a hero," she said, glancing up at Parker and risking a smile.

"How's that?"

"He drank blush wine."

Parker stared at her a moment without blinking. "I beg your pardon?"

"You prefer straight Scotch, right?"

"Yes." Parker was staring at her. "How'd you know?"

"You also get your hair cut by a real barber and not a hairdresser."

He nodded.

"You wear well-made conservative clothes and prefer socks with your shoes."

"That's all true," Parker agreed, as though he'd missed the punch line in a joke. "But how'd you know?" he asked again.

"You like your coffee in a mug instead of a cup."

"Yes." His voice was even more incredulous.

"You're a hero, remember?" She sent him another smile, pleased with how accurately she'd assessed his habits. "At least I've learned one thing in all of this, and that's how to recognize a real man."

"Paul and Tom weren't real men?"

"No, they were costly imitations. Costly to my pride, that is." She altered her position and pulled her knees beneath her chin, wrapping her arms around her legs. She'd consciously assumed a defensive position—just in case he felt the need to comfort her. "Before you leap to conclusions, I think you should know that the only reason I need a hero is for the sake of *Forever Yours*. You're perfect as a model for Michael."

"But you don't want to become personally involved with me."

"Exactly." Now that everything was out in the open, Bailey felt an immediate sense of relief. Now that Parker understood, the pressure would be gone. There would be no unrealistic expectations. "I write romances and you're a hero type. Our relationship is strictly business. Though of course I'm grateful for your…friendship," she added politely.

Parker seemed to mull over her words for several seconds before shaking his head. "I could accept that— except there's one complication."

"Oh?" Bailey's gaze sought Parker's.

"The kiss."

Abruptly she dropped her gaze as a chill raced up her spine. "Foul!" she wanted to yell. "Unfair!" Instead, she muttered, "Uh, I don't think we should discuss that."

"Why not?"

"It was research," she said forcefully. "That's all." She was working hard to convince herself. Harder still at smiling blandly in his direction, hoping all the while he'd leave her comment untouched.

He didn't.

"Well, then it wouldn't hurt to experiment a second time, would it?" he argued. Unfortunately she had to acknowledge the logic of that—but she wouldn't admit it.

"No, please, there isn't any need," she told him, neatly destroying her own argument with her impassioned plea.

"I disagree," Parker said, standing up and striding toward her.

"Ah..." She clasped her bent legs even more tightly.

"There's nothing to worry about," Parker assured her.

"Isn't there? I mean...of course, there isn't. It's just that kissing makes me uncomfortable."

"Why's that?"

Couldn't the man accept a simple explanation? Just once?

Bailey sighed. "All right, you can kiss me if you insist," she said ungraciously, dropping her feet to the floor. She straightened her sweatshirt, dutifully squeezed her eyes shut, puckered her lips and waited.

And waited.

Finally she grew impatient and opened her eyes to discover Parker sitting next to her, staring. His face was inches from her own. A smile nipped at the corners of his mouth, making his lips quiver slightly.

"I amuse you?" she asked, offended. He was the one who'd requested this demonstration in the first place. He was the one who'd demanded proof.

"Not exactly *amuse,*" Parker said, but from the gleam in his eyes she suspected he was fighting the urge to laugh out loud.

"I think we should forget the whole thing." She spoke with as much dignity as possible then got up to carry her cup into the kitchen. Turning to collect Parker's mug from the living room, she walked headlong into his arms.

His hands rested on her shoulders. "Both of those men were fools," he whispered, his gaze warm, his words soft.

Trapped between his body and the kitchen counter, Bailey felt the flutterings of panic. Her heart soared to her throat, beating wildly. He'd had his chance to kiss her, to prove his point. He should've done it then. Not now. Not when she wasn't steeled and ready. Not when his words made her feel so helpless and vulnerable.

Gently his mouth claimed hers. The kiss was straightforward, uncomplicated by need or desire. A tender kiss. A kiss to erase the pain of rejection and the grief of loss.

Bailey didn't respond. Not at first. Then her lips trembled to life in a slow awakening.

Like the first time Parker had kissed her, Bailey felt besieged by confusion and a sense of shock. She wasn't ready for this! She jerked herself free of his arms and twisted around. "There!" she said, her voice quavering. "Are you happy?"

"No," he answered starkly. "You can try to fool yourself if you want, but we both know the truth. You've been burned."

"Since I can't stand the heat," she said in a reasonable tone, "I got out of the kitchen." The fact that she'd just been kissed by him *in* the kitchen only made her situation more farcical. She brushed the hair back from her forehead, managed a false smile and turned around to face him. "I should never have said anything about the wedding dress. I don't know why I did. I'm not even sure what prompted that display of hysteria."

"I'm glad you did. And, Bailey, don't feel you have to apologize to me."

"Thank you," she mumbled, leading the way to her door.

Parker stopped to pat Max, who didn't so much as open his eyes to investigate. "Does he always sleep on your printer?"

"No, he sometimes insists on taking up a large portion of my pillow, generally when I'm using it myself."

Parker grinned. Bailey swore she'd never met a man with a more engaging smile. It was like watching the sun break through the clouds after a heavy downpour. It warmed her spirit, and only with the full strength of her will was she able to look away.

"I'll be seeing you," he said, pausing at the door.

"Yes," she whispered, yearning to see him again, yet in the same heartbeat hoping it wouldn't be soon.

"Bailey," Parker said, pressing his hand to her cheek, "just remember you haven't been the only one betrayed by love. It happens to all of us."

Perhaps, Bailey thought, but Parker was a living, breathing hero. The type of man women bought millions of books a year to read about, to dream about. She doubted he knew what it was like to have love humiliate him and break his heart.

"You look like you don't believe me."

Bailey stared at him, surprised he'd read her reaction so clearly.

"You're wrong," he said quietly. "I lost someone I loved, too." With that he dropped his hand and walked out, closing the door behind him.

By the time Bailey had recovered her wits enough to race after him, question him, the hallway was empty. Parker had lost at love, too? No woman in her right mind would walk away from Parker Davidson.

He was a hero.

"I'm afraid I did it again," Bailey announced to Jo Ann as they walked briskly toward their respective office buildings. The noise on the subway that morning had made private conversation impossible.

"Did what?"

"Put my foot in my mouth with Parker Davidson. He—"

"Did you see his name in the paper last night?" Jo Ann asked excitedly, cutting her off. "It was a small piece in the local section. I would've phoned you, but I knew I'd see you this morning and I didn't want to interrupt your writing time."

"I saw it."

"Dan was impressed that we even knew Parker. Apparently he's made quite a name for himself in the past few years. I never pay attention to that sort of thing. If it doesn't have to do with medical insurance or novel-writing, it's lost on me. But Dan's heard of him. He would, being in construction and all. Did you know

Parker won a major national award for an innovative house he designed last year?"

"N-no."

"I'm sorry, I interrupted you, didn't I?" Jo Ann said, stopping midstride. "What were you about to say?"

Bailey wasn't sure how much she should tell her. "He stopped by my apartment—"

"Parker came to your place?" Jo Ann sounded awestruck, as though Bailey had experienced a heavenly visitation.

Bailey didn't know what was wrong with Jo Ann. She wasn't letting her get a word in edgewise. "I made the mistake of telling him about the wedding dress in my closet. And at first I think he assumed I was married."

Jo Ann came to an abrupt halt. Her eyes narrowed. "There's a wedding dress in your closet?"

Bailey had forgotten she'd never told Jo Ann about Paul and Tom. She felt neither the inclination nor the desire to explain now, especially on a cold February day in the middle of a busy San Francisco sidewalk.

"My, my, will you look at the time?" Bailey muttered, staring down at her watch. It was half-past frustration and thirty minutes to despair. The only way she could easily extricate herself from this mess was to leave—now.

"Oh, no, you don't, Bailey York," Jo Ann cried, grasping her forearm. "You're not walking away from me yet. Not without filling me in first."

"It's nothing. I was engaged."

"When? Recently?"

"Yes and no," Bailey responded cryptically with a longing glance at her office building two blocks south.

"What does that mean?" Jo Ann demanded.

"I was engaged to be married twice, and both times the man walked out on me. All right? Are you satisfied now?"

Her explanation didn't seem to appease Jo Ann. "Twice? But what's any of this got to do with Parker? It wasn't his fault those other guys dumped you, was it?"

"Of course not," Bailey snapped, completely exasperated. She'd lost her patience. It had been a mistake to ever mention the man's name. Jo Ann had become Parker's greatest advocate. Never mind that she was also *her* good friend and if she was going to champion anyone, it should be Bailey. However, in Jo Ann's starry-eyed view, Parker apparently could do no wrong.

"He assumed you were married?"

"Don't worry, I explained everything," she said calmly. "Listen, we're going to be late for work. I'll talk to you later."

"You bet you will. You've got a lot more explaining to do." She took a couple of steps, walking backward, staring at Bailey. "You were engaged? To different men each time?" she repeated. "Two different men?"

Bailey nodded and held up two fingers as they continued to back away from each other. "Two times, two different men."

Unexpectedly Jo Ann's face broke into a wide smile. "You know what they say, don't you? Third time's the charm, and if Parker Davidson is anything, it's charming. Talk to you this evening." With a quick wave, her friend turned and hurried down the street.

By lunchtime, Bailey decided the day was going to be a disaster. She'd misfiled an important folder, accidentally disconnected a client on the phone and worst of all spent two hours typing up a brief, then pressed the wrong key and lost the entire document. Following the fiasco with the computer, she took an early lunch and decided to walk off her frustration.

Either by accident or unconscious design—she couldn't decide which—Bailey found herself outside Parker's office building. She gazed at it for several minutes, wavering with indecision. She wanted to ask him what he'd meant about losing someone he loved. It was either that or spend the second half of the day infuriating her boss and annoying important clients. She was disappointed in Parker, she decided. He shouldn't have walked away without explaining. It wasn't fair. He'd been willing enough to listen to the humiliating details of *her* love life, but hadn't shared his own pain.

Roseanne Snyder, the firm's receptionist, brightened when Bailey walked into the office. "Oh, Ms. York, it's good to see you again."

"Thank you," Bailey answered, responding naturally to the warm welcome.

"Is Mr. Davidson expecting you?" The receptionist was flipping through the pages of the engagement calendar. "I'm terribly sorry if I—"

"No, no," Bailey said, stepping close to the older woman's desk. "I wasn't even sure Parker would be in."

"He is, and I know he'd be pleased to see you. Just go on back and I'll tell him you're coming. You know the way, don't you?" She turned in her chair and pointed down the hallway. "Mr. Davidson's office is the last door on your left."

Bailey hesitated, more doubtful than ever that showing up like this was the right thing to do. She would have left, crept quietly away, if Roseanne hadn't spoken into the intercom just then and gleefully announced her presence.

Before Bailey could react, Parker's office door opened. He waited there, hands in his pockets, leaning indolently against the frame.

Fortifying her resolve, she hurried toward him. He moved aside and closed the door when she entered. Once again she was struck by the dramatically beautiful view of the bay, but she couldn't allow that to deter her from her purpose.

"This is an unexpected surprise," Parker said.

Her nerves were on edge, and her words were more forceful than she intended. "That was a rotten thing you did."

"What? Kissing you? Honestly, Bailey are we going to go through all that again? You've got to stop lying to yourself."

"My day's a complete waste," she said, clenching her hands, "and this has nothing to do with our kiss."

"It doesn't?"

She sank down in a chair. "I dragged my pride through the mud of despair for you," she said dramatically.

He blinked as though she'd completely lost him.

"All right," she admitted with a flip of her hand, "that may be a little on the purple side."

"Purple?"

"Purple prose." Oh, it was so irritating having to explain everything to him. "Do you think I enjoy sharing my disgrace? It isn't every woman who'd willingly dig up the most painful episodes in her past and confess them to you. It wasn't easy, you know."

Parker walked around to his side of the desk, sat down

and rubbed the side of his jaw. "Does this conversation have anything to do with the slightly used wedding dress?"

"Yes," she returned indignantly. "Oh, it was perfectly acceptable for me to describe how two—not one, mind you, but two—different men dumped me practically at the altar steps."

The amusement faded from Parker's eyes. "I realize that."

"No, you don't," she said, "otherwise you'd never have left on that parting shot."

"Parting shot?"

She shut her eyes for a moment and prayed for patience. "As you were leaving, you oh-so-casually mentioned something about losing someone you loved. Why was it fine for me to share my humiliation but not for you? I'm disappointed and—" Her throat closed before she could finish.

Parker was strangely quiet. His eyes held hers, his look somber. "You're right. That was rude of me, and I don't have any excuse."

"Oh, but you do," she said dryly. She should have known. He was a hero, wasn't he? She shook her head, angry with herself as much as with him.

"I do?" Parker countered.

"Yes, I should've figured it out sooner. Heroes often have a difficult time exposing their vulnerabilities. Obviously this...woman you loved wounded your pride. She unmasked your vulnerability. Believe me, I know about that from experience. You don't have to explain it to me." She stood up to go, guiltily aware that she'd judged Parker too harshly.

"But you're right," he argued. "You shared a deep

part of yourself and I should have been willing to do the same. It was unfair of me to leave the way I did."

"Perhaps, but it was true to character." She would have said a quick goodbye and walked out the door if not for the pain that suddenly entered his eyes.

"I'll tell you. It's only fair that you know. Sit down."

Bailey did as he requested, watching him carefully.

Parker smiled, but this wasn't the winsome smile she was accustomed to seeing. This was a strained smile, almost a grimace.

"Her name was Maria. I met her while I was traveling in Spain about fifteen years ago. We were both so young and in love. I wanted to marry her, bring her back with me to the States, but her family...well, suffice it to say her family didn't want their daughter marrying a foreigner. Several hundred years of tradition and pride stood between us, and when Maria was forced to choose between her family and me, she chose to remain in Madrid." He paused, shrugging one shoulder. "She did the right thing, I realize that now, much as it hurt at the time. I also realize how difficult her decision must have been. I learned a few months later that she'd married someone far more acceptable to her family than an American student."

"I'm sorry."

He shook his head as though to dispel the memories. "There's no reason you should be. Although I loved her a great deal, the relationship would never have lasted. Maria would've been miserable in this country. I understand now how perceptive she was."

"She loved you."

"Yes," he said. "She loved me as much as she dared,

but in the end duty and family were more important to her than love."

Bailey didn't know what to say. Her heart ached for the young man who had lost his love, and yet she couldn't help admiring the brave woman who had sacrificed her heart for her family and her deepest beliefs.

"I think what hurt the most was that she married someone else so soon afterward," Parker added.

"Paul and Tom got married, too… I think." Bailey understood his pain well.

The office was quiet for a moment, until Parker broke the silence. "Are we going to sit around and mope all afternoon? Or are you going to let me take you to lunch?"

Bailey smiled. "I think you might be able to talk me into it." Her morning had been miserable, but the afternoon looked much brighter now. She got to her feet, still smiling at Parker. "One thing I've learned over the years is that you can't allow misery to interfere with mealtimes."

Parker laughed and the robust sound of it was contagious. "I have a small surprise for you," he told her, reaching inside his suit pocket. "I was going to save it for later, but now seems more fitting." He handed her two tickets.

Bailey stared at them, speechless.

"The Pops concert," Parker said. "They're having a rock group from the sixties perform. It seems only fitting that Janice and Michael attend."

# *Eight*

It wasn't until they'd finished lunch that Bailey noticed
what a good time she was having with Parker. They'd
sat across the table from each other and chatted like old
friends. Bailey had never felt more at ease with him,
nor had she ever allowed herself to be more open. Her
emotions had undergone a gradual but profound change.

Fear and caution had been replaced by genuine contentment. And by hope.

After lunch they strolled through Union Square tossing
breadcrumbs to the greedy pigeons. The early-morning
fog had burned away and the sun was out in a rare display
of brilliance. The square was filled with tourists, groups
of old men and office workers taking an outdoor lunch.
Bailey loved Union Square. Being there now, with Parker,
seemed especially…fitting. And not just because Janice
and Michael did the same thing in chapter six!

He was more relaxed with her, as well. He talked freely
about himself, something he'd never done before. He was
the oldest of three boys and the only one still unmarried.

"I'm the baby of the family," Bailey explained. "Pam-
pered and spoiled. Overprotected, I'm afraid. My parents

tried hard to dissuade me from moving to California." She paused.

"What made you leave Oregon?"

Bailey waited for the tightness that always gripped her heart when she thought of Tom, but it didn't come. It simply wasn't there anymore.

"Tom," she admitted, glancing down at the squawking birds, fighting over crumbs.

"He was fiancé number two?" Parker's hands were locked behind his back as they strolled along the paved pathway.

Bailey couldn't resist wondering if he'd hidden his hands to keep from touching her. "I met Tom a couple of years after... Paul. He was, is, a junior partner in the law firm where I worked as a paralegal. We'd been dating off and on for several months, nothing serious for either of us. Then we got involved in a case together and ended up spending a lot of time in each other's company. Within three months we were engaged."

Parker placed his hand lightly on her shoulder as though to lend her support. She smiled up at him in appreciation. "Actually it doesn't hurt as much to talk about it now." Time did heal all wounds, or as she preferred to think, time wounds all heels.

"I'm not sure when he met Sandra," she continued. "For all I know, they might have been childhood sweethearts. What I do remember is that we were only a few weeks away from the wedding. The invitations were all finished and waiting to be picked up at the printer's when Tom told me there was someone else."

"Were you surprised?"

"Shocked. In retrospect, I suppose I should have recognized the signs, but I'd been completely wrapped up in preparing for the wedding—shopping with my bridesmaids for their dresses, arranging for the flowers, things like that. In fact, I was so busy picking out china patterns I didn't even notice that my fiancé had fallen out of love with me."

"You make it sound as though it was your fault."

Bailey shrugged. "In some ways I think it was. I'm willing to admit that now, to see my own faults. But that doesn't make up for the fact that he was engaged to me and seeing another woman on the sly."

"No, it doesn't," Parker agreed. "What did you say when he told you?" By now, his hand was clasping her shoulder and she was leaning into him. The weight of her humiliation no longer seemed as crushing, but it was still there, and talking about it produced a flood of emotions she hadn't wanted to face. It was ironic that she could do so now, after all this time, and with another man.

"Have you forgiven him?"

Bailey paused and nudged a fallen leaf with the toe of her shoe. "Yes. Hating him, even disliking him, takes too much energy. He was truly sorry. By the time he talked to me, I think poor Tom was completely and utterly miserable. He tried so hard to avoid doing or saying anything to hurt me. I swear it took him fifteen minutes to get around to telling me he wanted to call off the wedding and another thirty to confess that there was someone else. I remember the sick feeling in my stomach. It was like coming down with a bad case of the flu, having all the symptoms hit me at once." Her mind returned to that dreadful day and how she'd sat and stared at Tom in shocked disbelief. He'd been so uncomfortable, gazing at his hands, guilt and confusion muffling his voice.

"I didn't cry," Bailey recalled. "I wasn't even angry, at least not at first. I don't think I felt any emotion." She gave Parker a chagrined smile. "In retrospect I realize my pride wouldn't allow it. What I do remember is that I said the most nonsensical things."

"Like what?"

Bailey's gaze wandered down the pathway. "I told him I expected him to pay for the invitations. We'd had them embossed with gold, which had been considerably more expensive. Besides, I was already out the money for the wedding dress."

"Ah, the infamous slightly used wedding dress."

"It was expensive!"

"I know," Parker said, his eyes tender. "Actually you were just being practical."

"I don't know what I was being. It's crazy the way the mind works in situations like that. I remember thinking that Paul and Tom must have been acquainted with each other. I was convinced the two of them had plotted together, which was utterly ridiculous."

"I take it you decided to move to San Francisco after Tom broke the engagement."

She nodded. "Within a matter of hours I'd given my notice at the law firm and was making plans to move."

"Why San Francisco?"

"You know," she said, laughing lightly, "I'm not really sure. I'd visited the area several times over the years and the weather was always rotten. Mark Twain wrote somewhere that the worst winter he ever spent was a summer in San Francisco. I guess the city, with its overcast skies and foggy mornings, suited my mood. I couldn't have tolerated bright sunny days and moonlit nights in the weeks after I left Oregon."

"What happened to Tom?"

"What do you mean?" Bailey cocked her head to look up at him, taken aback by the question.

"Did he marry Sandra?"

"Heavens, I don't know."

"Weren't you curious?"

Frankly she hadn't been. He obviously hadn't wanted *her,* and that was the only thing that mattered to Bailey. She'd felt betrayed, humiliated and abandoned. If Tom ever regretted his decision or if things hadn't worked out between him and Sandra, she didn't know. She hadn't stuck around to find out. Furthermore, she wouldn't have cared, not then, anyway.

She'd wanted out. Out of her job, Out of Oregon. Out of her dull life. If she was going to fall in love, why did it have to be with weak men? Men who couldn't make up their minds. Men who fell in and out of love, men who were never sure of what they wanted.

Perhaps it was some flaw in her own character that caused her to choose such men. That was the very reason she'd given up on relationships and dating and the opposite sex in general. And she knew it was also why she enjoyed reading romances, why she enjoyed writing them. Romance fiction offered her the happy ending that had been so absent in her own life.

The novels she read and wrote were about men who were *real* men—strong, traditional, confident men— and everyday women not unlike herself.

She'd been looking for a hero when she stumbled on Parker Davidson. Yes, she could truly say her heart was warming toward him. Warming, nothing! It was *on fire* and had been for weeks, although she'd refused to acknowledge that until now.

Parker's dark eyes caressed hers. "I'm glad you moved to the Bay area."

"So am I."

"You won't change your mind, will you?" he asked

as they began to walk back. He must have read the confusion in her eyes because he added, "The concert tonight? It's in honor of Valentine's Day."

"No, I'm looking forward to going." She hadn't even realized what day this was. Bailey suddenly felt a thrill of excitement at the thought of spending the most romantic evening of the year with Parker Davidson. Although of course it would mean no time to work on *Forever Yours...*

"Think of the concert as research," Parker said, grinning down at her.

"I will." A woman could be blinded by eyes as radiant as Parker's. They were alight with the sensitivity and strength of his nature.

"Goodbye," she said reluctantly, lifting her hand in a small wave.

"Until tonight," Parker said, sounding equally reluctant to part.

"Tonight," she repeated softly. She'd seen her pain reflected in his eyes when she told him about Tom. He understood what it was to lose someone you loved, regardless of the circumstances. She sensed that in many ways the two of them were alike. During that short walk around Union Square, Bailey had felt a closeness to Parker, a comfortable and open honesty she'd rarely felt with anyone before.

"I'll pick you up at seven," he said.

"Perfect." Bailey was convinced he would have kissed her if they hadn't been standing in such a public place. And she would have let him.

The afternoon flew by. Whereas the morning had been excruciatingly slow, filled with one blunder after another, the hours after her lunch with Parker were trouble free. No sooner had she returned to the office than it seemed time to pack up her things and head for the subway.

True to form, Max was there to greet her when she walked in the door. She set her mail, two bills and an ad for the local supermarket, on the kitchen counter, and quickly fed him. Max seemed mildly surprised at her promptness and stared at his food for several minutes, as though he was hesitant about eating it.

Grumbling that it was impossible to please the dratted cat, Bailey stalked into her bedroom, throwing open the closet door.

For some time she did nothing but stare at the contents. She finally made her decision, a printed dress she'd worn when she was in college. The paisley print was bright and cheerful, the skirt widely pleated. The style was slightly dated, but it was the best she could do. If Parker had given her even a day's notice she would have gone out and bought something new. Something red in honor of Valentine's Day.

The seats Parker had purchased for the concert at Civic Center were among the best in the house. They were situated in the middle about fifteen rows from the front.

The music was fabulous. Delightful. Romantic. There were classical pieces she recognized, interspersed with soft rock, and a number of popular tunes and "golden oldies."

The orchestra was spectacular, and being this close to the stage afforded Bailey an opportunity so special she felt tears of appreciation gather in her eyes more than once. Nothing could ever duplicate a live performance.

The warm generous man in her company made everything perfect. At some point, early in the program, Parker reached for her hand. When Bailey's heartbeat finally settled down to a normal rate, she felt an emotion she hadn't experienced in more than a year, not since the day Tom had called off their wedding.

*Contentment.* Complete and utter contentment.

She closed her eyes to savor the music and when she opened them again, she saw Parker studying her. She smiled shyly and he smiled back. And at that moment, cymbals clanged. Bailey jumped in her seat as though caught doing something illegal. Parker chuckled and raised her hand to his lips, gently brushing her knuckles with a kiss.

The second group, Hairspray, performed after the intermission. Bailey found their music unfamiliar with the exception of two or three classic rock numbers. But the audience responded enthusiastically to the group's energy and sense of fun. Several people got to their feet, swaying to the music. After a while some couples edged into the aisles and started dancing. Bailey would have liked to join them, but Parker seemed to prefer staying where they were. She couldn't very well leave him sitting there while she sought out a partner. Especially when the only partner she wanted was right beside her.

Eventually nearly everyone around them rose and moved into the aisle, which meant a lot of awkward shifting for Parker and Bailey. She was convinced they were the only couple in the section not on their feet.

She glanced at Parker, but he seemed oblivious to what was happening around them. At one point she thought she heard him grumble about not being able to see the band because of all those people standing.

"Miss?" An older balding man moved into their nearly empty row and tapped Bailey on the shoulder in an effort to get her attention. He wore his shirt open to the navel and had no less than five pounds of gold draped around his neck. Clearly he'd never left the early seventies. "Would you care to dance?"

"Uh..." Bailey certainly hadn't been expecting an invitation. She wasn't entirely confident of the protocol. She'd come with Parker and he might object.

"Go ahead," Parker said, reassuring her. He actually seemed relieved someone else had asked her. Perhaps he was feeling guilty about not having done so himself, Bailey mused.

She shrugged and stood, glancing his way once more to be sure he didn't mind. He urged her forward with a wave of his hand.

Bailey was disappointed. She wished with all her heart that it was Parker taking her in his arms. Parker, not some stranger.

"Matt Cooper," the man with the gold chains said, holding out his hand.

"Bailey York."

He grinned as he slipped his arm around her waist. "There must be something wrong with your date to leave you sitting there."

"I don't think Parker dances."

It had been a long while since Bailey had danced, and she wasn't positive she'd even remember how. She needn't have worried. The space was so limited that she couldn't move more than a few inches in any direction.

The next song Hairspray performed was an old rock song from the sixties. Matt surprised her by placing two fingers in his mouth and whistling loudly. The piercing sound cut through music, crowd noises and applause. Despite herself, Bailey laughed.

The song was fast-paced and Bailey began swaying her hips and moving to the beat. Before she was sure how it had happened, she was quite a distance from her friend. She found herself standing next to a tall good-looking man about Parker's age, who was obviously enjoying the group's performance.

He smiled at Bailey and she smiled shyly back. The next song was another oldie, one written with young lovers in mind and perfect for slow dancing.

Bailey tried to make it down the aisle to Parker's seat, but the row was empty. Although she glanced all around she couldn't locate him.

"We might as well," the good-looking man said, holding out his hands to her. "My partner has taken off for parts unknown."

"Mine seems to have disappeared, too." Scanning the crowd, she still couldn't find Parker but then, the area was so congested it was impossible to see anyone clearly. A little worried, she wondered how they'd ever find each other when the concert was over.

She and her new partner danced two or three dances without ever exchanging names. He twirled her about with an expertise that masterfully disguised her own less-inspired movements. They finished a particularly fast dance, and Bailey fanned her face, flushed from the exertion, with one hand.

When Hairspray introduced another love ballad, it seemed only natural for Bailey to slip into her temporary partner's arms. He said something and laughed. Bailey hadn't been able to make out his words, but she grinned back at him. She was about to say something herself when she saw Parker edging toward them, scowling.

"My date's here," she said, breaking away from the man who held her. She gave him an apologetic look and he released her with a decided lack of enthusiasm.

"I thought I'd lost you," she said when Parker made it to her side.

"I think it's time we left," he announced in clipped tones.

Bailey blinked, surprised by his irritation. "But the concert isn't over yet." Cutting a path through the horde of dancers would be difficult, perhaps impossible. "Shouldn't we at least stay until Hairspray is finished?"

"No."

"What's wrong?"

Parker shoved his hands in his pockets. "I didn't mind you dancing with that Barry Gibb look-alike, but the next thing I know, you've taken off with someone else."

"I didn't *take off* with anyone," she said, disliking his tone as much as his implication. "We were separated by the crowds."

"Then you should've come back to me."

"You didn't honestly expect me to fight my way through this mass of humanity, did you? Can't you see how crowded the aisles are?"

"I made it to you."

Bailey sighed, fighting the urge to be sarcastic. And lost. "Do you want a Boy Scout award? I didn't know they issued them for pushing and shoving."

Parker's eyes flashed with resentment. "I didn't push anyone. I think it would be best if we sat down," he said, gripping her by the elbow and leading her back into a row, "before you make an even greater spectacle of yourself."

"A spectacle of myself," Bailey muttered furiously. "If anyone was a spectacle, it was you! You were the only person in ten rows who wasn't dancing."

"I certainly didn't expect my date to take off with another man." He sank down in a seat and crossed his arms as though he had no intention of continuing this discussion.

"Your date," she repeated, struggling to hold on to her temper by clenching her fists. "May I remind you this entire evening was for the purposes of research and nothing more?"

Parker gave a disbelieving snort. "That's not how I remember it. At the time, you seemed eager enough." He laughed, a cynical, unpleasant sound. "I'm not the one who chased after you."

Standing there arguing with him was attracting more attention than Bailey wanted. Reluctantly she sat down, primly folding her hands in her lap, and stared directly ahead. "I didn't chase after you," she informed him through gritted teeth. "I have *never* chased after any man."

"Oh, forgive me, then. I could have sworn it was you who followed me off the subway. Were you aware that someone who closely resembles you stalked me all the way into Chinatown?"

"Oh-h-h," Bailey moaned, throwing up her hands, "you're impossible."

"What I am is correct."

Bailey didn't deign to reply. She crossed her legs and swung her ankle ferociously until the concert finally ended.

Parker didn't say a word as he escorted her to his car,

which was fine with Bailey. She'd never met a more unreasonable person in her life. Less than an hour earlier, they'd practically been drowning in each other's eyes. She'd allowed herself to get caught up in the magic of the moment, that was all. Some Valentine's Day!

They parted with little more than a polite goodnight. Bailey informed him there was no need to see her to her door. Naturally he claimed otherwise, just to be obstinate. She wanted to argue, but knew it would be a waste of breath.

Max was at the door to greet her, his tail waving in the air. He stayed close to her, rubbing against her legs, and Bailey nearly tripped over him as she hurriedly undressed. She started to tell him about her evening, changed her mind and got into bed. She pulled the covers up to her chin, forcing the cantankerous Parker Davidson from her mind.

Jo Ann was waiting for her outside the BART station the following morning. "Well?" she said, racing to Bailey's side. "How was your date?"

"What date? You couldn't possibly call that outing with Parker a date."

"I couldn't?" Jo Ann was clearly puzzled.

"We attended the Pops Concert—"

"For research," Jo Ann finished for her. "I gather the evening didn't go well?" They filed through the turnstile and rode the escalator down to the platform where they'd board the train.

"The whole night was a disaster."

"Tell Mama everything," Jo Ann urged.

Bailey wasn't in the mood to talk, but she made the effort to explain what had happened and how unreasonable Parker had been. She hadn't slept well, convinced she'd made the same mistake with Parker as she had with the other men in her life. All along she'd assumed he was different. Not so. Parker was pompous, irrational and arrogant. She told Jo Ann that. "I was wrong about him being a hero," she said bleakly,

Jo Ann frowned. "Let me see if I've got this straight. People started dancing. One man asked you to dance, then you got separated and danced with another guy and Parker acted like a jealous fool."

"Exactly." It infuriated Bailey every time she thought about it, which she'd been doing all morning.

"Of course he did," Jo Ann said enthusiastically, as though she'd just made an important discovery. "Don't you see? He was being true to character. Didn't more or less the same thing happen between Janice and Michael when they went to the concert?"

Bailey had completely forgotten. "Now that you mention it, yes," she admitted slowly.

The train arrived. When the screeching came to a halt, Jo Ann said, "I told Parker all about that scene myself, remember?"

Bailey did, vaguely.

"When you sit down to rewrite it, you'll know from experience exactly what Janice was feeling and thinking because those were the very thoughts you experienced yourself. How can you be angry with him?"

Bailey wasn't finding it difficult.

"You should be grateful."

"I should?"

"Oh, yes," Jo Ann insisted. "Parker Davidson is more of a hero than either of us realized."

# Nine

"Don't you understand what Parker did?" Jo Ann asked when they met for lunch later that same day. The topic was one she refused to drop.

"You bet I understand. He's a... Neanderthal, only he tried to be polite about it. As if that makes any difference."

"Wrong," Jo Ann argued, looking downright mysterious. "He's given you some genuine insight into your character's thoughts and actions."

"What he did," Bailey said, waving her spoon above her cream-of-broccoli soup, "was pretty well ruin what started out as a perfect evening."

"You said he acted like a jealous fool, but you've got to remember that's exactly how Michael reacted when Janice danced with another man."

"Then he went above and beyond the call of duty, and I'm not about to reward that conduct in a man, hero or not." She crumbled her soda crackers into her soup, then brushed her palms free of crumbs.

Until Bailey accepted the invitation to dance, her evening with Parker had been wonderfully romantic. They'd sat together holding hands, while the music swirled and floated around them. Then the dancing began and her knight in shining armor turned into a fire-breathing dragon.

"You haven't forgotten the critique group is meeting tonight, have you?" Jo Ann asked, abruptly changing the subject.

Bailey's head was so full of Parker that she had, indeed, forgotten. She'd been absentminded lately. "Tonight?"

"Seven, at Darlene's house. You'll be there, won't you?"

"Of course." Bailey didn't need to think twice. Every other week, women from their writing group took turns hosting a session in which they evaluated one another's work.

"Oh, good. For a moment I wondered whether you'd be able to come."

"Why wouldn't I?" Bailey demanded. She was as dedicated as the other writers. She hadn't missed a single meeting since the group was formed two months ago.

"Oh, I thought you might be spending the evening with Parker. You two need to work out your differences. You're going to be miserable until this is resolved."

Bailey slowly lowered her spoon. "Miserable?" she repeated, giving a brief, slightly hysterical laugh. "Do I look like I'm the least bit heartbroken? Honestly, Jo Ann, you're making a mountain out of a molehill. The two of us had a falling out. I don't want to see him, and I'm sure he feels the same way. I won't have any problem making the group tonight."

Jo Ann calmly drank her coffee, then just as calmly stated, "You're miserable, only you're too proud to admit it."

"I am *not* miserable," Bailey asserted, doing her utmost to smile serenely.

"How much sleep did you get last night?"

"Why? Have I got circles under my eyes?"

"No. Just answer the question."

Bailey swallowed uncomfortably. "Enough. What's with you? Have you taken up writing mystery novels? Parker Davidson and I had a parting of the ways. It would have happened eventually. Besides, it's better to learn these sorts of things in the beginning of a... relationship." She shrugged comically. "A bit ironic to have it end on Valentine's Day."

"So you won't be seeing him again?" Jo Ann made that sound like the most desolate of prospects.

"We probably won't be able to avoid a certain amount of contact, especially while he's taking the subway, but for the record, no. I don't intend to ever go out with him again. He can save his caveman tactics for someone else."

"Someone else?" Jo Ann filled the two words with tearful sadness. Until Parker, Bailey had seen only the tip of the iceberg when it came to her friend's romantic nature.

Bailey finished her soup and, glancing at her watch, realized she had less than five minutes to get back to the office.

"About tonight—I'll give you a ride," Jo Ann promised. "I'll be by to pick you up as close to six-thirty as I can. It depends on how fast I can get home and get everyone fed."

"Thanks," Bailey said. "I'll see you then."

They parted and Bailey hurried back to her office.

The large vase of red roses on the reception desk was the first thing she noticed when she walked in.

"Is it your birthday, Martha?" she asked as she removed her coat and hung it on the rack.

"I thought it must be yours," the secretary replied absently.

"Mine?"

"The card has your name on it."

Bailey's heart went completely still. Had Parker sent her flowers? It seemed too much to hope for, yet... "My name's on the card?"

"A tall good-looking man in a suit delivered them not more than ten minutes ago. He seemed disappointed when I said you'd taken an early lunch. Who is that guy, anyway? He looks vaguely familiar."

Bailey didn't answer. Instead she removed the envelope and slipped out the card. It read, "Forgive me, Parker."

She felt the tightness around her heart suddenly ease.

"Oh, I nearly forgot," Martha said, reaching for a folded slip of paper next to the crystal vase. "Since you weren't here, he left a message for you."

Carrying the vase with its brilliant red roses in one hand and her message in the other, Bailey walked slowly to her desk. With eager fingers, she unfolded the note.

"Bailey," it said. "I'm sorry I missed you. We need to talk. Can you have dinner with me tonight? If so, I'll pick you up at seven. Since I'll be tied up most of the afternoon, leave a message with Roseanne."

He'd written down his office number. Bailey reached for the phone with barely a thought. The friendly—and obviously efficient—receptionist answered on the first ring.

"Hello, Roseanne, this is Bailey York."

"Oh, Bailey, yes. It's good to hear from you. Mr. Davidson said you'd be phoning."

"I missed him by only a few minutes."

"How frustrating for you both. I've been concerned about him this morning."

"You have?"

"Why, yes. Mr. Davidson came into the office and he couldn't seem to sit still. He got himself a cup of coffee, then two minutes later came out again and poured a second cup. When I pointed out that he already had coffee, he seemed surprised. That was when he started muttering under his breath. I've worked with Mr. Davidson for several years now and I've never known him to mutter."

"He was probably thinking about something important regarding his work." Bailey was willing to offer a face-saving excuse for Parker's unprecedented behavior.

"That's not it," the woman insisted. "He went into his office again and came right back out, asking me if I read romance novels. I have on occasion, and that seemed to satisfy him. He pulled up a chair and began asking me questions about a hero's personality. I answered him as best I could."

"I'm sure you did very well."

"I must have, because he cheered right up and asked me what kind of flowers a woman enjoys most. I told him roses, and a minute later, he's looking through my phone book for a florist. Unfortunately no florist could promise a delivery this morning, so he said he'd drop them off personally. He phoned a few minutes ago to tell me you'd be calling in sometime today and that I should take a message."

"I just got back from lunch."

So Parker's morning hadn't gone any better than her

own, Bailey mused, feeling almost jubilant. She'd managed to put on a good front for Jo Ann, but Bailey had felt terrible. Worse than terrible. She hadn't wanted to discuss her misery, either. It was much easier to pretend that Parker meant nothing to her.

But Jo Ann had been right. She *was* miserable.

"Could you tell Mr. Davidson I'll be ready at seven?" She'd call Jo Ann later and tell her she wouldn't be able to make the critique group, after all.

"Oh, my, that *is* good news," Roseanne said, sounding absolutely delighted. "I'll pass the message along as soon as he checks in. I'm so pleased. Mr. Davidson is such a dear man, but he works too hard. I've been thinking he needed to meet a nice girl like you. Isn't it incredible that the two of you have known each other for so long?"

"We have?"

"Oh, yes, don't you remember? You came into the office that morning and explained how Mr. Davidson is a friend of your family's. You must have forgotten you'd told me that."

"Oh. Oh, yes," Bailey mumbled, embarrassed by the silly lie. "Well, if you'd give him the message, I'd be most grateful."

"I'll let Mr. Davidson know," Roseanne said. She hesitated, as though she wanted to add something else and wasn't sure she should. Then, decision apparently made, the words rushed out. "As I said before, I've been with Mr. Davidson for several years and I think you should know that to the best of my knowledge, this is the first time he's ever sent a woman roses."

For the rest of the afternoon, Bailey was walking on air. At five o'clock, she raced into the department store closest to her office, carrying one long-stemmed rose. Within minutes she found a lovely purple-and-gold silk dress. Expensive, but it looked wonderful. Then she hurried to the shoe department and bought a pair of pumps. In accessories, she chose earrings and a matching gold necklace.

From the department store she raced to the subway, clutching her purchases and the single red rose. She'd spent a fortune but didn't bother to calculate how many "easy monthly installments" it would take to pay everything off. Looking nice for Parker was worth the cost. No man had ever sent her roses, and every time she thought about it, her heart positively melted. It was such a *romantic* thing to do. And to think he'd conferred with Roseanne Snyder.

By six-thirty she was almost ready. She needed to brush her hair and freshen her makeup, but that wouldn't take long. She stood in front of the mirror in a model's pose, one hand on her hip, one shoulder thrust forward, studying the overall effect, when there was a knock at the door.

Oh, no! Parker was early. Much too early. It was either shout at him from this side of the door to come back later, or make the best of it. Running her fingers through her hair, she shook her head for the breezy effect and opted to make the best of it.

"Are you ready?" Jo Ann asked, walking inside, her book bag in one hand and her purse in the other. She gaped openly at Bailey's appearance. "Nice," she said, nodding, "but you might be a touch overdressed for the critique group."

"Oh, no, I forgot to call you." How could she have let it slip her mind?

"Call me?"

Bailey felt guilty—an emotion she was becoming increasingly familiar with—for not remembering tonight's arrangement. It was because of Parker. He'd occupied her thoughts from the moment he'd first kissed her.

There had been no kiss last night. The desire—no, more than desire, the *need*—for his kiss, his touch had flared into urgent life. Since the breakup with Tom she'd felt frozen, her emotions lying dormant. But under the warmth of Parker's humor and generosity, she thawed a little more each time she saw him.

"Someone sent you a red rose," Jo Ann said matter-of-factly. She walked farther into the room, lifting the flower to her nose and sniffing appreciatively. "Parker?"

Bailey nodded. "There were a dozen waiting for me when I got back to the office."

Jo Ann's smile was annoyingly smug.

"He stopped by while I was at lunch—we'd missed each other..." Bailey mumbled in explanation.

Jo Ann circled her, openly admiring the dress. "He's taking you to dinner?" Her gaze fell to the purple suede pumps that perfectly matched the dress.

"Dinner? What gives you that idea?"

"The dress is new."

"This old thing?" Bailey gave a nervous giggle.

Jo Ann tugged at the price tag dangling from Bailey's sleeve and pulled it free.

"Very funny!" Bailey groaned. She glanced at her watch, hoping Jo Ann would take the hint.

Jo Ann was obviously pleased about Parker's reappearance. "So, you're willing to let bygones be bygones?" she asked in a bracing tone.

"Jo Ann, he's due here any minute."

Her friend disregarded her pleas. "You're really falling for this guy, aren't you?"

If it was any more obvious, Bailey thought, she'd be wearing a sandwich board and parading in front of his office building. "Yes."

"Big time?"

"Big time," Bailey admitted.

"How do you feel about that?"

Bailey was sorely tempted to throw up her arms in abject frustration. "How do you think it makes me feel? I've been jilted twice. I'm scared to death. Now, isn't it time you left?" She coaxed Jo Ann toward the door, but when her friend ignored that broad hint, Bailey gripped her elbow. "Sorry you had to leave so soon, but I'll give your regards to Parker."

"All right, all right," Jo Ann said, sighing, "I can take a hint when I hear one."

Bailey doubted it. "Tell the others that…something came up, but I'll be there next time for sure." Her hands were at the small of Jo Ann's back, urging her forward. "Goodbye, Jo Ann."

"I'm going, I'm going," her friend said from the other side of the threshold. Suddenly earnest, she turned to face Bailey. "Promise me you'll have a good time."

"I'm sure we will." *If* she could finish getting ready before Parker arrived. *If* she could subdue her nerves. *If*…

Once Jo Ann was gone, Bailey slammed the door and rushed back to her bathroom. She was dabbing cologne on her wrists when there was a second knock. Inhaling a calming breath, Bailey opened the door, half expecting to find Jo Ann on the other side, ready with more advice.

"Parker," she whispered unsteadily, as though he was the last person she expected to see.

He frowned. "I did get the message correctly, didn't I? You were expecting me?"

"Oh, yes, of course. Come inside, please."

"Good." His face relaxed.

He stepped into the room, but his eyes never left hers. "I hope I'm not too early."

"Oh, no." She twisted her hands, staring down at her shoes like a shy schoolgirl.

"You got the roses?"

"Oh, yes," she said breathlessly, glancing at the one she'd brought home from her office. "They're beautiful. I left the others on my desk at work. It was so sweet of you."

"It was the only way I could think to apologize. I didn't know if a hero did that sort of thing or not."

"He…does."

"So once again, I stayed in character."

"Yes. Very much so."

"Good." His mouth slanted charmingly with the slight smile he gave her. "I realize this dinner is short notice."

"I didn't mind changing my plans," she told him. The critique group was important, but everyone missed occasionally.

"I suppose I should explain we'll be eating at my parents' home. Do you mind?"

His parents? Bailey's stomach tightened instantly. "I'd enjoy meeting your family," she answered, doing her best to reassure him. She managed a fleeting smile.

"Mom and Dad are anxious to meet you."

"They are?" Bailey would have preferred not to know that. The fact that Parker had even mentioned her to his family came as a surprise.

"So, how was your day?" he asked, walking casually over to the window.

Bailey lowered her gaze. "The morning was difficult, but the afternoon...the afternoon was wonderful."

"I behaved like a jealous fool last night, didn't I?" He didn't wait for her to respond. "The minute I saw you in that other man's arms, I wanted to get you away from him. I'm not proud of how I acted." He shoved his fingers through his hair, revealing more than a little agitation. "As I'm sure you've already guessed, I'm not much of a dancer. When that throwback from the seventies asked you to dance with him, I had no objections. If you want the truth, I was relieved. I guess men are supposed to be able to acquit themselves on the dance floor, but I've got two left feet. No doubt I've blown this whole hero business, but quite honestly that's the least of my worries. I know it matters to you, but I can't change who I am."

"I wouldn't expect you to."

He nodded. "The worst part of the whole evening was the way I cheated myself out of what I was looking forward to the most."

"Which was?"

"Kissing you again."

"Oh, Parker..."

He was going to kiss her. She realized that at about the same time she knew she'd cry with disappointment if he didn't. Bailey wasn't sure who reached out first. What she instantly recognized was the perfect harmony between them, how comfortable she felt in his arms—as though they belonged together.

His mouth found hers with unerring ease. A moan of welcome and release spilled from her throat as she began to tremble. An awakening, slow and sure, unfolded within her like the petals of a hothouse rose.

That sensation was followed by confusion. She pulled away from Parker and buried her face in his strong neck. The trembling became stronger, more pronounced.

"I frighten you?"

If only he knew. "Not in the way you think," she said slowly. "It's been so long since a man's held me like this. I tried to convince myself I didn't want to feel this way ever again. I didn't entirely succeed."

"Are you saying you *wanted* me to kiss you?"

"Yes." His finger under her chin raised her eyes to his. Bailey thought they would have gone on gazing at each other forever if Max hadn't chosen that moment to walk across the back of the sofa, protesting loudly. This was his territory and he didn't take kindly to invasions.

"We'd better leave," Parker said reluctantly.

"Oh, sure…" Bailey said. She was nervous about meeting Parker's family. More nervous than she cared to admit. The last set of parents she'd been introduced to had been Tom's. She'd met them a few days before they'd announced their engagement. As she recalled, the circumstances were somewhat similar. Tom had unexpectedly declared that it was time to meet his family. That was when Bailey had realized how serious their relationship had grown. Tom's family was very nice, but Bailey had felt all too aware of being judged and, she'd always suspected, found wanting.

Bailey doubted she said more than two words as Parker drove out to Daley City. His family's home was an elegant two-story white stone house with a huge front garden.

"Here we are," Parker said needlessly, placing his hand on her shoulder when he'd helped her out of the car.

"Did you design it?"

"No, but I love this house. It gave birth to a good many of my ideas."

The front door opened and an older couple stepped outside to greet them. Parker's mother was tall and regal, her white hair beautifully waved. His father's full head of hair was a distinguished shade of gray. He stood only an inch or so taller than his wife.

"Mom, Dad, this is Bailey York." Parker introduced her, his arm around her waist. "Bailey, Yvonne and Bradley Davidson, my parents."

"Welcome, Bailey," Bradley Davidson said with a warm smile.

"It's a pleasure to meet you," Yvonne said, walking forward. Her eyes briefly connected with Parker's before she added, "at last."

"Come inside," Parker's father urged, leading the way. He stood at the door and waited for them all to walk into the large formal entry. The floor was made of black-and-white squares of polished marble, and there was a long circular stairway on the left.

"How about something to drink?" Bradley suggested. "Scotch? A mixed drink? Wine?" Bailey and Parker's mother both chose white wine, Parker and his father, Scotch.

"I'll help you, Dad," Parker offered, leaving the two women alone.

Yvonne took Bailey into the living room, which was strikingly decorated in white leather and brilliant red.

Bailey sat on the leather couch. "Your home is lovely."

"Thank you," Yvonne murmured. A smile trembled

at the edges of her mouth, and Bailey wondered what she found so amusing. Perhaps there was a huge run in her panty hose she knew nothing about, or another price tag dangling from her dress.

"Forgive me," the older woman said. "Roseanne Snyder and I are dear friends, and she mentioned your name to me several weeks back."

Bailey experienced a moment of panic as she recalled telling Parker's receptionist that she was an old family friend. "I…guess you're wondering why I claimed to know Parker."

"No, although it did give me a moment's pause. I couldn't recall knowing any Yorks."

"You probably don't." Bailey folded her hands in her lap, uncertain what to say next.

"Roseanne's right. You really are a charming young lady."

"Thank you."

"I was beginning to wonder if Parker was ever going to fall in love again. He was so terribly hurt by Maria, and he was so young at the time. He took it very hard…." She hesitated, then spoke briskly. "But I suppose that's neither here nor there."

Bailey decided to ignore the implication that Parker had fallen in love with her. Right now there were other concerns to face. "Did Parker tell you how we met?" She said a silent prayer that he'd casually mentioned something about the two of them bumping into each other on the subway.

"Of course I did," Parker answered for his mother, as he walked into the room. He sat on the arm of the sofa and draped his arm around Bailey's shoulders. His laughing eyes held hers. "I did mention Bailey's a budding romance writer, didn't I, Mom?"

"Yes, you did," his mother answered. "I hope you told her I'm an avid reader."

"No, I hadn't gotten around to that."

Bailey shifted uncomfortably in her chair. No wonder Yvonne Davidson had trouble disguising her amusement if Parker had blabbed about the way she'd followed him off the subway.

Parker's father entered the room carrying a tray of drinks, which he promptly dispensed.

Then he joined his wife, and for some time, the foursome chatted amicably.

"I'll just go and check on the roast," Yvonne said eventually.

"Can I help, dear?"

"Go ahead, Dad," Parker said, smiling. "I'll entertain Bailey with old family photos."

"Parker," Bailey said once his parents were out of earshot. "How *could* you?"

"How could I what?"

"Tell your mother how we met? She must think I'm crazy!"

Instead of revealing any concern, Parker grinned widely. "Honesty is the best policy."

"In principle I agree, but our meeting was a bit... unconventional."

"True, but I have to admit that being described as classic hero material was flattering to my ego."

"I take everything back," she muttered, crossing her legs.

Parker chuckled and was about to say something else

when his father came into the room carrying a bottle of champagne.

"Champagne, Dad?" Parker asked when his father held out the bottle for Parker to examine. "This is good stuff."

"You're darn right," Bradley Davidson said. "It isn't every day our son announces he's found the woman he wants to marry."

# *Ten*

Bailey's gaze flew to Parker's in shocked disbelief. She found herself standing, but couldn't remember rising from the chair. The air in the room seemed too thin and she had difficulty catching her breath.

"Did I say something I shouldn't have?" Bradley Davidson asked his son, distress evident on his face.

"It might be best if you gave the two of us a few minutes alone," Parker said, frowning at his father.

"I'm sorry, son, I didn't mean to speak out of turn."

"It's fine, Dad."

His father left the room.

Bailey walked over to the massive stone fireplace and stared into the grate at the stacked logs and kindling.

"Bailey?" Parker spoke softly from behind her.

She whirled around to face him, completely speechless, able only to shake her head in bemused fury.

"I know this must come as…something of a surprise."

"Something of a surprise?" she shrieked.

"All right, a shock."

"We…we met barely a month ago."

"True, but we know each other better than some couples who've been dating for months."

The fact that he wasn't arguing with her didn't comfort Bailey at all. "I… Isn't it a bit presumptuous of you…to be thinking in terms of an engagement?" She'd made it plain from the moment they met that she had no intention of getting involved with a man. Who could blame her after the experiences she'd had with the opposite sex? Another engagement, even with someone as wonderful as Parker, was out of the question.

"Yes, it was presumptuous."

"Then how could you suggest such a thing? Engagements are disastrous for me! I won't go through that again. I won't!"

He scowled. "I agree I made a mistake."

"Obviously." Bailey stalked to the opposite side of the room to stand behind a leather-upholstered chair, one hand clutching its back. "Twice, Parker, twice." She held up two fingers. "And both times, *both* times, they fell out of love with me. I couldn't go through that again. I just couldn't."

"Let me explain," Parker said, walking slowly toward her. "For a long time now, my parents have wanted me to marry."

"So in other words, you used me. I was a decoy. You made up this story? How courageous of you."

She could tell from the hard set of his jaw that Parker was having difficulty maintaining his composure. "You're wrong, Bailey."

"Suddenly everything is clear to me." She made a sweeping gesture with her hand.

"It's obvious that nothing is clear to you," he countered angrily.

"I suppose I'm just so naive it was easy for me to fall in with your...your fiendish plans."

"*Fiendish* plans? Don't you think you're being a bit melodramatic?"

"Me? You're talking to a woman who's been jilted. Twice. Almost every man I've ever known has turned into a fiend."

"Bailey, I'm not using you." He crossed the room, stood directly in front of her and rested his hands on her shoulders. "Think what you want of me, but you should know the truth. Yes, my parents are eager for me to marry, and although I love my family, I would never use you or anyone else to satisfy their desires."

Bailey frowned uncertainly. His eyes were so sincere, so compelling.... "Then what possible reason could you have for telling them you'd found the woman you want to marry?"

"Because I have." His beautiful dark eyes brightened. "I'm falling in love with you. I have been almost from the moment we met."

Bailey blinked back hot tears. "You may believe you're in love with me now," she whispered, "but it won't last. It never does. Before you know it, you'll meet some-one else, and you'll fall in love with her and not want me anymore."

"Bailey, that's not going to happen. You're going to wear that slightly used wedding dress and you're going to wear it for me."

Bailey continued to stare up at him, doubtful she could trust what she was hearing.

"The mistake I made was in telling my mother about you. Actually Roseanne Snyder couldn't wait to mention you to Mom. Next thing I knew, my mother was after me to bring you over to the house so she and Dad could meet you. To complicate matters, my father got involved and over a couple of glasses of good Scotch I admitted that my intentions toward you were serious. Naturally both my parents were delighted."

"Naturally." The sinking feeling in her stomach refused to go away.

"I didn't want to rush you, but since Dad's brought everything out into the open, maybe it's best to clear the air now. My intentions are honorable."

"Maybe they are now," she argued, "but it'll never last."

Parker squared his shoulders and took a deep breath. "It will last. I realize you haven't had nearly enough time to figure out your feelings for me. I'd hoped—" he hesitated, his brow furrowed "—that we could have this discussion several months down the road when our feelings for each other had matured."

"I'll say it one more time—engagements don't work, at least not with me."

"It'll be different this time."

"If I was ever going to fall in love with anyone, it would be you. But Parker, it just isn't going to work. I'm sorry, really I am, but I can't go through with this." Her hands were trembling and she bit her lower lip. She was in love with Parker, but she was too frightened to acknowledge it outside the privacy of her own heart.

"Bailey, would you listen to me?"

"No," she said. "I'm sorry, but everything's been blown out of proportion here. I'm writing a romance novel and you…you're the man I'm using for the model." She gave a resigned shrug. "That's all."

Parker frowned. "In other words, everything between

us is a farce. The only person guilty of using anyone is you."

Bailey clasped her hands tightly in front of her, so tightly that her nails cut deep indentations in her palms. A cold sweat broke out on her forehead. "I never claimed anything else."

"I see." The muscles in his jaw tightened again. "Then all I can do is beg your forgiveness for being so presumptuous."

"There's no need to apologize." Bailey felt terrible, but she had to let him believe their relationship *was* a farce, otherwise everything became too risky. Too painful.

A noise, the muffled steps of Parker's mother entering the room, distracted them. "My dears," she said, "dinner's ready. I'm afraid if we wait much longer, it'll be ruined."

"We'll be right in," Parker said.

Bailey couldn't remember a more uncomfortable dinner in her life. The tension was so thick, she thought wryly, it could have been sliced and buttered.

Parker barely spoke during the entire meal. His mother, ever gracious, carried the burden of conversation. Bailey did her part to keep matters civilized, but the atmosphere was so strained it was a virtually impossible chore.

The minute they were finished with the meal, Parker announced it was time to leave. Bailey nodded and thanked his parents profusely for the meal. It was an honor to have met them, she went on, and this had been an exceptionally pleasant evening.

"Don't you think you overdid that a little?" Parker muttered once they were in the car.

"I had to say something," she snapped. "Especially since you were so rude."

"I wasn't rude."

"All right, you weren't rude, you were completely tactless. Couldn't you see how uncomfortable your father was? He felt bad enough about mentioning your plans. You certainly didn't need to complicate everything with such a rotten attitude."

"He deserved it."

"That's a terrible thing to say."

Parker didn't answer. For someone who, only hours before, had declared tender feelings for her, he seemed in an almighty hurry to get her home, careering around corners as though he were in training for the Indianapolis 500.

To Bailey's surprise he insisted on walking her to the door. The night before, he'd also escorted her to the door, and after a stilted good-night, he'd left. This evening, however, he wasn't content to leave it at that.

"Invite me in," he said when she'd unlatched the lock.

"Invite you in," Bailey echoed, listening to Max meowing plaintively on the other side.

"I'm coming in whether you invite me or not." His face was devoid of expression, and Bailey realized he would do exactly as he said. Her stomach tightened with apprehension.

"All right," she said, opening the door. She flipped on the light and removed her coat. Max, obviously sensing her state of mind, immediately headed for the bedroom. "I'd make some coffee, but I don't imagine you'll be staying that long."

"Make the coffee."

Bailey was grateful to have something to do. She concentrated on preparing the coffee and setting out mugs.

"Whatever you have to say isn't going to change my mind," Bailey told him. She didn't sound as calm and controlled as she'd hoped.

Parker ignored her. He couldn't seem to stand still, but rapidly paced her kitchen floor, pausing only when Bailey handed him a steaming mug of coffee. She'd seen Parker when he was angry and frustrated, even when he was jealous and unreasonable, but she'd never seen him quite like this.

"Say what you want to say," she prompted, resting her hip against the kitchen counter. She held her cup carefully in both hands.

"All right." Parker's eyes searched hers. "I resent having to deal with your irrational emotions."

"My irrational emotions!"

"Admit it, you're behaving illogically because some other man broke off his engagement to you."

"Other *men,*" Bailey corrected sarcastically. "Notice the plural, meaning more than one. Before you judge me too harshly, *Mr.* Davidson, let me remind you that every person is the sum of his or her experiences. If you stick your hand in the fire and get burned, you're not as likely to play around the campfire again, are you? It's as simple as that. I was fool enough to risk the fire twice, but I'm not willing to do it a third time."

"Has it ever occurred to you that you weren't in love with either Paul or Tom?"

Bailey blinked at the unexpectedness of the question. "That's ridiculous. I agreed to marry them. No woman does that without being in love."

"They both fell for someone else."

"How kind of you to remind me."

"Yet when they told you, you did nothing but wallow in your pain. If you'd been in love, deeply in love, you would've done everything within your power to keep them. Instead you did nothing. Absolutely nothing. What else am I to think?"

"Frankly I don't care what you think. I know what was in my heart and I was in love with both of them. Is it any wonder I refuse to fall in love again? An engagement is out of the question!"

"Then marry me now."

Bailey's heart leapt in her chest, then sank like a dead weight. "I—I'm not sure I heard you correctly."

"You heard. Engagements terrify you. I'm willing to accept that you've got a valid reason, but you shouldn't let it dictate how you live the rest of your life."

"In other words, bypassing the engagement and rushing to the altar is going to calm my fears?"

"You keep repeating that you refuse to go through another engagement. I can understand your hesitancy," he stated calmly. "Reno is only a couple of hours away." He glanced at his watch. "We could be married by this time tomorrow."

"Ah…" Words twisted and turned in her mind, but no coherent thought emerged.

"Well?" Parker regarded her expectantly.

"I…we…elope? I don't think so, Parker. It's rather… heroic of you to suggest it, actually, but it's an impossible idea."

"Why? It sounds like the logical solution to me."

"Have you stopped to consider that there are other factors involved in this? Did it occur to you that I might not be in love with you?"

"You're so much in love with me you can't think straight," he said with ego-crushing certainty.

"How do you know that?"

"Easy. It's the way you react, trying too hard to convince yourself you don't care. And the way you kiss me. At first there's resistance, then gradually you warm to it, letting your guard slip just a little, enough for me to realize you're enjoying the kissing as much as I am. It's when you start to moan that I know everything I need to know."

A ferocious blush exploded in Bailey's cheeks. "I do not moan," she protested heatedly.

"Do you want me to prove it to you?"

"No," Bailey cried, backing away.

A smug smile moved over his mouth, settling in his eyes.

Bailey's heart felt heavy. "I'm sorry to disappoint you, Parker, but I'd be doing us both a terrible disservice if I agreed to this."

Parker looked grim. She stared at him and knew, even as she rejected his marriage proposal, that if ever there was a man who could restore peace to her heart, that man was Parker. But she wasn't ready yet; she still had healing and growing to do on her own. But soon… Taking her courage in both hands, she whispered, "Couldn't we take some time to decide about this?"

Parker had asked her to be his wife. Parker Davidson, who was twice the man Paul was and three times the man Tom could ever hope to be. And she was so frightened all she could do was stutter and tremble and plead for time.

"Time," he repeated. Parker set his mug down on the kitchen counter, then stepped forward and framed her face in his large hands. His thumbs gently stroked her cheeks. Bailey gazed up at him, barely breathing. Warm anticipation filled her as he lowered his mouth.

She gasped sharply as his lips touched hers, moving over them slowly, masterfully. A moan rose deep in her throat, one so soft it was barely audible. A small cry of longing and need.

Parker heard it and responded, easing her closer and wrapping her in his arms. He kissed her a second time, then abruptly released her and turned away.

Bailey clutched the counter behind her to keep from falling. "What was that for?"

A slow easy grin spread across his face. "To help you decide."

"The worst part of this whole thing is that I haven't written a word in an entire week," Bailey complained as she sat on her living-room carpet, her legs pulled up under her chin. Pages of Jo Ann's manuscript littered the floor. Max, who revealed little or no interest in their writing efforts, was asleep as usual atop her printer.

"In an entire week?" Jo Ann sounded horrified. Even at Christmas neither of them had taken more than a three-day break from writing.

"I've tried. Each and every night I turn on my computer and then I sit there and stare at the screen. This is the worst case of writer's block I've ever experienced. I can't seem to make myself work."

"Hmm," Jo Ann said, leaning against the side of the couch. "Isn't it also an entire week since you saw Parker? Seems to me the two must be connected."

She nodded miserably. Jo Ann wasn't telling her anything she didn't already know. She'd relived that night in her memory at least a dozen times a day.

"You've never told me what happened," Jo Ann said, studying Bailey closely.

Bailey swallowed. "Parker is just a friend."

"And pigs have wings."

"My only interest in Parker is as a role model for Michael," she tried again, but she didn't know who she was trying to convince, Jo Ann or herself.

She hadn't heard from him all week. He'd left, promising to give her the time she'd requested. He'd told her the kiss was meant to help her decide if she wanted him. Wanted him? Bailey didn't know if she'd ever *stop* wanting him, but she was desperately afraid that his love for her wouldn't last. It hadn't with Paul or Tom, and it wouldn't with Parker. And with Parker, the pain of rejection would be far worse.

Presumably Parker had thought he was reassuring her by suggesting they skip the engagement part and rush into a Nevada marriage. What he didn't seem to understand, what she couldn't seem to explain, was that it wouldn't make any difference. A wedding ring wasn't a guarantee. Someday, somehow, Parker would have a change of heart; he'd fall out of love with her.

"Are you all right?" Jo Ann asked.

"Of course I am." Bailey managed to keep her voice steady and pretend a calm she wasn't close to feeling. "I'm just upset about this writer's block. But it isn't the end of the world. I imagine everything will return to normal soon and I'll be back to writing three or four pages a night."

"You're sure about that?"

Bailey wasn't sure about anything. "No," she admitted.

"Just remember I'm here any time you want to talk."

A trembling smile touched the edges of Bailey's mouth and she nodded.

Bailey saw Parker three days later. She was waiting at the BART station by herself—Jo Ann had a day off—when she happened to glance up and see him walking in her direction. At first she tried to ignore the quaking of her heart and focus her attention away from him. But it was impossible.

She knew he saw her, too, although he gave no outward indication of it. His eyes met hers as though challenging her to ignore him. When she took a hesitant step toward him, his mouth quirked in a mocking smile.

"Hello, Parker."

"Bailey."

"How have you been?"

He hesitated a split second before he answered, which made Bailey hold her breath in anticipation.

"I've been terrific. How about you?"

"Wonderful," she lied, astonished that they could stand so close and pretend so well. His gaze lingered on her lips and she felt the throb of tension in the air. Parker must have rushed to get to the subway—his hair was slightly mussed and he was breathing hard.

He said something but his words were drowned out by the clatter of the approaching train. It pulled up and dozens of people crowded out. Neither Parker nor Bailey spoke as they waited to board.

He followed her inside, but sat several spaces away. She looked at him, oddly shocked and disappointed that he'd refused to sit beside her.

There were so many things she longed to tell him.

Until now she hadn't dared admit to herself how much she'd missed his company. How she hungered to talk to him. They'd known each other for such a short while and yet he seemed to fill every corner of her life.

That, apparently, wasn't the case with Parker. Not if he could so casually, so willingly, sit apart from her. She raised her chin and forced herself to stare at the advertising panels that ran the length of the car.

Bailey felt Parker's eyes on her. The sensation was so strong his hand might as well have touched her cheek, held her face the way he had when he'd last left her. When she could bear it no longer, she turned and glanced at him. Their eyes met and the hungry desire in his tore at her heart.

With every ounce of strength she possessed, Bailey looked away. Eventually he would find someone else, someone he loved more than he would ever love her. Bailey was as certain of that as she was of her own name.

She kept her gaze on anything or anyone except Parker. But she felt the pull between them so strongly that she had to turn her head and look at him. He was staring at her, and the disturbing darkness of his eyes seemed to disrupt the very beat of her heart. A rush of longing jolted her body.

The train was slowing and Bailey was so grateful it was her station she jumped up and hurried to the exit.

"I'm still waiting," Parker whispered from directly behind her. She was conscious as she'd never been before of the long muscled legs so close to her own, of his strength and masculinity. "Have you decided yet?"

Bailey shut her eyes and prayed for the courage to do what was right for both of them. She shook her head silently; she couldn't talk to him now. She couldn't make a rational decision while the yearning in her heart was so great, while her body was so weak with need for him.

The crowd rushed forward and Bailey rushed with them, leaving him behind.

The writers' group met the following evening, for which Bailey was thankful. At least she wouldn't have to stare at a blank computer screen for several hours while she tried to convince herself she was a writer. Jo Ann had been making headway on her rewrite, whereas Bailey's had come to a complete standstill.

The speaker, an established historical-romance writer who lived in the San Francisco area, had agreed to address their group. Her talk was filled with good advice and Bailey tried to take notes. Instead, she drew meaningless doodles. Precise three-dimensional boxes and neat round circles in geometric patterns.

It wasn't until she was closing her spiral notebook at the end of the speech that Bailey realized all the circles on her page resembled interlocking wedding bands. About fifteen pairs of them. Was her subconscious sending her a message? Bailey had given up guessing.

"Are you going over to the diner for coffee?" Jo Ann asked as the group dispersed. Her eyes didn't meet Bailey's.

"Sure." She studied her friend and knew instinctively that something was wrong. Jo Ann had been avoiding her most of the evening. At first she'd thought it was her imagination, but there was a definite strain between them.

"All right," Bailey said, once they were outside. "What is it? What's wrong?"

Jo Ann sighed deeply. "I saw Parker this afternoon.

I know it's probably nothing and I'm a fool for saying anything but, Bailey, he was with a woman and they were definitely more than friends."

"Oh?" Bailey's legs were shaky as she moved down the steps to the street. Her heart felt like a stone in the center of her chest.

"I'm sure it doesn't mean anything. For all I know, the woman could be his sister. I… I hadn't intended on saying a word, but then I thought you'd want to know."

"Of course I do," Bailey said, swallowing past the tightness in her throat. Her voice was firm and steady, revealing none of the chaos in her thoughts.

"I think Parker saw me. In fact, I'm sure he did. It was almost as if he *wanted* me to see him. He certainly didn't go out of his way to disguise who he was with—which leads me to believe it was all very innocent."

"I'm sure it was," Bailey lied. Her mouth twisted in a wry smile. She made a pretense of looking at her watch. "My goodness, I didn't realize it was so late. I think I'll skip coffee tonight and head on home."

Jo Ann grabbed her arm. "Are you all right?"

"Of course." But she was careful not to look directly at her friend. "It really doesn't matter, you know—about Parker."

"Doesn't matter?" Jo Ann echoed.

"I'm not the jealous type."

Her stomach was churning, her head spinning, her hands trembling. Fifteen minutes later, Bailey let herself into her apartment. She didn't stop to remove her coat, but walked directly into the kitchen and picked up the phone.

Parker answered on the third ring. His greeting sounded distracted. "Bailey," he said, "it's good to hear from you. I've been trying to call you most of the evening."

"I was at a writers' meeting. You wanted to tell me something?"

"As a matter of fact, yes. You obviously aren't going to change your mind about the two of us."

"I…"

"Let's forget the whole marriage thing. There's no need to rush into this. What do you think?"

# *Eleven*

"Oh, I agree one hundred percent," Bailey answered. It didn't surprise her that Parker had experienced a change of heart. She'd been expecting it to happen sooner or later. It was a blessing that he'd recognized his feelings so early on.

"No hard feelings then?"

"None," she assured him, raising her voice to a bright confident level. "I've gotten used to it. Honestly, you don't have a thing to worry about."

"You seem…cheerful."

"I am," Bailey answered, doing her best to sound as though she'd just won the lottery and was only waiting until she'd finished with this phone call to celebrate.

"How's the writing going?"

"Couldn't be better." Couldn't be worse actually, but she wasn't about to admit that. Not to Parker, at any rate.

"I'll be seeing you around then," he said.

"I'm sure you will." Maintaining this false enthusiasm was killing her. "One question."

"Sure."

"Where'd you meet her?"

"Her?" Parker hesitated. "You must mean Lisa. We've known each other for ages."

"I see." Bailey had to get off the phone before her facade cracked. But her voice broke as she continued, "I wish you well, Parker."

He paused as though he were debating whether or not to say something else. "You, too, Bailey."

Bailey replaced the receiver, her legs shaking so badly she stumbled toward the chair and literally fell into it. She covered her face with her hands, dragging deep gulps of air into her lungs. The burning ache in her stomach seemed to ripple out in hot waves, spreading to the tips of her fingers, to the bottoms of her feet.

By sheer force of will, Bailey lifted her head, squared her shoulders and stood up. She'd been through this before. Twice. Once more wouldn't be any more difficult than the first two times. Or so she insisted to herself.

After all, this time there was no ring to return, no wedding arrangements to cancel, no embossed announcements to burn.

No one, with the exception of Jo Ann, even knew about Parker, so the embarrassment would be kept to a minimum.

Getting over Parker should be quick and easy.

It wasn't.

A hellishly slow week passed and Bailey felt as if she were living on another planet. Outwardly nothing had changed, and yet the world seemed to be spinning off its axis. She went to work every morning, discussed character and plot with Jo Ann, worked an eight-hour day, took the subway home and plunked herself down in front of her computer, working on her rewrite with demonic persistence.

She appeared to have everything under control. Yet her life was unfolding in slow motion around her, as though she was a bystander and not a participant.

It must have shown in her writing because Jo Ann phoned two days after Bailey had given her the complete rewrite.

"You finished reading it?" Bailey couldn't hide her excitement. If Jo Ann liked it, then Bailey could mail it right off to Paula Albright, the editor who'd asked to see the revised manuscript.

"I'd like to come over and discuss a few points. Have you got time?"

Time was the one thing Bailey had in abundance. She hadn't realized how large a role Parker had come to play in her life or how quickly he'd chased away the emptiness. The gap he'd left behind seemed impossible to fill. Most nights she wrote until she was exhausted. But because she couldn't sleep anyway, she usually just sat in the living room holding Max.

Her cat didn't really care for the extra attention she was lavishing on him. He grudgingly endured her stroking his fur and scratching his ears. An extra serving of canned cat food and a fluffed-up pillow were appreciated, but being picked up and carted across the room to sit in her lap wasn't. To his credit, Max had submitted to two or three sessions in which she talked out her troubles, but his patience with such behavior had exhausted itself.

"Put on a pot of coffee and I'll be over in a few minutes," Jo Ann said, disturbing Bailey's musings.

"Fine. I'll see you when I see you," Bailey responded, then frowned. My goodness, *that* was an original statement. If she was reduced to such a glaring lack of originality one week after saying farewell to Parker, she hated to consider how banal her conversation would be a month from now.

Jo Ann arrived fifteen minutes later, Bailey's manuscript tucked under her arm.

"You didn't like it," Bailey said in a flat voice. Her friend's expression couldn't have made it any plainer.

"It wasn't that, exactly," Jo Ann told her, setting the manuscript on the coffee table and curling up in the overstuffed chair.

"What seems to be the problem this time?"

"Janice."

"Janice?" Bailey cried, restraining the urge to argue. She'd worked so hard to make the rewrite of *Forever Yours* work. "I thought *Michael* was the source of all the trouble."

"He was in the original version. You've rewritten him just beautifully, but Janice seemed so—I hate to say this—weak."

"Weak?" Bailey shouted. "Janice isn't weak! She's strong and independent and—"

"Foolish and weak-willed," Jo Ann finished. "The reader loses sympathy for her halfway through the book. She acts like a robot with Michael."

Bailey was having a difficult time not protesting. She knew Jo Ann's was only one opinion, but she'd always trusted her views. Jo Ann's evaluation of the manuscript's earlier versions had certainly been accurate.

"Give me an example," Bailey said, making an effort to keep her voice as even and unemotional as possible.

"Everything changed after the scene at the Pops concert."

"Parker was a real jerk," Bailey argued. "He deserved everything she said and did."

"Parker?" Jo Ann's brows arched at her slip of the tongue.

"Michael," Bailey corrected. "You know who I meant!"

"Indeed I did."

During the past week, Jo Ann had made several awkward attempts to drop Parker's name into conversation, but Bailey refused to discuss him.

"Michael did act a bit high-handed," Jo Ann continued, "but the reader's willing to forgive him, knowing he's discovering his true feelings for Janice. The fact that he felt jealous when she danced with another man hit him like an expected blow. True, he did behave like a jerk, but I understood his motivation and was willing to forgive him."

"In other words, the reader will accept such actions from the hero but not the heroine?" Bailey asked aggressively.

"That's not it at all," Jo Ann responded, sounding surprised. "In the original version Janice comes off as witty and warm and independent. The reader can't help liking her and sympathize with her situation."

"Then what changed?" Bailey demanded, raising her voice. Her inclination was to defend Janice as she would her own child.

Jo Ann shrugged. "I wish I knew what happened to Janice. All I can tell you is that it started after the scene at the Pops concert. From that point on I had problems identifying with her. I couldn't understand why she was so willing to accept everything Michael said and did. It was as if she'd lost her spirit. By the end of the book, I actively disliked her. I wanted to take her by the shoulders and shake her."

Bailey felt like weeping. "So I guess it's back to the drawing board," she said, putting on a cheerful front. "I suppose I should be getting used to that."

"My best advice is to put the manuscript aside for a few weeks," Jo Ann said in a gentle tone. "Didn't you tell me you had another plot idea you wanted to develop?"

Bailey nodded. But that was before. Before almost all her energy was spent just surviving from day to day. Before she'd begun pretending her life was perfectly normal although the pain left her barely able to function. Before she'd lost hope...

"What will putting it aside accomplish?" she asked.

"It will give you perspective," Jo Ann advised. "Look at Janice. Really look at her. Does she deserve a man as terrific as Michael? You've done such a superb job writing him."

It went without saying that Parker had been the source of her inspiration.

"In other words Janice is unsympathetic?"

Jo Ann's nod was regretful. "I'm afraid so. But remember that this is strictly my opinion. Someone else may read *Forever Yours* and feel Janice is a fabulous heroine. You might want to have some of the other writers in the group read it. I don't mean to be discouraging, Bailey, really I don't."

"I know that."

"It's only because you're my friend that I can be so honest."

"That's what I wanted," Bailey admitted slowly. Who was she kidding? She was as likely to become a published writer as she was a wife. The odds were so bad it would be a sucker's bet.

"I don't want to discourage you," Jo Ann repeated in a worried voice.

"If I'd been looking for someone to tell me how talented I am, I would've given the manuscript to my mother."

Jo Ann laughed, then glanced at her watch. "I've got to scoot. I'm supposed to pick up Dan at the muffler shop. The station wagon's beginning to sound like an army tank. If you have any questions give me a call later."

"I will." Bailey led the way to the door and held it open as Jo Ann gathered up her purse and coat. Her friend paused, looking concerned. "You're not too depressed about this, are you?"

"A little," Bailey said. "All right, a lot. But it's all part of the learning process, and if I have to rewrite this manuscript a hundred times, then I'll do it. Writing isn't for the faint of heart."

"You've got that right."

Jo Ann had advised her to set the story aside but the instant she was gone, Bailey tore into the manuscript, leafing carefully through the pages.

Jo Ann's notes in the margins were valuable—and painful. Bailey paid particular attention to the comments following Michael and Janice's fateful evening at the concert. It didn't take her long to connect this scene in her novel with its real-life equivalent, her evening with Parker.

*She acts like a robot with Michael,* Jo Ann had said. As Bailey read through the subsequent chapters, she couldn't help but agree. It was as though her feisty, spirited heroine had lost the will to exert her own personality. For all intents and purposes, she'd lain down and died.

*Isn't that what you've done?* her heart asked.

But Bailey ignored it. She'd given up listening to the deep inner part of herself. She'd learned how painful that could be.

*By the end of the book I actively disliked her.* Jo Ann's words resounded like a clap of thunder in her mind. Janice's and Bailey's personalities were so intimately entwined that she no longer knew where one stopped and the other began.

*Janice seemed so...so weak.*

Bailey resisted the urge to cover her ears to block out Jo Ann's words. It was all she could do not to shout, "You'd be spineless, too, if you had a slightly used wedding dress hanging in your closet!"

When Bailey couldn't tolerate the voices any longer, she reached for her jacket and purse and escaped. Anything was better than listening to the accusations echoing in her mind. The apartment felt unfriendly and confining. Even Max's narrowed green eyes seemed to reflect her heart's questions.

The sky was overcast—a perfect accompaniment to Bailey's mood. She walked without any real destination until she found herself at the BART station and her heart suddenly started to hammer. She chided herself for the small surge of hope she felt. What were the chances of running into Parker on a Saturday afternoon? Virtually none. She hadn't seen him in over a week. More than likely he'd been driving to work to avoid her.

Parker.

The pain she'd managed to hold at bay for several

days bobbed to the surface. Tears spilled from her eyes. She kept on walking, her pace brisk as though she was in a hurry to get somewhere. Bailey's destination was peace and she had yet to find it. Sometimes she wondered if she ever would.

Men fell in love with her easily enough, but they seemed to fall out of love just as effortlessly. Worst of all, most demeaning of all, was the knowledge that there was always another woman involved. A woman they loved more than Bailey. Paul, Tom and now Parker.

Bailey walked for what felt like miles. Somehow, she wasn't altogether shocked when she found herself on Parker's street. He'd mentioned it in passing the evening they'd gone to the concert. The condominiums were a newer addition to the neighborhood, ultramodern, ultra-expensive, ultra-appealing to the eye. It wouldn't surprise her to learn that Parker had been responsible for their design. Although the dinner conversation with his parents had been stilted and uncomfortable, Parker's mother had taken delight in highlighting her son's many accomplishments. Parker obviously wasn't enthusiastic about his mother's bragging, but Bailey had felt a sense of pride in the man she loved.

*The man she loved.*

Abruptly Bailey stopped walking. She closed her eyes and clenched her hands into tight fists. She did *not* love Parker. If she did happen to fall in love again, it wouldn't be with a man as fickle or as untrustworthy as Parker Davidson, who apparently fell in and out of love at the drop of a—

*You love him, you fool. Now what are you going to do about it?*

Bailey just wanted these questions, these revelations,

to stop, to leave her alone. Alone in her misery. Alone in her pain and denial.

An anger grew in Bailey. One born of so much strong emotion she could barely contain it. Without sparing a thought for the consequences, she stormed into the central lobby of the condominium complex. The doorman stepped forward.

"Good afternoon," he said politely.

Bailey managed to smile at him. "Hello." Then, when she noticed that he was waiting for her to continue, she added, "Mr. Parker Davidson's home, please," her voice remarkably calm and impassive. They were going to settle this once and for all, and no one, not a doorman, not even a security guard, was going to stand in her way.

"May I ask who's calling?"

"Bailey York," she answered confidently.

"If you'll kindly wait here," He was gone only a moment. "Mr. Parker says to send you right up. He's in unit 204."

"Thank you." Bailey's determination hadn't dwindled by the time her elevator reached the second floor.

It took Parker a couple of minutes to answer his door. When he did, Bailey didn't wait for an invitation. She marched into his apartment, ignoring the spectacular view and the lush traditional furnishings of polished wood and rich fabric.

"Bailey." He seemed surprised to see her.

Standing in the middle of the room, hands on her hips, she glared at him with a week's worth of indignation flashing from her eyes. "Don't Bailey me," she raged. "I want to know who Lisa is and I want to know *now*."

Parker gaped at her as though she'd taken leave of her senses.

"Don't give me that look." She walked a complete circle around him; he swiveled slowly, still staring. "There's no need to stand there with your mouth hanging open. It's a simple question."

"What are you doing here?"

"What does it look like?"

"Frankly I'm not sure."

"I've come to find out exactly what kind of man you are." That sounded good, and she said it in a mocking challenging way bound to get a response.

"What kind of man I am? Does this mean I have to run through a line of warriors waiting to flog me?"

Bailey was in no mood for jesting. "It just might." She removed one hand from her hip and waved it under his nose. "I'll have you know Janice has been ruined and I blame you."

"Who?"

"My character Janice," she explained with exaggerated patience. "The one in my novel, *Forever Yours.* She's wishy-washy, submissive and docile. Reading about her is like...like vanilla pudding instead of chocolate."

"I happen to be partial to vanilla pudding."

Bailey sent him a furious look. "I'll do the talking here."

Parker raised both hands. "Sorry."

"You should be. So...exactly what kind of man *are* you?"

"I believe you've already asked that question." Bailey spun around to scowl at him. "Sorry," he muttered, his mouth twisting oddly. "I forgot you're doing the talking here."

"One minute you claim you're in love with me. So

much in love you want me to marry you." Her voice faltered slightly. "And the next you're involved with some woman named Lisa and you want to put our relationship on hold. Well, I've got news for you, Mr. Unreliable. I refuse to allow you to play with my heart. You asked me to marry you..." Bailey paused at the smile that lifted the corners of his mouth. "Is this discussion amusing you?" she demanded.

"A little."

"Feel free to share the joke," she said, motioning with her hand.

"Lisa's my sister-in-law."

The words didn't immediately sink in. "Your what?"

"She's my brother's wife."

Bailey slumped into a chair. A confused moment passed while she tried to collect her scattered thoughts. "You're in love with your brother's wife?"

"No." He sounded shocked that she'd even suggest such a thing. "I'm in love with you."

"You're not making a lot of sense."

"I figured as much, otherwise—"

"Otherwise what?"

"Otherwise you'd either be in my arms or finding ways to inflict physical damage on my person."

"You'd better explain yourself," she said, frowning, hardly daring to hope.

"I love you, Bailey, but I didn't know how long it would take you to discover you love me, too. You were so caught up in the past—"

"With reason," she reminded him.

"With reason," he agreed. "Anyway I asked you to marry me."

"To be accurate, your father's the one who did the actual speaking," Bailey muttered.

"True, he spoke out of turn, but it was a question I was ready to ask…"

"But…" she supplied for him. There was always a "but" when it came to men and love.

"But I didn't know if your feelings for me were genuine."

"I beg your pardon?"

"Was it me you fell for or Michael?" he asked quietly.

"I don't think I understand."

"The way I figure it, if you truly loved me you'd do everything in your power to win me back."

"Win you back? I'm sorry, Parker, but I still don't get it."

"All right, let's backtrack a bit. When Paul announced he'd found another woman and wanted to break your engagement, what did you do?"

"I dropped out of university and signed up for paralegal classes at the business college."

"What about Tom?"

"I moved to San Francisco."

"My point exactly."

Bailey lost him somewhere between Paul and Tom. "*What* is your point exactly?"

Parker hesitated, then looked straight into her eyes. "I wanted you to love me enough to fight for me," he told her simply. "Don't worry. Lisa and I are not, repeat not, in love."

"You just wanted me to think so?"

"Yes," he said with obvious embarrassment. "She reads romances, too. Quite a few women do apparently. I was telling her about our relationship, and she came up with the idea of using the 'other woman' the way some romance novels do."

"That's the most underhand unscrupulous thing I've ever heard."

"Indulge me for a few more minutes, all right?"

"All right," she agreed.

"When Paul and Tom broke off their engagements to you, you didn't say or do anything to convince them of your love. You calmly accepted that they'd met someone else and conveniently got out of their lives."

"So?"

"So I needed you to want me so much, love me so much, that you wouldn't give me up. You'd put aside that damnable pride of yours and confront me."

"Were you planning to arrange a mud-wrestling match between Lisa and me?" she asked wryly.

"No!" He looked horrified at the mere thought. "I wanted to provoke you—just enough to come to me. What took you so long?" He shook his head. "I was beginning to lose heart."

"You're going to lose a whole lot more than your heart if you ever pull that stunt again, Parker Davidson."

His face lit up with a smile potent enough to dissolve her pain and her doubts. He opened his arms then, and Bailey walked into his embrace.

"I should be furious with you," she mumbled.

"Kiss me first, then be mad."

His mouth captured hers in hungry exultation. In a single kiss Parker managed to make up for the long cheerless days, the long lonely nights. She was breathless when he finally released her.

"You really love me?" she whispered, needing to hear

him say it. Her lower lip trembled and her hands tightened convulsively.

"I really love you," he whispered back, smiling down at her. "Enough to last us two lifetimes."

"Only two?"

His hand cradled the back of her head. "At least four." His mouth claimed hers again, then he abruptly broke off the kiss. "Now, what was it you were saying about Janice? What's wrong with her?"

A slow thoughtful smile spread across Bailey's face. "Nothing that a wedding and a month-long honeymoon won't cure."

# *Epilogue*

Bailey paused to read the sign in the bookstore window, announcing the autographing session for two local authors that afternoon.

"How does it feel to see your name in lights?" Jo Ann asked.

"You may be used to this, but I feel... I feel—" Bailey hesitated and flattened her palms on the smooth roundness of her stomach "—I feel almost the same as I did when I found out I was pregnant."

"It does funny things to the nervous system, doesn't it?" Jo Ann teased. "And what's this comment about me being used to all this? I've only got two books published to your one."

The bookseller, Caroline Dryer, recognized them when they entered the store and hurried forward to greet them, her smile welcoming. "I'm so pleased you could both come. We've had lots of interest." She steered them toward the front where a table, draped in lace, and two chairs were waiting. Several women were already lined up patiently, looking forward to meeting Jo Ann and Bailey.

They did a brisk business for the next hour. Family, friends and other writers joined the romance readers who stopped by to wish them well.

Bailey was talking to an older woman, a retired schoolteacher, when Parker and Jo Ann's husband, Dan, casually strolled past the table. The four were going out for dinner following the autograph session. There was a lot to celebrate. Jo Ann had recently signed a two-book contract with her publisher and Bailey had just sold her second romance. After weeks of work, Parker had finished the plans for their new home. Construction was scheduled to begin the following month and with luck would be completed by the time the baby arrived.

"What I loved best about *Forever Yours* was Michael," the older woman was saying to Bailey. "The scene where he takes her in his arms right in the middle of the merry-go-round and tells her he's tired of playing childish games and that he loves her was enough to steal my heart."

"He stole mine, too," Bailey said, her eyes linking with her husband's.

"Do you think there are any men like that left in this world?" the woman asked. "I've been divorced for years, and now that I'm retired, well, I wouldn't mind meeting someone."

"You'd be surprised how many heroes there are all around us," Bailey said, her gaze still holding Parker's. "They take the subway and eat peanut-butter sandwiches and fall in love—like you and me."

"Well, there's hope for me, then," the teacher said jauntily. "And I plan to have a good time looking." She smiled. "That's why I enjoy romance novels so much. They give me encouragement, they're fun—and they tell me it's okay to believe in love," she confided. "Even for the second time."

"Or the third," Parker inserted quietly.

Bailey grinned. She couldn't argue with that!

\* \* \* \* \*

# #1 *New York Times* Bestselling Author
# DEBBIE MACOMBER

### Sometimes, where you *think* you're going isn't where you end up...

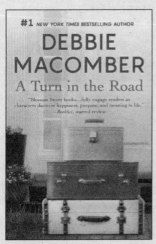

In the middle of the year, in the middle of her life, Bethanne Hamlin takes a road trip with her daughter, Annie, and her former mother-in-law, Ruth. They're driving to Florida for Ruth's fiftieth high school reunion. A longtime widow, Ruth would like to reconnect with Royce, the love of her teenage life. She's heard he's alone, too...

Bethanne herself needs time to reflect on a decision she has to make—whether or not to reconcile with her ex-husband, Grant, her children's father. Meanwhile, Annie's out to prove to her onetime boyfriend that she can live a *brilliant* life without him!

So there they are, three women driving across America. They have their maps and their directions—but even the best-planned journey can take you to a turn in the road. Or lead to an unexpected encounter—like the day Bethanne meets a man named Max...

### Available now, wherever books are sold!

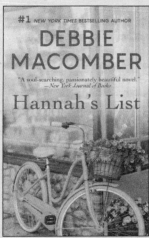

# Get 2 Free Books,
## <u>Plus</u> 2 Free Gifts –

**just for trying the *Reader Service!***

# DEBBIE MACOMBER

| | | | | | |
|---|---|---|---|---|---|
| 33019 | ALASKA HOME | ___ | $7.99 U.S. | ___ | $9.99 CAN. |
| 32918 | AN ENGAGEMENT IN SEATTLE | ___ | $7.99 U.S. | ___ | $9.99 CAN. |
| 32798 | ORCHARD VALLEY GROOMS | ___ | $7.99 U.S. | ___ | $9.99 CAN. |
| 31894 | ALWAYS DAKOTA | ___ | $7.99 U.S. | ___ | $9.99 CAN. |
| 31888 | DAKOTA HOME | ___ | $7.99 U.S. | ___ | $9.99 CAN. |
| 31883 | DAKOTA BORN | ___ | $7.99 U.S. | ___ | $9.99 CAN. |
| 31868 | COUNTRY BRIDE | ___ | $7.99 U.S. | ___ | $9.99 CAN. |
| 31864 | THE MANNING GROOMS | ___ | $7.99 U.S. | ___ | $9.99 CAN. |
| 31860 | THE MANNING BRIDES | ___ | $7.99 U.S. | ___ | $9.99 CAN. |
| 31829 | TRADING CHRISTMAS | ___ | $7.99 U.S. | ___ | $9.99 CAN. |
| 31580 | MARRIAGE BETWEEN FRIENDS | ___ | $7.99 U.S. | ___ | $8.99 CAN. |
| 31551 | A REAL PRINCE | ___ | $7.99 U.S. | ___ | $8.99 CAN. |
| 31441 | HEART OF TEXAS VOLUME 2 | ___ | $7.99 U.S. | ___ | $8.99 CAN. |
| 31413 | LOVE IN PLAIN SIGHT | ___ | $7.99 U.S. | ___ | $9.99 CAN. |
| 31341 | THE UNEXPECTED HUSBAND | ___ | $7.99 U.S. | ___ | $9.99 CAN. |
| 31325 | A TURN IN THE ROAD | ___ | $7.99 U.S. | ___ | $9.99 CAN. |
| 31917 | BECAUSE IT'S CHRISTMAS | ___ | $7.99 U.S. | ___ | $9.99 CAN. |
| 31535 | PROMISE TEXAS | ___ | $7.99 U.S. | ___ | $8.99 CAN. |
| 33018 | ALASKA NIGHTS | ___ | $7.99 U.S. | ___ | $9.99 CAN. |
| 31624 | ON A CLEAR DAY | ___ | $7.99 U.S. | ___ | $8.99 CAN. |
| 31903 | WEDDING DREAMS | ___ | $7.99 U.S. | ___ | $9.99 CAN. |
| 31907 | THE KNITTING DIARIES | ___ | $7.99 U.S. | ___ | $9.99 CAN. |
| 31926 | THE SOONER THE BETTER | ___ | $7.99 U.S. | ___ | $9.99 CAN |

*(limited quantities available)*

| | |
|---|---|
| TOTAL AMOUNT | $ _____ |
| POSTAGE & HANDLING | $ _____ |
| ($1.00 for 1 book, 50¢ for each additional) | |
| APPLICABLE TAXES* | $ _____ |
| TOTAL PAYABLE | $ _____ |

*(check or money order—please do not send cash)*

To order, complete this form and send it, along with a check or money order for the total above, payable to MIRA Books, to: **In the U.S.:** 3010 Walden Avenue, P.O. Box 9077, Buffalo, NY 14269-9077; **In Canada:** P.O. Box 636, Fort Erie, Ontario, L2A 5X3.

Name: _____

Address: _____ City: _____

State/Prov.: _____ Zip/Postal Code: _____

Account Number (if applicable): _____
075 CSAS

Harlequin.com

\*New York residents remit applicable sales taxes.
\*Canadian residents remit applicable GST and provincial taxes.

MDM1217BL